Crimson Falls

ings
ress, Inc.

Terry Lloyd Vinson

Crimson Falls

The newest arrival appeared from the eastern edge of the property, jogging across the snow-coated grass between a sizeable two-car garage and the main property. Hopping onto the winding walkway, he slowed what had been a frantic pace only when the two men grew to within a few dozen feet.

"McCarron, I want to put this out there right from the get-go," the man said—his breathing amazingly unfazed—once he'd halted forward momentum but continued to jog in place, his workout ensemble made up of dark green sweats, tar-black joggers and a crimson WKU toboggin that currently matched his rose-glow cheeks. "Being that I've been half-expecting you to make an appearance since such a miraculous resurrection, I will allow this one-time visit onto my property. Once you depart that entrance gate, do not think of returning or I will have you carted off to the county lockup. Tell me you understand."

"Looking good, your highness, but then you always were one for keepin' up appear—"

His square, clean-shaven jaw seemingly chiseled from the finest marble, the vibe given off by the sixtyish former mayor of Crimson Falls was undeniably gruff and utterly void of slack.

"I've got both the police chief and county sheriff on speed dial, McCarron. Tell me you understand."

"Loud *and* clear, Mister Mayor. Joggin' out all that built-up guilt, are we?" Gunther shot back, all signs of his initial cheeriness—however faux—having vanished in lieu of a veritable death-stare. "Pray tell, why the relocation from the ol' stompin' grounds from which you were so highly regarded? I heard tell you hightailed it outta Crimson Falls as soon as that second term was up, roughly six months after the incident that left me the walking carrot stick ya see before ya now."

"None of your business, McCarron. I suggest you ramp this up and limit the trivialities. You've got five minutes," the older man said calmly enough but with a building impatience, arms crossed and head titled slightly back as to challenge all comers.

"Or less, if I so decide. I wouldn't waste it on veiled insults, random speculation or insignificant small talk." With his V-shaped torso, thick neck and toned arms and shoulders—all made more evident by the sweatshirt's overt snugness, Kerry Hammock was the picture of senior health personified, a lifestyle he'd adopted since his teen years as a former Wildcats' star linebacker.

Crimson Falls

Terry Lloyd Vinson

A Wings ePress, Inc.
CrimeThriller Novel

Wings ePress, Inc.

Edited by: Jeanne Smith
Copy Edited by: Heather O'Connor
Executive Editor: Jeanne Smith
Cover Artist: Trisha FitzGerald-Jung

All rights reserved

Wings ePress Books
www.wingsepress.com

Copyright © 2022 by: Terry Lloyd Viinson
ISBN 978-1-61309-498-3

Published In the United States Of America

Wings ePress, Inc.
3000 N. Rock Road
Newton, KS 67114

Dedication

To Liza, for always understanding.

Prologue

Standing just outside the ramshackle trailer's entrance, the raven-haired young woman's deep frown reflected in her cell phone's darkened screen. Jagged smudges trailed from the corner of each eye from a mix of tears and oversaturated eyeliner.

Whispering barely audible curses into the cloaking darkness of the surrounding forest—the profanities easily drowned out via a veritable concerto from an unseen army of crickets and katydids—she repeatedly used the forefinger of her right hand to pummel the flip phone curled into her left palm in a futile attempt to obtain a usable signal.

She could only guesstimate five to seven minutes had passed since she'd watched haplessly as her car sped away, the shadowy figure behind the wheel navigating the gravel and dirt trail with predictable recklessness before spinning sideways onto the paved road fronting the property. Slowing only slightly to adjust to its new terrain, tires squealing their disapproval, her aged but dependable ride quickly vanished behind a thick wall of head-high indigo shrubs, scattered red oaks and three-story high weeping willows.

Backstepping into the trailer's dusky threshold, she briefly perused the woefully unfurnished space for a landline, though with the begrudging understanding it was pure folly, considering the trailer's desolate locale. Huffing in frustration, she exited yet again, this time onto a weed-infested lawn, her pink, Punic tank top soaking through at the underarms and white sneakers coated in dandelion shrapnel.

Scanning the tree line just past the main road, she snorted aloud and, pocketing the cell, wiped sweat-coated palms onto tight-fitting blue jeans before reversing and reentering the structure with slumping shoulders, all the while mumbling to herself concerning the idiocy of ever expecting to spot telephone poles nearby.

The woman stood at the center of the sparse living room and, sighing deeply while using bare forearms to wipe moisture from each eye, sat defeatedly on the lone piece of actual furniture present, a worn leather couch that reeked of cheap cologne and recently applied antiseptic spray.

Chin drooping and sneakers nervously tapping the linoleum, she ran splayed fingers through her short-cropped hair.

"So what you gonna do? C'mon girl, what's it gonna be?" she murmured, the actual words mostly muffled through jaws so tightly clenched the teeth within hardly parted.

"You gotta decide like...*RIGHT NOW!*" she shouted, raising her head and lunging from the sagging sofa, hugging herself as if chilled despite interior temperatures in excess of eighty degrees. "You can't...*cannot* have it both ways, so...stop trying to figure out how."

Following yet another quick peek outside—she'd tilted her head in opposite directions and briefly paused each time to ensure the absence of oncoming car lights or the hum of an approaching engine—she turned on a squeaking heel and traversed a narrow, dimly lit hallway leading to the rear of the structure.

Unlike the cheap, fiberglass-based doors she'd passed on either side along the way, a gray metal barrier fronted the rear room, a stainless-steel hasp pulled away from a similarly fortified latch from which loosely hung a comically oversized gold combination padlock.

Beyond the heavy, slightly creaking doorway, she squinted into a cloak of utter blackness, save for the scant light provided by the hallway's only illumination.

A groping hand fumbled for and eventually found a light switch, a faint click preceding the gradual ignition of a trio of hanging rows of fluorescent tubes spaced roughly three feet apart.

"Oh...oh *my*," she whispered in unabashed awe, lower jaw hanging like a broken shutter as she half-stepped inside a space that appeared, at least at first glance, to be the equal in square footage of the entire front half of the trailer, if not grander. Suddenly, all her initial guilt and festering shame magically melted away, replaced by a steely, iron-willed determination to finish a job she'd willingly agreed to take on.

With shaky hands, she set the cell's photo feature before beginning the tour with the device raised chest high and a posed forefinger clicking away at two to three second intervals.

She tiptoed to the center of the room before executing a gradual spin, her breath coming in short gasps, careful to still the grip on the phone while snapping each individual shot.

To her left stood a trio of what appeared to be reinforced metal TV trays adorned with separate Bunsen burners, behind which sat a circular conference table perhaps eight to ten feet

3

wide, stacked with both unboxed and boxed beakers and glass tubes of assorted sizes. To her right were piled a dozen or more clear plastic containers, bookended by a waist-high metal table on either side, each holding an assortment of bottled liquids, only a few of which were labeled as either ammonia, rubbing alcohol or paint thinner. In the far-left corner of the square space, and stacked shoulder high, were bags of generic cat litter, while the opposite corner featured assorted cardboard boxes with the tops cut away to reveal clear pill bottles of various dimensions.

Coughing into an open palm, she only then became aware of a faint burning at the back of her throat and a rapid buildup of clear mucus within each flaring nostril. With watering eyes, she lowered the phone to her side and stepped toward the door before freezing in mid-lunge. Hanging from framing nails protruding from the inner door frame were a group of chemical face shields, at least two of which possessed dual respirators and goggles.

At that moment, gnawing nervously at her lower lip as the pulse in her temples pounded like twin bass drums, the woman hopped back just far enough to bring the masks into the tiny frame of her cell's camera. Thinking ever so briefly of the one currently navigating her missing vehicle, a single spasm of remorse gripped her gut in a sudden burst of nausea. As before, she was able to justify her actions by visualizing "the big picture" and how what she was doing would someday bear positive fruit for the one she currently so cruelly betrayed.

Figuring a final shot necessary as the ultimate *coup de grace*, she stepped through and just past the steel door's frame before turning to line up a portrait to capture the gist of just what the room represented.

The shadow, like that of a giant swooping bat, fell across her line of vision just a split-second before the blow landed at the base of her neck, sending her sprawling face-first onto the linoleum.

Rolled roughly onto her back, she was acutely aware of two distinct facts despite drifting into impending unconsciousness: the surprise assault had effectively jarred the cell from her grip and, much more concerning, a bizarre sensation of numbness was slowly spreading up each sporadically twitching leg and into her lower back.

The woman managed to pry a single eyelid slightly ajar; a dark, blurry shape was leaning over her seemingly paralyzed frame. The blood-filled orb, lid fluttering madly, drifted slowly toward the same floor that seemed to be engulfing her like quicksand.

The blurred object initially appeared to her as a human leg and foot, but as it began to sway back and forth with pendulum efficiency, she was able to identify it by name only as a hammer of the sledge variety.

"W-whuuu...Gu-guuunnneee?..." she babbled toward her mystery attacker through trembling lips, her last coherent thought before a series of similarly vicious strikes followed, that perhaps, just perhaps, she was getting *exactly* what she deserved.

One

Fall 2022
Tuesday, 15:43 hours

Crimson Falls, Kentucky
Police Department Headquarters

The boy sneaked sporadic peeks past his mother's ample backside at the man sharing the miniscule waiting area, having openly gasped at the initial sighting as the strange-looking individual had struggled mightily to clear the glass, double-door entrance.

"Mama, is it human?" he'd whispered, though within the nearly deafening silence it was akin to a full-throated shriek.

"Shush now, Markie," his mother spat back with a light pat to the boy's left shoulder. "That's not polite. We mustn't stare nor make judgments of those whose plight is not known to us, understand?" Much like her wide-eyed offspring, she seemed somehow clueless that every hissed word was dramatically amplified by the cramped space. Not surprisingly, her meek warning provided little in the way of relief, nor did it prevent a series of increasingly frenzied tugs at her dress.

"But it...he moves funny, like one of my Transformer. .Look Mama, *look*. I think he's gonna fall over."

"I won't tell you again, young man. Be quiet and leave the man be. People have...problems you can't understand."

"Like the man behind the glass, you mean? Yeah, bu-but this one's different, he's standing up. Well, kind of anyw—"

"Mark Allen Brock!" she brayed, a loud pop echoing as flat, bare palm met the back of a pudgy hand. "That's enough now! I mean it!" she concluded with a low hiss, pulling the boy around until he faced forward and directly into a slightly scarred, aged oak counter.

At their backs, a metallic screech scraped across hard tile floor, followed by a resounding sigh that signaled either fatigue or intense pain, or perhaps both. The voice that followed was a deep, rich baritone that, considering its source, might naturally have been mistaken as coming from someone else altogether.

"Not a problem, ma'am. I take no offense. Boy's never seen anything like me. Youthful curiosity is only natural."

The woman had openly flinched at the intrusion, instinctively yanking the boy snugly against her side, the bulk of which virtually swallowed him whole. In replying without turning about, the shakiness in her voice was apparent, despite a most valiant effort.

"It's fine, mister. I raised my boy better. You're kind to say it doesn't bother you, but he knows not to gawk and then speak aloud at what...amazes him."

"You say something, Miss Renfro?" a male voice echoed from behind the thick clear glass that separated authorized personnel from inquiring citizen.

7

"No, no, just take your time," the woman replied with noticeably less apprehension, leaning forward to speak through a small circular space in the glass, one of two such openings to allow for clearer communication. "We're fine out here. Got yourself another customer, though."

"Be right there. Just pulling the hard copy for the statements that were attached," the voice said, containing roughly half the scorching bass output of the newest arrival.

In the relative quiet that followed, the light hum of central heating and a consistent pecking at the glass double doors reigned from a light spattering of blowing sleet that was gradually transforming the historic streets of Crimson Falls to the equivalent of an outdoor hockey rink. Through those same doors, a gloomy gray winter afternoon prevailed, low-hanging clouds effectively cloaking any warmth a visible sun might create while crying icy specs of equal indifference.

"All right, here we are," the still-unseen clerk announced as a multi-sectioned rolling file retracted noisily, his seated shadow emerging slowly from the dimness beyond. "There were a few necessary redactions on the reports, you might notice. Just the usual: social security numbers, DL numbers, and there was one mention of the boy, um, a juvenile that had to be taken out. You know the drill, Miss Renfro."

"No problem, I understand," the rotund woman responded amiably, digging into the wide maw of her oversized purse with both hands as if to retrieve an object bulky or hefty enough to require such. "How much is the damage?"

His bearded chin—a grayish growth styled to a pointy lower edge—hovering mere inches above the countertop, the wheelchair-bound clerk, a headset sitting slightly askew atop a mostly bald dome, glanced upward while mentally calculating and blindly stapling a dozen or so pages of legal bond together in a single, neat stack.

"Let's see, at thirty cents per page," he offered a nod and slight smile showcasing the slightly crinkled dimples of middle age, "that'll be four dollars and fifty cents, Miss Renfro."

Pulling two quarters from a cash box hidden beneath the counter, he reached over and pushed them through a narrow space into her waiting palm before following up with the requested reports.

"You take those down to the county seat to file the order of protection."

The woman folded the pages neatly and, after tucking them into the open purse, regained her grip on the child and took a cautious step, as if wary of bumping the man at her back, despite a full yard of open space between them.

"Yes, sir, the procedure is quite familiar these days, sad to say. Never could muster much confidence in a piece of paper protecting me and mine, but a body has to start somewhere."

"Yes, ma'am, a body certainly does. Good luck now and happy holidays."

As if to avoid coming face-to-face with the man, she executed a slow-motion left face before leading the boy toward the exit while maintaining a slumping posture and speaking to him in a soft whisper that was, yet again, completely negated by a sudden, deafening silence.

"Mark, I'm warning you now, I got no more patience for your misbehaving. Keep this up and Santa is gonna have second thoughts about that new bicycle. You just stare straight at those doors and nowhere else, you hear?" her deep Southern drawl altering the final two words to "ya heah?"

As the two sidled past the stiffly posed man, the woman offered the slightest of nods without actually meeting his eyes.

"Good boy," he heard her conclude while pulling the side door ajar and guiding the child through the opening, her wide hips following his lead with the sound of a cotton dress roughly brushing the door's squared edge.

"Yes, sir. How can I help you?" the clerk inquired, pale, bare elbows propped atop the counter, a pair of black-framed glasses balanced at the tip of his nose like a counterweight.

Sauntering forth in a jerky shamble, the man briefly appeared fated to take a forceful header directly into the glass partition before righting his gait with his face parked mere inches from its surface, his upper body leaning noticeably to the right. Ghostly pale of complexion, he sported a pencil-thin black mustache and matching eyebrows that were in stark contrast to the salt-and-pepper strands of hair protruding from underneath a well-worn, crimson beret.

"You a one-man army in there?" he inquired through a warped grin, head tilted slightly to the left. The seated man simply nodded sheepishly while flipping over each hand and exposing bare palms.

"The one and only full-time records clerk duly employed by the fair city, yes sir."

"Seems a bit much, if ya don't mind an outsider's take. I mean, lots of history to maintain in those rollin' files, I'd wager."

"More than people would think for such a supposedly quiet and crime-free community. You seeking employment in this particular field?"

The man with the deep baritone threw his head back and not so much as merely laughed but howled like a baying wolf.

"Sorry. Just thinkin'...we'd be quite the pair, wouldn't we? Couple of paper-pushin' crips takin' turns weirdin' folks out until they felt so rattled they forgot why they even walked in, much less what report they'd originally sought. You notice that one?" He gestured stiffly with a thumb toward the entrance. "Did everything but dig her way through the nearest wall to sidestep my presence? At least the kids are honest about their fascination. Hell, with the circus freakshows of old goin' the way of cassette tapes and payphones, I reckon I'm about the best show in town."

"Well, we do offer online services," the clerk stated, straight-faced, arms folded loosely across his chest, "for those unnerved by disabilities."

"Nice. And no, not seekin' employment, just all law enforcement-type incidents involving...," he paused to scoot back, the execution so awkward it briefly appeared he would topple over, and, reaching into a front pants pocket, retrieving a folded piece of yellow legal pad, "...a foursome of locals."

"Background checks?" the clerk inquired, using pinched fingers to acquire the still-folded page and then spreading it out onto the counter to survey the scribbled names announced there.

"Affirmative. Kinda why I was askin' if ya had help. I'm thinkin' a couple of those might be, well, extensive and time-consumin', and I'm needin' it like yesterday, if ya get my drift."

Alternating glances through the lenses of his spectacles and over the top edge of the frames, the clerk finally locked eyes with the customer, who had relocated back to his original position, albeit tilting a little more to the left than the right.

"I see. Well, a couple of these I'm fairly familiar with, as is anyone who's resided in these parts for a spell. Which are you thinking will be so...wide-ranging in their involvements with our department?"

"Not rightly sure except for McCarron," the man answered, gesturing to his note with the forefinger of his black-gloved right hand, a noticeable tic causing the left side of his mouth to spasm upward as if attempting a rather grotesque Elvis impersonation. "Bad dude *that* one. The others are a crapshoot, but I wouldn't be surprised if their rap sheets contain a stain or three. This here fishin' expedition is more about catchin' up with the last decade or so."

The seated man nodded and, backing the chair before smoothly steering it toward a wall-file that held various forms, returned with a single sheet, at which he immediately targeted a felt-tip pen.

"Understood. We offer two distinct types of background checks: full involvement or arrest only, the former covering the whole shebang to include traffic accidents and field interviews, the latter only charged offenses but including misdemeanor cites."

"Best go with the whole shebang version. I take it they carry vastly different sticker prices."

"Free of charge."

The clerk saw the other man's eyes widen with apparent surprise and pushed forward with an explanation.

"A recent development since the COVID outbreak, when customer contact was limited. Later the city decided they could survive without it."

"Cool. *Definitely* the whole shebang then."

The clerk cleared his throat noisily while filling in assorted blanks in the blue-tinted form.

"Will do. We do require a copy of an ID."

"No sweat. State ID suffice?"

"Yes sir, or a driver's license."

The clerk heard the man cackle between metallic scraping noises but avoided looking up from the form to openly gawk at the man's spastic movements.

"Appreciate the thought, but I don't think I'll see a reinstatement of cruisin' privileges anytime soon, sad to say, though that's probably a good thing, considerin' the potential hazards that might arise."

The clerk grunted with a noncommittal nod before reaching to retrieve the offered card, glossy and without flaw, as if only recently laminated.

"You...possess a legal DL, do ya?" the man inquired with obvious fascination.

"Yes, sir," the clerk nodded without looking up. "Utilize it on a daily basis, *legally*."

"Amazing, I mean...considerin'. I heard they could customize the steerin' wheel with special knobs and such."

"Indeed they can. So if you're ever interested in regaining the power of personal freedom that only driving can res—"

"Appreciate it, bro, but no. Won't be around, I mean *these parts* anyhow, to think about enrollin' in drivin' lessons for gimps classes."

What sounded like a half dozen separate phones blared in not-quite synchronized harmony just as the clerk had shrugged while studying the front of the state ID, which featured the man's comically grimacing mug and various personal info.

"Crimson Falls Police Department, Records Division. Please hold," the clerk stated flatly into the headset's mic, his android-like lack of emotion triggering a wide smile from the man posed crookedly on the other side of the glass.

The phones again blared in jagged unison just moments later, the clerk's brief roll of the eyes and sour scowl not lost on his live customer, who giggled aloud, leaning forward with his chin layered in grayish stubble resting on an upturned fist.

"Crimson Falls Records Division, please hold," the clerk repeated with casual aplomb not missing a beat as still more blank spaces were expertly filled.

"Joe and Josephine Public can be quite the handful, I'd imag—" the leaning man had begun, only to halt in mid-word at the sound of a rear interior door being pushed ajar and just as rapidly slammed shut.

This new arrival, small-framed, lithe and graceful, sprinted forth with ballerina-like agility to pose at the seated clerk's immediate left, the mic of her own headset bobbing beneath her chin like a recently cut wire.

"They piling up on you, Wes? Kinda slow on the console; allow me."

"Thanks, Mag. Line one, if you dare. Hey, you mind copying this for me on the way?" The man referred to as Wes inquired through a tight smile, the card pulled gently from his grip just as he trained his full attention back to the man whose slightly crooked nose sat mere inches from kissing the glass barrier. The woman, distinct facial features identifying her as being of Asian descent and in the age range of middle to late twenties but surely no older than low thirties, began speaking through her headset while shuffling over to a nearby copier.

"Should have this ready for you by midday tomorrow, being as I'll probably need to access our archived records, some of which are located over in the city hall basement," Wes was explaining as the young lady reached over his left shoulder to return the state ID, laying it atop the request form before backing so smoothly it was as if she'd donned skates while simultaneously explaining to some unheard caller the proper procedure for obtaining a crash report.

"I'll give you a ring when I get 'em all packaged up, to include the required redactions, you understand. I'll need a home phone or cell number, mister um...," he paused, pen hovering over paper, eyes briefly scanning the copied ID and, lids fluttering as if struck by a sudden gust, executing a textbook double take from paper to man and back again, "...McCarron?"

"Eight-five-nine, six-one-seven, four-eight-seven-five," the man offered, elbows balanced atop the narrow shelf, eyes having narrowed considerably, any semblance of the earlier good humor having thoroughly evaporated.

"That's a landline. While I do own a mobile device, I'm stubbornly choosy about allowin' access."

"Not a problem. I'll be in touch."

"Mid-morning a possibility?"

"I'll do my best, Mister McCarron, but as you observed, I'm kind of in one-armed paperhanger territory here. Mag, um, Maggie there is our day dispatcher and can't always assist as she just di—"

"Wes, is it?"

"Wesley. Wesley Grant."

"Gunther. Wesley, I can imagine you get the bum's rush on a regular basis, but in my case it ain't a matter of dramatics or merely blowin' smoke for the sake of doin' so. I need that info as fast as you can possibly get it to me. Time is extremely limited, ya might say."

"You live here in town, Mister McCarron?"

"Gunther."

"Gunther, you reside nearby?"

"A few miles to the south but within posted limits. The McCarron place on Old Sawmill Road."

"You possess dependable transportation?"

Gunther smiled mischievously.

"I'll manage. Bused in on Trailways a few days back. About as comfortable as your basic sardine can and nearly as aromatic, but desperate times and all that..."

"If you don't mind my asking, how *are* you getting around?"

"Wes, this is normally about the time I'd tell ya to pound sand for terminal nosiness, but bein' as we share at least one trait in semi-common, from one crip to another, I've been catchin' rides with a relative."

Wes Grant nodded knowingly while gently pushing the man's ID back through the provided space.

"Tell you what. If you can manage to catch a ride over by say, nine AM, I'll have it all prepped and ready to go. I'll come in early enough to see it's so."

"Wesley, I cannot express my appreciation strongly enough without embarrassin' myself."

"Forget it," the clerk replied, beaming and holding both hands up in mock surrender. "From one crip to another, it's the *least* I can do."

Before departing, his exoskeleton leg braces clanking and humming with fine-tuned precision, Gunther McCarron lifted a pale hand and, utilizing the thumb and forefinger to create the mythical "finger-gun," placed the seated clerk directly in the line of fire before snapping off multiple shots, all the while sporting a wide, toothy grin that revealed at least two voided spaces.

Before switching focus to the on-hold caller, Wes watched the man trudge android-like from the front entrance concrete walkway and, several potentially painful missteps later, duck into an aged blue Ford pickup—the driver of said chariot hidden in the shadows—and glide slowly away.

"So who was the mystery man anyhow?" Maggie Childers inquired, cradling a mug of steaming coffee in both hands and standing posed half-in, half-out of the connecting dispatch office, this only after all callers had been duly dispatched and the counter clear of further interruption.

The initial temptation to spill was nearly unbearable, though Wes had managed to remain stubbornly mum, at least for the time being.

"Typical amateur-hour expedition. As usual, the local PD seems to be ground zero for digging up dirt from one's past."

Maggie, her strikingly dark eyes practically twinkling with gossip-fueled glee, sipped noisily before responding.

"Smarmy cuss, obvious disabilities aside. That whole 'gimps like us' thing didn't rile you even a little?"

"Not at all. We are a smarmy clan, for sure," he fired back with a playful wink, strategically cloaking his computer screen by backing the wheelchair flush with the edge of his desk.

Mercifully, as he struggled to come up with an equally clever epilogue to put a proper bow on the snappy dialogue, the dispatch phone blared to life. Instead, while backing into the relative darkness of the other room, it was Maggie who fired the final salvo.

"Dunno Wes, personally I see no similarities. I mean, here you are, articulate, professional man on wheels, but that guy, sheesh, the bionic man meets Foghorn Leghorn."

A half hour into researching the requested names via updated and older computer systems, Wes hit the proverbial gold mine. Though far from shocked, as he'd long-since retained many of the details involved, it had after all been nearly a decade and a half since the incident.

While listening to Maggie deal with the sporadic calls, the majority tied to icy roads and the drivers not accustomed to navigating them calling in to report they were currently parked in a nearby ditch, the veteran clerk's darting eyes alternated steely glances from the recently obtained ID photo to the glow of the computer monitor.

Unaware of the rapid beating of his heart and the fresh moistness layering the palms of both hands, Wesley Grant hadn't felt such a delirious mix of trippy apprehension and steely resolve in years, decades, perhaps ever.

It would be nearly three and a half hours, to include a trip to the aforementioned archives at the old city hall building (his specially equipped Camry—a hand throttle located on the left of the steering wheel—handling the black ice with remarkable ease), before he would call it a night, the promised materials duly pulled and requiring only a quick read-over and basic redaction before release.

Not surprisingly, sleep would not come easy, and he was up and about before five the next morning and keying the PD's front entrance by a quarter till six, all concerns of potentially hazardous roadways reduced to an afterthought in comparison to the mission at hand.

The epiphany struck at straight up six-thirty, as he had been placing the copied reports and all accompanying forms and statements in chronological order. As prompt and reliable as they came, Maggie would surely arrive for her shift by quarter of seven at the latest—taking over from the sheriff's county dispatcher—the RAV4 she drove reducing the icy roads to a minor inconvenience at best. Thus, Wes wheeled back out of the front entrance at exactly six-forty, with the monumental decision to expand his duties to include home delivery of requested police reports already made.

From the *Crimson Falls Gazette* Sports Page
Dated Sept. 12

Wildcats stun the Broncos 32-14 behind the two Ds: Defense and Dalton
(Friday night, Barton Field)

Powered by Dalton Crane's three rushing TDs and a stifling defense that held the Barton running game to a paltry forty-one yards on twenty-eight carries (exactly one-hundred yards short of Crane's own tally), the underdog Crimson Falls Wildcats won their first season opener since the 2015 season in grand style.

Two

Having trekked dicey two-lanes littered with patches of black ice cloaked beneath a dusting of snow, Wes veered off the curvy, pothole-littered Old Sawmill Road onto a sporadically paved drive, passing a brick mailbox with the name *"McCarron"* painted in faded black lettering onto an equally faded shade of red.

It would be another ten minutes-plus—the upsloping, ice- and snow-slicked drive seriously affecting his unloading time— before he'd find himself parked at the bottom of a trio of concrete steps leading to a split-level ranch style home's front entrance, an oversized manila folder sitting across his lap, a cell phone shoved flush to his left ear.

"Mister McCarron? Yes sir, it's Wesley Grant from the police department. I know it's a little early, but I've completed your request and decided to just drop them by and save you a trip. The less vehicles on these roads, the better."

Scanning his surroundings, his cheeks glowing red from a stiff morning breeze, Grant identified a few telltale signs of neglect in what would otherwise be considered a high-end home in terms of resale value. A few loose shingles, a crooked window seal, peeling paint in various spots. Nothing a few thousand dollars couldn't make right.

"Yes sir, I'm right outside. Thought about honking the horn, but it does take me a bit to unload the chair and strap myself in. Yes sir, I could use a cup at that. Oh, well, sure, I do have a few minutes. Roads aren't really that nasty. Um, not sure how I can access your front door, though, without combat-crawling. A back entrance? Oh sure, um, just follow the walkway. Be there in in a few. If not, send out help for a possible rollover."

His squinting eyes, the bifocal portion of his glasses partially fogged from his own steamy breath, perused a path of concrete tiles that slinked around the side of the house's brick base and dead-ended atop a paved patio leading directly to a ground-level entrance.

A shirtless man wearing a contorted grin and decked out only in cut-off jean shorts and flipflops met him at the back door, the tightly coiled exoskeleton braces at his thighs, knees and calves showcasing pencil-thin legs long since drained of their livelihood.

"Welcome to the McCarron estate, Mister Grant, you are both a gentleman and a scholar," the man beamed, assorted strands of hair sticking out like quills, and backed away to allow space for the passing chair. "But I gotta warn ya, the ol' homestead here is just chock full of the rattlin' bones of some tired old specters."

As Wesley cleared the narrow entrance and entered a relatively bare, surprisingly spacious kitchen, his host executed a stiff half-bow.

"Roll on in here, my man, and join us spooks in a cup of joe."

Wesley Grant felt a chill run up his spine that had little to do with such dramatics and everything to do with the performer.

~ * ~

Roughly seventy hours earlier, a man sat with heavily braced legs splayed and arms crossed, the gray stubble on his chin resting on his upper chest, a low hissing sound barely audible through flaring nostrils. Outside the Crimson Falls combination bus station and car rental, a light snow descended onto grounds still too warm to properly welcome their frosty arrival, thus instantly altering each icy flake to its original liquid state. Tucked warmly inside the aged transportation hub's walls, there resided perhaps two dozen scantily padded empty seats and exactly four of the taken kind, all other guests recently having deboarded the afternoon arrival from Louisville.

In the seat to the slumbering man's left sat his lone piece of luggage in the form of a worn brown duffel, against which a folded wheelchair leaned. A few rows back and over resided a young couple whose whispered pronouncements concerning the man's unique ensemble (crimson beret, faded blue jeans, leather jacket, spit-shined hunting-style boots accented by the coiled straps, sealed backpack and a squared hard shell that appeared straight out of a futuristic sci-fi movie) were made inaudible by a never-ending stream of elevator music being pumped in from overhead.

A short time later, the station deserted save for his own napping self, a series of gentle tugs at the left sleeve of his leather jacket brought him back to the land of the living.

The kneeling man at his side wasn't immediately familiar, but quickly enough identified as his deceased mother's younger brother, Dexter, a short, stout man in his late fifties to early sixties who wore his hair in a tightly wound ponytail trailing his back, the "do" unnaturally dark considering his advanced years, thus more than hinting at chemical alteration.

What instantly came to mind concerning "Uncle Dex" was the man's sometimes irritating and always bizarre penchant for hardly ever speaking. That, and a faint memory regarding prison time done upstate, the associated crime a mystery Gunther wasn't about to broach, at least not yet, considering the decade-plus since the pair had shared the same space.

Now as then, his uncle wasn't merely a man of few words, but of no words whatsoever, instead using assorted nods, scowls and the occasional grunt to convey communication. That the man seemed to pay no mind to his nephew's physical disability nor the state-of-the-art equipment strapped to his frame like a second skin, nor why he'd reached out after such a lengthy absence for assistance in reclaiming the family home was, in retrospect, perfectly in character with the morose, tight-jawed elder of Gunther's past (he recalled his father's rather blunt assessment of Uncle Dex being that *The man possesses all the emotion of a picked cabbage*").

The ride from the station to the McCarron home had taken approximately twelve minutes, his uncle's battered and mud-spattered Ford pickup never tempting to surpass or even match posted limits. Main Street, Crimson Falls had, Gunther noted, undergone a few important changes since his last trek down its two-lane path, though he couldn't be sure this lack of familiarity wasn't due to a woeful lack of memory.

A quaint little village of just under two-thousand citizens fourteen years ago, Wikipedia reported the current population at just under twenty-eight hundred, this rather dramatic increase no doubt tied to the construction of an Amazon hub warehouse in 2017 that employed around two-hundred full-time employees.

As for the main drag, there were clothing and shoe stores, not one but two pharmacies (both promising *"prompt, 24-hour service"*) and, bookended on both the north and south sides, separate grocery chains. Among these, most all vaguely familiar as holdovers, stood something called a "Vape Store," sharing space with a Verizon Wireless. Also new, at least as far as he could recollect, was the addition of a fourth red light seen as they'd departed Main for the red ridge split—basically a pair of two-lanes headed in opposite directions out of town. Sadly, it appeared the town's lone movie theater, the Crown Cinema Three, must have closed during the COVID outbreak and had yet to find a new owner.

Though nothing specific came to mind, Gunther knew he'd spent many the lazy hour tucked inside the building directly next to the old movie house, now boarded up and vacant but at one time one of the town's few hotspots for simply hanging out. The exact name escaped him, as did so many specific details these days, Billy Bob's Billiard House or The House of Pool or Strike, Spare, or Split. Something similarly corny, an old-school haven for those whose idea of high-dollar entertainment included a casual game of pool, darts or pinball, all served with the coldest beer in the county and a pulled pork sandwich to equal any restaurant in three states.

As the aged Ford spat, sputtered and shimmied toward the split to eventually veer left toward Old Sawmill Road, Gunther took note of at least the third roadside sign—this one fronting a combination gas station and garage—announcing the weekend's (and perhaps the year's or even decade's) upcoming highlight event.

Grinning beneath a strategically placed hand, Gunther had felt the inexplicable need to hide this sudden display of emotion from his uncle, who most likely wouldn't have inquired into its origin if featured beneath a glaring spotlight or announced through a bullhorn. As with a parallel road sign he'd spotted near one of the main drag's pharmacies and a full-blown banner hanging over the entrance to the local Waffle House, the hyperbole of each message displayed was essentially the same, though with minor variations. The majority ran from the rather generic "Go Wildcats! Slam the Red Raiders!" to the infinitely more graphic "Wildcats will GUT the Raider's 'red'!" to the more family-friendly (Waffle House banner version) "CF Wildcats to rock the D. Raiders THIS SATURDAY!!"). As they approached the homestead, Gunther made a mental note to attend this locally historic event, if at all possible, for nothing more than pure sentimentality.

Stepping gingerly from his uncle's rickety ride, always a dicey maneuver even on the flattest and driest of terrains, much less the crack-infested pavement fronting the McCarron home, he was forced to lean heavily upon a loudly creaking passenger door to prevent crashing face-first onto the cold, jagged asphalt.

"You mind snaggin' the duffel and chair for me, Dex?" he requested without turning, while trudging stiffly to stone steps rife with their own potential dangers.

His uncle did so without reply, leaving the truck running while hauling the overstuffed bag over one shoulder and curling the folded chair with the opposite hand, all the while careful to maintain a yard's distance as his nephew scaled the four steps with the precision and cautious apprehension of a man tiptoeing through a live minefield.

Steps successfully scaled and front door keyed, Gunther pushed the heavy oak entrance inward, flaring nostrils instantly assaulted by a hybrid scent that was equal parts stale abandonment and, strangely enough, homey familiarity. The former was as understandable as the latter was bizarre, considering the place hadn't experienced human occupancy in just over a year and, as for the latter, he hadn't set foot inside its walls in just over fourteen.

Sniffing generously, he took instant pleasure in the simple joys of *déjà vu.*

Uncle Dexter shattered his daze just moments later, roughly tossing the duffel onto light gray cut-loop carpet while reaching around the door to lean the chair against an adjacent wall, before hopping back from the entrance as if forbidden to access some invisible wall of detention.

"You're always welcome on these grounds, Dex," Gunther had offered, arms outspread within the spacious living area, made all the roomier by a conspicuous absence of furniture, except for a black leather recliner parked between matching end tables, all fronting a large screen plasma atop a squared marble stand. The surrounding walls, once adorned by an assortment of pastoral paintings and framed black-and-white photos handpicked from his dad's collection, stood as blank and gray as any stereotypical prison rampart.

His last known elder nodded as if to refuse the offer, though he did tilt forward with arms crossed and lips parting in minute fractions as if forcefully pried.

The words came just as Gunther's patience had worn until he was on the point of inquiring if his uncle still possessed an operational tongue.

"You might want to think about limiting your time here. Not just the house, but the town and general area as well."

"Sounds like you might be privy to some information vital to my plight, Dex."

His mother's brother's eyes, usually an unreadable blank slate, narrowed with surprising guile.

"The newspaper and TV vultures will soon swarm. Bank on it."

Gunther met his elder's stare with equal intensity, his freakishly disproportionate features on full, graphic display as he twisted his torso and head halfway around, with painfully thin legs still pointing inward like the fractured gams of a mangled flamingo.

"This close to year's end? They're all about feel-good stories around the holidays. Still, if so, it's an annoyance I can handle. That it?"

"Can't say for certain."

His uncle's eyes fell to the carpet and lingered.

"What I'm saying is you might not wanna find out. Put the place on the market and just go. Start fresh with new surroundings."

"You know I can't do that. Not yet anyhow. Didn't come here to profit by sellin' off what little's left. Wish I still had their vehicles. I'd put one of 'em under the tree for ya in a few weeks." Gunther nodded past his uncle to his idling pickup, which was coughing, gargling and spatting like an asthmatic wino. "Seems like you've been drivin' that old brontosaurus since my high school days."

"Had to auction 'em off for, well you know. Your dad had a grand old Chief Cherokee they sold for parts. Delores' Regal fetched a fair price at least. She wasn't driving much at the end anyhow. Besides," his uncle's arms fell loosely to his sides as if released from bondage, "no choice."

"Damn shame all the way around, right?" Gunther peered downward at himself as if to validate the point. "All that for a down payment on the ultimate junker *without* a warranty."

The silence between them was as jarringly sudden as it was solemn.

"Sure you don't want some java?" the nephew resumed, his legs twisting gradually around to join their connected torso. "Gotta be a coffee maker in there somewhere and I've got a fresh bag of *Death Wish* stashed in the duffel along with some fig newtons and at least ten separate species of pharmaceuticals. Can't legally hand over the latter, but the first two are free of charge to family, no small offer considerin' that small bag of DW ran me almost twenty bucks. Gotta admit, though, it's a hell of a lid-lifter. Got a taste of it in rehab and, brother, it was instant addiction."

As if to answer nonverbally, his uncle began backing off the porch, a hand raised in apparent farewell.

"What you going to do for future transport?"

"I'll work it out. The town's grown. Must have a version of *You-bra*, right?"

A tiny smile, barely recognizable as such, temporarily creased his uncle's craggy mug.

"Uber, I think it's called, and I doubt it. You have my cell number. Ring me. I'm semiretired as it is and get up way too early since Libby left."

"Libby?"

"Most recent ex."

"There's a scorecard?"

"Think there's been two since you...went away."

Libby—Liberty Delbert McCarron by marriage—had been Dexter's third wife; she had vamoosed their less than happy home nearly a year ago, following an always-shaky three-year run, supposedly in the arms of a Lexington car mechanic she'd met online. Marriage had not been good to the McCarron or Bonner (his mother's family) clans. Save for Gunther's parents, the unions were usually about as permanent as home interest rates.

Gunther couldn't help but smile at his uncle's awkward wording, though considering the man's limited vocabulary, he wasn't about to offer a verbal thesaurus.

"Well, I surely appreciate the free taxi offer. Remember, you're always welcome, compadre."

The two shared a final, amiable yet undeniably gauche nod, Dexter stepping forward just long enough to reach in and reseal the front door.

Sure enough, a coffee maker existed, as did an unused bag of sugar and unopened box of individual half-and-half creamer. The fridge, humming smoothly and fully cooled, held a fresh (at least according to date) dozen eggs, a gallon of milk and a full case of bottled spring water.

A casual perusal of the kitchen cabinet interiors unearthed at least a dozen assorted cans of soup and veggies, saltine crackers and even twin boxes of Oreo cookies.

"Bless ya, Uncle Dexter," Gunther whispered several minutes later, while sitting at the kitchen's dining table—the lone piece of furniture except for two accompanying chairs—nibbling an Oreo with a glass of cool milk sitting close by. "Bless your cotton-pickin', tongue-tied heart."

~ * ~

"Cream and sugar?"

"Pardon?"

"You take it full ebony or well-doctored?"

Gunther stood with his back to the visiting clerk, who'd parked his wheelchair at the far side of the dining table opposite his host, absently stroking the outside of the closed manila envelope with a probing forefinger.

"Oh, unaltered is fine, thanks."

A gradual turn, accomplished in one slow, ultra-precise movement and two stiff, robotic steps forward, and Gunther stood at the opposite side of the table, leaning—his back as stiff and straight as an ironing board—to set down two separate bowls, one filled with individual coffee creamers and the other with powdered sweetener.

"There ya go, stout enough to darken the teeth and steam clean the gullet," he quipped, a hybrid grimace *slash* grin ever-present while wrestling table and chair simultaneously before finally managing to seat himself, braced legs spread out so far under the table they lightly tapped the side of his guest's wheelchair.

As if to test the claim, Wesley Grant sipped noisily and, replacing the cup atop the cloth tabletop, nodded in apparent satisfaction.

"Nice. Not sure whether to sip it or spoon it."

"Breakfast? Afraid the mornin' menu is limited to either Little Debbie oatmeal cakes or some store-brand granola bars sure to crack your molars."

"Tempting, but think I'll pass. Trying to cut back after the poundage I packed onto home base over Thanksgiving."

Gunther's half-smile, half-smirk hardly wavered while he stirred in a heady mix of four creamers and three heaping helpings of pure cane sweetness.

"Got'cha. Least I could do for ya for droppin' these off."

"No hassle. Halfway on my way anyhow. Hope they're of some use to you."

Reaching over after a quick taste test of his own severely modified brew, Gunther slid the folder forward, touching its slick outer edge with a probing forefinger while eyeing his guest through a tight squint.

"Some interestin' readin', I take it?"

"Not particularly, at least for the majority of what I dug up. Buuuut," the guest emphasized while reaching up to tuck thick strands of shaggy brownish-gray hair behind each ear, "there were a few tidbits that caught my eye during the redaction phase."

"Safe bet it was more of a knuckle punch. Some familiar names present, I'd wager."

Wes nodded without verbal reply, his latest sip drawn out to at least twice the previous effort's duration.

"Goes without sayin' then," Gunther concluded, leaning back as far as the suit's backpack would allow.

"Not my business, Mister McCarron. Got to admit, though, something has been praying on my mind ever since you waltzed up to the records window."

Head tilting slightly to the left, Gunther's dramatically cocked brows seemed to indicate silent permission for the other man to continue.

"I'd heard and seen pictures, but never saw that sort of...," he gestured with the raised coffee cup toward Gunther's general person, "...equipment up close and personal. Is it, well, as seamless and streamlined as they say?"

"The best twenty-first-century technology has to offer, for those fortunate minorities with the means to throw down a cool sixty to seventy-five grand for the privilege. Oh, and please call me Gunther."

Wes Grant's eyes widened, his lips pursing in a pained wince.

"Dang. I figured they weren't cheap, but that's at least thirty-grand more than I was guesstimating. Oh, and it's Wes."

"Lesser models run for just over forty thousand, ballpark figure, Wes. This here deluxe SuitX Exoskeleton model is the full bells-and-whistles version, battery-charged edition. See, like any other electronic device, I gotta keep 'er plugged in whenever she's not in use. A larger-scale cell phone, ya might say."

"Impressive, I mean considering."

"Course, ya gotta understand that what you see before you *is* the broke-in version. Took me and a veritable pit crew of physical therapists roughly three months of strappin', strainin' and screamin' before I could even manage to stumble from one wall to another like a human pinball. Not a pretty sight, I'm here to tell ya. I still have the occasional morning I end up face-first on the turf."

"Still, worth all the effort, I'd imagine."

"Well, yeah, I mean considerin' the alternatives," Gunther began, pausing to shrug. "Nothin' personal. Got my own set of wheels for backup.

"Besides, it ain't like most have the choice, I mean financially. If I was King Crip, all paraplegics could snag one free of charge and I'd have all the best eggheads workin' on a similar model for the Quads."

"Not a problem," Wes replied between sips. "Anyway, I've grown quite accustomed to life on wheels in just over a decade of navigation. Still, a person does appreciate change now and then, and the whole bionic man thing does appear to have its advantages over a permanent squat."

"It does, no question, though it ain't like I don't utilize the ol' rollin' chariot myself occasionally for the same reason. Obvious advantages aside, strappin' this on and haulin' it around all day does tend to wear."

"I see."

"Yeah, the whole 'suitin' up' process gets real tiresome when all ya really want is a quick roll outta the hay to go take a dump. So, what got ya?" Gunther inquired, following a brief respite for respective sips and subsequent sighs.

"What's that?"

"What put ya there?" he nodded, gesturing with a raised pinkie toward the chair.

"Oh, oldest cliché in the book. Car crash."

"Spinal or brain?"

"Depends on who you ask. My ex will tell you brain. Doctors all settled on spine."

Rolling his eyes, Gunther grinned and tipped his coffee cup as to toast.

"I was told my own was a little of both but mostly spinal and neck, a paralysis stew if ya will. No need to go into the hows. I'm sure ya read enough to get the gist. As for the whys, well, therein lies the rub.

"But things could be worse," he concluded with a cocked brow.

"Locked-in syndrome?" Wes offered.

"Bingo. Had an uncle on my ma's side who rotted away flat on his back for years from Lou Gehrig's. Hell on earth, that one."

Another short silence, any initial awkwardness having been quickly erased by the naturalness of their banter.

"Tell the truth. What do you miss most?" Wes asked, perhaps or perhaps not to alter the direction of the conversation.

"You first," Gunther fired back, winking playfully. "You've had longer to want, at least consciously."

"Might sound corny, but just being able to *stand* over a urinal."

Gunther paused briefly to properly take in the weight of the remark before flashing a thumbs-up gesture.

"Yeah, there is *that*, now that ya mention it. One of the few remainin' strictly genuine male traits left standin', ya might say. Least that's what I hear."

"What about you?" Wes inquired with a slight uptilt of the chin and through squinting eyes equally as hound-dog droopy as his host's, despite the recent shot of caffeine.

"Oh, no contest, though it has to be placed in the category of 'in memory of,' but that's easy. Doggy-style."

"Swimming?"

Gunther's cocked brow spoke volumes.

Executing a textbook spit take, Wes Grant was helpless to hold back the fountain of hot liquid he shot across the table, nor was he able to successfully quell the spillage dripping forth from each flared nostril. Handing over a palmful of paper napkins, Gunther's wild cackle sent them both into a minute-long laughing jag that left both straining for breath in the aftermath.

"Just a couple of wild and crazy paraplegics," Gunther finally managed, hugging himself to soothe the throbbing pain at his ribs.

"Got to appreciate an honest man," his guest whined, wiping brownish dribble from each flaring nostril.

Cups empty, the two bid each other farewell with a firm handshake, the lengthy duration of which wasn't lost on either, the wheelchair-bound police records clerk wishing the similarly aged, similarly disabled man "good reading" before waving the normal research and copy fees associated with acquiring said reading materials.

A light snow descended from what appeared to be an infinite formation of light gray clouds as Wes pulled back onto Old Sawmill Road, all thoughts of the potential hazards of traipsing atop steadily worsening pavement conditions utterly lost amid a building fog of apprehension.

At precisely nine-thirty-eight AM, settling into the handicapped parking spot reserved solely for his use, the Crimson Falls police department's lone full-time clerk decided he was long overdue for a vacation, as in posthaste.

From the *Crimson Falls Gazette* Sports Page
Dated Sept. 19
(Friday night, Falls Field)

In a hard rain and muddy track, Wildcats rout the Tigers 41-6

A consistently hard rainfall and muddy field conditions did little to slow the Wildcats on either side of the ball, the offense grinding out over three-hundred yards on the ground—one-seventy-eight by halfback Dalton Crane, to include two long touchdown runs—and holding the visiting Cordova Tigers to under one-hundred yards in total offense, while forcing four fumbles.

Three

"Tofu? She offered. "It *is* fried, tough guy, in case you're worried about misplacing your man card."

"Not unless Dan managed to conceal a chicken nugget or two in there somewhere."

"If he values his life, he'll avoid such shenanigans."

"You know, such a remark *could* be construed as the intimidation version of domestic simple assault."

"I joyfully confess. So enough fluff already, tell me, and I mean the *truth*, why this sudden urge for time off?"

Forking up a large bite of the aforementioned soymilk dish with a side of brown rice, Maggie Childers regarded her co-worker with a suspicious smirk, complete with arched brow and slight tilt of the head, her dark coif curled into a tight bun that, from afar, resembled a perfectly rounded, ebony cabbage ripe for picking. The pair inhabited their usual lunchtime table, a booth in the rear out of earshot of the small crowd—no more than a dozen or so—sharing the pre-noon rush at The Glutton's Dream diner, the owner and head chef of which was Maggie's lesser half of over a decade, Dan.

"I told you, Mag, I'm just feeling the faint flames of burnout. First the state audit, a week of pawing through random reports and another spent correcting the numerous hits. Or how 'bout the sixteen accidents and a dozen incidents in the past four days? Not that I'm counting, but hey, you took the majority of the calls turkey day and all the forced family fun that annually ensues."

"Pinheads behind the wheel and cabin fever casualties," she conceded between bites, "grumpy guts filled with dressing, yams, pumpkin pie and bootleg booze. Powder-kegs lit with the joys that only a houseful of hated kinfolk can bring."

Relieved to see her expression mellow, Wes balanced a spoonful of steaming chili in front of pursed lips and gently blew.

"Exactly. You know the drill."

"Rarely alters course, does it? Good ol' small town America."

Saltine in hand, Wes seized the opportunity to further divert her curiosity.

"Sure you don't want some R and R yourself? I got plenty of room at the Love Pad."

"Don't go tempting," she replied, winking playfully. "Life with Dapper Dan has ensured I'm constantly in need."

"Well, my lady, with such low expectations, I'm sure to sa-sa-satisfy."

Heads bowed, the two were giggling like naughty teens sharing a dirty joke, when a shadowy figure appeared at the side of the booth as if having magically teleported there.

"You two been sneaking a certain green, leafy substance from the evidence room again?"

Patrolman Phil Strickland was average in stature but heavy in bulk, a dedicated, lifelong weightlifter whose uniforms always seemed on the cusp of splitting from even the slightest flex. It was also well known, save apparently to Dan Childers, that Phil and Maggie had been an item—both on and off duty—for quite a spell.

"Phillip," Wes nodded, pushing the mostly empty bowl of chili to the center of the table. "Hot on the trail of the mad streaker?"

Maggie snickered, reaching back and delivering a playful slap to the officer's tree-trunk-thick left thigh.

"Alias Baron Von Shrunken-Pecker."

Figuring that was his cue, Wes bit.

"Alias Frost-testicle the Snowman."

"Alias Nanook of the Nipple."

"Alias the Abom-nipple Snowma—"

Eyes rolling with apparent disgust, the patrolman ended the banter, evidently stopping far short of rating it even remotely witty, with a low, snakelike hiss.

"Good grief, *enough* already."

Amazingly, in the past four nights, as nighttime temps had averaged just under twenty degrees, there had been an equal number of sightings of a naked Caucasian male sprinting buck naked down both Main and three of its cross streets, those being Oak, Shackleford and Spring.

"More like winter hallucinations reported by a grouping of either widowed or old maid boozers, all well past middle age," Strickland replied sourly, one palm rubbing his square jaw while the other performed a similar service atop his crewcut. "Wilma Jenkins, last night's witness, probably hasn't been laid since the Bubba Clinton administration. Horny old hag with a Southern Comfort buzz was just seeing what she *wanted* to see." He paused, peering past the food counter and into the open kitchen, no doubt to pinpoint Dan's exact location before applying a brief massage to Maggie's right shoulder. "You off at five or thereabouts?"

Before replying, Maggie shot Wes a mischievous wink as if to say, "watch as I seduce the haplessly overheated po-lice officer."

"Affirmative and not a second later, why?"

As Strickland spoke out of the side of his mouth with his eyes darting about like pinwheels, Wes mused that the man appeared borderline unstable. Then again, he'd never quite understood what his officemate saw in Phil Strickland, a divorced father of two teenage girls who at times came off about as authentic as your basic social media "celebrity," a walking talking pestilent know-it-all with all the authenticity of a counterfeit twenty featuring Andrew Jackson sporting a nose ring.

As far as what Phil was getting out of their relationship, well, that was obvious. Maggie was not merely an exotic beauty, but was smart as a whip and exuded charm.

"I'm thinking of burgers and brew at Sid's around, say, six-thirty?" Phil mouthed, removing his hand as if from a hot stove as Dan emerged from the kitchen holding serving plates.

A lanky, balding gent fifteen years his lovely wife's senior, Dan Childers was about as talkative as a geranium and twice as jolly, his normal expression being the pained grimace of a man suffering either severe intestinal disorders or raging hemorrhoids, or perhaps both.

Though not his place to approve or disapprove of his co-worker's reckless tryst, Wes often wished he were as oblivious to the affair as was poor, clueless Dan.

"Roads are snot-slick up north, Ace," Maggie shot back, casually sipping green tea from a cup so petite Wes referred to them as "mug-ettes."

"You sure you want to risk us sliding into a ditch with only Tiny or Ears to pull us out? Tongues would wag like a terrier on amphetamines."

"Tiny" referred to PD Chief Will Crockett, a giant of a man at six-six and roughly two-hundred-seventy-five pounds of

Stonehenge hardness. A former noseguard for Crimson Falls' last and lone state football champs back in the early nineties, he'd blown out his knee as a freshman at Bowling Green and soon began a twenty-five-plus year career in law enforcement, starting with a decade's-long turn as a state correctional officer. Gruff and intimidating when the need arose, to those close to him he was a kind, teddy bear of a man.

As for "Ears," that was Jerome Griffey, a reliable if not overzealous patrolman with a penchant for making misdemeanor molehills into felony-related mountains. A straightlaced, "strictly by the book" type, the barely twenty-three-year old's unfortunate nickname came not so much from the size of those particular body parts but the way they appeared to protrude from his close-shaved noggin like separate windmills.

"Fine, whatever then," Phil conceded with a shrug. "How about tuna sandwiches and chips at my place?"

Maggie grinned across the table at Wes, shaking her head as if to say, "see what I have to put up with just for a decent lay?"

"Oh, to swoon. Canned Chicken-of-the Sea and stale Golden Flake. A girl's romantic dream come to life, on wheat or white?"

When the squat officer's pinched features remained unchanged, she sighed wearily and resumed, "Like I have a better offer. Five-forty-five or thereabouts, Romeo, and make sure the bread isn't riddled with yeast spots."

Departing with a surly grunt, the veteran patrolman headed for the counter to pick up whatever carryout order he'd previously phoned in.

"So who's gonna man the console in your absence?" Maggie inquired before finishing off her tea with a resounding slurp.

Wes replied while watching Phil pay for his bagged lunch, leaning near the register to flirt with Dan's teenaged niece.

"Cindy Lou, who else?"

"That dusty old relic? Thought she retired from parks and rec over the summer."

"Nope, still humping it part time."

Maggie frowned.

"Would you mind not using the word *humping* when speaking of Cindy Lou? Tofu can be a bear to digest as it is."

Wes finished the last of his iced tea, grimacing in the aftermath.

"Be nice. She's just trying to stay busy since Ray passed."

"It appears she's been staying plenty busy at the Donut Hole, buying 'em out of Boston Cremes."

"I said be nice. Besides, she's the only former records clerk still on the city payroll and knows the system fairly well."

Both paused to finish off their respective entrées, their eyes darting about the mostly vacant eatery until Maggie's gaze relocked firmly onto his own, that earlier hint of suspicion having returned in both expression and tone.

"Kinda short notice, wasn't it?"

"Been brooding on it for a while. Didn't want to wait till later in the month when all the Christmas shenanigans kick in. Chief approved it without batting an eye or cocking a brow. Maybe I ought to worry."

And just like that, all signs of mistrust evaporated.

"Probably realizes it's overdue. Plans?"

"Well, let's see. Hiking's out, as is running the Boston Marathon or auditioning for that Gladiators reboot I keep hearing about."

Maggie's sour grimace spoke volumes of his rather feeble attempt at low-brow humor.

"Jeepers creepers, Ace. About as comical as someone pulling the bolts outta that rolling throne of yours."

"Nothing special. Might drive down to Huntsville to see Sandy's folks. Maybe binge-watch some overdue Netflix offerings."

"Sandy's fol—you're yanking my chain, right?"

Raising his fork and swaying it back and forth, the faux scowl Wes displayed was easily identified as such even with the burgeoning grin that accompanied it.

"Hey, they're good folks. Her mom makes a chocolate pie straight from the ovens of our heavenly host."

"Just seems weird, Wes. I mean, your ex-battleaxe's parents are your closest friends out of state?"

"Did I mention her mother's chocolate pie?"

"You, sir, are a wildman," Maggie stated, straight faced.

"No argument."

"You will be back in town for the—the..." she rolled her eyes and pretended to swoon, "...the big game on Saturday?"

"Wouldn't miss it. Just hope all this Dakota-like weather is a memory by then."

"Weather dot com says light snow showers and/or sleet with temps in the mid-thirties by kickoff. Best leave the windbreakers in the closet and go for the parka."

As Dan Childers was not only a former Wildcats' standout at right guard and had even once served (on an interim basis) as an assistant coach, he and his less-than-enthralled spouse had season tickets and fifty-yard-line seats, much to her very vocal chagrin. This in mind, Wes was forever able to apply a playful jab whenever the opportunity arrived. Needless to say, what with this season seeing the team's miraculous resurgence, the opportunities to land sporadic haymakers at her expense were many and plentiful.

"Perfect. Anyhow, I'll make sure to roll over to your...*assigned* seating area before that first whistle pierces the darkness of Crimson Falls stadium. Could be a special night, especially if the team pulls it off. Yep, the *assigned* seating area will surely be the place to be, all right."

"Sow-weeeee," she murmured with sincere misery, jabbing her own fork into what remained of her tofu and rice.

Reaching over and gently sweeping the back of his left hand with a meticulously manicured nail, the pout she displayed, though surely meant to express sadness, could've just as easily been defined as playfully seductive.

"All joking aside, I'm gonna miss ya in the trenches, Wheels."

Blushing despite his best efforts, Wes had always loved that nickname as something only the two of them shared during particularly whimsical moments. As was routine, a ritual of sorts, he responded in kind using his own pet name for her.

"Same here, Legs. Hey, it's just a week. We'll survive. Least you have Officer No-Neck to keep your feet warm and Dan to fry your eggs."

In response, she delivered a light jab to his left shoulder, all the while giggling like a girl twenty years her junior.

"If Dan fried my eggs the way he was *supposed* to, maybe I wouldn't need my feet warmed."

Rarely a man lost for words, Wes nonetheless found himself unable to drudge even the weakest of comebacks. In lieu of this, he merely bowed his head in defeat, while checking his wristwatch.

"Let's roll, Mag. Straight up eleven-thirty," he said, scooting over to first unfold and then reboard his chair.

"Back to the salt mines we go. I got the check."

Snugly strapped in, Wes watched his friend and co-worker of nearly a decade stroll to the counter and offer her perpetually grim, droopy-eyed spouse an obligatory wave while paying strictly Wes' part of the bill—Dan had, though reluctantly according to Mag—agreed years ago to write off her own daily lunch order as a freebie.

Steering himself toward the exit and navigating around the pre-noontime crowd that was beginning to file in—though smaller than normal due to the frigid temps and slick roads—Wes was struck by what he could only describe as a premonition.

A virgin to such phenomenon, he wasn't quite sure how to react other than to temporarily freeze up and halt his chair's forward progress a few feet short of the entrance.

"What's wrong? You okay?" he heard Maggie inquire behind him, her voice weirdly muted as if asking from a far distance.

"Dan's chili lighting you up already?" she continued, this time with maximum clarity.

"Nah, just waiting on you, slowpoke," he replied, allowing her to steer him through the exit as an entering couple held it ajar.

As they made their way quietly down the snow-dusted sidewalk toward the nearby PD building, the Main Street traffic irregularly light for approaching the noon hour, Wes struggled to properly define the omen he'd experienced, save for feeling an overwhelming pulse that spoke of dread and foreboding. Bad things. Bad people. Bad *times*.

"Penny for your thoughts, Wheels," Maggie quipped, hugging herself tightly across her department-issued, fur-lined, dark blue jacket with *CFPD* stenciled on the back in bright gold.

"Blank slate, Legs," he replied with as much jocularity as he could muster, despite the feeling that he'd recently been gut punched with such force that the perpetrating fist had yet to depart his butterfly-bloated midsection.

At that moment, he truly wished he could enjoy their light, comfortable banter without the sudden, weighty anchor of apprehension, for something was telling him that a specific recent event might dictate that it be the last such dialogue they might ever share.

~ * ~

Approximately twelve hours after Wesley Grant had dropped the files off in his sweaty palms—he'd done his best to conceal all semblance of nervousness in the man's presence—Gunther McCarron lay sprawled on an aged but well-kept leather recliner in his childhood home, attempting but failing to rub the fatigue from sagging, badly bloodshot eyes.

The file contents had been all he had expected and somehow less, containing a few surprises but no actual jolts of shock—the latter he'd both hoped for and sincerely dreaded.

As for the surprises, he was never sure if such details had merely been lost in the jumbled haze his memory banks had become since waking, or if they were true revelations of events he'd never been privy to.

Of the four incident reports, the oldest having occurred in the fall of 1999 and the most recent, the summer of 2007, only two were of much use for his quest, and he'd reread both at least a dozen times throughout an otherwise unspectacular day tucked inside the house where he'd grown up.

The first of interest, though easily the lesser of the two, involved a harassment/stalking charge brought against him in the spring of '07.

The second, same year but a little further down the calendar, represented the granddaddy of them all and involved such combinations as arson, aggravated assault and homicide.

Hugging the manila folder to his bare chest, he drifted off into a fitful slumber at half past midnight, despite having downed a full pot and a half of coffee as the day and late evening had progressed. Though physically incapable of "tossing and turning" in true nocturnal fashion, he was instead limited to an assortment of facial gestures (from pained grimaces to open-mouthed silent screams), barking grunts and drawn-out snores that, when inhaled through the mouth and exhaled through flaring nostrils, mimicked a tea kettle at full boil.

Thursday, 0630 hours

Rudely awakened by the sound of his cell phone blaring at full volume (to the tune of Rascal Flatts' "Mayberry") his mind felt as leaden as his lower extremities—an extreme hangover without benefit of alcohol—meaning of course that he'd passed out without benefit of his nightly meds. Struggling to roll over within the sunken confines of the ancient couch, he spotted the foursome of prescription bottles within arm's reach on the nearby ottoman, accompanied by a half-empty bottle of Evian.

"Weeelll, never...too early or too late...to overly medicate," he mumbled to himself, sitting up and staring down at an open palm containing a single gabapentin, a luvox, a baclofen and the lone over-the-counter representative, two Aleve. In the aftermath of strapping himself into the exoskeleton, he barely avoided tumbling headfirst into the ottoman before righting his gait with a series of head jerks and arm windmills. While reaching for his cellphone, which he'd used as a paperweight of sorts for the manila folder, he first took note of the text message awaiting his acknowledgement. A message that had, unbeknownst to him in his earlier catatonic state, been received at just before 5:30 AM.

One and a half hours, two hard-boiled eggs and a large mug of steaming Death Wish later, he sat at the dining table with the cell in hand perusing the magic web carpet ride known as Google when a gentle series of three knocks, each timed precisely two seconds apart, echoed from the back door.

"If that's my Uncle Dexter, you've got the key. Step on in. If not, you might as well get comfortable as it's gonna take me a minute or five for a proper greeting."

Decked out in a black, ankle-length duster and an ivory felt Stetson, his uncle strolled into the kitchen holding a McDonald's bag, which he tossed onto the dining table directly between his sulking nephew's parked elbows.

"Morning, dude. Ya really should've called. Had eats already."

"Egg and cheese biscuits and hash browns. Have 'em for lunch."

His nephew stared at the grease-stained bag.

"Take it into consideration. *Danke.*"

"Going to need a ride today?"

"Actually, believe I've got that covered."

Dexter grunted, his face revealing nothing of its origin.

"Need any groceries? Medications? Bottle of Jack Black?" he finally inquired while pulling a pack of Marlboros from his jacket, having spouted that final offer without cracking a smile.

"Nope. Appreciate the offer, though, especially that happy water bit."

Shifting uncomfortably in the narrow high-back chair, Gunther sighed heavily, the folder pinned tightly to the tabletop as if to prevent his uncle from snatching it away.

"Listen Dex, I don't want ya to think you're somehow...responsible for my upkeep. I mean, it ain't like I don't think it's commendable, but it just ain't neces—"

"Digging up old bones can be hazardous."

Following a short pause, during which time his uncle's expression remained like carved marble, Gunther's face creased with a sudden flush of anger as he pounded a gnarled fist against the tabletop with enough force to topple his empty coffee mug.

"To those responsible, ya mean? Well, let's just say I'm countin' on it!"

"I can't protect you, Gunny. Even in my prime, which I can't even recall at this point, I couldn't have."

"I ain't askin', Dex, but I didn't come back to settle in as the new town crip. I came back...came back *here* for answers. If I step on some sensitive toes in the meantime, well maybe those toes *deserved* to be stomped on."

His uncle, staring down at the tiled floor, shuffled his booted feet from side to side like a bashful child.

"And what are *you* going to uncover that the state and feds couldn't?"

Gunther's shoulders sagged, the burst of rage having abruptly abated.

"Remains to be seen."

The two fell into a stilted silence, during which time they exchanged labored sighs but no actual dialogue. Surprisingly, it was the stoic elder who resumed.

"I...understand your need for...closure, for justice, but in your, well...," Dexter paused to gesture toward his kin as if to acknowledge the whole package, "...the way you are now, how exactly are you planning on extracting it?"

"With all due respect to my last livin' elder, you have no clue what my...needs are. No one but me can hope to meet them, and honestly I ain't rightly sure myself. But I do know it's less about me and more about, well, it ain't *just* about me."

"Tell you what I *do* know, Gunther. There's going to be people who not only resent you for playing some half-assed, amateur detective, but are downright pissed-off and willing to hurt you over it."

The younger man shrugged, sporting a droopy, severely warped grin that mimicked a recent stroke victim.

"Agreed, and I accept that. Hell, from certain individuals I *expect* some serious blowback."

"Let me ask you this then," his uncle inquired, reaching to pull the back door ajar. "If you find the person you seek, what will...what *can* you do in that moment but play hapless victim a second time, only this time around, you surely won't survive."

"Dex, all I can tell ya is this: there has to be a reason I survived that *first* time. I aim to find out if that's so. If, as you called it, my half-ass, amateur private dick imitation leads to nothin' but more dead ends or even the same dead ends, then at least I know I tried."

"That's the problem, Gunther!" the older man barked, as close to real emotion as his nephew had ever seen him. "You won't let it. You won't let it lead to nothing. A hundred dead ends or a thousand, you'll keep pushing till somebody pushes back and I can't...I can't protect you."

Leaning back, chair legs squeaking their disapproval, the younger man crossed spindly but surprisingly toned arms—literally muscle and bone—across his narrow chest. The warped smile had long since departed, replaced by the hangdog expression of the mentally or physically drained, or in this case, most likely both.

"Uncle Dexter, understand this is *my* quest and no one else's. Whatever happens to me, be it simple frustration or a showdown I can't possibly win, I've pre-accepted. But I can't just weave and wobble through what years I've got left not knowing. Solving all or just a part of this is all I've got."

With that, his uncle merely nodded, shutting the door halfway before a final inquiry.

"You sure you don't need a taxi service? Cheapest rates in town. Free for relatives, as long as they supply an occasional cup of joe."

"Thanks again. I'll take ya up on it sooner than later!" Gunther offered, flashing a peace sign in farewell just as the door sealed.

There would be another knock at the same door a half-hour later, where a well-fed (Gunther had indulged with a Mickey D's biscuit after all), fully dressed (suited up and strapped-in), medicated and ready to roll host would greet his chauffeur for the day with a handshake and a nod, all the while pondering the mystery of said driver's motivation.

~ * ~

Fourteen hours earlier, Wednesday's late evening temperatures having dropped below the twenty-degree mark for the fourth-straight night (though thankfully with no additional frozen precip on the way), Wes sat on the edge of the bed staring blankly at the cell phone resting on his bare palm as if it were some alien artifact only recently teleported. Sandy's number stared back accusingly, and the finger that levitated mere centimeters over the "call" icon had frozen there as if blocked by some unseen forcefield.

Having been separated for just over five years and officially divorced for just over two, the pair spoke via phone or Skype at least once a week and this week's call was overdue by a full day. Knowing Sandy the way he did, it was only a matter of hours or perhaps minutes before she mistook this for forgetfulness on his part—he had, admittedly, been exhibiting symptoms of early-stage dementia for some time now—and checked up on him. At least he'd been reasonable enough to choose a phone call over a video chat, immediately dismissing the latter option as far too chancy considering his current state of mind and lack of skill in hiding same if viewed on camera. For at least the dozenth time since his arrival home that evening—his Camry fishtailing just slightly several times along the way—he thanked the powers that be that she hadn't lost her job to COVID cutbacks all those months ago and that the drive from Louisville to Crimson Falls was just lengthy enough to prevent any surprise visits. Only a matter of time, he realized, once she became privy to the news. She'd burn tread like a veteran NASCAR racer blitzed on amphetamines within minutes, not hours, of finding out.

Sighing deeply, he briefly scanned the mostly bare walls— save for a framed UK Wildcats poster proclaiming their 2012 National Championship—of the modest, one-bedroom apartment he'd occupied since the divorce, the phone's protective case growing slick with sweat. Taking a peek through the open bedroom door into the sparse living room, he offered the glow of the television screen casual interest at best.

Still hours away from leaving a voice message for Gunther McCarron, a much easier task in comparison to ringing his former partner, he gradually lowered a visibly shaking forefinger downward.

Despite sitting prone for nearly a full hour and going over what could and couldn't be said numerous times during that duration, he commenced to mumble like a drunken stew bum the moment she answered.

"H-hiya San. How goes...so, um, h-how's the weather?"

Roughly six minutes later, the discarded cell lay on a nearby table, Wes briefly worrying that the thundering in his chest and pounding at his temples was possibly a precursor to a massive coronary, massive stroke, or both.

From the *Crimson Falls Gazette* Sports Page
Dated Sept. 26

Crimson Falls moves to 3-0 for the first time in over a decade with a resounding 34-12 thrashing of visiting Baymont
(Friday night, Falls Field)

Behind junior quarterback Shane Mills' two-hundred-twenty-eight yards passing and three TDs, two to wideout Jeremy Dixon, and an opportunistic defense that forced four Black Bear turnovers, the Wildcats moved to their first 3-0 start in twelve seasons.

Four

"Something on your mind, Mister McCarron?"

"Ya might say that, Mister Graves."

"Grant."

"My bad. Recallin' monikers was never my strong suit in better times, and the whole extended coma thing hasn't done anything to improve that shortcomin'."

"No sweat. So you had a question?"

"Several in fact. Just gimme a second to get better situated."

Wrestling with the Exo-suit's twin ergonomic seven-G forearm canes, shoulder and leg braces and battery backpack, even managing to jab his own upper forehead with the former and barely missing an eye in the process, Gunther panted and gasped as if having scaled a steep mountainside.

"No rush whatsoever. My time is your time," Wes said if for no other reason than to distract from his passenger's struggles to regain a semblance of comfort. As his transfer from chair and its loading into the Camry's back seat were seemingly effortless when compared to his passenger's plight, there was a twinge of guilt he'd felt compelled to address.

"I guess there is a price to pay, no matter the level of technology involved."

"Ya might...say that. Doesn't help...that...I was...never the patient...type," came the breathy reply. "And I ain't gonna lie. This...thrice-day grapplin' gets...old fast. Makes a...body want to...stay put, if ya...can dig it?"

Reaching beneath the ankle-length duster he was sporting for the day's travels, Wes flipped it inside out to reveal the clear bag strapped to his upper thigh.

"Dig it I can, courtesy of this little stowaway. Have to severely limit my liquid intake to avoid numerous, sometimes awkward pitstops to offload."

"Sooo, we comparin' battle scars like that scene from *Jaws*, are we?" Gunther grinned, thick beads of sweat coating his forehead, cheeks and nose. In response, Wes reached over and shifted the car heater to a lower setting.

"Not a chance. Just saying. Didn't notice a similar holster hanging on your person, so...," he shrugged, hands held palms up as if to surrender, "...nope, I got nothing else."

"Happy to say I've found the crede method works enough to keep me both bagless and diaper-free, though the frequent UTIs that come with the territory are no picnic. Can ya mail a package without soiling the surroundings?"

"Mail a...oh, yeah, that can be a problem, but over the years I've maintained the routine well enough to avoid stinky spills...you?"

Gunther frowned, nostrils flaring as if inhaling double of the subject matter at hand.

"Oh, I can feel it comin' on well enough but stoppin' the dam from breakin' open, so to speak, can be a bear. Since I'm still fairly new to the process, there have been a few missed calls, fortunately none in public, though."

"Well, if you feel that dam is in danger of cracking anytime during our travels, don't be shy in addressing the conductor."

His passenger's hearty laugh, deep and joyous, came as a palpable relief.

"Will do. And hey, don't get me wrong. This here gear is a miracle once you're upright, but sittin', especially in cramped spaces, is kinda like an astronaut from an old sci-fi flick goin' through the decompression phase, if ya get my drift."

"I don't and I do. So, I'm ready to field those long-delayed questions anytime you're ready to fire away."

Reaching up to readjust the beret, pushed awry during his earlier struggles, Gunther coughed roughly into a palm before resuming. If anything, his deeper-than-the-ocean-floor baritone had discovered an even more cavernous level in the aftermath. It was like listening to a lifelong smoker bark through a cracked bullhorn that only served to enhance the gravelly effect.

"Oh yeah, *that*. Mainly just ponderin' why you'd take time from your daily duties to haul my lifeless carcass around the county and beyond. I mean, I saw how busy you were what with playing one-man army back at the station."

Sucking in a deep, labored breath, Wes faced his fellow paraplegic, arms crossed as if he were suddenly chilled despite the building warmth inside his parked ride, and locked eyes with him, as if doing so would somehow validate the statement to come as being unquestionably sincere.

"Fair enough. Okay, I'm not going to even try to blow smoke here. Once I was tasked to retrieve and read the...that specific incident report involving you and the young lady for the usual redaction purposes, well, it did pique my curiosity. Lots of water has gone by beneath the Crimson Falls overpass in what? Thirteen years?"

"Little over fourteen actually. Please proceed."

Wes nodded in obvious awe.

"That's a mess of seasons. Anyway, the town has seen upwards of a dozen murders, countless rapes and even a child abduction in that stretch. Shangri-la it isn't, though you'd never know it from the blasé attitude of its citizens, half of which still leave their front doors unlocked twenty-four seven, whether they're at home or not. Your, um, *that* case is, without a doubt, still the most talked about, well, more like whispered about by most, and second place isn't even close.

"At the time, I wore a county deputy's badge and *still* remember where I was when I first heard about it. I'd wager most law enforcement types on duty that night within a fifty-mile radius have that in common."

"So basically, you're just bein' nosy," the other man stated blandly, the slight tilt of his head and squint of his eyes, coupled with the flat, almost accusatory tone of his voice temporarily making Wes regret his choice of narrative.

"Well, hey, it's not just that...I mean...I...I guess I see a man with similar...struggles as myself and I'm, well, naturally drawn to help him ou—"

"Just yankin' your chain, dude," Gunther intruded with a leather-gloved hand raised up and out. "Truth is, I've been warned about media vultures tappin' on my front door hopin' for an exclusive update or some such malarky, so I figured it was still...now what did they used to call it? Hot copy? Hard to believe after all these years. So far so good. Guess no one's spilled the beans about my surprise arrival. Well, make that my surprise survival. Just a matter of time now I guess, 'specially since I ain't exactly plannin' on keepin' the lowest of profiles."

"Tell you what, Mister McCarron," Wes replied, reaching down to put the Camry in gear, "I'll do my best to maintain secrecy as long as possible, not just for you but for my own self-preservation."

His passenger cocked a quizzical brow.

"Oh yeah? Why's that?"

"As far as my inner circle knows, I'm taking a short sabbatical to lie around in my bloomers, stuff my face with chips and dip and binge-watch Netflix."

Though appearing briefly lost on the relevance of the "Netflix" comment, Gunther nodded agreeably enough.

"By the way, it's no sin to go bald, you know," Wes jabbed while backing cautiously from the paved drive as several frozen puddles had formed at its smooth edges.

"Well, that was random. Who says it is?" Gunther replied, bending to adjust the braces at his calves, one of which had snagged on his seatbelt.

Having successfully navigated them onto the roadway, Wes gestured with upturned eyes toward his passenger's scalp, where his familiar crimson beret sat slightly askew.

"That stylish head warmer you're always sporting. You purposely going for the south-of-the-border dictator look?"

"When it ain't completely numb, my noggin gets cold, okay? Besides," he replied, smiling wryly while surveying the pot-hole ravaged two-lane ahead, "sure saves time from stylin' the pathetic combover that's my lone alternative. I've got an extra at home, a real Fidel Castro special. Ya might think about it. Besides, the chicks dig it."

"Uh-huh, hard pass."

"Might think about paintin' that gray shrub hangin' off your chin like dried spinach while you're at it."

"Hey," Wes barked back, stroking his beard with a gloved hand until it sat as pointy as any stereotypical devil of biblical lore. "This baby screams wisdom and knowledge."

"My man, what it screams is week-old soup and crackers. Take my advice, head on over to Kroger and seek out the shampoo and shaving isle. It's called *Just for Men*. Take a decade off all that...wisdom of yours."

"Advice duly noted and discarded. Wait, how is it you're wise to over-the-counter whisker watercolors when it hasn't been a thing since you were pulled from the ice, so to speak?"

"Whiskey water-...oh, the hair-painting thing. Saw a commercial and took note in case I never decide to recultivate my own cookie duster."

"Cookie duster? See that one carved in stone somewhere, grandpa?"

"And speaking of what passes for boob-tube entertainment these days," the passenger inquired with a pronounced sneer, "what happened to *King of the Hill* or *Malcolm in the Middle?* Saw some nasty crap on cable last night called *My Nine-hundred-pound Wife.* Disgustin' as steppin' in a fresh stack of dog droppin's but damned if I could look away."

"*My six-hundred-pound Life,* I think you mean. Yeah, the so-called reality shows rule the roost, sad to say. Guess that's only natural though, considering the thousand or so channels looking to fill time slots. Cheap is in and quality out."

"Apparently," Gunther nodded agreeably, a small smile creasing his thin lips. "Wonder when it airs again. They still sell *TV Guides?*"

"Just a click away these days," Wes replied, briefly removing his right hand from the wheel and mimicking pressing a remote with a flexing thumb.

"Figures. And movies are all steaming these days, I see. You'd think I'd been away fourteen blessed years or somethin'."

"Or something, and it's *streaming.*"

"Oh, kinda like the urine presently fillin' my adult underoos."

The driver grinned despite himself. "Something like that, only without that soothing yellow shading."

The pair briefly fell silent and stared straight ahead, sharing similarly sardonic grins as the Camry neared a four-way stop, a nearby road sign advertising the best in both room and board

(Holiday Inn Express) and fast-food eats (McDonald's, Taco Bell and KFC) that Crimson Falls had to offer.

"So, Mister McCarron, just to verify the address I entered into the GPS, the system isn't recognizing the street name as viable."

"Honesty, I didn't expect it to," Gunther interrupted casually, "bein' as that was the name the locals gave it, not the highway commission. But you do know of the place?"

Taking a left, away from the aforementioned businesses and the main part of town as a whole, Wes replied while checking both the rearview and side mirrors, each confirming they were indeed lone travelers on a path far less traveled than normal due to the numerous patches of ice.

"Let's just say it rings familiar."

"Cool. I...haven't had a chance to check out the area since I got back and figured, well, might as well start at the beginnin', right?"

Weaving them around and past a number of assorted-sized, battlefield-worthy potholes, Wes shrugged indifferently.

"You're the boss."

Thursday, 0916 hours

"Oh, um, couldn't really say, Miss Jamison. Far as I knew, his biggest plan was to veg out at home or maybe take a ride down to see your folks."

As soon as those final nine words slipped from her tongue, Maggie wished there existed some magical rewind function to retrieve and/or delete their uttering.

"Well, how bizarre. Spoke with him just last night and he mentioned nothing of the sort, much less a trip down to Huntsville."

Sandy Grant Jamison, all five-foot-seven and just over two-hundred pounds of barely restrained southern debutante rage disguised as overt politeness, her plump jowls glowing as red as a pair of overripe tomatoes, growled from between pearly-white gritted teeth while, amazingly maintaining an unwavering, not to mention unnerving, grin.

"Maybe he wanted to surprise your folks and thought telling you might spoil it."

Maggie instantly regretted her impromptu tap dance and broke eye contact with the predatory beast on the other side of the glass. Sitting at a nearby desk, Cindy Lou Harrison stared straight ahead at her computer monitor, though occasionally her beady eyes would gravitate toward the source of the conversation, as all the while she used the pointy end of a ballpoint pen to scratch deep into a hilariously fluffed silver mane that Maggie had secretly coined "Retro Hell from Prell" look.

"Trust me, Maggie, my parents are not into *surprises.* Wesley knows better. Well then...," she sighed, pushing her considerable bulk from the outer counter, the ankle-length dress and floppy hat she sported like some experimental, unfinished psychedelic tapestry, "...I drove three hours on potentially dangerous roadways just to surprise that blockhead." Her Stepford-wife-like smile had suddenly transformed into something infinitely more sinister. "It does appear the surprise is on little ol' me."

"You drop by his place or try calling?"

"Well, not until I got into town, but yes, and all attempts went straight to voicemail."

Shuffling her feet nervously, Maggie bit into her lower lip while dredging up the only answer that managed to crawl to the surface. Sandy Grant Jamison had always made her antsy, as she'd never known which of the woman's many personalities to prepare for, from the sickly-sweet dispositioned Southern belle to the teeth-grinding pit bull or the wild-eyed, schizophrenic hybrid of both.

"Maybe he's on the road and can't answer."

The unnatural gleam in the woman's eyes, the slightly off-kilter pose—hands on hips, head slightly tilted, double chin upturned—along with the hammy, honey-dripping drawl left little doubt in Maggie's mind which persona currently held dominance.

"Well, bless his heart. We surely wouldn't want him breakin' any traffic laws, would we now?" came the reply, literally drenched in sarcasm and delivered with a wink less playful than mocking.

"Um, well he could have his phone turned off, or maybe it's charging," Maggie babbled, unaware that as Wesley's ex had gradually backed toward the PD building exit, she herself was slowly headed in the opposite direction behind the protective glass.

"Good to see you, Maggie. Ya'll take care now," Sandy had concluded with a dismissive wave, having spun around on a heel with a subtle grace which belied her considerable bulk.

Maggie blurted a high-pitched response once the hefty form had vanished beyond the resealed double door.

"Y-yeah, you too...," it began, though the conclusion, whispered harshly through an exasperated sigh, birthed a brief but undeniably wide, toothy grin from Wesley's interim replacement, "...and may you snap a cankle, you psychotic bitch."

Moments later, the whooshing sound of the double doors reopening caused the veteran dispatcher to flinch as if she'd stepped onto a live, sparking wire, that is until the looming, gargantuan shadow quickly transformed into that of Chief Will Crockett.

"Hey, wasn't that Wesley's ex I saw stomping on down the street like a...like a..."

"Mad hippo? Thunder herd of one? Yes sir, that it was. Or should I say, there it blew."

The chief, a hulking and intimidating figure to those who took such traits at face value, was forced to lower his head—the tip of his wide-brim, trooper-style cap lightly tapping the window, presumably to hide the smile surely plastered there.

"Now now, Miss Childers, remember you are a professional," he stated flatly upon straightening, though still unable to meet his subordinate's eyes.

"She searching for Wes?"

Maggie nodded, the dispatch phone ringing just as her lips parted to reply.

"Driving through and thought she'd surprise him," she offered, backing into the gloomy confines of her workspace.

The big man stood silently in the aftermath, no doubt contemplating, and far from the first time, the strange relationship between his veteran records clerk and the man's ex-spouse.

Tipping his cap in Cindy Lou Harrison's direction—the large and hardly in-charge interim clerk nodding faintly in reply—he then strode back to the spacious confines of his own office at the sound of the records phone chiming.

By the time he collapsed into the genuine leather couch fronting a wide, cherry oak desk, both so generously funded by the city council a few years previously, Will Crockett's thoughts had turned to a wild, completely unsubstantiated rumor he'd heard tossed around at Dan Childers' eatery, that of a pale, shambling, ghostlike figure having returned to town; a figure he knew damn well shouldn't even be alive, much less mobile.

Thursday, 0921 hours

"Hard to believe they ever saw fit to pave this lonely stretch."

"Happened about five, maybe six years ago, I think."

Unlike the state road they'd just departed, the curvy, unmarked two-lane was not only pothole free, but a definite improvement overall, as if specially maintained despite appearing, at least thus far, to lead absolutely nowhere of consequence.

"I can only guesstimate that somebody with deep pockets moved nearby," Gunther mused, using the slightly gnarled fingers of his left hand—referred to with a sly grin as "the claw of injustice"—to scratch a buildup of gray stubble beneath his chin.

"You would guesstimate correctly," Wes replied, using the left-hand gear to shift the Camry on coast through yet another endless series of extreme curves, the surrounding landscape an ocean of swells dominated by leafless oaks, twisted pines and matted, freeze-dried weeds, the lone sign of life the occasional prickly holly with its seemingly winterproofed, red-berried leaves.

"Man named Jensen bought up a huge stretch for his farming enterprises. From what I heard, he paved the road from one end to the other from out of his own pockets."

"Bottomless pockets, I surmise."

"Uh-huh. Raises livestock mainly but also works over a thousand acres of corn and nearly as much in tobacco."

"Tobacco?"

Wes nodded, utilizing the opposite handle to accelerate just enough to navigate the Camry over a steep grade but instantly letting off as they crested, the edges of each shoulder of roadway showcasing sporadic patches of snow-coated ice.

"Has contracts with several third-tier cigarette companies, all based in Southeast Asia."

"Impressive. So there's *still* gold in them-there cancer sticks."

"Apparently. Less consumers just means higher prices."

"Yeah, so I've noticed. Not just smokes either. Need a twenty just to grab a burger, fries and a soda at the Golden Arches. It seems the cost of livin' has inflated like a Macy's parade float in my absence."

Yet another series of winding curves finally revealed a mostly straight, flat stretch, easily the lengthiest since they'd departed the main highway, and soon after, the first manmade structure.

Already driving ten miles per hour slower than the posted 35 MPH limit, Wes intentionally coasted to a slow roll as they passed a trio of planked, wooden edifices, all featuring gabled roofs and twin open bays.

"Tobacco barns," Wes explained. "Enough to outnumber the homes down this road three to one."

"I didn't see any road signs when we pulled off the highway. They still call it 'bootlegger alley'?"

"MapQuest had it listed as 'Jensen Acres Way' I believe, no doubt since his buyup in oh-eight or nine."

"Well," Gunther shrugged, leaning forward and squinting through the driver's side as if to spot something familiar. "Man buys up practically half the county, I guess he has the right."

"From what I've heard, Jensen has the market on ego as we—"

"Hang on, hang on, wait...a...minute. Hold up, hold up," Gunther chimed in, face practically flush with the chilled window glass, his breath instantly fogging up the bottom portion. "I think it's...pretty sure it's...steady as she...goes. Riiiiight...there!"

Steering the Camry off the main road and onto what once might've been a well-used gravel drive—just faint remnants of its prior use intact due to expansive weed growth and a glut of weather-beaten potholes—Wes braked to a stop as the path began a gradual U-turn.

Once they'd rolled to a complete halt, Wes noticed his guest staring at the steering wheel and its modified handles.

"Not as complicated as it looks," he said, cutting the engine.

"Well, one of man's greatest strengths is the power to adapt." His passenger nodded. "Nobody knows that better than our kind, right?" he concluded, turning back to the passenger window.

"Well, well," he sighed as the passenger window descended with a low hum. "Not sure what I expected, but a bigger bag of nothin' is hard to imagine."

Wes cleared his throat and paused briefly before replying in case his passenger hadn't yet concluded his thought.

"The report said something about thermite use or some super-flammable mix of chemicals being the reason for such damage."

"Yeah, I think the exact phrasin' in that fire department supplemental said even the ash leftover was still partially flammable. Definitely an educated firebug at work."

A brief, studied silence allowed for the acknowledgement of a light flaking being produced via a dull gray sky, the sullen passenger finally turning to the equally somber driver with lips parted as if to speak but temporarily unable to recapture the power to do so. Gloved hands clenched and shaking at Gunther's lap, eyes blinking rapidly and throat hitching, a low, guttural growl preceded the words that rushed out in rapid-fire succession, their tone of desperation palpable.

"The t-thing is, is this: to you, to my uncle, to the whole blamed town, and mostly to whoever fried this place to the ground, it's been over fourteen winters, ya see? B-but, but to m-me...," he stammered, forcefully jabbing his own chest with a firmly clenched fist, "...it's literally been months, man! A few short flips of the calendar.

"Everything I see, hear and read about the...that night might be moldy old news for everybody else concerned, but to my crippled old ass, it's all still a seepin', open wound and here I am, voluntarily rippin' out the stitches. You...you get me, Grant?"

The driver's darting eyes and blank-slate expression said more than his mumbling retort ever could.

"Gunther, I'm...not su—"

"You think I just showed up out of the blue to relive this wakin' nightmare? Dude, it ain't like I've been livin' my best life at some faraway locale and just bidin' my sweet time to limp down memory lane. I woke up not knowin' who I was, who all the people sportin' light blue or white smocks were, and over the months that followed had to relearn not only how to shit, shower and shave, but how I came to be this...the walkin' pile of *mostly* inoperable rot ya see before ya."

"So you were...you've been incapacitated all this time?"

Reaching into the back seat for his canes, Gunther appeared to have decompressed significantly save for the glowing red sheen adorning both cheeks.

"If incapacitated means in"—he bent to secure the knee and ankle bracelets—"and out of a coma, that about sums 'er up. From what...they told me, I'm the longest livin' survivor in the state of such a...well, *state*."

"Fourteen years, my god. It's just amazing you're able to, that you've been able to recover to even this degree," Wes replied, instantly regretting the implication of his words, but helpless to recover without coming off sounding apologetic for all the wrong reasons.

If his passenger appeared offended, it was impossible to detect; the man's demeanor and gravelly tone remained unchanged.

"Yeah, well, they tell me I did regain varyin' degrees of consciousness, sometimes for as much as a week at a time, but that was mostly just brain waves."

Reaching back for his chair, Wes briefly considered not broaching the subject but quickly discovered the power of curiosity easily trumped bashfulness.

"I can only imagine the medical bills."

"Astronomical is underplayin' it, my man. Forced my folks to refinance the homestead not once but twice and sell off everything but their own hides, up to and including my dad's lifesavings, a trio of CDs and even his IRA. Even with all that, there was a balance of somethin' in the league of a million point five that only disappeared through the efforts of a crackerjack financial lawyer they'd hired from Chicago, who ensured both their life insurance policies went into the till."

"I heard of their individual passing, may they rest in peace. Cancer took your father first, I think? Benjamin, wasn't it?"

"Yeah. Prostrate, 'bout a year and a half back. Mother had expired about five years earlier from a brain embolism. Personally, I'm not underestimatin' the power of stress in cuttin' 'em both down before their time."

"From what I understand, pillars of the community."

Gunther turned to the other man and nodded stiffly, chin jutted and narrow chest as pumped with as much pride as he could manage.

"Appreciate it. *So* unlike the jackass they sired it's truly amazin' we were kin at all. Anyhow, all said I was left the homestead and the remainder of the policies. I tell ya, Wesley, and you can believe this or not, I won't judge ya regardless, but my decidin' to return to the scene of the crimes, that's plural, is as much a tribute to them as my own selfish need to know. I would hope they'd want me to search out the person or persons responsible for practically endin' their only son's life and pretty much their own as well."

His chair unfolded into position just outside the driver's door, Wesley determined to ask the question despite the forthcoming answer appearing quite obvious.

"We taking a stroll onto the old stomping grounds?"

With the aid of the cane strapped to his right forearm, Gunther pushed his own door ajar and gradually levitated his booted right foot out onto the frozen clay surface.

"If ya don't mind. I'm a sucker for nostalgia."

Though forced to navigate the uneven surface of the matted trail onto equally rutted grass, Gunther moved with a consistent determination through a mostly bare landscape, save for the occasional patch of pig or horseweed.

As the path had proven downright unpassable due to a seemingly infinite collection of ruts and furrows, Wesley decided to forego crossing onto the grassy perimeter in fear of getting stuck.

Instead, he sat back and watched in awe as the other man pressed bravely on, seemingly without a trace of the same trepidation. While doing so, he felt the cell vibrate in his left front pants pocket for at least the third time since departing the McCarron house. As with the previous calls or texts, he felt a level of indifference so uncommon from his norm that it served both to shock and enliven.

"So, how's it look to you?" he inquired, instantly dreading the question as seeming overly anxious in terms of personal curiosity.

Standing at the center of the sparse clearing with his back turned to his inquisitor, Gunther's rounded shoulders sagged, his normally light, upbeat tone grew downbeat and sober.

"Damn strange. I mean, ya gotta understand, it seems like a matter of a few short months, not...all those years, since I trekked these exact grounds, only it looked a helluva lot different. Felt...different. Even the surroundin' woods don't seem right. I mean, they look vaguely familiar, but they don't feel like they're from the same time or place, which I guess if ya think about it, they really ain't. It's like, my mind transplanted 'em here from another time. Jeez if I don't sound as unstable as I feel, just breathin' this airspace again."

"Well, like you said, it's like yesterday to you. Such weird vibes would have to be considered normal under the circumstances," Wes replied, giving great effort not to come off patronizing. In the still, silent moments that followed, both men seemed to drift into their own individual dazes.

Wesley, his own trance so deep and razor-focused he hardly noticed the descending flakes coating his scalp, beard and even eyebrows, was rudely snapped to by the sound of an approaching motor, echoing loudly from the east and just around the sharp curve that had preceded their own arrival in the center of the clearing.

A late model GMC pickup, sleek black with comically jacked tires and a window tint as jet-black as its paint job, sped a few hundred yards past before braking hard and reversing at roughly a third of its earlier pace.

"Looks like company," Wes heard Gunther bellow without turning, instead focusing on the backing truck with no small amount of building trepidation.

"Probably just wonderin' who dares trespass on such hallowed grounds."

The truck spun onto the dirt and gravel path, peeling off the hard pavement with a brief but resounding squeal.

"Safe bet they're not the auto club," Wes heard himself quip, steering his chair over a series of shallow ruts that nonetheless served to rattle his kidneys and teeth simultaneously. Just as Gunther shuffled up to his left, the truck rolled up like a stalled Panzer less than a dozen feet from where the pair sat and stood, respectively, and less than half that distance from the parked Camry.

"Looks like they got the jump on us, Tex," Gunther whispered from the right side of his mouth, though in his deep baritone he might as well have bellowed through a bullhorn.

The driver and passenger doors flew ajar as if set on a precise timer, offering an initial image of the inhabitant's boots being of the cowboy and work variety.

"You fellas lost?" asked the driver—black cowboy boots and matching fedora intact—his cocky façade and the lit smoke hanging from his lower lip doing nothing to offset an appearance so comically baby-faced he seemed to possibly have yet to discover the necessity of weekly or even monthly shaving.

"Damn, Chet," spat the other with an equal serving of smarmy cockiness, this one a short, chubby longhair decked out in torn blue jeans, black workboots, a leather vest and U of K baseball cap. "Nobody told me Mister Jensen was holding Special Olympic tryouts. Check out the rad hat on the bird-legged one."

Nodding solemnly, Gunther glanced over at his wheelchair-bound ally.

"And who says the younger generation ain't respectful?"

Flashing a wry smile, Wes calmly shrugged, his windblown combover topped with freshly fallen snow.

"If you're looking to buy, I doubt Mister Jensen is selling," the one identified as Chet announced while giving the older men a sardonic once-over.

"Maybe they're thinking of opening one of those institutes for the disabled, you know, or a nursing home," the other chimed in, having seemingly already lost interest when his initial jab fell flat.

"No, nothin' like that, fellas. We're just lookin' around. Truth is, I used to homestead here," Gunther offered, gesturing with a slight nod toward the bare patch a few dozen feet over his left shoulder. "So many years ago you two were probably still milkin' mama's tit."

"Horseshit," chubby sneered, no doubt taken aback by the older man's weaning remark. "Ain't nobody lived around here except for the boss, whose estate is about two miles further south. You believing this handicrapper, Chet?"

The slimmer teen, obviously the alpha of the two, merely rolled his eyes, the brim of his faded briar fedora littered across its slanted border with piled flakes.

"Ah, cork it, Hoss, he's just yanking our goobers."

"Probably his *specialty*," the one called Hoss grinned as whatever dim bulb he possessed lit to its brightest capacity with what was most likely a rare witticism. "Bet these two *share* each other's canes, you figure?" In both drawing out and pronouncing the word "figger" and accompanying the comment with a playful wink, the man-boy's overestimating of his own rapier wit was quickly established by Gunther's wordless response: a seductive wink of his own, followed by an equally lustful pursing of the lips.

Executing a full-body shiver, the man-boy leapt over as if to actually hide behind his friend.

"Awwww gross, man! I knew it! That ladies' hat on pencil legs seals it. These two are a couple!"

"Gay gimps," Chet spat, echoing his pal's open disgust. "Sheeeeeiiiit, I could've gone my whole life without this knowledge or even worse, the nasty image currently polluting my brain."

This time, it was the wheelchair-bound chauffeur turning to his client; each sported similar smirks.

"Kids today, huh?"

"Two shiny examples of modern tolerance," Gunther sighed, lowering his head disappointedly, "and just when I thought our kind was beyond persecution."

When the younger pair backed away as if from a floating black cloud ripe with plague, it was the shorter, stockier of the two who fired the final verbal shot, albeit in a shaky tone ripe with repulsion.

"Hey, what you two sickos do in the dark ain't beans to us, but just know we're reporting your trespassing to Mister J's security chief."

Raising his right cane airborne, Gunther tucked the handle-end beneath his chin and, utilizing his thumb and forefinger, mimicked firing several shots in their massive ride's direction.

"You boys keep a cool tool now, ya hear? Goooooo, *Wildcats!*" he concluded, wildly waving the cane while bellowing over the roar of the Ram's engine and in the aftermath, nearly tipping over.

As if to escape an approaching avalanche, the truck backed onto the snow-coated pavement and spun out with equal ferocity, leaving the two men staring blankly ahead into an increasingly heavy net of snowfall.

"Well, I thought that went well enough," Gunther stated blandly, having regained his balance.

"Left our mark on those impressionable young souls, I'd say," Wes added, forced to purse his lips to refrain from giggling aloud. "May I suggest we depart memory lane before I wind up being booked into my own workplace?"

Stepping back as if to allow access, Gunther executed a slight bow while waving a cane in the direction of the Camry.

"After you, good sir."

Avoiding the deepest of several nearby ruts, Wes wheeled around the other man as if to purposely circle his slightly warped form.

"By the way," he said flatly while passing his passenger on the right-hand side, "your ladies' hat is hanging a tad crooked."

"A thousand unemployed comedians...," Gunther grumbled, though he did make a mental note to check the beret's position upon reentering their ride.

Roughly five minutes later, once they'd properly reboarded sans all or at least a portion of their respective equipment, the Camry pulled onto the roadway and headed back the way they had come.

"Keep a cool tool? *Really*?" the driver inquired, brow cocked toward his suddenly solemn, silent passenger.

"Too dated?"

"Not if that coma started in the swinging sixties."

Soon the Camry sat idling at the cusp of the highway.

"So, where too, Mister McCarron?" Wes asked, scanning a roadway deserted for as far as the eye could see.

"Don't know about you, but all this sightseein' has my innards gaspin' for grub. Plus I need to swallow down my lunch meds, which are damn near a meal all on their own. Is there still a barbecue place just down the way?" his passenger said, pausing to yawn before gesturing east with an outstretched thumb. "The

Pig's Foot or The Swine's Knuckle or somethin' similar. Stupid name but damn good chicken and ribs."

As Wes turned right, the car's back tires went into a slight slide atop the freshly coated asphalt, which he quickly deescalated by adjusting the accelerator gear handle.

"Same menu, but different name. Goes by The Prize Sow these days and is known county wide. I have to say, I'm impressed."

"My taste for only the finest things in life?"

"Nope. Your powers of selective memory."

Gunther shrugged his rounded shoulders, gazing out the passenger window into mostly barren pasture and farmland, left abandoned until spring re-sprung, the fresh ivory coating just starting to collect on their hard, frozen hides.

"Well, you know, a man's gotta maintain priorities, even when comatose."

Nervously gnawing his lower lip, Wes, the younger man—by a scant year and a half—secretly pondered the limits of both the older man's memories and the order of his priorities.

From the *Crimson Falls Gazette* Sports Page
Dated Oct. 9

A Classic shoot-out ends in 43-37 victory for resilient Wildcats
(Friday night, Falls Field)

Dalton Crane's thirty-nine-yard TD run with just over a minute to go lifted the Wildcats to a six-point win on a cool, crisp night on the home field, this despite having fallen behind 17-0 in the first quarter and trailing 24-13 at the half. Quarterback Shane Mills added two TD passes in a furious second-half comeback that saw the Wildcats outscore the visiting Renegades from Pearl City 30-13 in the final two quarters.

Five

"Dex—Mister McCarron has *every* right in the book to have you removed for trespassing, Mister Briggs, and if I need to reiterate this point, it'll be with us communicating through steel bars, are you with me?"

An imposing individual via his sheer size alone, Will Crockett was downright terrifying when riled, this rare state of anger normally diagnosed via a threesome of easily identifiable symptoms. *One*: His usually calm, low manner of speaking rose several octaves until reaching full-blown predatory growl status.

Two: Veins the size of cable cord protruding from his tree-trunk thick neck.

Three, and most telling by far: He would, whether consciously or unconsciously, tip the front brim of his trooper-styled, campaign cover hat downward until his searing gaze was effectively cloaked. Probably a good thing, those exposed to his rage would agree, figuring the man's eyes might fire potentially fatal twin-lasers if not strategically blockaded.

The targets of his building ire, an eclectic trio that squirmed, sidestepped and circled him as if he were on display, had successfully triggered symptom two and were inching dangerously close to the final stage.

"Sheriff, we can still claim first amendment rights, correct? I mean, even a native Kentuckian should be able to count that high!"

The twenty-something male, bespectacled, toothpick thin and sporting spiked, multi-colored hair, was decked out in skinny jeans and a gray sweatshirt with the words "T(AIL)W(AGS)D(OG) Storm-Trooper" in bold black lettering and waving his bony fist airborne as if to fire up a mob that was comically nonexistent.

"Son, I don't care what internet gossip rag employs your services, but I'm gonna give you and your fellow media brethren exactly thirty seconds to depart Dexter McCarron's property," Crockett snarled, stepping squarely into the smaller man's personal space, a gnarled hand moving slowly toward his headgear. "And I can guarantee you that *this* native Kentuckian can indeed count that high."

"Perhaps then you can clear up some things for us, Sheriff," a slight, red-haired female chimed in, pointing her cell at Crockett, her natty and textbook professional appearance the direct opposite of her younger peer's. To her right, a heavyset man sporting an overly pale, moon-shaped visage and clipped Hitler-style mustache typed so furiously into his own communications device it appeared both hands were in the throngs of an involuntary spasm.

As the strange twosome lunged forward, the chief instinctively backed away a step, hands on hips and jaw set tight just as a Ford Focus adorned with PD insignia pulled onto the snow-coated dirt drive.

"Number one, young lady, I'm the chief of police, not the...a sheriff. That would be a county distinction. Number two, I'd be more than happy to grant an official interview to whatever local law enforcement subject you'd care to broach. But not *here* on a man's private property in sub-freezing weather, and especially seeing as he doesn't want you here."

"Small town, small minds, *big* secrets," the twenty-something blurted, his bearing screaming the perfect definition of slacker, throwing up both puny arms in apparent disgust, the sincerity of which was highly questionable. "And here I always thought *In the Heat of the Night* was just more Hollywood malarky."

Smoothly snapping a pair of cuffs from his utility belt with one hand and a taser with the other, the chief cocked a brow while clearly displaying both.

"Your thirty seconds have long since expired, people. Now for the last time, voluntarily disperse or the young patrolman and I will *assist* you in doing so."

Having jogged over from his patrol unit, Jerome Griffey's eyes bugged at the sight of his usually mild-mannered boss openly threatening a threesome that hardly appeared the type to warrant such fury.

"Chief, everything copasetic here?"

"You see, son?" Crockett stared down the slacker while gesturing toward his young subordinate with a stiff nod. "Co-pa-se-tic. We use big words here too, but only to differentiate reality from Hollywood malarky.

"Everything's just dandy here, Officer Griffey. These fine examples of modern media journalism were just leaving Mister McCarron's property, weren't we, folks?"

"So how about that interview, Chief Crocker?" Moon-Face, Hitler-'stache bellowed over his shoulder as the trio slumped back to their individual rides. The chief, rolling his eyes, replied gruffly while striding toward the home's front porch as Griffey slowly trailed the departing parties.

"Crockett, you know, like *Davy*. Ring my office in a few hours, 859-356-4785, and I'll see about fitting you in."

He joined Dexter at the porch railing, the two silent as the trio of vehicles pulled away in mini-procession fashion, Moon-Face, Hitler-'stache's gray Kia SUV leading the way at a snail's pace, followed by the female reporter's Jeep Cherokee and the slacker's Dodge Charger.

"Now just what in the name of good sense was that all about, McCarron?" Crockett finally asked calmly, tipping his cap back until it resembled an ill-fitting sombrero.

Wearing only a brown, short-sleeve tee, knee shorts and wool socks, his thick, graying hair sticking out at all possible angles, Dexter took a full thirty seconds to respond, as if pondering several options.

"They're looking for my nephew," he finally replied, though only when the chief had turned toward him as if to repeat the query.

"And why would three separate news rags, two of them out of state, be searching out your kin?"

"Gunther McCarron."

As the chief patiently waited for a follow-up, Jerome Griffey stepped onto the first of three porch steps and halted, removing his department-issued cap and shaking off the fresh, fluffy buildup from its brim.

"Duly noted," the chief finally retorted, his tone rapidly losing its coolness. "For what purpose?"

"You have access to the full story, Chief."

"I do, do I?"

"In your police files, or crime incidents, whatever you call them."

"Why don't you save me some reading? I mean, I'm standing here now."

"I'd prefer not to."

"You got somewhere to be?"

Nostrils flaring, his unblinking gaze never leaving the wide expanse of desolate farmland fronting his property, Dexter's shoulders visibly tensed.

"Honestly no, but it's a long story and I'm...I just don't feel up to it."

"Chief?" Griffey inquired timidly, leaning forward as to whisper to his visibly perturbed superior.

"Yeah, Jerome?"

"Should I trail those three? I mean, see where they might be headed next?"

The chief waved him off with a meaty hand while never shifting his gaze from his reluctant guests.

"Negative. Just head on back to town and resume patrolling. I'm determined to uncover that particular nugget of info myself and without ever leaving these premises.

"You mind if we talk inside, McCarron? You might feel all cozy and warm out here in your civvies, but I'm freezing my wide ass off."

With obvious reservations and looking as if he were about to take a long walk off a short pier, Dexter eventually turned toward the screen door, pulled it wide and invited the larger man inside with a less-than-enthusiastic wave of a hand.

Thursday, 1018 hours

The sleek, charcoal gray Charger sat parked on a narrow gravel shoulder, its motor idling so quietly one would have had to practically be sitting on its hood to notice. Its driver and leaser— with less than a full month remaining contractually, a short-term rental just long enough to impress without the long-term financial burden draining his meager savings—had positioned its slick bulk just past a sharp bend in the road and behind an overgrowth of shoulder-high Dwarf Burford Hollies. Lying back as far as the driver's seat would allow, Kevin Briggs, ace reporter—at least in his own estimation—for the semipopular online e-zine *Tail Wags Dog*, barked into the cell fastened to his right ear, a freshly lit joint pinned between the thumb and forefinger of his free hand.

"I'm telling you, Jo, this boy was about one more hillbilly-hick remark away from needing bail money," he crooned in a nasally whine that, unbeknownst to all but himself, was easily the most off-putting in a checklist of personality defects. "So yes, as usual here I sit in Dogwood, taking one for the team, right? You just remember that when annual raises are passed out, right Jo? Joanne, you listening to me or TikTok?"

Briggs took a a deep pull from the joint and held it, the Dodge's interior steaming up like a sauna with malfunctioning ventilation, the webzine reporter—twenty-four and a two-time college dropout— forced into a full minute of listening without interruption, that is until both nostrils spewed smoke and his mouth freed to reassume a more natural state.

"I get it, Jo, I get it. So, the human veggie resprouts after twelve ye—what's that? Oh yeah, whatever, *fourteen* years then, and heads back to the scene of the crime.

"Or maybe, just maybe, he just heads home 'cause that's where home is? A veggie reburying its roots into familiar ground. Could be I'm wasting my precious time here in Huck Finn's backyard for a steaming turd of a nonstory, right?"

Thin, fish-bone-pale face pinched in discomfort, Briggs started to suck in another drag but paused, his already shrill tone going full-throttle Girl Scout with a skinned knee.

"Yeah, yeah, I got the scoop from our boy at the hospital. Dude was sweating bullets and twitching like a crank addict a half-hour out of rehab, no doubt nursing a pain-pill jones of Everest proportions.

"Yeah, I'd say it was well worth the moolah invested. Of course, I made sure the video and audio took. Lighting was dim as a mole's asshole in that janitor's basement but it'll suffice. "Wh—? Th-that's a big no, sister. I told you I no longer get blazed on duty. You know, that whole maturity thing we all scoffed at in our late teens. Right, right, well I *am* a professional, Jo-Jo. Waking and baking is only acceptable when chillin' between the barricades of one's own castle. You take me for an idiot? Dude gets caught puffin' the hay in this state probably winds up with a life sentence, right?"

Shifting his narrow rear and leaning back until he basically was lying across both the passenger and driver seats, he took a more conservative puff of the joint to cut the odds of any involuntary coughing fit proving him a liar.

"Warmer than home base you say? It is to laugh, Joanne. Check out weather dot com and you'll note with no small amount of irony it is currently coming down with a frequency so far unmatched in our little old home state. Worst of all, here I sit barely off the shoulder of the road and I can't imagine these toothless hicks have the first clue on how to steer anything more complicated than a prize bovine on snow-covered roads. My precious baby might as well have a target painted on its back en—"

The sudden, brutal jolt, delivered as if on cue, spun the Charger's back end into the center of the roadway, Briggs' spindly frame bouncing off the dash with enough force to break three ribs and shatter his specs, driving jagged shards of progressive lenses into the flesh of his cheeks, nose and left eye. Adding insult to a half-dozen injuries, he'd also swallowed what little remained of the joint and shook himself to semiconsciousness roughly thirty seconds past impact via a smoke-filled coughing jag that did little to soothe his fractured midframe.

Managing to pull himself into a semi-seated position on the driver's side, he became aware of the faint buzzing of his editor and employer's mousy voice from wherever his cell had been tossed.

Scanning with his one unblurred eye and groping wildly for the palm-sized Galaxy, on which he'd blown two complete paychecks just weeks earlier, Briggs involuntarily ceased all forward movement and briefly considered he'd somehow snagged his sweatshirt on the door handle.

Moments later, as he was being dragged arms-first through the shattered driver's window, the razor-sharp glass left in the crash's wake serving to peel away both shirt and the soft flesh beneath, *Tail Wags Dog*'s self-proclaimed ace reporter somehow understood, with no small amount of stark terror, that a roadside rescue wasn't the intention.

Thursday, 1041 hours

Careful to maintain a speed ten miles per hour under the posted limit, Wes steered them to the requested eatery with nary an additional slide or slip atop an increasingly slick roadway.

"Well, it's only ten-forty," Wes commented, noting the dirt/gravel parking lot fronting the restaurant—Gunther finding its classically aged, undeniably dogged yet charming look only vaguely familiar—sat mostly empty. "Hope they serve brunch. Steak and eggs would sure hit the spot."

With his baggy eyes, sagging shoulders and raspier-than-usual pronouncements, Gunther appeared on the verge of a much-needed nap.

"Aw, don't sweat it, Wes. By the time we've properly outfitted our wasted husks and wheel and limp respectively toward the nearest open booth, they're liable to be chargin' dinner prices."

Parking in the lone marked handicapped space, Wes allowed the engine to continue idling, thus keeping the heater operational as his passenger began the arduous task of refitting, re-hooking and re-snapping the dozen or more straps, hooks and snaps of the exoskeleton. A few minutes in, the faint sound of passing gas accompanied Gunther's familiar concerto of groans and moans as he was forced to all but plant his face against the dash to reach the suit's ankle straps.

"Oh, that ain't good," he grimaced, head turned toward the driver. "My apologies for the less-than-rosy aroma, partner. More times than not it's like tryin' to plug a dam with a butterfly net. Hopefully that wasn't a wet one, but damned if I ever know till I survey the damage or worse yet, leave a brown stain on the furniture."

Twisting around to retrieve the folded chair from its assigned space, Grant giggled despite himself and the promised odor, as foul and rancid as prewarned.

Approximately twenty minutes later, they sat across from one another in a surprisingly well-padded booth, Wes sipping plain black coffee and Gunther his own well doctored-up version, complete with six packs of sugar and three creams. Having removed his ever-present beret ("wearin' a hat inside an eatery is a sure sign of redneck indifference," he'd remarked with dead seriousness), it revealed a thick head of graying hair, the bulk of which was only partially flattened by the constant gear wearing.

"You're how old, Grant? Forty-four or five?"

"Three."

"Holdin' up well, considerin' how, you know, the permanent lack of mobility can age our kind."

Wes simply nodded to acknowledge the back-handed compliment.

"How about you?"

"Let's just say though I do qualify as your elder, it's dang near nose to nose, and don't even try to insinuate I cloak it well, though I've been told a few more years of slow healin' is in order to possibly slow the inevitable."

"Less than a year out of a fourteen-year coma, correct?" Wes asked, steaming cup levitating just beneath parted lips.

"A state Rip Van *Wrinkle* record holder, they tell me."

"I'd say your merely sitting here upright *and* coherent is nothing short of miraculous." With that, Wes held the cup out as if to propose a toast before reversing direction and taking a noisy sip.

"Well," Gunther grinned, mimicking the toasting gesture. "Same to you, Mister Grant."

"Sorry, but our respective conditions are not comparable in any form or fashion," Wes winked back, exaggeratingly so. "Other than sharing similar disabilities, the Herculean effort you alone can claim is head, shoulders and useless limbs ahead of the curve, at least in our fair commonwealth."

The other man leaned in, nearly toppling over both his half-filled cup and a napkin dispenser with the effort.

"Nothin' personal, Wes, but there are times that overworked dialogue you favor comes off a tad snobby, not to mention hintin' ya might be a little light in the loafers."

"My sincere apo—whoops, I mean *my bad.* Do my best to dummy it down and man it up, at least when we're in public."

Pawing through their respective dishes of steak and eggs (Wesley) and pulled pork barbecue sandwich and fries (Gunther) in relative silence as the clock on the wall approached the noon hour, the pair happily accepted coffee refills from a painfully young-looking waitress who, despite her glued-on smile, couldn't fully disguise her skittishness in their presence.

Sliding a mostly cleared plate to the center of the table, Wes leaned back and belched silently behind the back of a hand before speaking.

"So, where to next, boss? The day is still mostly young."

Gnawing his last fry, having gulped down a handful of pills with water as a chaser, Gunther checked the watch strapped onto his spindly left wrist.

"You know Reddenville pretty well, do ya?"

"Fairly. Bought my last ride there."

"The Camry with all the gimps-r-us extras?"

"The very same. There's a pretty decent medical supplies shop up the—"

Gunther interrupted, wincing as if that last mouthful of fried potato might be riding the express elevator back to the top.

"Don't tell me. The Hammock Used Car Emporium."

"As a matter of fact, yeah. Best deals this side of a Lexington back alley."

"Figures. Well then, kinda like those seven degrees of separation that links half the world population to Kevin Bacon, you've all but pressed flesh with our next interviewee."

Though intrigued, something in both the other man's tone and expression advised Wes to merely nod and switch subjects.

"So, before we slip and slide on back out into the elements, something's been praying on my mind since we teamed up, boss."

"Shoot."

"When you woke from the coma, I mean permanently came to, what was it like? I mean, I'm imagining every time-travel flick I've ever seen."

Eyes suddenly agleam, the other man leaned back and paused as if prepping a response that he could mentally file away for future use without even minor alternations.

"We covered our slim age difference a while back, right?"

Wes nodded, bearded chin resting on upturned fists.

"In reality, at least *my* reality, I'm still in my late twenties and, if not quite still in my prime, not that far removed and surely not a shriveling turnip approachin' middle age. It's like I went to bed one way and woke up this soggy, saggy mess of mostly defective parts.

"For me, as you and I sit here jawin' in a place I used to occasionally frequent, mere months have passed away since that night, but everything, I mean *every* damn thing, has changed. This whole scene, bein' back in town, seein' these places and things again, is way beyond just textbook weird. It's...I..."

"Surreal."

Only able to feebly snap the fingers of his right hand, Gunther nonetheless did so with as much gusto as he could manage.

"Bingo, *that,* in spades."

"I can only imagine. But why Hammock? I mean, I get the connection, but for what purpose?"

"Well, if you're thinkin' it's some kinda guilt-trip fueled apology tour for what just knowin' me did to his little girl, think again. For now, that's all I'm gonna say."

Head twisting awkwardly one way and then another, Gunther spotted their waitress leaning against the bar, hawking them unapologetically, and attempted to gesture her over with a dramatic roll of the eyes.

"What say we pay up and vamoose? Appears the blizzard has subsided to a light flakin', but I'll wager the roads to the county line are slick as buzzard snot. By the way, Hammock's estate is just over the state line, 'bout halfway to Reddenville."

When he saw his appointed chauffer begin to remove a wallet from a jacket pocket, Gunther raised a shaky hand palms out, the minimal effort to do so birthing a twisted scowl.

"Nope. Put it away. Your money's no good here, sailor. I got this and any other expenses we might incur along the path of this magical mystery tour, agreed?"

Having somehow teleported his own billfold from parts unknown, Gunther then tossed a pair of folded twenties and a single ten onto the tabletop.

"That ten-spot's all yours, honey. Don't pee it all away in one place," he said, greeting the blushing waitress with a wink while retrieving and refitting his beret, either oblivious or apathetic to the sneer of disgust she'd flashed in the aftermath.

"Um, Gunther, the younger generation is, well, more sensitive these days about such...terms."

"Yeah, so I've heard. Too bad. What fun is life goin' through it all tight-assed and offended? C'mon partner, let's shag."

"Your time is my time, Kemosabe," he quipped in wry response while remounting his chair, neither his light tone nor bemused expression revealing the gnarled knot of building apprehension mutating just below the falsely calm, cool surface.

Thursday, 1024 hours

"Appreciate your time and the clarification, as well as the coffee, McCarron. It does serve to help clear up the mystery of why those media types were circling your place like vultures, though I've got to say it also manages to birth quite the checklist of new questions."

Will Crockett stood on the top porch step of Dexter McCarron's modest two-bedroom abode, arms crossed and eyes squinted as if attempting to penetrate the steady net of descending snow.

"I fear for my nephew, Chief," Dexter replied after a lengthy pause, posing just inside the parted screen door, his words as weary as his browbeaten, hangdog expression. "He's as frail and brittle physically as he is scarred emotionally, and to a degree no other man nor woman can rightly claim."

White vapor spewing from each flared nostril, the chief nodded silently, leaving the homeowner to resume what was most likely the lengthiest stretch of continual dialogue he'd spoken in years.

"If today is any indication, it appears he's gonna be hounded on a regular basis, least till the new wears off. Of course, the draw to the news types is as much *how* he got into his current condition in the first place as the recent miraculous resurrection.

"I warned him, but he inherited the stubborn gene from our side of the family. I just wish there were some way to keep the buzzards at bay other than having you and your department on speed dial."

"Fears and suspicions duty noted," the chief reassured with a tip of the cap. "I'm going to have to reacquaint myself with the details of that...his case, being as I was still employed as a CO up at Blackburn back in oh-seven."

"CO?" Dexter inquired, a fresh smoke parked between pursed lips.

"Corrections. My first official law enforcement gig. I'd put in nearly five years before joining the PD early in oh-eight."

"I did some time up in Green River back in the late nineties."

"You a former turnkey?"

A mild shrug and faint smile preceded the reply.

"Guest. Took my meals and bunked down courtesy of this fair state's taxpayers for just under three years."

Joining the chief at the edge of the planked porch, the homeowner was substantially dwarfed in both height and bulk.

"Kind of surprised you didn't already know, considering your line of work."

The chief shrugged. "A man's past discrepancies are just that as long as he walks the straight and narrow in the present."

"Fair enough, though I figure now you might be curious as to what put me there."

"None of my business, Mister McCarron," the chief replied, without meeting the other man's gaze, the latter having appeared increasingly haggard as the morning wore on.

"Appreciate your respecting my privacy face-to-face and all, Chief, just don't believe everything you read about me or my nephew in the official records I'm fairly certain you'll be perusing soon. Gunther was far from perfect, not saying otherwise, but laying a false rap on someone is easily accomplished when that person is unable to defend himself."

"Again, I don't make it a habit of judging folks by their kin's past run-ins with the law, nor do I judge a man solely on his past."

With that, Crockett turned and offered a final tip of his hat.

"I'll keep in touch, Mister McCarron, and if you find yourself overly concerned with your nephew's dealings within my jurisdiction, feel free to give me a ring. Meanwhile, my people and I will do our best to allow him some peace from those who stalk and harass for the purpose of headlines, ratings and internet hits."

Face briefly hidden by a puff of rising smoke, the homeowner merely grunted his acknowledgement before turning back and vanishing behind the screen and inner door.

Moments later, parked behind his cruiser's wheel with the engine humming and heater cranked to maximum warmth, Will Crockett removed his cap and, laying it on the passenger's seat, reached up with both hands to vigorously massage a mostly bald pate in hopes of at least partially quelling a building migraine.

"Well now, Mister top law dog," he whispered wearily, "it does appear you have some serious perusing to do."

Thursday, 1113 hours

"Ma'am, might I bother you to radio your superior to inform him we're waiting?"

Peering up over the edge of black-rimmed glasses, Cindy Lou was still in the process of properly chewing a bite of roast beef on rye, her other fist filled with an oversized mug of sweet tea, and was forced to swallow prematurely in order to properly reply, which in turn triggered a brief coughing jag and subsequent sips of tea.

Appearing not the least bit concerned that the obviously aged, overly rotund records clerk might literally choke to death in her presence, the slight, auburn-haired female stood on the opposite side of the glass wearing an expression as sour as her disposition.

"It's been almost an hour after all, and I...we do have other places to be."

"Maggie?" Cindy announced between sips, a forefinger raised airborne as a gesture of acknowledgement to the requestor. "Can you buzz the chief and tell him he still has company waiting?"

"Who might that be?" Maggie could be heard inquiring from the perpetual gloom of the dispatch office.

"Beth Connors of the *Louisville Post* and, um, hold on," the red-haired, thin-faced, pixie-like figure responded sharply, pausing to back away from the window, the space being quickly filled by a figure roughly twice her physical stature, or at least in terms of thickness.

"Randy Grimes, *Dayton Post-Dispatch*."

"Got it," Maggie replied, the radio echoing a quick blast of static as she prepped the call.

Resembling the moon-faced man's preteen sibling, Beth Connors rejoined him at the glass, her narrow face pinched with frustration.

"Ma'am, might I inquire how much longer it's going to take to acquire the requested reports?"

Cindy Lou Harrison paused to reply before shoving the last of her sandwich between dentures so ivory white they practically smoldered.

"Miss, you two happened to walk up and make said request just as my lunchbreak commenced. Being as I suffer from low blood-sugar content if undernourished, I have no choice but...renourish. Rest assured I will pull and copy those records within the next five to ten minutes, that is, if I'm allowed to *complete* the process of feeding in relative peace."

"Hmmph," Beth Connor whispered in the general direction of her rival news gatherer, having strategically turned her back from the glass, "that sow and the word undernourishment go together like liver and chocolate mousse."

"Chief's on his way, Cindy," Maggie relayed. "Said the roads are trickier than this morning but at least it's just flaking now."

Putting the finishing touches on her meal, Cindy Lou pushed away from the desk normally occupied by Wesley Grant and stood, facing the window and sporting a tight, wholly insincere smile.

"Chief Crockett is inbound, folks, so just get comfortable. While you have your meeting, I'll be readying those reports."

Emerging from the dispatch room, Maggie sauntered over as if to speak with Cindy Lou but with her eyes darting continuously toward the window.

"Media types from as far as Dayton? What gives? Safe bet they're not here to cover the game," she whispered out of the left side of her mouth, casually thumbing through a random pile of unrelated papers.

"Indeed. Scribbled this name on the notepad and said they wanted everything we had on him."

Snatching the note from Cindy Lou's bare palm, Maggie ducked into the nearby rolling cabinet for maximum privacy. Upon her exiting, she found the interim records clerk busily pecking away at the nearest terminal.

"Sooo, anything on this McCarron guy?" she hissed, her chin practically resting on the older woman's rounded shoulder.

"Nothing in the newer system," Cindy Lou answered in a similarly muted tone, though still amplified by the lack of surrounding noise to drown it out. "That's since twenty-thirteen, I think. The chubby guy said it might've been an older incident. Lemme check the old RMS system, if I can remember my darn password."

The dispatch phones rang out just as she'd attempted accessing the department's archived electronic files, many of which had been scanned in for posterity a few years earlier, sending Maggie into a mad dash toward the source but not before spouting a parting "keep me posted."

Just as the veteran civil servant had managed to put a case report number to match the provided name, the double doors leading into the department flung open, followed by the familiar thumping of heavy boots smacking tile.

"Hello again, good people of the press. Kindly follow me," Chief Crockett brayed in an overly cheery tone instantly recognized by Cindy Lou Harrison as being solely of the caustic variety.

Minutes later, as the report she'd sought flashed across the wide monitor in all its handwritten glory, Cindy Lou began to peruse the narrative and soon forgot all about reporters, the chief and even the half-eaten pack of powdered donuts sitting mere inches from the keyboard.

**From the *Crimson Falls Gazette* Sports Page
Dated Oct. 16**

The Wildcats show little mercy in 56-8 road win, move to 5-0 on season
(Friday night, Benton Field)

Building a quick 21-0 first quarter lead, the Crimson Falls squad continued their unbeaten season, the home Benton Devils (1-4) showing little resistance as Wildcats' quarterback Shane Mills threw for two touchdowns and ran for two more in just a little more than a half's work. The 5-0 start marks the first such unbeaten streak to begin a campaign since the 1998 squad that ended the year with a close loss in the second round of the state playoffs.

Six

"You're kiddin'? One blessed property damage report from six years ago? Never figured the snobby jackass for John Gotti, but I expected more. Then again, money talks."

Wes cleared his throat noisily, slowing the Camry to ten miles beneath the posted 45 MPH limit as they neared a steep grade where a ton-and-a-half truck labored, spewing thick plumes into an overcast sky.

"In a manner of speaking, yes, only these days it can be done legally. You ever heard of *expungements*?"

Leaning back with his eyes closed, Gunther's weak shrug was barely visible.

"Can't say I have."

"Means basically the expungement of records."

"So?"

"*Erasure* of records."

The passenger's already gaunt face visibly tightened, his jaw set tight as if expecting the worst.

"Ya mean, criminal records?"

Wes paused, briefly considered fibbing or at least underplaying the truth.

"Affirmative. It's become all the rage of late. Fairly cheap and far too easy."

"Yet another legal dodge for all those whiny-ass victims of circumstance out there. So, we're talkin' misdemeanor type charges, right? Traffic tickets, petty thefts and the like."

"Pretty much across the board if the charge qualifies, depending on circumstances."

Gunther's chin dropped as if unhinged, his normally drooping eyes stretched saucer wide.

"Ya mean like felony thefts or even a killin'?"

"Never expunged a full-blown homicide, but more than a few aggravated assaults, and yes, larcenies are fairly routine and involve lifting car parts or routine shoplifts. The majority of what I see in Crimson Falls involves drug possession and the accompanying paraphernalia, and of course it's usually alcohol-related."

"Wipes it clean, does it?"

"Without a trace as far as background checks and the like are concerned."

"Damn. Where were all these bleedin' hearts when I started runnin' afoul of John Q. Badge?" Gunther concluded with just a hint of a smile.

"Never too late," Wes offered, to which his passenger merely scoffed without added dialogue.

Accelerating past the rumbling ton and a half, which had taken a left onto an unmarked, unpaved one-lane, Wes nodded toward a sign reading "Reddenville – 9 Miles" and was relieved to see the roadway ahead appeared only sporadically snow covered, hinting that everything east of Crimson Falls hadn't received as heavy a downpour, at least in the past few hours.

"So to digress, you hintin' hard-ass Hammock has taken full advantage of this craze?"

"I'd say so."

"I take it you ain't at liberty to divulge any specifics."

"You'd be correct."

"If I guess, can ya just nod yes or no?"

"You know the answer."

"Not even a grunt if I'm close?"

"Gunther..."

"Okay, I get, I *get* it, but I'd wager a year's worth of exo-batteries *and* adult diapers on domestic violence bein' a chart-topper and maybe a driving while zonked or two bein' another."

Stone-faced, Wes stared straight ahead without so much as an eye twitch or nostril flare.

"Yeah well...," McCarron resumed, red-faced, the veins in his thin neck visibly throbbing, "...well, unless that pit-bull prick found Jesus soon after my forced sabbatical, I stand by said claims. Hell, even if he *did*."

Steering them through a four-way stop, a nearby sign announcing assorted fast-food eateries and hotel chains as upcoming attractions, Wes couldn't help but toss a final jab his guest's way, if for no other reason than to add some much-needed levity.

"So I'm guessing this isn't apt to be one of the cheerier reunions on your current tour?"

"Oh, I wouldn't say that," the other man said, turning toward his host and brandishing a wide, warped grin that could only be labeled as maniacally unstable. "I'm hopin' to depart the Hammock estate with nothin' less than palpitations of warmth in my heart and a tingle in my privates. Sad thing is," he concluded, the overdone smile melting into more of a demented leer that a staring Grant found less than comforting, "the former might leave me dead as a hammer and the latter I would never even feel."

They turned onto Belle Road a few minutes later, and soon after, coasted off onto a wide paved entrance complete with a custom swing gate, rod iron lettering spelling out *The Hammocks* running its barred frame.

"We sure he's even home?" Wes offered. "Or better yet, even if he is, that he'll be open to invite *you* in?"

"Wesley, my man," Gunther retorted, executing a series of neck stretches as if loosening up for an impending skirmish. "He'll either see me now or see me later. Logic dictates he'll want to get it over with."

The gate swung back with a static hum just as Wes had prepared to inquire how they were to announce themselves, a curved two-lane path beckoning beyond.

"Ya see?" his passenger quipped with an accompanying wink. "Hard-Ass knows I'm here. It's almost like the telepathic bastard bugged me all those years ago, maybe paid one of the rehab docs to plant a tracking device 'neath my skullcap. Well," he sighed before leaning down and then back to resecure the exo's many straps, "let's not keep Mister Mayor waitin'."

Navigating them past the entrance, Wes felt inclined toward self-preservation.

"Steady. Whatever you suspect, just remember you're on his turf."

The other man's lone response was a single, unreadable, guttural grunt of either simple acknowledgement or cutting defiance. As the Hammock estate, a split-entry red brick ranch, came into view around the final of three lengthy bends atop smooth asphalt, Wesley had a sinking feeling it was the latter.

Thursday, 1143 hours

Resecuring his cap with dual tugs of the wide brim, the chief stood to tower over the seated pair fronting his desk and casually retrieved a fur-lined, department-issued jacket from the back of the high-back chair which served as his personal throne on a daily basis for sometimes up to fourteen hours a day.

Twenty-plus minutes, he'd decided, had been ample time in their presence, though admittedly they had managed, purposely or not, to fill in a few blanks on his own budding investigation's mental checklist. It was time he shared those few but perhaps vital details with a subordinate and, if needed, filed the paperwork necessary to keep it active on the departmental docket.

"Listen folks, I understand the fascination and desire to share Mister McCarron's story. Thing is, I cannot force the man to cooperate if he chooses to remain steadfast and uncooperative to your journalistic plight, nor will I harbor harassment on your part. I can, on your behalf, go to the man and inquire an official yay or nay. Can't guarantee a timeline on an answer, but I can promise to get back to you as soon as I do receive an answer."

"Can you at least procure a phone number, Chief?" Moon-Face Hitler-'stache inquired in a whiny, nasal tone that had grown old at light speed. "We find human interest stories get stale in record time."

"Or at the very least, an email addy?" Wispy-Woman added between gnaws on the eraser end of a number two pencil. "I give my word to no communicative abuse." She raised three fingers in the classic "Scout's-honor" gesture.

Moving casually toward the office door and hoping this rather obvious hint would expedite their own departure, Crockett halted with his massive left hand completely enveloping the doorknob in half-twist mode.

"I'll see what I can do, on both counts. By the way, what happened to your third wheel?"

The two exchanged a quick glance before shrugging in almost perfect synchronization.

"Not a clue," Moon-Face, Hitler-'stache replied first, immediately followed by Wispy-Woman's equally bland "couldn't care less."

"Chief, for the record, please do not lump us in with that online scum. Speaking for myself, I actually earned a journalism degree," she continued, standing only after inserting the toothmark riddled pencil behind her right ear.

"Same here. Briggs' type got their diplomas from the correspondence courses offered at YouTube or TikTok U. GRMDs at their lowest."

Apparently reading the chief's befuddled expression, Moon-Face, Hitler-'stache expounded while wriggling free from a chair far too constrictive for his pudgy frame.

"Gossip Rag Master's Degree."

Pulling the door ajar, Crockett revealed the first thing resembling a smile since making their acquaintance.

"Not too hard to earn, I'd imagine."

"IQ of a houseplant," Wispy-Woman confirmed, skipping past his huge frame and into the narrow hall.

"*Tail Wags Dog* makes *TMZ* read like the *New England Journal of Medicine*. Rancid, low IQ sludge always shooting for the lowest of common denominators," added Moon-Face, Hitler-'stache, forced to turn sidewise to squeeze by the chief's own considerable, albeit muscle-toned, bulk.

"Yeah, I kind of figured Briggs wasn't here digging around for the human-interest aspect of the story but more the human tragedy," the chief conceded, gently shutting the door behind him and trailing the two reporters into the lobby.

Having secured an unlit electronic cigarette between pursed lips, Wispy-Woman faced the glass peering into the records division, where Cindy Lou stood with twin manila folders perched between chubby hands.

"It appears Miss Harrison has your reports ready," the chief concluded, turning back toward the murky hallway from which they'd just emerged. "Good hunting, folks, but remember what we discussed. If you are lucky enough to locate the enigmatic Mister McCarron, respect his wishes for privacy."

"You got it, Chief," Moon-Face, Hitler-'stache said, flashing a thumbs-up before joining his competitor, whose own half-hearted farewell consisted of a slight nod and the briefest flash of a smile, while posing behind the clear glass like suspects in a two-person lineup.

"I'll need to get a copy of an ID from each of you," Cindy said monotonically, peeking over bifocals perched so precariously they appeared on the cusp of freefall.

Once each had provided the requested document in the form of their respective driver's licenses and the rotund clerk had retreated to make copies, Moon-Face leaned down and in, and, wearing the smarmy grin of a drunken sailor, whispered to Wispy-Woman as if trying out a particularly intriguing come-on line.

"Can you believe ol' Sheriff Podunk and that speech? Like we were student reporters from the local junior high school, right?"

Grimacing, she sidestepped away before replying in full voice, to which Moon-Face, Hitler-'stache openly flinched, "Nothing personal, Grimes, but your breath could peel paint."

Less than five minutes later, the pair departed the Crimson Falls Police Department building, each without acknowledgment of the other, moving with similar purpose while flipping through the collection of stapled papers they'd procured.

The surprisingly robust snowfall of midmorning had transitioned to a light flaking as their respective vehicles departed a mostly empty lot and sped off in opposite directions.

Tucked snugly away within the pleasantly dim confines of the office of chief of police, Will Crockett was calmly instructing Maggie Childers to dispatch day patrol to the rural home of Gunther McCarron for the duration of their shift.

Having done so, Maggie leaned back with a fresh cup of decaf and perused her own personal copy of a long-dormant incident report completed over fourteen years earlier that was suddenly experiencing what retro radio disc jockeys used to describe as "heavy airplay."

Thursday, 12:39 hours

Cell phone tucked tightly to her left ear, the woman leaned her considerable bulk forward from the edge of the bed with each thick elbow propped atop its corresponding knee while staring into a full-length mirror attached to the hotel room door.

"Well, it *is* the road conditions, but, well, that's not nearly all," she explained, the deep concern in her voice as palpable as her expression was shockingly bland, considering the former. "Wesley just...isn't himself. I think it's the approaching anniversary of the crash. Most years he can shrug it off, but there's something different this time. He's sullen and withdrawn as those earliest years of dealing with his...the restrictions."

Leaning back, she slung one pudgy foot forward and then the other, tossing her flat, black leather loafers against a far wall with a low thump in the process. As the party on the other end replied, their sympathetic retort buzzing through the receiver like incessant radio static, the woman's pale, full cheeks expanded and deflated with apparent boredom.

"Pat, you're a jewel. You can't know how much I appreciate your understanding. I...it's...I somehow just *know* I can't leave him alone this time. Not just yet. Marital status aside, I'm his permanent keeper, and I don't begrudge him that."

More static, a weary roll of the eyes from its recipient, her rolling orbs temporarily locking on an overturned plastic, label-free pill bottle lying atop a nearby lamp table, dozens of its oval contents trailing from the tabletop onto the deep, shag carpeting below.

"Thanks again, Patricia, and you can just hold off on ordering the new yoga mats and having the squat machine repaired till I hop back into the saddle on Monday. Okay, see you then. You bet. Bye."

Tossing the cell onto a nearby pillow, she lay back with a resounding sigh, thick arms flopping off each side of the narrow twin bed.

Standing nude in front of the bathroom mirror a half hour later, she would sporadically mumble to herself through gritted teeth while casually studying the plethora of tribal tattoos adorning the majority of the flesh from just below the neckline to her slickly shaved groin region. One in particular, a dark crimson phoenix rising from directly between ample breasts, received an intense audit, its yellowish flames briefly rising and wings visibly flapping until a vigorous shake of the head ended their respective actions.

Moments later, standing beneath a steady stream of water hot enough to completely engulf the room in a drifting cloud of steamed fog, she slowly and precisely whispered every curse word and combination thereof she had ever heard, personally used or even thought of using in her forty-one years.

Drying off and shockingly out of breath from the experience once the impressive checklist of profanities and assorted vulgarities were concluded, the former Mrs. Sandy Grant felt strangely soothed and calmed by it, akin to a self-exorcism of sorts.

"Oh darlin' Sandy baby," she cooed seductively, having donned a Jokeresque grin revealed in all its frozen, frightening, warped glory only after wiping thick condensation from the mirror with a pale, pudgy paw, "you are one powerful pill, you are, and you sneak up like a delayed oxy with a moonshine chaser. A true blue and gorgeously tattooed Georgia (pronounced '*Jaw-gah*') peach. Sweet, tangy and ripe for the pickin'. Not to be trifled with or underestimated and definitely not as stump-dumb as you appear."

With that, she head-butted the mirror into a thousand glass fragments, the thin streams of blood that soon trailed from her wounded scalp left unattended until they streaked her forehead and cheeks like a freshly drawn tribal marking.

Thursday, 12:25 hours

"Well my, my, *my*, those cruel wicked rumors weren't merely idle gossip after all. Gunny Mac, as I live, breathe and walk upright on...my...own, a privilege I was so selfishly taking for granted until this very moment!"

Gangly and thin in a thick wool coat and baggy jeans, the man paced in front of the pair with his hands tucked behind his back, his beady eyes and rat-like appearance a perfect match for the screeching, whiny tone accompanying it.

"Marty Farty!" Gunther bellowed in reply, having lowered his head to gaze unblinkingly upon the man's weasel-like movements and exaggerated gestures as if studying some exotic, rarely spotted species. "Dude, lookin' at you makes me wonder if my coma was fourteen years or closer to thirty. I can only guess such dramatic agin' means you and meth are still an item?"

"McCarron, are you seriously going to stand, well, more like *lean* there resembling a recently exhumed corpse and make remarks concerning *my* looks?"

"I am. I mean, least we know what brought *me* to this stage."

"By stage you mean a barely human meat mannequin held together by bones of twig and skin of parchment? Fair enough, though you'll excuse me if I call *severe* hypocrisy on the hot-ice remark."

McCarron shot a bemused glance at Wes, whose eyes darted about wildly as if to find a suitable distraction.

"Whatever ya say there, muscles. Now, putrid and parchment I ain't too sure about, but I can surely resemble that bones of twig description.

"Burnin' question is, what mudpuddle of near fatal disease or self-inflicted jackass behavior did you step in to secure such a pale, lifeless, near-death appearance?"

Pacing having ceased to a dead stop in light of this latest salvo, the ratty man's oily grin faded, replaced by a pained grimace.

"Father knows you're here. He'll be down in a minute."

"Ya know, it's kinda chilly out here, Marty Far—"

"Do you really think for a moment you'd ever be allowed access to the *interior* of the Hammock estate? Gunther...*really*. Is it even scientifically possible that an almost nonexistent IQ has dipped to single-digit levels due to being rendered chronically comatose?"

"I'd say about as possible as some pansy-ass, deadbeat butt-clown still livin' at home and spongin' off dear ol' dad in his forties. Say Marty, ya still trollin' the middle schools for the love of your life or have ya graduated to high school gals in your older age?"

Briefly dropping the casual façade of mere annoyance, their lanky host—his spindly arms seeming to hang past knobby knees and halfway down equally slender calves—flashed a deep scowl that accentuated rodent-like facial features: close-set, oversized eyes, overlong beak and nearly lipless mouth.

"Says Mister Clean," he growled, noisily clearing his throat and regressing to a less predatory stance, the rage-filled expression reverting back to one of mere irritation.

"Hey, nothin' personal, Mart. It's just, well, I seem to recall rumors of some pretty lurid accusations that daddy big-bucks subsequently squashed with assorted payoffs to some highly pissed-off parents. Alleged only, I'm sure. I mean hell, lookin' at ya, why would a studly, handsome fella such as yourself need to force himself on the chicks? That is, unless we're talkin' the Girl Scout types I heard ya favored."

To this, Wesley audibly snickered, the target of the verbal onslaught shooting him a hateful, squinty glare that lingered for a full five seconds before beady, rat-like eyes refocused on the originator.

"Riddle me this, McCarron," he snarled, frail arms crossed. "How does it feel to wake from a fourteen-year slumber just to find out you're not only a shriveled stack of uselessness, but also, at least in the minds of most in these parts, a soulless killer? Should've been you burned down to a pile of black soot that night, pal, not your victim."

Gunther flinched, mouth stretched into a parody of sudden, intense pain, a clenched fist resting against his breastbone.

"Arrow...straight to the...ticker, Ma-Ma-Marty," he grimaced before quickly dropping the act and staring Hammock down with an intensity that appeared nothing if not sincere.

"Better go fetch daddy now, junior. Romper Room has lost its charm. Time for the adults to consult."

Warped, frozen scowl intact, the lanky greeter turned and departed without further comment, leaving the shivering pair abandoned atop the cold, snowflake-specked pavement. After a moment, Gunther stumbled clumsily back until he and his traveling companion stood and sat, respectively, evenly facing the massive abode like a pair of debating surveyors.

"Martin Hammock, lone surviving heir to his dad's fortune," he said matter-of-factly, as if the two had not just spent the last several moments trading brutal body-shaming insults. "Still the same creepy prick, only a damn sight uglier and no doubt just as deceptively dangerous as ever."

"The vibe of camaraderie was palpable," Wes cracked, straight-faced and visibly shaking the folds of his jacket.

His expression that of someone whose senses are being bombarded by a most malodorous odor, Gunther gave no clue he appreciated his driver's attempt at levity.

"Amazin'. The more things change, the more they stay the same. Once a worthless, greedy, blood-suckin' parasite always a...," he paused, sighing deeply before concluding, "...well, ya get the gist. You could wait in the ride, ya know. Crank the heater and some tunes just to drown out all the drama."

The chaired man just stared straight ahead, unwavering,

"And miss such warm, heartfelt reunions? Not on your life."

"Suit yourself, but I'm freezin' my nads off out here."

"How would you know?"

"Good point, but the odds are on my side."

"Well, at least neither of us have to worry about frostbitten toes."

Leaning hard to the left in the face of a stiff gust from the other direction, Gunther's purple-tinted lips parted and appeared to stick to the teeth beneath.

"True that. Those bad boys could freeze up and snap off and neither of us would even notice till they rolled outta our socks."

"And to think people waste sympathy on such as us."

"Right?" Gunther's smile faded even as his naturally drooping eyes widened. "Oh geez, here comes the former king of Crimson—Falls, that is."

The newest arrival appeared from the eastern edge of the property, jogging across the snow-coated grass between a sizable two-car garage and the main property. Hopping onto the winding walkway, he slowed what had been a frantic pace only when the two men grew to within a few dozen feet.

"McCarron, I want to put this out there right from the get-go," the man said—his breathing amazingly unaffected—once he'd halted forward momentum but continued to jog in place, his workout ensemble made up of dark green sweats, tar-black joggers and a crimson WKU toboggin that currently matched his rose-glow cheeks. "Being that I've been half-expecting you to make an appearance since such a miraculous resurrection, I will allow this one-time visit onto my property. Once you depart that entrance gate, do not think of returning or I will have you carted off to the county lockup. Tell me you understand."

"Looking good, your highness, but then you always were one for keepin' up appear—"

"I've got both the police chief and county sheriff on speed dial, McCarron. Tell me you understand."

His square, clean-shaven jaw seemingly chiseled from the finest marble, the vibe given off by the sixtyish former mayor of Crimson Falls was undeniably gruff and utterly void of slack.

"Loud *and* clear, Mister Mayor. Joggin' out all that built-up guilt, are we?" Gunther shot back, all signs of his initial cheeriness—however faux—having vanished, a veritable death-stare in its place.

"Pray tell, why the relocation from the ol' stompin' grounds in which you were so highly regarded? I heard tell you hightailed it outta Crimson Falls as soon as that second term was up, roughly six months after the incident that left me the walking carrot stick ya see before ya now."

"None of your business, McCarron. I suggest you ramp this up and limit the trivialities. You've got five minutes," the older man said calmly enough but with a building impatience, arms crossed and head tilted slightly back as if to challenge all comers. "Or less if I so decide. I wouldn't waste it on veiled insults, random speculation or insignificant small talk." With his V-shaped torso, thick neck and toned arms and shoulders—all made more evident by the sweatshirt's overt snugness, Kerry

Hammock was the picture of senior health personified, a lifestyle he'd adopted since his teen years as a former Wildcats' star linebacker.

"Well, yes sir, will do sir, though veiled ain't nearly what I had in mind, boss, but since my time is so limited, guess I'd better skip to the chase. Oh, this is Wesley Grant, by the way. He's helpin' me get around town."

Wesley nodded faintly, never quite locking eyes with their host but nonetheless aware of the man's searing gaze.

"I know of Mister Grant. Must say I'm disappointed with a former lawman's choice of company."

"Just a good guy basically offerin' a helpin' hand to one in need. Not that he owes you any explanation."

"Fair enough. Now please expedite your point, McCarron."

"Well hell, mayor, can't we just catch up like old acquaintances? Hear ya snagged a new wife of just over legal age. Buy stock in Viagra, did we?"

"To the point or beat feet," the older man fired back. A tiny smile creased lips shiny from balm as he concluded, "Though I'd be sympathetic if such a hasty exit might not be so prompt, well...," he gestured with a gloved hand in the general direction of Gunther's feet, which sat comically askew, "...considering."

"Same ol' Mayor Tenderheart, always so considerate of the feelings of others."

Groaning, the older man's gaze was forced skyward by a dramatic roll of the eyes.

"I save consideration for those I deem worthy. Needless to say, former dealers of illegal schedule drugs and potential murderers do not even sniff making the list. Best spit out what you came to say and be quick abou—"

"Just *this* then, Hammock: don't you for a minute think this phenomenal second chance I've been given didn't happen for a reason?."

The older man's face severely crinkled, the effect so dramatic he briefly appeared his actual age.

"Meaning?"

"She told me things, slick. Things you wouldn't want gettin' out to your adorin' public."

"Did she now?"

Head tilted severely to the left either for dramatic effect or to ease a building pressure in the general area, the lengthy pause Gunther executed was surely for the former and left his trademark beret hanging slightly crooked.

"Oh yeah," he finally shot back with a playful wink that could have, under different circumstances, been mistaken for a facial tic. "Seems like just yesterday, so you'll have to excuse me for reacting this way. Just standin' in your company is twistin' my gut worse than the most severe bout of IBS."

"That feeling is definitely mutual. In fact, I'm not sure how much more I can tolerate. If it's accusations you're here to toss around, McCarron, I can match you heave for heave. You see...," the older man replied while pacing a six-to-eight-foot stretch, sending flecks of frozen precip sailing into the equally frigid grass, "...state and federal investigations aside, I know you had more to do with what transpired that night than merely act as tragic witness and co-victim. I'm also thoroughly convinced that if she had never met you, my daughter would still be alive. There isn't a day that goes by that I don't curse myself for doing something, *anything* to keep her from your...evil influences, though of course her *true* intentions were quite heroic. At least there is that."

Head thrown back like a baying wolf—albeit of the crippled, sickly variety—the perpetually wobbly man, being held upright by the most advanced exoskeleton known to mankind, nearly toppled over from the act. His seated companion frantically rolled his chair over as to get between him and the cold, hard pavement, while simultaneously bending to retrieve the red beret that had flown free during his associate's impromptu howl.

A semblance of balance regained, Gunther shot Wesley an appreciative glance as the seated man reached up to replace the beret before turning his full attention back to their increasingly agitated host.

"Correction one: Stepdaughter, Hammock, *stepdaughter,* and from what I've gathered, the atypical stepchild in more ways than one.

"Correction two: Everything that girl knew about evil she learned at home. Between you and that half-weasel, half-jellyfish son of yours, it's nothing short of a miracle she escaped with a semblance of sanity or a shred of dignity.

"Finally, as far as accusations go, let's just say when they do come to public light, you'd best be prepared to call in every favor you got from whatever political connections you still hold in this state, 'cause in the aftermath you can swallow down enough age-defyin' vitamin supplements to KO Godzilla, lift the Titanic's weight in the gym or jog to China and back and it won't diminish the back-blow that's comin'. From what I understand about the power of social media these days, the tide of public perception can turn in a blink. If I were you and Junior Perv, I'd be lookin' to relocate, and soon."

Swaying forward, his slight upper body appearing to magically levitate over an equally scrawny lower half—this as a bald man dressed in a knee-length black parka and roughly the size of a Panzer came sprinting from the direction of the main house like a bull elephant—Gunther was either oblivious or uncaring that the volume of his tone had reached glass-shattering levels.

"But hey, look at the bright side, Mister Mayor, 'least then you and that creepy as fuck son of yours can hide away in the same dim basement once the story breaks and get some of that special father and biological son personal time!"

"Is everything all right here, Mister H?" the walking, talking tank asked so timidly Wes nearly guffawed aloud despite the building cloud of tension permeating the chilled air.

"No problem, Chet. These two were just leaving, weren't you, boys?"

Gunther stubbornly stood his ground, hands visibly shaking and teeth audibly grinding, forcing his driver and erstwhile partner to intervene: first via rolling his chair between the two men—the left side wheels briefly sticking between pavement and grass—and secondly by breaking the thirty-second pause in exchanged dialogue.

"Let's go," he said with remarkable calm, eyes moving smoothly between Kerry Hammock and the grimacing man-mountain he could only assume was employed as estate security. "I might not be able to feel frostbite, but it won't stop even the deadest of toes from snapping off in the aftermath."

"Good day, gentlemen, and goodbye," Kerry Hammock concluded before twisting around and jogging off even as his sizable companion *slash* bodyguard remained rigid, as if there were an actual chance the paralyzed twosome might somehow become aggressive.

Practically beaming, Gunther regarded his seated companion, wearing a wide smile of pure satisfaction.

"Well, that certainly went better than expected. How's 'bout a coffee break? I think one of the waitresses at the Sow was givin' me the eye."

Despite a severe case of nerves that had his hands shaking beneath the blanket lying across his lap, Wesley's tone was astonishingly calm.

"Sounds like a plan, Stan."

Wheeling and lumbering, respectively, back to the Camry, the two men did so in complete silence, the assigned driver's expression as pinched and unpleasant looking as the passenger's was openly smug.

Thursday, 1218 hours

Gnawing a chocolate chip protein bar between sips of steaming black coffee, Patrolman Phil Strickland had parked his assigned Expedition just to the east of the McCarron house on a flat, gravel shoulder overlooking a steep, rocky ravine currently painted in freshly fallen snow.

"Nothing moving out here, Mag. Then again, if this McCarron guy is as incapable of self-propelled movement as they say, he could be holed up in there. Didn't you say you saw him at the counter a couple of days back?"

"Yeah. He was upright, but just watching him move around was downright painful. I swear he looked like one of those animatronic characters from that *Five Nights at Frankie's* game."

"Freddy's," the bulky, bald officer corrected her with a cheesy grin she could easily visualize in her mind's eye.

"Yeah, *that*. Anyway, Cindy Lou had to pull the reports on him for these media types. You remember hearing about the Hammock case, right?"

"The murder-arson thing from like twenty years back? I was in middle school or someth—"

Her voice rife with gossip-fueled glee, Maggie barreled forth like a runaway freight with no patience for either her lover's apparent disinterest or any unrelated details he might add.

"More like fourteen. Well, he's the dude they found laid out just beyond the burning trailer, beat nearly to death. Gunther McCarron. Former all-county linebacker with the Wildcats, or so Cindy Lou said. Before our time here, obviously. So I guess the chief's thinking those reporter types aren't about to leave town without their exclusive, huh?"

"Sounds like." Not bothering to expound in fear of yet another interruption, the patrolman briefly removed the cell from his ear and stretched it out the length of his muscular right arm, burping softly before shoving it snugly back into home base. In the aftermath, he pondered why he bothered with such politeness in the company of a woman who freely passed gas beneath the bedcovers they sometimes shared.

"Can't really blame them, right?" the excitable dispatcher resumed. "Fourteen years lying there like an unpicked melon, nobody giving you a chance of being anything but a slowly wilting houseplant and you not only snap out of it, but are coherent enough to return to revisit the scene of the crime. I'm surprised *Hard Copy*, *TMZ* and *Dateline* aren't camping at the county line."

Swallowing down the last of the protein bar, the thick-necked peace officer paused for a sizeable gulp of java that was fast growing much too lukewarm for his tastes, his mistress' use of the word "melon" bringing to mind her own flawless pair, and thus, birthing a small, lustful smile.

"Heard he's got an uncle around somewhere," he grunted, barely finishing the refrain before being cut off yet again.

"Dexter McCarron, his last surviving kin. That's where the chief and Ears ran off a trio of 'em from this morning. Two from Dayton and Louisville no less, plus some online webzine.

"The first two came here to collect past reports straight from being run off McCarron's uncle's land. Only one that didn't show was the webzine vulture, and he's the one Will is most worried about as far as not taking the department's no stalking policies seriously."

"We know what this individual was driving?"

"Late model Dodge Charger, gray two-door dandy."

"Easy enough to spot. So, back to the coma miracle guy, was the case cleared or what?"

Maggie's voice cracked with preteen delight at the inquiry.

"Negative, at least according to the few supplementals attached from the state bureau. Cold case city, unless there's an update floating around KBI we aren't privy to."

"Possible," he tossed out blandly, hoping to change a subject that had increasingly grown stale in the face of more pressing issues, at least in his one-track mind.

"So anywho, what you up to after shift?"

Any and all signs of the earlier exhilaration having instantly evaporated from her tone, she suddenly sounded on the verge of powering down.

"Warm cocoa and Amazon Prime."

"I got Prime at the house. Not sure about cocoa, but got some of that herbal tea with all those assorted flowery flav—"

"Misplace your calendar, Phil?"

"No, what does that me—"

"It's Thursday, remember? One of two weeknights that Max subs for Dan so he can leave early?"

"Well, I figured you could tell him you got saddled with some emergency call or something."

If her voice had been only a tad chilly before, it was arctic frigid now.

"Not going to happen, lover boy."

"Aw, c'mon now, half an hour, that's all I'm asking."

He could imagine twin trails of frosty condensation spewing from her flaring nostrils.

"No means no, slick. Just tuck it back in your pants and remember what we talked about: be *its* master, not *its* slave."

"Yes, ma'am," he conceded with sincerity, secretly aroused by how, all these many months later, this sexy, exotic minx so effortlessly kept him at bay with a simple alteration in tone or deportment, though he wouldn't dare confess this, no matter the level or technique of torture. "How about lunch?"

"As long as you mean actual food and no nooner tomfoolery."

"Vittles my lady, *vittles*. Ears is relieving me around one. Meet me at Sow about one-thirty?"

"Fine, fine. Make it one-forty-five. I'll get Cin to relieve me. Now, back to the McCarron case. I heard his poor folks spent every penny keeping him plugged into life support all those years but died before ever seeing him, well, rise from the grave."

"Yeah, pretty tragic stuff all right," Phil mumbled in disheartened reply, having already fallen into auto-pilot mode while mulling a suddenly eventless evening ahead.

Oppositely, the comely dispatcher who had captured if not his eternal love, surely his transient lust, seemed inexhaustible concerning the subject matter at hand.

From the *Crimson Falls Gazette* Sports Page
Dated Oct. 23

Backups give strong showing in the Wildcats' 54-7 Rout of Carver Hills
(Friday night, Falls Field)

For the second straight contest, Wildcat starters on both sides of the ball played little in the second half, this after cultivating a 28-0 lead at the break. Backup tailback Gene Bogart tallied 141 yards on the ground, including a 60-yard scamper late in the third quarter that put the game on ice against a woefully mismatched Pirates squad from Carver Hills (now 2-4 on the season).

Seven

Thursday, 13:10 hours

Wincing as if sipping bitter gruel instead of freshly ground coffee, Gunther McCarron had barely placed the mug back atop the table when the clutching hand began to tremor with gradually increasing ferocity, culminating in the attached fingers curling into his palm like the petals of a withering plant.

"You...all right?" he heard Wesley inquire from what sounded like a faraway mountaintop, his eyesight suddenly so horrendously out of focus that the man sitting just across the table appeared as if he were nothing more than a large brown blur.

"Gunther, can I...you need your meds?" the voice continued, its volume wildly distorted from static-filled whisper to booming retort, depending on the word.

"Jus...j-just n-need...a sec...to re...reboot," he managed, feeling as though someone else's tongue and lips were being utilized and being completely unaware of the assortment of spasms currently decimating his facial expression, most notably a left eye tic and upper lip twitch.

"Is he gonna...okay?" a foreign voice, young and female, chimed in, no doubt the waitress so unfortunate as to be assigned their server. "Do we need to like, call nine-one-one?"

Blinking madly even as he heard Wesley reply with a mostly garbled message meant to console the obviously shaken teen, the source of their concern found the focus slowly returning to his right eye only.

"N-no, ju-just spas-spasticity," he mumbled, instinctively aware only of the dozen or so patrons currently inhabiting The Prize Sow and their collective stares. "B-be g-good as...g-gold an-any...se-second now. No sw-sweat, n-no strain, re-really."

A full ten minutes passed, wherein the power of sight, still slightly fuzzy but serviceable, was regained even as the mass spasms mostly ceased, save for the occasional twitch of his upper lip. During this time, their youthful server had slunk away and the gawkers had gone back to their business, the novelty of watching a sickly, crippled man wearing a red beret slowly disintegrate, having quickly passed upon his gradual healing.

"You had me worried. I mean worried in a *how-can-I-manage-CPR-from-a-damn-wheelchair* worried," Wesley was saying, the man's bare forehead glistening from a coating of fresh sweat.

"Guess I've just...overextended is all. It...that only happens when I've overloaded the circuits to near short-circuit levels. Usually just takes swallowin' down a couple of gabapentin or baclofen to reverse the effects. Gimme a sec while I seek the magical cure."

A full minute of digging the desired meds from a front pants pocket and another to remove them from their respective bottles ensued, the inevitable epilogue mercifully brief as he gulped down a trio of oval tablets, with the assistance of a half-glass of ice-less water. Head bowed weakly and narrow shoulders slumped in the aftermath, Gunther briefly reached out for the coffee mug as if to polish off the fast-cooling brew, but quickly relented as the fingers groping for the mug had yet to regain complete flexibility.

"Worst part is how sudden it hits ya, like a bolt from the blue. No warnin' either, or hardly a symptom when the meltdown is about to commence. Hell, I was fixing to blame the java about the time someone poured molasses in both eyes and the mitt started shakin' like a wino on a three-day bender. You gotta know the feelin', right?"

Wes, cupping his own steaming mug, seemed to consider for a moment before responding.

"Nothing like that. Not even *close*. Maybe the occasional phantom shooting pain or throbbing sensation from a calf or thigh. Most of my chronic pains involve the lower back."

As if magically teleported into their midst, a man stood poised at the edge of their table, booted feet spread wide and hands on hips. Narrow of face and bloated of belly, the former sporting a walrus-thick salt-and-pepper mustache, the latter hanging over his belt like an oversized, overextended water balloon, he wore a dark crimson *Wildcats* jacket that was little more than a windbreaker, matching, well-worn baseball cap, light gray sweatpants and black, knockoff Wolverine work boots.

"Sorry to interrupt, gents," he said softly, bent forward and hissing like a leaky tire, "but might I steal a moment of your time?"

The pair silently studied him, their eyes similarly squinting, until Wes switched focus to his companion, figuring the stranger might be an old, as-of-yet unidentified acquaintance. Instead, Gunther turned his own eyes back to the tabletop, where he groped for the coffee mug with the hand unaffected by spasms.

"Just state your business, mister. I ain't in the mood nor physical state for games, or isn't that obvious?"

"Just figured to save you some time tracking *me* down, McCarron," the stranger answered, bending with both elbows balanced atop the table until their gazes met straight on.

"Yeah? And why would I be trackin' you exactly?"

"Same reason you departed the Hammock estates about an hour back, I'd surmise. Only serves to reason if you're on some sort of misguided mystery tour of accusing and laying blame, my name would definitely need checking off whatever short list you're following."

Leaning back as far as the well-cushioned booth—and the suit's battery pack—would allow, Gunther looked the thick-bodied stranger up and down as if judging a prize bovine at a county fair. In turn, the stranger removed the ballcap to reveal wavy brown locks with just a touch of gray around well-concealed ears. Similar to the caterpillar-bushy 'stache, an equally fluffy unibrow had been successfully cultivated.

"To be fair, it has been a duration of many years since we last stood within one another's personal space and though I haven't changed *nearly* as much as yourself, time has seen fit for some slight alterations."

Pausing another five ticks and thus allowing two quick, noisy sips, Gunther's eyes widened only slightly as if to possibly play down the situation.

"McKay. Yeah, I'd say those...slight alterations ya mentioned had me thrown for a loop, most notably that massive cookie duster that's the perfect example of a 'stache wearin' the man. Well, that and..." he paused for a leisurely, lingering gaze upon the man's ample gut, "...the love affair ya seem to have developed with Dunkin' Donuts."

"More like hops and barley," the man replied with a light, playful pat of his own breadbox, though the predatory grin he flashed was anything but.

"So what can I do for ya, Shannon?"

"So glad you asked. Simple really. Plainly put, you can stay the hell away from me and mine, McCarron. I've got nothing to say to you and there's nothing you can possibly say or do to change my opinion of you. Push it and I'll sue you for slander. I'm in good standing in this community, you see, and I'm not about to allow an ancient, dried-up sliver of excrement to stick to my shoes and stink up such a well-earned reputation."

"Dried up sliv—" Gunther started to mimic, forehead creased in comical befuddlement, while turning to address a suitably blasé Wesley, who was keeping busy fidgeting with what little remained of a cinnamon danish. "Did he just, in a kind of fruity, roundabout way, refer to me as an old turd?"

"That's how I would define it, yes."

"Thought so." With that, the beret-wearing paraplegic turned back to the recent arrival. "So tell me, Coach K—that is what the kids call ya, right?"

Pushing himself upright—both knees popping loudly with the effort—Shannon McKay did not verbally respond, though his gaunt cheeks gained a measure of rosiness.

"How did ya even know I was here? I mean, should I be seekin' out stalkin' charges?"

"As crude and droll as ever. Hammock called me and said you'd just left his place. I figured, *knew* I would be next on your little bait and blame tour. Now, I know we both probably share similar suspicions concerning the other's involvement in a certain night's tragedy, but speaking frankly, my interest in the subject matter has waned substantially over the years. As for your own, just read the reports, sport. Not only was I not, in any form or fashion, tied to the crime scene, neither was anyone else I ran with at the time. Cliched as it sounds, life does go on, yeah?"

Gunther nodded, stifling a yawn.

"Rumor has it. I'll have to take your word, well, considering."

"Let me put it as simple as I know how," McKay resumed, red-faced and seemingly oblivious of the other man's words, much less their intentionally sardonic meaning. "I'm not gonna play, McCarron, so let's drop it right here and now, and then proceed to keep our distance, agreed?"

A single hand raised—weakly, with several fingers curled inward—Gunther waved an invisible white flag of surrender.

"Fair enough, Coach, fair enough. Soooo, our boys gonna kick some Red Raider hiney this coming Saturday, or what?"

"Yeah, well, about that. McCarron, how about doing the town and especially my...the team a favor and stay as far away from that stadium as possible. Just looking at you makes me an instant believer in jinxes."

"Hey, not *nice,* Coach. I'm a star alum, remember? Class of ninety...somethin'."

Lowering both his gaze and tone, the high school gridiron mentor's thick upper body appeared to puff and swell even as both hands clenched into fleshy, purple-knuckled wrecking balls.

"You're a black cloud of bad luck, mister. Bad luck, bad choices and bad vibes. I didn't come in here to swap spit or hug out our differences. You and I hardly saw eye to eye all those years back. I highly doubt a change is imminent —nor do I even want to know. I want no part, no serving, of...whatever shit-soup you're stirring. I swear, McCarron, as permanently stoved-up as you appear, I won't hesitate to exacerbate the condition, read me?"

Lurching back, Gunther let his jaw collapse and his eyes grow wide with comic shock, though his reply wasn't nearly as muted.

"You publicly threatening a paraplegic, Coach? Tsk tsk tsk. What would your adoring public, better yet all those kids who look to ya like a role model, think of such thuggish shenanigans?"

McKay stood stiffly and afforded his surroundings a quick, paranoid glance, sighing in apparent relief when no one within earshot showed even a passing interest in the conversation.

"My apologies. Violence never solves anything, but a well-timed lawsuit sure as hell *can*. I've said all I came to say. *Not* nice seeing you again, Gunther."

Before sauntering away, Shannon McKay peered over as if only then noticing Wesley's presence.

"I know you?" he inquired with a brisk rub of a stubble-riddled jaw.

Wes only briefly met the large man's gaze before refocusing it across the table to his traveling companion, whose earlier eye tic had returned with a vengeance.

"Just two ships that passed in the hallways too long ago to matter."

"Well, consider yourself banned from my presence as well, seeing as you willingly chose to buddy-up to such trash."

"Best see yourself out now, Coach," Gunther grumbled through a thick scowl, though his tone had lost all verve. "The big game calls and I know your precious time is limited. Go Wildcats."

With that, McKay offered a low grunt before huffing off in a staggering, swaying gait that, crazily, reminded Wesley of John Wayne's infamous cowpoke stroll.

"Nice enough fella, despite that highly indicative walk."

"Yep. Seemed a tad defensive, though."

"You've got supporters coming out of the woodwork."

"Well, you know," Gunther concluded with a weak shrug and even feebler wink, the facial tic having noticeably subsided since the coach's departure, "it's those friendships you make in your youth that last a lifetime."

"I take it this surprise cameo appearance saved us a trip?"

"Not really, 'least not on today's docket. I am lookin' forward to seein' the old fieldhouse again. Nothin' like the stink of old gym socks and mildewin' jock straps to jog the memory."

"Nice. Pretty sure I'd elect to stay in the car."

"You play back in the day?"

Wes shook his head and flashed a weak smile.

"Kicked butt at *Super Mario*."

"Thought so. Nothin' personal, but I never figured you as the jock type."

"Hey, nerds had goals and dreams, too."

"Speakin' for myself, I only played to draw the chicks. Hated practice. Hated the whole process. Didn't give two shits if we won or lost most of the time, but ya always had to act otherwise."

The two men fell silent for several moments, each pushing their respective cups toward the center of the table.

"Ready to motivate?" Wes finally asked, tucking a folded twenty beneath his cup's saucer.

"A wise move. Sit here much longer and the battery on my walkin' suit is apt to refuse walkin' orders, so to speak. That, and it feels like my scrawny butt cheeks are melding into these cushions. Well, not *feels* exactly, but I do seem to be sinkin' within the folds."

It was precisely one-forty-three PM when the two made their way toward the exit, cutting a wide swath through the scattered patrons, most of whom put forth their best—if not shamelessly obvious—effort not to stare.

Thursday, 1333 hours

Poking her toboggan-covered head out from underneath the vehicle's propped hood, Maggie wasn't even aware of her own audible swearing.

"Should I call for a priest?" she heard someone ask over an engine humming so smoothly it practically purred.

"Say again?" Maggie said, turning to stare into the dark interior of an idling, black SUV, the shape within having yet to come clearly into focus, though the voice was vaguely familiar.

"You know, last rites an' all?"

The figure leaned closer to the passenger window, her bulky form filling the ample space within, the full, plump face dominated by an almost ear-to-ear smile that struck Maggie as less jovial than downright creepy.

"Miss Jami—...Sandy?"

"Guilty as charged, hon. You need a lift somewhere? Ya'll still have that auto parts place down by the railroad tracks? Might just need a battery."

"Actually, if you have a set of cables, I think we might be able to jump 'er to life."

"Sorry, I never seem to remember to get those back from a co-worker I let swipe 'em last winter season. You on your lunch break?"

Hands on hips and face creased with conflict, Maggie scanned the sparse, all-but-empty lot—save for the chief's SUV, Cindy Lou's aged Civic and a pair of long-decommissioned Crown Vics—and sighing heavily, regarded her potential savior with a thin, sad smile that was less appreciative than simply an admission of defeat.

"Matter of fact, I'm famished," the veteran dispatcher confessed timidly and not without instant regret at the thought of breaking bread with Wesley's ex, a woman she'd long branded a soulless harpy, despite her co-worker and close friend's insistence otherwise.

"The Glutton, I presume?"

Maggie frowned as if suddenly assaulted by an offending odor.

"Ugh. Familiarity breeds contempt. How's The Prize Sow sound? I know it's kind of out of the way, but hey, lunch is on me. Least I can do."

"How about your disabled ride?"

"Oh, I'll get Ph—...um...Officer Strickland to run over to Bates Auto and snag it a new power source. He's actually...meeting us at the Sow."

The SUV's passenger door flung open and the dispatcher's flaring nostrils soon filled with the stout aroma of citrus air freshener.

"Oh, got'cha. Well, hop on in, little sister. Truth be told, I was on my way to tie on the old feedbag when I heard you voicing your displeasure with your car's mechanical shortcomings from about two streets over."

Tucked within the SUV's warm, expansive folds, the pair were soon departing Main Street for the first of several unmarked two-lanes eventually leading to the state highway on the town's western edge.

Having removed the worn, CFPD-issued and -embroidered toboggan, Maggie tucked both it and her similarly castoff gloves into her lap, her host choosing to remain tightly tucked within her own winter ensemble, to include thick wool jacket, North Face gloves and faux fur Cossack hat, all in the same matching ebony shade as her sleek, late-model ride.

"Appreciate it again, Sandy. Your timing was impeccable."

"Think nothin' of it, hon. I'm just glad to have the company. I simply despise eating alone."

In lieu of cracking an inadvertent grin at this rather ironic line—from which Maggie's mischievous mind instantly belched forth many a one-liner, the most prominent being "then you must keep constant company, honey,"—she instead switched subjects at breakneck speed.

"Still managing that gym?" she muttered between forced nibbles on the pinkie nail of her left hand, the act serving to disallow the wide smile that begged for release.

"Roger that," came the enthusiastic reply, accompanied by an equally chipper thumbs-up. "Business has been going gangbusters since Covid dang near shut us down a couple of summers back. Lots of extra pounds found their way onto people's breadbaskets and rear ends in twenty-twenty, including yours truly, as you can probably tell."

"Oh, well, no, you look fi—"

"Been hitting the mat pretty hard after hours the last few weeks, though. Tell ya this much, it ain't nearly as easy to work off all the Twinkies and Ho-Hos when middle age comes callin', so be careful what ya fuel up on now, young lady, and you'll save yourself multiple rolls of grief later on."

Maggie knew all too well—via Wesley—the other woman's past feats of Herculean physicality, to include competitive powerlifting and bodybuilding.

"Duly noted. So, any luck with finding Wes?"

"Pardon?"

"I know you were trying to get in touch with him."

"Oh that. Nope, no luck as of yet. Voice mailbox is still jampacked. I swear, that man can be so...absentminded and unorganized, shocking considering his line of work."

"He's a card, all right," Maggie replied casually, though not about to participate in trading backstabbing barbs concerning Wes with his ex.

"I'll smoke 'im out eventually. He can run but he can't hide, right?"

Maggie merely nodded with a barely audible grunt, staring out the passenger window as the light flaking that had begun at midmorning continued unabated.

"Maggie, I guess you know 'im better than anyone but myself, so give it to me straight. How's he doin' these days? I mean, *really* doing? It's just...I always have the feeling he's putting on an act whenever we do talk, playing down whatever might be eating at him."

Clearing her throat, Maggie was already regretting the decision to accept Sandy Jamison's supposed good Samaritan act, as it had mutated very quickly to a form of interrogation.

"Well, Wes is mostly mum about anything outside of work. Pretty serious dude most of the time. Rarely rears his head outta that shell, you know."

"I just...worry so about his health. If he's taking his meds or eating like he should, you know. You didn't know him before the incident, did you?"

Maggie nodded stiffly, her mind racing for an avenue of escape from the current subject matter.

"Well, you can imagine how different a man he was. Losing the use of one's limbs has gotta be one of fate's cruelest gut punches, especially for one as virile as Wesley."

"I'm...sure it's...an extreme adjustment."

"Hope I'm not getting too personal here, but it's just us ladies, right?"

"Y-yeah, it's just..."

"Early in our marriage—I mean those first few years are all about learning each other's habits, right? I wasn't exactly a wealth of experience in the sack, after all," Sandy giggled girlishly in so uncharacteristic a tone that Maggie actually felt the stereotypical cold chill race up her spine despite the well-heated truck interior. "I nicknamed Wes my...," the giggle, shrill and grating, briefly interrupted yet again, "...sledgehammer. He was...relentless and so, so uninhibited. *Lord* but he made me lose myself. I probably miss the intimacy almost as much as he—"

"Hey, um, Sandy, this is a little awkward."

"But what I'm getting at is, to lose this element of one's life, the complete devastation to a man's psyche has to be catastrophic."

Unwilling and/or unable to shift her focus from the passing countryside, Maggie frantically sought to change the subject but was, so very uncharacteristically, mentally gazing at an utterly blank slate of options.

"I'm...I'd imagine it would—"

"I guess it's possible, probable even, he might seek out a kindred spirit, ya think?"

"Kindred...spirit?"

"You know, someone who might share the hardships and, well, loss of what was. Kinda like AA only for the disabled."

"I guess it's...yeah, I could see that. I'd guess Louisville or Lexington might offer some sort of group therapy for para—""

"Scuttlebutt has it Crimson Falls was recently reintroduced to just such an individual."

With that, Maggie discovered the proper motivation to at least face forward, a lightbulb of renewed interest all but glowing over her comically puffy hairdo.

"True enough, though I have a hard time visualizing Wes and Gunther McCarron having much in common other than the, well, obvious. That McCarron is one weird bird."

Navigating the SUV past a sputtering, smoking, Jurassic-era Chevy four door, Sandy Jamison kept her beady blues parked straight ahead, though with the obviously drawn-on left brow cocked severely.

"Oh, you're acquainted?"

"Vaguely, but he's a hard one to forget. Came into the PD a few days back to pick up the records pertaining to his case. Surprisingly spry, well you know, considering."

"Fifteen years comatose, right?"

Inexplicably recharged, Maggie's eyes boggled with gossip-fueled joy, her distaste for the present company all but forgotten.

"Longest on record to wake up functional, at least in this state."

"So he just...wheeled into the station out of the blue?"

"*Walked* into the station. Well, sort of."

At this specific divulgement, it was the driver's turn to exhibit wide-eyed, jaw-dropping shock, the top of her Cossack hat tipping back from the sudden flinch, revealing the bottom edges of a tan-shaded band-aid just below the hairline.

"Upright, ya mean? But how in blue blazes? I mean, I heard he was fully paralyzed from the neck down!"

"Bionic man technology at its finest. Will, um, Chief Crockett said it was one of the newest models of exoskeletons. Uses some kind of electrical charge to stimulate nerve endings or some such Star Trek shit...um, crap. He wasn't exactly what I'd call graceful, kinda robotic if I'm being honest, but amazing to see. Like witnessing something futuristic in real time, if that makes sense."

"Unbelievable. A mobile paraplegic. I'm guessing you don't find such contraptions in the bargain bin at the local Dollar General."

"Not hardly. Cin—...a co-worker researched 'em and said the price tag ranged anywhere from sixty to one-hundred grand."

A quick shake of her head—the furry Cossack hat miraculously resetting in the process—the driver clicked her tongue while exiting from one narrow two-lane to another, the SUV effortlessly ascending a steep incline coated in a wintry mix that all but obliterated any signs of the aged asphalt beneath.

"Amazin' what medical science can accomplish these days, for a price. Must be nice for those in the upper two percentile."

"Yeah but, I gotta say he looked kind of, well, creepy," Maggie instantly countered. "It was like he was being pulled along by puppet strings. I tried not to stare but I'd never seen anything like it. Like...him." Suddenly, as if just becoming aware of who she was utilizing as a sounding board, Maggie's lips clamped as if forced shut by compressed air.

"Dang. Sounds like some kinda robot. Guess it's the better of two options though. I mean, I do wish Wesley had the necessary funds. I'd love to see him show some initiative to gain extra mobility if given the shot."

In lieu of a verbal reply, the passenger—having resumed her earlier stare-down of the passing countryside—merely shrugged without commitment.

The SUV hummed along atop a mostly deserted path as the pair fell into a silence that was rapidly growing, at least for the passenger, painfully awkward. Though XM radio was cranking out the classic country tunes, the volume was set too low to create the required diversion.

"Sooo...," Sandy finally blurted while passing a sign announcing the desired eatery's imminent appearance, "...can you think of any other place he could be? I mean locally other than maybe with this McCarron character? You sure he didn't mention anything that might afford me a clue?"

Maggie's focus remained fixed, her gestures, earlier so openly animated, stilted to the point of utter lifelessness.

"None that come to mind other than his saying he just needed some downtime from the office. You want me to give 'im a ring?"

"Been there, done that and then some. Voice mailbox is still one overstuffed tick."

"Overstu—...oh, yeah. Weird. Well, I guess he really did mean to live off the grid for a while. Recharge the ol' batteries and all that."

The driver grunted, pulling into a mostly sparse parking lot, though behind a threesome of vehicles with the same lunchtime destination, oblivious to the probable significance of a departing Camry that passed by them without fanfare.

"Recharge from what? Combing through the eight or ten police reports that come through that station in a week's time? Not exactly inner-city Detroit."

Maggie felt her face grow red with ire at not only the woman's smarmy tone, but the sudden descent into her trademark sour disposition that arose whenever she spoke of Wesley's choice of careers after the accident, as if this alone and not her own blatant selfishness, had eroded and eventually ended their marriage.

"It's not *Mayberry*, Sandy. Never was, and sure as hell isn't now."

Another repellent grunt, this scoff accompanied by a pouty, scrunched expression that instantly raised her passenger's BP well past the stable range.

"Yeah well, he could've switched gears from pushin' paper and sniffin' holsters. Wes is a damn smart man, though he's always had a penchant for keeping that fact well concealed. He could've done so much better."

The SUV parked in one of a half-dozen available spaces fronting the establishment, a light snow still pecking the windshield and evaporating almost instantly.

"Considering what the man's been through, I personally give him a ton of credit," Maggie countered, no longer even trying to conceal her displeasure, while yanking on the toboggan. "A lesser person could never have endured so many potentially fatal body blows to the psyche, and to face it alone the way he did."

"Meaning *what* exactly, darlin'?"

Sandy Jamison's overly toothy grin, her lips withdrawn like a growling wolf and tight, predatory squint did more to halve the younger woman's continued rant than the bile-retching query complementing it.

Wary but undeterred, Maggie plowed forward, though with a noticeably tamer tone.

"Meaning he was and is the bravest individual I've ever met..."

"You ever straddle his ride, Childers?" Jamison snarled, tongue clicking annoyingly in the aftermath.

"Excuse me?"

"Check under his hood back there in the dark catacombs of records when no one else was around? Maybe pull the shades over that glass window and sneak back behind the rolling file for a little handicapped hanky-panky? A little disabled dick on the sly, ya might say."

Dark eyes pulled wide, Maggie Childers' open-mouthed gasp only served to further fuel Jamison's bile-filled rant, leaning in as if to eventually plant a big, wet kiss on her shocked passenger.

"C'mon now, Maggie, ain't no secret that you've boned every officer that's pinned on a badge in Crimson Falls in the last decade, so why not bang the town cripple to continue satisfying that insatiable, never-ending bucket list?"

Even before she could control it, the smaller woman's right arm swung over the dash—the gloved, open hand avoiding brushing the windshield by less than an inch—only to be halted in mid-swing barely halfway to its intended target. Jamison's gnarled mitt easily enveloped the smaller appendage it currently held captive, the former gradually constricting with anaconda efficiency.

"Kinda sensitive for the town floozie, ain't we?"

"F-fat piece of shit...," Maggie whined with increased shrillness; the intended growl of guttural rage having instantly dissipated in the face of impending, multiple fractures.

"I always suspected, ya know. Small wonder he never touched me those last few years we shared a bed, not with Little Miss Saigon around to inflate his egg noodle."

"Bu-bullshit and y-you know it," Maggie huffed, struggling in vain to retrieve her lost hand, the digits of which were being slowly crushed to the snapping point. "Y-you...dumped h-him like...bad tr-trash. He b-became a...b-burden t-to you...an em...embarrassment."

"You...don't...*know*...shit," came the raspy reply, each word punctuated by increased pressure on fingers already numb and purple-shaded beneath their individual leather wrappings.

Squirming in the seat until her back was planted firmly against the door, Maggie—tightly-clamped eyes now streaming hot tears onto cheeks glowing rose-red—had managed to worm her left hand from its own glove and was just moments from reaching over in an attempt to claw at the other woman's eyes when the right was unceremoniously released, the abruptly-freed appendage smacking the dash with a muffled thump.

"Wh-what's *wrong* with you?" she inquired, wincing in obvious pain while twisting around in the seat and pushing the passenger door ajar just enough to plant a single boot out onto the snow-coated terrain.

Shifting the SUV into reverse, Sandy Jamison stared straight ahead, though mindful to check the rearview and notice a marked CFPD vehicle parked in the rear of the lot.

"When you see or hear from Wesley, please let him know that he and I need to converse, and please feel free to overdramatize our set-to here. Hell, tell him I twisted your titties for all I care. And Maggie...," she paused, right eye shifting like a single brown marble even as her head's position remained unchanged, "...tell him I *won't* be leaving town until he and I share some personal space."

"Lady, you need help," Maggie started to reply, her left boot suddenly scraping the moving pavement as the SUV lurched back.

"Jump out or be dragged, bitch. Your choice," she heard Sandy Jamison spit before practically diving from the vehicle and barely avoiding executing what would've surely been a painful and, at the very least, embarrassing breakdance *slash* splits routine.

Standing with hands on hips, Maggie watched the sleek utility vehicle streak out of the lot and back onto the highway like an ebony missile, whitish vapor spewing from its tailpipe in a thick tapered stream.

"Bat-shit crazy," she whispered softly, turning to find the patrolman she'd come to meet for lunch and, massaging fingers she'd briefly feared might have been fractured, pondering whether or not to mention any or all portions of the story to him.

In the end, as the frequent lovers greeted in a back booth bathed in shadow and shared coffee and eats, she decided to keep all details of the bizarre confrontation to herself, all the while nagged unmercifully not only by Jamison's outlandish "floozie" remark, but the even wilder accusation that she and Wesley had somehow been romantically involved.

By the time she'd resumed her afternoon shift nearly an hour later, the uncontrollable shaking of both Maggie Childers' hands had little to do with either recent physical trauma or the frigid temperatures.

Thursday, 1421 hours

"Looks like you've got company."

Droopy lids parting just enough for semi-visibility, Gunther grunted as if to acknowledge familiarity with the pickup parked halfway down his drive, a grayish fog spewing from its aged tailpipe.

"Someone you know, I presume?"

"My uncle Dexter. A worry-wart of the highest order."

Wesley steered the Camry just to the left of the idling truck, its passenger eyeing them through the rearview but unmoved behind the wheel.

"I know the sort. Have a co-worker that shares the very same characteristic. Hey, just my take, but you might want to cut his visit as short as possible. You're looking about as fresh as year-old cabbage."

"Probably smell worse."

"You need a sabbatical something fierce."

"Thanks for not sayin' coma. Had my fill."

"You gonna need my services tomorrow?"

"If you're offerin'."

"I am."

"I got your cell. Might wanna wait till I give you a ring. I'm feelin' a lengthy nap is in order."

"Notice you didn't say *coma* either. Sharp."

Passenger regarded driver with a warped smile and playful wink.

"You sure we didn't hang out in a past life? Suckin' down brews and nibblin' pretzels at the local bar? With workin' legs, of course."

"Highly doubtful we ever would've. Without our shared disability, all this witty banter would just seem rote and, dare I say it, only mildly amusing?"

"Yep, I concede," Gunther replied, leaning down and openly struggling to ensure his leg straps were secured. "When ya start usin' terms...," he panted, rearing back up with a huff, his pale visage sporting a shiny coating of sweat "... like witty banter and words like rote, you...make said case an unbeatable one."

The passenger door was pushed ajar in spaced segments, as the individual responsible moved with all the vim and vigor of that heavily medicated type recently released from major surgery.

"Take your meds and get some rest, McCarron. Call me when you need me."

With both feet planted as firmly as he could manage, Gunther pushed himself upright and, following a brief but potentially troublesome wobble, remained so.

"Yes, m-mother and thanks...again," he managed before using a well-placed elbow to push the door shut with as little force as was necessary for a proper seal.

The idling pickup's engine was cut just as the Camry successfully backed onto the road, Dexter McCarron exiting his vehicle only after the other had pulled away.

"You're a popular sort, I'll say that," the elder stated, decked out in his customary black ensemble, to include tinted Ray-Bans, Stetson fedora, ankle-length duster and scuffed work boots.

Greeting his uncle with a slight nod and pained grimace, Gunther halted mid-step, his foot dragging so severely it dug a clear outline into the flake-coated concrete.

"You...m-mind helpin' me into...the house, Dex? Batteries...about to conk out, and I...ain't just talkin' about this...contraption."

Without further dialogue, his uncle did just that, tucking a supportive shoulder beneath an armpit and all but carrying his nephew—the husk-like lightness of his frame like that of a slight, teenaged boy instead of full-grown man—up the porch steps and into the house.

~ * ~

"So, this patrolman was stakin' out the place?"

"Yeah, that jug-eared one with the spastic mannerisms. Guess they're rotating."

"He say why?"

Gunther's shockingly emaciated frame lay across the couch, the exoskeleton having been stripped away and its battery placed within a charger that was its usual home for the better part of twenty hours a day.

"Said it was to keep the media at bay. The chief figured they might congregate here after leaving my place."

"Three of 'em, you say?"

"Two men and a woman. All from different newspapers, or what suffices these days on the internet."

"What? They figurin' on doin' round-the-clock surveillance?"

Parked on a nearby ottoman, Dexter had yet to remove the Ray-Bans, allowing his nephew a warped reflection of his own form and ghostly visage.

"Didn't say. Probably just a few days unless a crime wave of some sort pulls 'em away."

"Or interest in my story wanes. From what I understand, it don't take much baitin' to redirect 'em to fresher tragedies. 'Sides, it ain't like they're gonna burn the house down with me in it, right? Pretty simple solution, if ya think on it."

When his uncle didn't bite—as stoic, statuesque and nonverbal as ever—Gunther inhaled deeply and resumed.

"They knock, I don't answer. I mean, unless they're into home invasions, that should turn the trick."

"They might not give up so easy."

The younger man scoffed, albeit weakly.

"I'll be old news by first of next week."

Seemingly unconvinced if facial expressions were to be believed, his uncle donned a frozen mask of disdain, though with characteristic silence.

"Relax, Dex. Brew yourself a cup of joe and stay awhile. I may look like death walkin', but it's just a disguise."

"Gotta go. Got some runs to make before the sun goes down. I left a folder on the kitchen table."

"I didn't see you carry anything in."

"It was in the truck. You fell asleep and I went out and got it."

"What is it?"

"You'll know it when you see it."

Gunther rolled his eyes, the physical equivalent of bench pressing a small car in his current state.

"A true man of mystery. Who knew?"

"No mystery. Just a friendly reminder of what was and what still *is*."

The younger man regarded the older through splayed fingers of the hand laid across his forehead.

"Um, yeah, okay then, whatever. Hey, grab it for me, will ya? I can peruse it while I lie here vegetatin'."

Dexter shook his head, rising with a resounding grunt.

"Nope. Sleep now. Read later. You resemble a freshly laid cadaver. I'll let myself out. Told the officer I'd let 'im know when I left the property."

"Ten-four. Tell 'em to keep the sirens and gunfire to a minimum, will ya?"

"Call if you need anything."

"Got ya on speed dial."

"Rest well, Gunny."

Closing his eyes, Gunther heard his uncle's boots trail toward the front door, the now-familiar creak swinging inward but the sound of its reclosing a non-occurrence.

Instead there was a lengthy pause, wherein Gunther felt his leaden lids begin the arduous task of rising in the face of unyielding curiosity.

"Your buddy's back," he heard Dexter announce blandly, his uncle standing with a bare palm parked at the center of the glass screen door.

"Should I tell him to leave you be?" his uncle resumed as his nephew pulled himself semi-upright within the couch's folds.

"Nah. If he's back this quick, there must be a pretty good reason."

The man in black exited without further dialogue, the somehow soothing hiss of the screen door following his departure.

Roughly five minutes later—Gunther had timed the other man's efforts to depart the vehicle and secure himself into the wheelchair down to that of a veteran pit-crew member—Wesley first knocked lightly before entering the kitchen through the back door.

"Hello in there!"

"Livin' room, sport."

Wheels departed tile for deep shag carpet, like under-lubricated roller skates relocating from a rink's highly waxed surface for a grassy knoll, and a final sharp, cautiously executed turn around the edge of the couch followed.

"Well, since it's only been a half-hour since ya beat feet, I can only figure you forgot somethin' pretty vital."

Staring into his own blanket-covered lap, the other man shrugged awkwardly, his cheeks visibly reddening.

"It's kind of, well, embarrassing, but I need a favor."

Gunther's left brow cocked dramatically.

"Ask me, brother. Anything but sex."

"You got an extra room I can crash in?"

"Definitely. What's up?"

"Let's just say that I hadn't been at all vigilant in checking either text or voice messages. I'd just rather not go home tonight."

Twisting around to gesture down a darkened, nearby hallway, Gunther retrieved a remote device from somewhere on the couch and, a few well-aimed jabs later, effectively lit up the narrow space.

"No sweat. My castle is your castle. Last room on the right. Has its own private john equipped with towels, toiletries and such."

"Words cannot express my thanks."

"I owe you, obviously, and hey, if ya feel like jawin' about it, ya know where to find me. For now, that's right on this here combination recliner and cruise ship disguised as an everyday sofa."

"Take your meds?"

"Yes, mother. You?"

Wesley displayed a raised forefinger.

"Right before beddy-bye to ensure maximum slumber effects."

"A real pro, you are. I'd ask you to stay but I really do need to crash for a few hours, if not days. There's a flatscreen in the bedroom and food in the fridge."

With a final nod, the other man adjusted the chair via a semi-wheelie but stopped short before rolling away.

"You really overdid it today playing robo-detective. Ever hear of pacing yourself?"

"Point taken, but ya see, I get the distinct feelin' my time is severely limited for solving this here mystery."

"Not if you stop driving yourself like a man possessed. I, like no one else within limping distance, know the strain this can put on severely compromised systems such as ours. Slow down, Gunther, or you won't be around to solve anything."

Allowing his threadlike frame to collapse onto the couch, Gunther's condescending reply was uncharacteristically devoid of all good humor.

"All due respect to your own hard-luck story, Grant, but you and I are about as similar in terms of a current state of trauma as Spam and filet mignon."

At just past nine PM, the muted flatscreen showcasing a marathon of vintage *Mission Impossible* episodes, Wesley felt his eyelids growing heavy despite having a myriad of frenzied thoughts and accompanying fears, the latter severely reducing the odds of impending full-REM sleep.

Of the twenty-something missed calls, eighteen had been from Sandy, with over a dozen of those having collected since noon. Similar to these, but easily the more frightening of the two forms of communications, however, were the astonishing *forty-six* text messages, many of them the five-to-six-word variety, but a few full-blown short-story length. There had also been three missed calls from Maggie and a brief but foreboding text which read simply: *The ex-missus is trailing your scent, young man. If I were you, I'd find the deepest, darkest of caves till the heat is off. Luv ya—mean it.*

As for the dozen or so voicemails, the gist of what was requested from his ex-spouse had been concise and clear-cut, her naturally volatile nature ramping up significantly as the messages had progressed to the point of barely restrained hysterics. Powering down both the television and his cell, he pondered the irony of Gunther's earlier proclamation concerning his time being "severely limited."

As purely a precautionary measure—Maggie was, after all, both a good friend and a known worry-wart—Wes had rung her up and supplied a purely off-the-cuff cock-and-bull tale of having rented a cabin just north of Independence to do a little fishing. His pal had seemed both relieved and a tad skeptical, and more of the latter than the former, if her tone was any indication.

Stripped to his boxers and a green tee, he lay atop the overly firm twin bed in near total darkness and whispered hoarsely to himself between gnashed teeth, his wheelchair parked strategically in front of the locked bedroom door.

"Really horrible odds, buddy boy, and that betting line is only gonna grow narrower by the hour," he muttered with both hands tucked behind his head, pondering the impossibility of staying effectively hidden away from certain prying, predatory eyes within the severely limited confines of the Crimson Falls' city limits.

In keeping with the day's overall mood, he was rocked awake by a booming chorus of thunder at just past midnight, moments after finally having drifted off. Save for a sporadic nap of a five-to-ten-minute duration, deep sleep would elude him thereafter.

From the *Crimson Falls Gazette* Sports Page
Dated Oct. 30

Unbeaten Wildcats stir up a Halloween-themed cauldron of trouble to the tune of 41-14 against Warriors
(Friday Night, Warrior Field)

Fueled by star tailback Dalton Crane's 186-yard, 2-touchdown performance on the ground, Crimson Falls moved to 7-0 on a drizzly Halloween eve with little resistance from the hosting Jefferson Warriors (3-4), who were also victimized by three turnovers and an anemic offense that netted barely 150 yards on the evening.

Eight

Will Crockett stood at the entrance to the dimly lit dispatch office, his massive bulk shielding all prospective illumination from the well-lit records section at his back.

"Mag, who's on this morning?"

"Jake's in for Phil till Sunday."

Jake Douglas was a part-timer, the only such position in the department, an always-dependable fill-in for all shifts whenever vacation or sick days intervened and, having just reached his sixtieth birthday, a retired corrections officer from several in-state penal institutions.

"Pardon my failing memory, but when is C.J. due back from vacation again?"

C.J. (Charles Jacobs), a three-year veteran to the force, had departed with the wife and kids to her folks' place in West Virginia the week of Thanksgiving.

"Twelve December."

"That young man has always had impeccable timing. Seems to me his last sabbatical kicked off a few days before that eight-car pileup on the forty-five."

Maggie smiled wryly. "Your *selective* memory is aces, Chief."

"What's Jake's twenty?"

"Patrolling out by Morrow Lake. Had a call about some campers out by the reservoir."

The chief reached up with his free hand—his left cupped a steaming cup of black java—to apply a light scratch to the balding dome tucked beneath the ever-present, wide brim cap.

"Harrison Trail?"

"The very same."

"Move 'im closer to town and tell him to peel eyes for a late model gray Charger, Michigan license HOTSHOT1. Might want to concentrate on the area in and around the McCarron place."

"Got it," she said, adjusting her headset and clearing her throat. "HQ to unit three."

"Unit three, come on," came the gruff reply through faint waves of barely audible static.

"BOLO a newer model gray Charger; Hotel, Oscar, Tango, Sierra, Hotel, Oscar, Tango, One. Last seen nearer town limits. Request location shift to concentrate on the area of the McCarron place on Old Sawmill Road and Little Bear Creek areas. Over."

"Ten-four, HQ, headed that way now. Over."

"If contact sighted, Unit One requests immediate notification. Over."

"Understood. Specifics on a probable navigator of said ride? Over."

"Hang on, three."

With that, Maggie turned to Crockett and shrugged.

"White male, slim build, early to mid-twenties. Likely possessing a sour disposition but hardly a threat."

Once the dispatcher had conveyed the info and the intended officer had duly received, she switched radio traffic to speaker and, removing the headset, regarded her superior with a pinched expression he knew all too well.

"So *give* already, boss. I'm dying here."

Having already turned to depart—the dispatch room flooded with newfound light—the chief halted half-in, half-out, a noisy sip previewing his response.

"Seems the youngest and easily most irritating of those three reporters we ran off from Dexter McCarron's house yesterday has never shown back up or even checked in with his employers."

"Oh yeah, Keith Braggs or something. Jerome mentioned he was quite the lippy millennial, that one."

"Kevin Briggs, and yeah, he was. Keep me posted."

Maggie waited until the thumping echo of the chief's size thirteens was thoroughly muffled by the closing of his office door before practically levitating from her assigned throne and darting into the records section, where Cindy Lou Harrison sat behind one of three available desks, gnawing on a granola bar.

"You take the call about this Briggs bozo?"

"Indeed I did," the fill-in clerk replied between crunchy bites, a large brown chunk having wedged its way between her front two teeth, however porcelain-based they might be, a playful wink executed between pauses.

"Why, Maggie, are we being nosy?"

"Darn tootin' we are. So what's the name of this online rag he works for anyhow?"

"*Hair of the Dog* or some similar idiocy. No doubt based out of somebody's mother's basement."

"We know the locale of that proposed basement?"

"She didn't say, but I'd guess from that accent, not from these parts. Definitely well above the Mason-Dixon line."

The dispatcher's eyes practically twinkled with curiosity.

"She? Who was this, girlfriend, wife...worried parent?"

Swallowing down the last of the snack, her flowery blouse littered with its jagged shrapnel, Cindy Lou paused for a quick sip of canned Sprite before resuming.

"His boss, I'd surmise. Maybe his editor, I dunno. Did sound mighty concerned, though. Said they'd been talking on their cells when she heard what sounded like a crash and then the call cut off. Hadn't heard from the young man since."

"Did he tell her where he was before the call dropped?"

"She didn't say."

"She give you the number?"

"Number?"

"Cell number."

"His or hers?"

Unable or simply unwilling to cloak her building exasperation, the dispatcher's dark eyes rolled.

"Either! Jeez Cindy..."

The older woman's rotund face glowed with sudden excitement.

"Mag, you thinking about tracing 'em?"

"Bingo."

"So, how is that done anyhow?"

"Triangulation. Depends on how many towers the call bounced from."

"Wowsa. I always wondered how they did that on all the cop shows..."

"Cindy Lou, focus."

Cindy Lou sat up stiffly as if from a sudden, generous charge of electricity.

"Surely."

"Our phones record, yeah? Incoming numbers, I mean."

Scooping up the nearest device from its cradle, the veteran city clerk punched a few select buttons before leaning down in order to read the number flashed across its tiny display.

Moments later, the number having been haphazardly scribbled on a Post-it note, a surprisingly subdued—at least on the outside—Maggie Childers briefly discarded her sworn duty as city dispatcher just long enough to make a beeline to her boss's office.

Friday, 0834 hours

"Well, good mornin' sunshine. There's coffee and danish on the kitchen table, though the former ain't exactly fresh and the latter is of the packaged variety."

Gunther sat upright, though slightly askew on the couch, a manila folder lying across his lap, an empty mug and danish-stained paper towel splayed across the nearby ottoman.

"Appreciate it on both counts," Wesley replied, rolling slowly past his seated host, whose pitch-black pjs, matching fuzzy slippers and severely cow-licked hairdo birthed a smile he was careful not to reveal until he'd wheeled out of the other man's visual range.

"A little light reading?" he inquired upon reentering the living room with a steaming mug in one hand and a matching set of danishes in the other.

"Practically feather-weight," Gunther answered, a pair of reading glasses having been pulled from parts unknown sitting precariously at the very tip of his nose, which was buried in the pages he sporadically flipped.

"Medical or police journal, I presume?"

"Can't get one past you, Sherlock. I knew there was a reason I wanted you around other than our shared penchant for nonworking limbs."

Parked on the opposite side of the ottoman and directly facing the other man, Wesley sipped noisily and winced.

"Well, want to share or should I just continue with the telepathic vibe?"

"Police report from all those years ago. Seems my uncle shares the same mind-readin' skills as yourself, as a trip to state police HQ in Lexington was gonna be our very next sojourn. Least, till he saw fit to save us the trip. Well, at least for *now*, anyhow."

"Anything there surprise you?"

"Investigator's name was Sandra Tanner," Gunther said, loosely gesturing toward the iPad taking up couch space to his left. "Amazin' what one can learn from a simple Google search. Tanner left the po-po less than six months after filing the report, when she'd had it closed administratively until, and I quote, any new leads surfaced to justify reopening the case. Chick was only twenty-eight when she resigned to enter the private security sector. Makes a body wonder just how dedicated she was to diggin' up any of those alleged leads, what with one foot possibly planted firmly inside the civilian world."

"Then again, that *chick* might've sincerely run into the proverbial dead end and had to move on or was forced to do so by a superior."

"Yeah, maybe. Just to sate my own curiosity, I did some probin' to see what she's been up to of late. Found her in one of those people search motors."

Wes smirked, though it was mostly hidden behind the raised coffee mug.

"Engines."

"Uh-huh. So, no mention of recent employment, just that she had relocated to Myrtle Beach and that she was raisin' two teenaged girls. Hmmm, couple of tweeners, huh? Only figures she popped those out soon after tossin' away the badge. No spouse mentioned either, even though the most recent address I dug up was in one of the more affluent areas."

Pausing, a suddenly strikingly pale Gunther peeked over the wire-rims and winked, though the gesture was anything but playful. "Life sure is funny, ain't it? As in many times more ironically bizarre than knee-slappin' humorous? Coincidences abound in this case, or am I just bein' one of those annoyin' conspiracy theorists?"

Upon his guest remaining conspicuously silent and cautiously sipping from the steaming mug, Gunther resumed in a tone that was equal parts patronizing and confrontational.

"C'mon, talk to me, brother. We've shared space and broken bread over the last few days. I'd say you probably know me as well as anyone these days, at least this pitiful version of me.

"Am I overreaching here? Has my outer shell cracked beyond repair just recently or did I come off as nutty as Aunt Martha's fruit cake the second ya met me?"

"All honesty, I'd need more...all the facts to voice...to form an opinion. So far it's been dribs, drabs and stale police reports."

His host's shoulders, round and narrow as a rule, slumped almost into nonexistence, his voice trailing off weakly. "Fair enough, though I gotta tell ya, dribs and drabs is kinda my high mark, at least at this stage of the investigation. Remember, I've made a living out of incapacitation of late. Can't know now what I never knew before, right?"

"Pure genius."

"What can I say? Never was much of a conspiracist unless viable proof existed to steer me that direction and this here essay...," he nodded toward the folder, which he then closed with a visibly shaking hand, "...hardly provides that. Dry as a week-old biscuit and almost as stimulating. Talk about clear as mud, it was like she wrote it up usin' some kinda paint-by-numbers tutorial for police reports."

A brief silence allowing the low hum of the central heat to dominate, Wesley spoke up only after finishing his coffee with a final, slurping gulp.

"So, since I take it we're not booking a flight to a certain South Carolina beach, what's the plan?"

His thin frame collapsing into the couch's deep cushions until it appeared he was being swallowed whole, Gunther's wan smile was as sickly as his overall deportment, as shockingly pale and gaunt as the living, breathing phantom he was slowly transforming into.

"Well, as a matter of fact, since you're askin'..."

Friday, 0931 hours

Lips pursed with pressure sufficient to tint them a purplish hue, Maggie stared down the nearby landline as if to intimidate it into ringing.

"Nothing yet?" she heard Cindy Lou ask—at least the third such inquiry in the last half-hour—from somewhere within the adjoining room.

"Negative. That *would* require the phone actually ringing!" she brayed in return, eyes rolling at the boneheadedness of the veteran clerk's query, though she couldn't deny sharing at least the same level of impatience.

"Oh yeah, *right.* Smartass," came a reply so shamelessly immersed in sarcasm the dispatcher couldn't help but grin.

In the meantime, with only three calls since her shift had begun at seven AM—two involving dogs running at large—it allowed Maggie to dwell on and delve further into that bizarre meeting *slash* confrontation with Wesley's ex the day before, all the while unconsciously massaging the lingering soreness of her right hand.

In the aftermath of the inexplicable standoff, she'd called his cell several times and left her third voice message in as many days, all requesting he get back to her post-haste concerning his ex-wife and her borderline psychotic behavior.

In truth, she was happy for the distraction of the missing reporter as her worry for her friend's whereabouts grew by the hour, especially considering that daily communications between the two was routine, even on their days off, the simple act of responding to a missed call normally instantaneous.

She couldn't help but wonder if the sole reason for the sudden request for time off hadn't been to bury his head in hiding from Sandy. Considering the woman's schizophrenic ways, who'd blame him? Certainly not the police department's unofficial "floozy," she mused with palpable bitterness.

Gnawing teeth expertly relocating from the pinkie to index finger of her left hand, she pondered for at least the dozenth time that morning what possible cave or cavern her co-worker was presently cowering down in, just as, to emphasize the level of this self-inflicted daze, the chief was able to saunter up and stick his head through the open door without being either heard or seen.

"Any word from Douglas?" he asked, leaning half in but leaving just enough space to avoid blocking the opening in full-eclipse fashion.

"Negative."

"How about the phone track?"

"Strike two, boss."

"Well, it takes time. Smart money is that the kid is holed up in a Motel Six a couple of hundred miles between here and Flint with a busted iPhone and is too stone-stupid to know how to use a landline."

Maggie nodded, scooping up a Post-it note which featured a barely readable name and number recorded in a haphazard, chicken-scratch fashion that was solely her own.

"Oh, I did finally manage to reach an actual manager at Verizon and emphasized the term 'police priority' more than once. Hopefully he'll treat it as such."

The chief lunged forward a step, the room a shade murkier from the effort.

"Outstanding. If it helps, his employer did mention a friend finder app on his cell and possibly even Grinder."

"The more options the better, I've heard. If he had his GPS turned on, the odds increase exponentially."

"Logically, yeah. Listen, I'll be out to the high school. Pep rally is at noon and I figured we might need a presence."

When the dispatcher's left brow arched dramatically, he expounded with a sigh. "For support, I mean. Phil's meeting me there. I might even say a few words."

"As all former legends of Wildcats' gridiron lore should," she nodded and flashed an exaggerated thumbs-up. "Will the Chill...Sacket Crockett, the man, the myth, the sack 'em and stack 'em marvel."

"Uh-huh, *sure*. None of these kids were even a tingle in their folks' genitals when I was playing. I'll be lucky if they don't heckle me off the gym floor."

"Tingle in their folks'...," Maggie eyes upturned as if to search for the proper definition.

"Keep me posted, CO Childers, if you please."

"Affirmative, Will the Chill, um, I mean Chief. Knock 'em dead!"

Upon departure, the big man's disagreeable grunt was mostly drowned out by the thumping echo of his boots on the hardwood flooring.

Roughly three and a half minutes later, just as she'd begun to a peel a banana for her mid-morning snack, Maggie was nearly jolted from her chair as the landline rang out, the numbered display clearly identifying VERIZON.

Friday, 10:22 hours

The two men, one sitting and the other upright but obviously leaning against a waist-high chain-link fence for support, stared out onto the empty field, its grassy surface more gray than green from unreasonably cold temps, the paved running track beneath their feet riddled with dead, blowing leaves.

"Amazin' how little things have changed, at least from this vantage point."

"Small town schools do seem to hold up, usually for budgetary reasons."

"If so, they just blew the whole wad on those newly painted lines."

"Gunther, for a man out of time, you possess the wisdom of an authentic sage."

As Gunther gazed toward the other side of the field at the stone bleachers that served as the visitors' seats—as opposed to the aluminum seating for the home team—Wesley found his tone both strangely soothing and inexplicably unsettling at the same time, like that of a potential suicide victim having come to terms with his maker before the act.

"Talk about homefield advantage," the leaning man said. "That honkin', squared slab of rock over there did and still does apparently have the desired effect on any visitors hopin' to make a dent. I tell ya, sittin' on a cold boulder for three hours has a tendency to turn cheers to cries of discomfort."

"Yes, well, that's what homefield is all about, I guess."

"You ever play?"

Wesley allowed himself a sneak into the gray, thus-far snow-free skies—the local weather report said there was only a thirty percent chance—before answering.

"You've inquired previously."

"Re-ed-u-mi-cate me."

"Football no. Played a year of roundball, well, more like warmed the bench for the starters, before facing the rather obvious truth that athletics was never going to be more than a spectator sport."

"I know we were separated by a few grades, but danged if I remember ya."

"Be shocked if you did. Graduated from a school just outside Louisville. Didn't move here until after graduation."

"Geez, I just assumed you were a Wildcat alum."

"Location wouldn't have changed the fact that I was a lousy athlete." Wesley shrugged, popping a semi-wheelie and briefly facing in the opposite direction in order to give the home team press box at the top of the aluminum bleachers a once-over before spinning gracefully back around.

"Rumor has it you were quite the gridiron madman in your days."

"I was no Lawrence Taylor, far from it, but I could scrap when properly motivated, and Coach Wilkes appreciated scrappers as much as the stars. He understood that a successful team needed a mix of both. I read he passed a few years back."

The sitting man nodded, though his upright cohort continued to face straight ahead, his mind's eye apparently transfixed within a memory-laced universe only he was privy to.

"Lung cancer. Sad. He was only in his mid-sixties."

"Tough cookie but fair. All he asked was ya gave it all ya had. Weird that we never made state with those teams. Came within a hair my senior year. Eight, one, and one, with the only loss comin' to, well, guess who?"

"Who is...Dawson High, Alex?"

"Bingo. Always a thorn in our side. Much as I despise that prick McKay, deep down I'm hopin' these boys can flip the script against 'em tomorrow night."

"You and an entire town."

Chin dropping, his bony elbows balanced atop the fence's rounded pole, Gunther suddenly looked on the verge of collapse, his heavily strapped legs buckling at the knees.

"Hey, you okay...," Wesley began, instinctively rolling the chair forward as if to somehow break the man's impending fall.

Raising his head, normally pale cheeks streaked in red patches and scattered streams of flowing perspiration—this despite a palpable chill hovering just over forty degrees—the other man displayed the flat palm of his right hand, albeit a badly shaking one.

"Y-yeah, multiple cramps, a-above and below. Happens every...now and then, sci-fi suit be damned. Just...need a second to allow 'em to pass."

Numerous sighs, a series of pained grunts and a short coughing jag later, he appeared to straighten to his previous position, his tone back to that of someone having come to terms with his impending fate, however tragic.

"You gonna make it or should we head on back?"

"Easin' up as we speak," came the raspy reply, though vastly improved from the previous dialogue. "Ya know," he paused to give his head a gentle shake from side to side, as if to wipe away any remaining cobwebs, the ever-present beret as characteristically unmoved as usual, as if stitched to his scalp, "comin' back here has served the purpose I'd hoped, though not without some unforeseen side effects. Weird I don't feel nearly as cold as I should, that is, the few parts that still retain the power of workin' nerve endings. You okay to hang for a spell, partner?"

Wesley nodded before reaching back to retrieve and pull forward the hood of his UK hoodie.

"I'll hang as long as you need me to, boss."

"Appreciate it more than you know. I need...to get this out and I ain't sure any other locale will serve as a better platform. Made sure my batteries were fully charged overnight in the hopes it...this place...would provide the proper motivation. Damned if it hasn't. Heart's been poundin' like a triphammer since we parked outside the concession."

Re-tucking the blanket over his knees, the seated man nodded as if readily prepped for whatever might come.

"Fine then. I'm here to listen, not judge."

With that, Gunther McCarron twisted clumsily around, one of his thigh straps briefly snagging a chain link before letting go with a muffled snap. Facing the home bleachers, he cleared his throat as if to address a full house.

"I met her here that first time. Complete chance. *Fate*, ya might say, if you're inclined to buy into such Harlequin romance crap-o-la."

"Wendy?"

Wesley instantly regretted the interruption, though the other man hardly seemed to notice, his normally semi-squinted, naturally beady eyes pulled wide and gleaming like polished marbles.

"She wasn't the classic beauty, ya know? Not some long-legged glamour queen with the textbook hourglass figure. Wasn't the type to sport the prom tiara, but she was hardly some ugly ducklin' either. Attractive enough to catch this boy's eyes, though I'd guess my peer group at that time would've rated her no higher than 'kinda' pretty or just 'cute' enough to pass for it. But ya see, it wasn't Wen's looks, man, it was Wen herself. The whole package. As much as I despise terms like bubbly, lively, or, lord help me, *chirpy*, she was any and all similar definitions in spades, only not in the annoyin' way I usually associated with such words. Charm, man, Wendy Hammock had it in spades. The queen of charisma.

"Honestly, at that point in my life I was as shallow as they come about the opposite sex, as in, it was all about the rack first and rear end second with the face a distant third and personality comin' in bottom-barrel last in the rankings. Stereotypical trade-school doofus turned part-time truckdriver, welder, handyman, basically anything to avoid bein' pigeon-holed into a 'career' by definition while earnin' just enough green to barely pay the bills. You know, the whole *growin' up meant growin' old* horseshit that my kind all but copyrighted as a built-in excuse to elude personal responsibility.

"I'd just turned twenty-eight and could claim exactly three semi-steady girlfriends, two of whom I'd shacked up with for a short time before the new eventually wore off. Marriage was a four-letter word and all that jazz, if you can dig it. Wasn't lookin' for anything deeper than to occasionally satisfy the carnal urges and to be honest, couldn't understand why anybody ever would. I'd seen many a friend and co-worker discover what they'd all sworn at the time was true love and watched most of 'em end up in divorce court as penance. From soulmates to soul-*eaters*, man. Not in the plans for this boy, ya know? Selfish, I know, but I'd always been labeled as being of the strange bird species."

The seated man started to reply but simply nodded instead in the understanding that the man behind the sermon was speaking as much to himself as to his present company.

"So, I was back in town for the first time in over nine years, havin' beat feet right after graduation and callin' everywhere, from Bowling Green to Huntsville to Atlanta and finally Nashville, home.

"Still had a pad in the Music City, in fact, and wasn't really thinkin' about replantin' roots here. I'd been keepin' up with the team some and saw they were a cat's whisker from nabbin' a state playoff spot and took a few days off to come see 'em lace 'em up against Booneville. The plan was to suck down a few cold ones after the game with Justin and Carl before headin' on back across the Tennessee line the next day. Oh, Justin bein' Justin Vincent and Carl Delaney, two of my best buds back in the day, both of 'em also in town for the game. Weird how life can toss you the ultimate curveball, standin' there as flatfooted and oblivious as the lunkheaded fool I was, and well, still most certainly am.

"Oh, I did head on back the next day, basically to pack my gear and leave my roomies in the lurch, all due to a conversation that in hindsight lasted no more than an hour, or maybe even less. Never shared those planned brews with the buds, no siree. The guys ended up leavin' without me, no doubt seein' I'd misplaced what little good sense I had. Now, here comes that fate factor, or as Wendy had referred to it later, 'kismet.' I mean, life is all about timin' and placement, right? If she'd been seated one person over on either side of me or in a row behind or in front, we probably never would've locked eyes or said a blessed word to one another. As it was, she sat directly to my left, those metal bleachers about as comfy and warm as squatting on a frozen lake. It was a nipple-raiser that night, kinda like what we're standin' in today, only with an even stouter gust, if I recall. The minute she offered me half her blanket to warm my buns by, smilin' at me like I was some helpless, shakin' pup she'd just rescued from the pound, I wasn't about to go all bashful. And man oh man, that *smile*. Radiant is the word. As far as I was concerned, the stadium could've pulled the plug on the overhead lights just to toss the spotlight on those pearly whites.

"First off, she'd come with a girlfriend, so there was at least a chance she was single. Well, there's strike one, as none other than Shannon McKay held the claim to that priceless deed. Strike two was findin' out her stepdad was none other than your honor the mayorship, Kerry Hammock, so the value of that aforementioned deed had just ascended waaayy beyond this boy's line of credit, or so it seemed at the time.

"Anyhow, we broke the ice talkin' football and not much else, as she was a Wildcat alum who'd left town for Duke University, got her degree in public relations and was settlin' down roots in Covington. Twenty-three the night I made her acquaintance, looked all of eighteen, but was unusually wise and mature for that age. A helluva lot wiser and a damn sight more mature than the man-boy five years her senior. I tell ya, Wes, I flipped for her mangy mullet over bootheels that very first night at Falls Field. Problem was, though I didn't view it as insurmountable by any stretch, was the whole 'Shannon McKay is my boyfriend' thing blockin' any progress for future rendezvous.

"Seems she'd been dating the arrogant jack-wagon for over a year and they'd even set a date for future nuptials. Found this out only after dredgin' up the courage to ask her out as the game clock neared the five-minute mark of the fourth quarter. Gotta be honest, I didn't have a clue of who was winnin' and didn't rightly care. Weird though, that she didn't seem the least bit offended by my offer, just kind of shrugged and said she really couldn't, considering the engagement and all. Man, from there I ran with the outside chance that this wouldn't be our first and last hookup, even goin' as far as inviting her for a burger and beer at the Suds 'n' Spuds café in Reddenville, as I'd lined up a job there the week following."

Falling silent, the standing man's eyes widened to match an equally broad smile creasing a previously stoic mug.

"Holy *hell*, the Suds 'n' Spuds! I can't believe that came back to me without even a mild strain. I mean, there are moments I forget how to tie my boots or that the adult diaper goes on *under* the pants, but that slid off my tongue so naturally I could almost taste those chili-burgers and fries I used to fancy at the place."

"Sad to say, pretty sure the Suds caught fire six, seven years back and they never rebuilt," Wesley chimed in cautiously, as if fearing he might be shattering some unspoken protocol in interrupting the man's stroll down memory lane.

"Shame. They served some of the best homecooked grub in this county. Anyhow, long story short, I talked her into it without havin' to twist an arm, offer a cash bribe or grovel at her feet. About a week or so later, there we were sittin' across from one another with no boyfriend or chaperonin' girlfriend in sight. Spoke volumes of her dedication to makin' it work with McKay, right? Never hinted at any guilt in her actions, either. She was happy to be there. This much I knew just from starin' into those gorgeous green eyes. True confession, partner...," Gunther paused, chin lowered as if to whisper some deep, dark secret, "...never experienced a happier moment in my whole blessed existence than the moment I saw her saunter into that restaurant, all decked out in a hooded parka and knee-high snow boots like she was on her way to a ski lodge, that toothy smile as contagious as any airborne virus."

Wesley was, despite a solid effort, unable to refrain from laughing aloud, his head thrown back with such force that the chair rolled several inches. Upon regaining his composure, he peered up into the other man's perplexed, squinty-eyed visage and nearly relapsed.

"You sir...," he managed in a hoarse whisper, "...are a hopeless romantic, not to mention a poet of unusual skills."

"You're a married man, right?" Gunther inquired, seemingly unfazed by the other man's lighthearted ribbing.

"I was."

"So, it's snagged you at one time or another. Maybe for just a short time, but long enough to corner and cage ya into submission till nothin' else mattered."

"You mean attraction?"

"More than that. Attraction, especially the physical type, passes, sometimes after a single session in the sack. Nope, I ain't talkin' merely carnal obsession, though I guess that's always the startin' line. Wendy blocked out everything around me, man, like a flesh and blood eclipse. She was all I could see or wanted to see. That constant twinkle of those eyes, the slight, sexy rasp of her voice when she grew excited, her...every...single...gesture. Magical. Mystical. Mesmerizin'. No lie, it was exhilaratin' *and* scary as hell at the same time, till I didn't know myself anymore, though I did know one thing for certain. I wanted to spend every single second I could with her, circumstances or location be damned. Just her and me."

"That is obsession defined, Gunther," Wesley offered with a tilt of the head.

The standing man's rebuttal was primed by a stubborn jutting of his chin, arching of his brows and an openly cocky backward lean that the chain-link fence absorbed without obvious strain.

"Yeah, maybe, but ya see, it didn't fade. That's the difference. In the short time we were an item, I never felt any change from that original rush. No lie. Seven months on and off, mostly on, and that initial charge maintained the same current, at least for me."

"No offense, but half a year, *on* and *off,* isn't exactly a marathon," the seated man countered, to which his opposition in the building debate merely smirked. "Then again, personally I can't say my own fiery affair with primal lust lasted more than two or three *weeks* and even that might be exaggerated. Maybe it's the act of marriage itself that can help douse the flame. With San...in my case, it might as well have been a bucket of ice water. Once this...," he gestured with a solemn nod to his lower torso and blanket-covered legs, "...became the new reality, it was definitely *turn out the lights, the party's over.* A man and wife can't just be about being roommates, even amiable ones, and I had to accept that as being a major part of her deci—"

It wasn't until he'd peered up from his own folded, gloved hands to the standing man's blank slate of an expression and distant stare into the stands—mouth slightly agape and lower lip hanging as if sleeping upright—that Wesley became aware of his own accidental rant.

"Sorry. Got lost in my own 'it's better to have loved and lost than to never love at all sermon.' Carry on, Gunther. I promise I'll transform back to all ears and no mouth."

"Talkin' about new realities," Gunther resumed, hardly skipping a beat but surprising Wes with the proof that he had been listening, at least to a degree. "Try this one on for size, fourteen-plus years is what the calendar might claim, but in my mind, it's been less than a year since she and I sat side by side in those stands and more like a single winter's passin' since we last shared space, intimately, if you can dig that."

Wesley nodded silently, intent on not verbalizing whatever words might naturally spew forth, as the other man had turned slowly toward him with a look that defined the word "haunted."

As he resumed, Gunther McCarron's normally raspy, ravine-deep voice broke sporadically, as if on the very cusp of cracking like the thinnest crystal tossed against a wall of granite.

"I swear that some mornings I wake up smellin' the scent of her, even though she never stepped a single foot inside my folks' house. In the dark of night, sacked out and on the verge of driftin' away, I've heard her whisper. Almost every night I can...I dream of touchin' her, of her...touchin' me. I can...still taste her, man. The back of her neck, her lips, those warm, rosy cheeks. Worst of all, especially since I got back to town, I swear I've *seen* her. Around a corner near that new hardware store on Main or strollin' between cars in the Big Star grocery parkin' lot. Of course, she's only there for a split second before evaporatin' like the mornin' fog at sunrise, but long enough to make it feel like somebody's taken a hammer drill to the center of my chest."

Pausing to first catch his breath and then whistle weakly between lips chapped by the chill, Gunther resumed only after bowing his head as if to pray.

"They say the passin' of time heals, ain't that supposed to be the deal?"

"It's been theorized."

"Well, problem is, to me almost no time *has* passed, and as far as that healin' part goes, I'm runnin' flat outta time at a record pace, like a flipped hourglass damn near void of descending sand."

Backing the chair until it sat perfectly centered atop the marked running track's middle of five rows, Wesley's mind groped for just the right reply to inject some much-needed positivity.

"McCarron, you're a hell of a lot stronger than you give yourself credit for."

"I'm a puppet gradually fracturin' beneath the strings!" the standing man brayed, briefly leaning hard to the left from the effort. "Cut or yank too hard on the right one and the melted disaster servin' as my core will collapse in on itself like a fallen cake."

Sighing heavily, the short but volcanic spurt of energy immediately left him, leaving him paler and more physically deflated than ever.

"Sorry for snappin', bud. Truth is, this battery-operated miracle is losin' its mojo. The clock is tickin' at warp speed and buildin' toward light mode. Hey, and just between us cripples...," he hesitated, bending down slightly and whispering behind the back of a skeletal hand, "...Doc Jarrett, supposedly one of the top neurosurgeons in the business, advised me to convalesce for another six months to a year before even attempting any type of normal existence, and even then, bionic-man suit included, he suggested assisted livin'."

The seated man winced as if suffering a painful intestinal disorder.

"So why rush it? Why...risk it?"

"They wouldn't allow me to take my sweet time, Wesley."

"They?"

"Really? I gotta spell it out?"

"But...so blatant paranoia dictated you risk your life, or at least severely shorten the span of your life, to come back here and do what exactly, Gunther?"

For the first time since arriving at Falls Field, the two locked eyes, neither daring to break contact.

"To *solve* this thing, Wesley, and while I'm still coherent enough to pull it off. Got to close the case for my own sanity and maybe, just maybe, release a couple of restless souls from a fourteen-year purgatory."

Somehow managing to maintain eye contact, Wesley wheeled forward before executing an expert spin that left the chair in a direct line across from the other man.

"And how exactly do you propose to solve it? What do you hope to uncover that both local and state authorities failed to dig up all those years ago? I...know I have no right to question your motives, but if the constant effort of grasping for invisible straws is going to literally kill you, then what's the purpose?"

The gaunt figure beneath the crimson beret looked away for just a flash, lips pulled into the thinnest of smiles.

"I can't and do not expect you or anyone else to understand, but trust me, the straws I'm gropin' for are hidin' in plain sight even as we speak."

Tossing up gloved hands in frustration, Wesley's exasperated reply was bookmarked by a shrill catcall that both men couldn't help but find unintentionally hilarious.

"Fine, but just know I would gladly offer my services to do a little grasping of my own, but to what end if there's no logical solution?"

"Well, well, ask and ye shall receive, at least in theory," Gunther announced, pumping a gnarled fist while staring off to their right to the sight of a slight young woman strolling purposefully their way, decked out in a maroon, ankle-length fur-collared coat, white knit beanie, black boots and a light brown scarf pulled up to cloak all but her pale blue eyes.

"Deep throat, I presume?" Wesley quipped, smoothly steering the chair in the approaching visitor's direction.

"No porn star there, bud," Gunther replied straight-faced, both his tone and mannerisms instantly revitalized. "That'll be Miss Janet Griffin, local investigative reporter extraordinaire."

"Mister McCarron?" she inquired, voice muffled only somewhat through the scarf, having stopped short a dozen feet or so from the gawking pair.

Gunther stepped forward, this after a precarious release and push-off from the fence's bracing and bowed down as low as his badly warped frame would allow.

"Yes, ma'am. Just call me Gunther, or Gunny, if you prefer. Kinda prefer the latter, considerin' our present locale, as it was my nick back in the day when this field behind us was littered with my cleat prints. This fella here is my friend and escort, Wesley Grant. Don't mind if he don't stand. He's kinda, well, *me* without the robotic assistance."

Executing separate nods toward each man, she replied only after reaching up to remove the scarf. Though a prominent nose and matching overbite prevented the woman—Wesley guesstimated her age between thirty-five and forty—from achieving conventional beauty status, he was instantly reminded of a younger actress from the eighties with similar features whose named escaped him but not the movies she'd graced, those being *Ferris Bueller's Day Off* and *Dirty Dancing*.

"Gentlemen. Um, might I suggest we continue the conversation in warmer climes? This wind is apt to freeze my lips to my teeth in mid-sentence."

"How 'bout the press box?" Gunther suggested, though it was obvious from Miss Griffin's pained grimace she'd more than likely have preferred a local eatery, or at least something offering indoor heat.

"Um, yes, sure. Anything would beat this outdoor meat locker." She shrugged, blue eyes darting while no doubt wondering how the two challenged individuals in her presence could possibly reach the structure at the top of the bleachers. As if reading her thoughts, Gunther gestured to a paved walk to the left of the track that appeared to lead behind the stacked aluminum seats.

"There's a handicapped path leadin' up. We could meet ya up there if you'd preferred to climb."

The woman hesitated, gloved hands waving about randomly as if suddenly attaining the power of independent thought, before tucking them away into her coat's oversized pockets.

"Might help me to fight this chill at that. Meet you there."

The two men watched her begin to ascend before departing for the curved path with Wesley allowing Gunther to lead at his own pace, the man's recent struggles to maintain even a semi-steady gait seemingly growing worse by the hour.

"No chance meeting, I'm guessing," he inquired, once they'd cleared the rear of the bleachers and began the slow, arduous ascent up the winding stone pathway while dodging as many of the numerous cracks and holes littering its aged surface as possible.

"Offered her an exclusive pow wow my first day back in town, figurin' vultures from other towns would come callin' soon enough."

"Any particular reason? I mean, the *Crimson Falls Gazette* isn't exactly hot copy outside the few thousand residents within the city limits."

"Her dad was a fair, squared away dude, at least accordin' to my old man."

"Her father?"

His pace having slowed considerably since the incline had gradually increased, Gunther's breathing grew noticeably labored.

"Oh yeah, I keep forgettin' you're...not a lifer. Mark Griffin. Ran the paper startin' in the...middle eighties. I figure his kid must...be cut from the same cloth. Then again, I'm also hopin' she don't mind mixin' in a heapin' helpin' of sensationalism with the scoop...I'm prepped to provide."

"To what end?"

Though he faced Gunther's horribly bent back, Wesley practically felt the wide, mischievous smile creasing the man's gaunt visage.

"Let's just say ya can't hope...to catch a prize trout...without the proper bait."

By the time they'd reached the archaic wooden structure—its narrow entrance held firmly ajar by the unrelenting mid-morning gusts, the publishing editor of the *Crimson Falls Gazette* was forced to assist her prize interviewee inside, his ghostly complexion and gasping breath hinting that any conversation might be forced to relocate to a local emergency room.

From the *Crimson Falls Gazette* Sports Page
Dated Nov. 7

Wildcats 8-0 after 18-16 nail-biter against Booneville's Lions
(Friday Night, Falls Field)

Despite an uncharacteristic five turnovers, Crimson Falls remained unbeaten with an 18-16 win over a scrappy Booneville squad coming off four straight wins of their own. Quarterback Shane Mills tossed a 26-yard TD to tight end Brad Vincent to put the Wildcats up 18-9 with just three minutes remaining, this after a grueling, defense-dominated first half that saw both teams scoreless. Booneville (now 6-2 on the season) managed a last second touchdown but was unable to recover an onside kick as time expired.

Nine

Jake Douglas, his uniform hanging loosely from his rail-thin form, leaned back in a chair across from Cindy Lou's desk, an ever-present toothpick protruding from thin lips. Upon request from the chief, who was on his way back from the high school, the part-time patrolman had returned to the station with nothing new on the matter of the missing reporter.

"Cruised by his place at least a half-dozen times, Maggie. Nary a sign. Probably got ponged there while he was stakin' out the place, grew bored with it and hit the road."

"Pinged, Jake," Cindy Lou corrected without looking up from the paperback romance novel she was currently perusing.

The toothpick magically levitating from one side of his mouth to another, Jake eyed the veteran clerk with obvious disdain. Ancient scuttlebutt around the PD was the two had been an item decades earlier when Jake was working as a guard at

Brisbain, a correctional facility twenty miles north of town, but this had never been confirmed nor disputed by either party, both of whom had been married at the time. Watching them interact like an old married couple seemed to lean toward verifying the former.

"Ping, pong, *whatever*. Ya'll know how impatient today's kids are. A stakeout probably equates to waiting no more than a half hour."

Maggie chewed nervously on a pinkie finger, having rolled the dispatch chair half into the records office. As fond as she was of Jake Douglas and his old-school ways and attitude, she secretly wished it were the younger, infinitely more eager and energetic Charles Jacobs working the shift.

"Yeah, could be. I don't know. Just feels wrong is all. Something's been off around here since that McCarron guy showed back up."

"Stranger in town, strangeness soon follows," Cindy Lou mumbled, her spectacles hanging precariously from the tip of her nose.

Douglas scoffed, standing to hitch his belt around an almost nonexistent waist, the toothpick sticking straight up from his bottom lip like a wooden syringe.

"Oh, *mumbo jumbo*. I do remember the case, though. Nasty business that. Real shame about the girl. From what I understand, the wrong one died, at least from a potential standpoint."

Perhaps just to even the score, it was Cindy Lou's turn to jeer.

"Yeah, well, from what *I* heard, she couldn't keep her jeans fastened. All the college degrees in the world don't mean squat if one doesn't possess even a semblance of self-control."

The entrance swinging open with a familiar creak, followed by the equally recognizable sound of heavy, thumping boots essentially cut off whatever rebuttal the retired correctional officer had surely concocted.

"Jake," Chief Crockett leaned down until his mouth was even with the window's oval opening.

"Hiya, boss."

"No charcoal Charger cruising about?"

"No sir."

"Nothing unusual out by McCarron's place?"

Sauntering up to the window, Douglas nodded, his belt sinking slightly past his narrow hips until it appeared on the verge of falling to his ankles.

"Nothing visually out of place. Of course, the snow had melted off all around so whatever alien tracks might've graced the surrounding shoulders had long faded. If you want, I can ride on back out there and check on foot around his place."

Tugging at his own belt, the chief shook his head dismissively.

"Don't bother. We've wasted enough man-hours as it is. That kid is probably partying down over in Myrtle on his boss's dime. You on till three?"

"That I am. Headed back out onto the mean streets here in a jif."

"How'd it go at the pep rally, boss? Sign many autographs?" Maggie inquired just as the big man had started to depart the window for the nearby hall.

"Principal James wisely omitted that part of the program. I was, however, obliged to mention my own playing days, to which the majority of the kids just stared blank-eyed as if I were speaking of dinosaur bones and dusty fossils, both of which I definitely identified with when all was said and done. Ah well, go Wildcats."

"Go Wildcats," both Cindy Lou and Maggie repeated, the former in a robotic monotone that screamed indifference.

Jake Douglas groaned as he started to exit the room, stopping short with his hand on the door handle.

"I got a bad feeling they're gonna get waxed. This town's just too hyped up for it and that kinda pressure can have a bad effect on kids unaccustomed to it. Hope I'm wrong, but a similar thing happened back in the late nineties and that Dawson team mowed 'em down but good."

"Keep that glass half-empty, JD," Cindy Lou quipped blandly, to which Maggie stifled a giggle.

"Oh, hey Maggie, spotted Wesley's Camry out by the Juniper cutoff," Jake Douglas offered off-handedly while exiting into the lobby. "Figured a man who takes a vacation about every five years wouldn't choose to spend it milling about town."

Her grin having wilted like a fresh bloom beneath a heat lamp, Maggie paused before hopping up and sprinting toward the window.

"You sure it was his...Wes's Toyota?"

The older man never turned, just slowed his walk toward the entrance.

"Yep, fairly certain. He was turning onto the highway and I was a few vehicles behind. Appeared he had a passenger with 'im but with that dark tint I couldn't make 'em out. Hey, maybe he and Jacobs are vacationing together." He winked, pulling the door ajar and stepping out. "Later gators."

Maggie's mind raced onto assorted tracks simultaneously while watching Douglas vanish past the entrance door, foremost within a veritable mishmash of frenzied thoughts being why her friend would blatantly lie or mislead her when they'd spoken the previous afternoon.

This, coupled with the psychotic, stalker-like behavior of his ex, and the sudden constriction at her gut was no mystery. Could Sandy have finally run him down—if not actually over, considering the woman's venomous attitude—and was she the figure Jake had seen in the Camry's passenger seat? Abruptly, inexplicably, Maggie felt a palpable wave of fear for her friend's safety, though to voice such concerns to anyone but the source himself would serve no purpose but to enhance her rep as a slightly ditzy, overly paranoid drama queen (this according to both her perpetually grumpy spouse and perpetually mouthy lover). For the time being, she'd cool her jets and, once off-shift later that afternoon, shoot Wes a friendly text in the mode of "how's the fishing" or some such malarky.

It wouldn't be until later that afternoon that Phil would casually mention someone offhandedly saying seeing Wes and a sickly man decked out in some sort of "full-body brace" breaking bread down at the *Sow* a day earlier. To this not at all nonchalantly *received* revelation, the normally ultra-imaginative Maggie Childers could dredge nary a single sherd of logical speculation, the text she'd left Wesley a few hours earlier having been relegated to nonsensical fluff that had, at least thus far, gone (justifiably) unanswered.

Friday, 11:13 hours

Blowing into his clutched palms to soothe the frigid numbness, Wesley knew he should be irate, but found little in the way of actual incentive to blow his top. As he and Gunther had successfully scaled the sloped pathway to the press box, he'd been kindly asked to take a powder until the interview was completed. Nothing personal, Gunther had insisted, just a matter of certain details not being safe for those close to him to know in case of future retribution. Flattering in a sense, the remark also struck Wesley as weirdly covert, as if the man he'd met only days before was somehow testing his loyalty.

He'd watched Crimson Falls' lone "investigative" reporter assist her prize interviewee into the structure and seal the door behind them, all the while never acknowledging the chairbound third-wheel of the party with even a second glance.

In lieu of sitting outside and thus losing additional feeling in his face and hands, Wesley had instead retreated to the comfort (and warmth) of the Camry, where the hum of the heater's fan gradually served to thaw.

Approximately eighteen minutes after he'd left the two to converse in utter secrecy and privacy, he tuned the radio to XM soft rock classics and, leaning the driver's seat to its maximum rear setting, closed his eyes and sighed deeply to the soothing sound of REO's "I Can't Fight This Feeling."

The banging at the driver's window, a threesome of echoing thumps spaced roughly a half-second apart, was at first so startling he thought it part of some elaborate dream sequence. That is, until, sitting upright with both hands gripping the wheel with white-knuckled shock, he peered through the driver's window through bleary eyes to see a familiar grimace staring back, with mere inches separating it from their own.

"Wha-what are y-you...do-doing h-here?" he mumbled, groping for the correct button to lower the window with one hand while using the thumb and forefinger of the other to rub the drowsiness from each drooping eye.

"My question exactly!" the hulking figure barked, squatting down until they were literally face-to-face. "Confirm for me, please, that you've lost your ever-loving mind, mister, being that I cannot, for the life of me, fathom an alternative conclusion!"

Dressed in baggy blue jeans, bloodred turtleneck sweater, unbuttoned light blue jean jacket and a denim, gray baseball cap with the words "Walk it Off" in bold black lettering, Sandy Jamison kneeled with balled fists balanced atop the driver's door, her breath coming in short, huffy snorts that her ex-spouse recalled ever-so-vividly from when they'd shared the intimate moments of man and wife. He could only imagine a bull elephant or horny hippo finding such a noise arousing but surely no other creature of god.

"Sa-Sandy, give me a min—...second, please. I was...nap—
...sleeping and dang neared drenched my drawers when you—"

"You didn't come home last night, lover boy. Anybody I
know?"

Struggling to push the seat to its upright position, Wesley
was afforded a chance glance past his ex-wife's beefy left
shoulder and spotted a lumbering figure making his way around
the corner of the bleachers in painstaking fashion.

"Li-listen, San, I don't have a lot of...the time to...he's...," he
stammered, pointing in the general direction of where Gunther
was slowly descending, a strong whiff of his former spouse's
scent—a heady mix of Ben-Gay and a Calvin Klein knockoff—
essentially clogging his flaring nostrils.

"Well, you're gonna make time, mister! I've been chasing
your carcass all over this county and, to put it mildly, we need to
talk!"

"Listen, let me call you—"

"Nope, *negatory*. Left you a month's worth of texts and
voicemails in the last two days already! You're not getting away
from me this time."

Eyes darting spastically from his one-time soulmate's
perpetual scowl to the shuffling figure growing closer by the
second, Wesley was finding it increasingly difficult to mask the
building panic in both his tone and movements.

"You staying in town? I can swing by later..."

Slapping the top of the Camry with bare palms, Sandy
grinned in the aftermath of his exaggerated flinch as if to openly
enjoy the response.

"Yeah, I've been staying in town, buddy boy, most recently at
the very house you and I once purchased as a couple! Simple
logic dictated you might actually show up last evening, that is
unless you had some super special reason not to, right? I've
heard stories, mister. Oh lawd, have I now! Now, kindly exit and

ride with me, or if you prefer, we can take your heap. Your call. Either way, I'm not letting you out of my sight..."

Rising with a huff, she kept both massive mitts in place as Wesley reached over and placed bared palms atop her own, applying just enough pressure to gain her unwavering attention.

"Sandy, whatever stories you've heard are probably true. Now listen closely and whatever you do, do not turn around. Get back in your vehicle and drive away. You're going to have to trust me, pumpkin. I promise I'll see you at the house in a few hours. No later than say...three PM. Now...leave."

"How stupid do you think I am, buster? I'm not going..."

Pushing downward with as much force as he could muster, Wesley found secret pleasure in hearing her pained groans of shock.

"You've got less than three minutes tops, honey-pie."

"Three minutes till what..."

Once a final, forceful double squeeze evoked yet another shocked gasp, he released his grip and, sticking his head from the open window, growled between tightly gritted teeth. As with the surprisingly feminine yelps, her teary, wide-eyed reaction was additional gravy to an already satisfying entrée of retaliatory abuse. Despite her gruff, intimidating demeanor, Wesley and Wesley alone knew how to turn the tables with matching bile.

"Sandra my dear, move your fat ass right now and drive away quietly and calmly or I'm liable to run you over just to confirm your presence here."

"You'd...better show up, mister. D-don't make me have to find you again," she muttered, shaking a forefinger while backing stiffly away, though obviously having lost the majority of her earlier bite.

Fingers of both hands tapping nervously on the steering wheel, Wesley watched the black SUV back out from the parking spot directly behind his own and exit the small lot located just to the right of the running track, thus no more than ten or twelve yards from where the two men had earlier entered through a narrow fenced opening.

It wasn't until the vehicle had completely vanished behind the nearby fieldhouse that he allowed himself to regain the power of breathing, the first labored sigh spewing forth just as the cell phone in his lap sounded off at full volume, a braying siren that, within the Camry's tight confines, initiated a second full-blown spastic flinch within a five-minute span.

"Y-yeah, wh-what?" he stuttered upon pinning the slim, slick device to a chilled ear, having found the requestor's flashing number at least vaguely familiar.

"So who was the chick-a-poo, Doc? Didn't know ya preferred 'em, now how do I put this without offendin', big-boned?"

Considering the near full-blown breakdown of just moments earlier, he found Gunther's voice, however sarcastic the tone or inane the query, remarkably soothing. Peering toward the weaving path, he saw the man had made it nearly halfway down but had stopped for a much-needed rest, that is if his slightly labored breathing was any indication.

"Oh, her. High school faculty wondering if I was looking for something or someone in particular. Once I told her I was a former alum and star linebacker just pining for the old days on the eve of the big game, she all but swooned."

"Ain't that considered identity theft?"

"Hey, if it triggers such gleeful admiration, it's fair game, big shot."

"Got'cha," retorted the winded man with an accompanying chuckle. "Whatever makes 'em drop the panties."

Wesley laughed despite himself while nervously scanning the lot and roadway beyond one final time to ensure their continued privacy.

"Classy. You gonna make it all the way down, Admiral Byrd, or am I gonna have to send up a St. Bernard with a bottle of tonic?"

"Engine light is still flashin' red hot. Coolin' system ain't what it used to be."

"Take your time. I'm fine and cozy in here."

"Nice to know. By the way, who or what the hell is an admin burr?"

Struck utterly speechless, Wesley lowered the driver's window and flashed an enthusiastic thumbs-up just as the other man tucked his own cell away and resumed the downhill jaunt.

"Miss Griffin decide to set up housekeeping up there?" he inquired, gesturing with a slight nod in the direction of the press box once Gunther had gotten settled into the passenger seat, the man's breathing as hollow and raspy as his complexion was wraithlike.

"She'd parked...out front. Real sparkplug, that one. Think I...*know* I made the right choice for an earpiece. That tiny keyboard on her phone was practically smokin'. She wanted to record the conversation but, well, the prospect kinda creeped me out, ya know?"

"Modern media and their gadgets, right?" Wesley chided, the sarcasm apparently lost on his winded passenger. "Um, you do know the *Gazette* only runs one hard copy issue a week, right?"

Falling back against the headrest, Gunther closed his eyes and inhaled deeply before replying.

"Normally, yeah, that is unless they push a special edition through the printer, not to mention the online version with updated headlines."

"Hmm, that newsworthy, is it?"

"You be the judge."

"No sneak preview for your fellow gimp?"

A wide smile broke across a face that was appearing to grow frighteningly gaunter by the minute.

"Let's just say there's a few folks gonna wake up tomorrow spittin' bile into their cereal bowls, at least one whose squirmin' discomfort will be totally justified."

"And the other?"

"Collateral damage."

"Do the words libel or slander mean anything to you?"

Turning his head slowly toward the other man, Gunther McCarron's uncharacteristically calm demeanor and similarly tranquil tone defined a man at complete peace.

"My man, in the fiery courtrooms of hell, I'll have 'em right where I want 'em."

The Camry pulled from the vacant lot just as a light rain began to fall and a few straggling students decked out in various winter garb, their faces cloaked by hoodies, shambled toward the nearby fieldhouse from the main high school building.

"Must be a mid-day practice," Wesley offered blandly, his mind secretly reeling from his passenger's sudden switch in deportment.

"Safe bet. Clock's tickin' on the biggest day in their young lives."

He forced a smile so insincere he felt his lips might actually stick to his teeth from the force applied to keep it in place.

"So who you got? And try to avoid being a homer, mister alum."

Staring out the passenger window and thus hiding whatever expression accompanied his prediction, the shock factor of the prognostication wasn't merely the content, but the surprisingly cold, unsympathetic delivery.

"Red Raiders in a cakewalk," he lipped grimly, accompanied by a mild shrug possibly less intentional than an involuntary spasm. "Only stands to reason, bein' as my presence alone seems to cast a cold, black cloud over everything in its path. Birthplace be hanged, I feel nothin' for this town anymore. Nothin' personal there, Mister Senior Records Clerk, but as far as I'm concerned, Crimson Falls, Kentucky is soured grounds that can go up in smoke in a similar fashion as a certain mobile home all those years ago."

To this, Wesley could only swallow hard and steer them away from the school grounds with an inexplicable sense of urgency, as if fleeing the most hazardous of chemical spills.

Friday, 1643 hours

Jerome Griffey had set some lofty goals. Goals that did not include wasting his formative years playing small-town cop where he was routinely referred to not by his job title, given or family name, but by the size and positioning of his ears. Since grade school it had been "hey ears," or "hey, mind if we park under one of your overhangs? Looks like rain," or the routine inquiry, "how they hangin', Dumbo?", and those constituted the *polite* references. Never mind the endless jabs, jokes and gags, more than a few of which bordered on sadistic. Since joining the force three years previous as a skinny, naïve local with nary a clue or care of future aspirations, he'd gradually crafted a taunt, muscular frame within the confines of his modest two-bedroom home's basement gym while simultaneously boning-up on all available video and audio police training tapes from both state and federal sources.

Recently divorced from his high school sweetheart, he no longer had the distraction of marriage and its endless trappings to hold him back. Sara had simply never understood his passion for law enforcement, instead pushing him to leave the PD at every opportunity to pursue a degree in business management or some such mundane garbage. With that, and her incessant badgering about their starting a family, the split had been nothing short of a two-ton load of bricks falling from his shoulders.

As far as fine-tuning his craft, albeit in a limited capacity, the last two years of qualifying at the local range saw him win department sharpshooter status and, unbeknownst to all, he'd recently contacted both the state police and highway patrol concerning applying requirements, though admittedly he considered each just another career stepping-stone toward securing a slot within the bureau of federal investigation.

Thus, in order to reach this treasured goal, the young man sporting the bushy unibrow, Popeye forearms and birthed with ears possessing an unseemly buildup of cartilage in the auricle was fiercely determined to build as impressive a resume as the mostly tranquil burg of Crimson Falls would allow, something a bit more impressive than mundane traffic tickets or the occasional DUI, public intoxication or pot bust.

As he'd reported in for the evening shift, a dull glimmer of something different had emerged with word of the missing reporter whose cell had pinged last near the Gunther McCarron place. Even as the perpetually lifeless Jake Douglas had filled him in on the fruitlessness of a continued search—the chief hadn't even bothered to brief him while departing for the night— Jerome figured further investigating couldn't hurt amid what promised to be a fairly eventless evening on patrol.

Tomorrow night, the big game loomed as did limitless opportunities for misdemeanor arrests for everything from drunken brawls, drunken driving and assorted drunken revelry and shenanigans of all kinds. Conversely, tonight would mostly likely be the lull before the storm. If so, Jerome saw no harm in retracing the steps of a tired old man who most likely couldn't have spotted a clue if it tugged at his saggy britches and introduced itself as such.

A knock on the door of the McCarron house found no response, though the driveway being vacant meant little as the lone resident, as far as anyone knew, and for obvious reasons, owned no motorized transportation. Walking around the side of the home, he noted little of interest save twin narrow—no more than two inches in width—ruts in the surrounding grass and gravel trailing a circular paved path, thus all but verifying the story Maggie had passed on back at the station: that for whatever reason, Wesley was indeed playing gentlemen's gentleman to the town's newest returning citizen. Noting the tracks ended at the wide, rear door of the ranch-style home, Jerome applied an obligatory, and equally fruitless, knock before giving the spacious back yard and wood-line beyond a quick onceover and soon after backing from the drive.

If not for inadvertently pulling a few feet onto a narrow shoulder just off the jagged pavement—the rear right tire sliding further off the roadway as he'd accelerated—he might've never exited the vehicle to visualize just how far from sliding into the nearby ditch his assigned cruiser really was. As fate would have it, while kneeling to inspect the deep rut the tire had carved into the loose dirt and gravel surface, Jerome spotted several pointed shards of assorted sizes of what appeared to be charcoal-shaded fiberglass; just the type associated with modern-day car bumpers and fenders.

A quick inspection in and around a waist-high wall of Dwarf Burford Hollies serving as the ravine's makeshift perimeter yielded nothing further, though his heart pounded at the prospect of discovering a wrecked Charger buried within. He pocketed the found shrapnel and, mind racing with possibilities, steered the cruiser carefully back onto the pavement.

The radio mic levitating near parted lips, Jerome debated briefly before placing it back in its bracket without ever radioing in as initially intended. As both Strickland—the senior patrolman and a shameless glory-hound—and old man Douglas had covered the same grounds and reported no such findings, he wasn't about to open even the slightest possibility of either, nor even the chief himself, confiscating the possible evidence before casually dismissing him from further investigation. Might seem like small potatoes at the moment, but escalation to something much bigger wasn't out of the realm of possibility. Perhaps this outwardly innocent find would be the beginning of building the dossier required to take that first step up the law enforcement ladder. Be it foul-play related or simply a missing person, at least it would trump the plethora of ordinary traffic tickets, drunken drivers or domestic disturbances currently riddling his pathetically simplistic resume.

Thus, following a quick stop for fresh (black, no sugar) coffee and a chocolate-caramel power bar at the local Honey-Badger-Mart, he sat in a dark corner of the parking lot flipping through the tiny notepad that was his constant companion when on shift. The 5G tower in Lexington had registered a faint but definite second ping just after the first, this one originating in the general area of Main Street and McRae Crossing.

Though these were oft-times labeled as little more than unreliable static echoes and thus usually dismissed as such, the young lawman figured that with so very little transpiring on the main drag as darkness began to settle in beneath a thick banking of potentially threatening skies, there was literally nothing to lose in checking it out, barring any incoming calls that required his immediate presence.

At a quarter till seven, as the first echoing blast of distant thunder sounded off from the east of town, he made a slow, deliberate turn off Willoughby Drive onto McRae Crossing, at first oblivious to the most notable of several scattered homes littering the narrow two-lane.

Reaching a dead end a few hundred yards past a long-abandoned tobacco barn, he circled back and, just as he'd reached to radio in his twenty, Jerome braked upon realizing the small brick and siding abode on the corner of Willoughby and McRae Crossing was suddenly familiar for a reason. He couldn't remember the last time he'd cruised the area on patrol, but did recall visiting the house in question, that being his rookie year on the force a little more than three winters ago. The barbecue and beer bash had been hosted by the homeowner—with more than a little assistance from the PD staff—who was celebrating a decade with the department in the role of records clerk *slash* office manager. Personally, he'd always sensed something a bit off about the crippled clerk though he'd never been able to pin down specifics other than an inexplicable contrast of personalities and perhaps his own juvenile unease and unabashed awkwardness around the handicapped man.

As for Grant's now ex-spouse—whom he vividly recalled as a cloyingly obnoxious drunk, not to mention undeniably intimidating due to her hulking physique—to think of her was to openly shudder with a heady mix of disgust and, no denying it, fear. He'd never met, before or since, a more mismatched couple, at least from an outsider's perspective, with Wesley Grant being the calm, soft-spoken type and his spouse—Sandra or maybe Sharon, he couldn't remember—the shrill, bombastic blowhard with the pit bull temperament cleverly cloaked by an endless barrage of saccharin-sweet, Southern-belle homilies. At least, he mused, such dramatic differences explained their inevitable split and subsequent divorce.

Jake had mentioned something about spotting Wesley's Camry around town, or maybe someone else had done the spotting—the semi-retiree was an infamous gossip hound and thus reveled in passing on such nonverified tidbits. Bizarre, considering Maggie had hinted the crippled clerk had journeyed to some faraway scape for a week of fishing and general R&R. Worth a check, if for no other reason than to quell his own building curiosity.

Pulling onto the relatively short dirt and gravel drive, Jerome balked at even reaching for the mic once parked less than a dozen feet from a planked ramp leading into the dark and seemingly deserted home's unscreened front entrance. Jerome stepped gingerly from the cruiser, a light shower abruptly mutating as larger drops of rain thumped the bill of his department-issued ballcap and a brief flash of lightning illuminated an otherwise murky landscape.

The young patrolman sighed deeply and exhaled, his own vaporish output forming a billowy cloud of condensation he was forced to step into and through while sauntering up the rain-slickened ramp, boot heels digging in and the groping fingers of gloved hands loosely grasping opposing wooden rails upon a purposely gradual ascent.

Friday, 12:11 hours

Though it had been nearly a decade since he had last partaken in the act of smoking, as Wesley sat in the otherwise deserted waiting room, his lone company a wall-mounted TV with the sound muted, he felt a sudden, shockingly intense craving to light up.

The Crimson Falls ER waiting room consisted of exactly nine strategically spaced chairs—a "temporary" precaution made permanent since the COVID outbreak—a soda and snack machine and the aforementioned-television, the age-old tradition of printed materials to peruse long-since abandoned for hygiene and infectious disease considerations.

Nostrils involuntarily flaring from a constant barrage of antiseptic which lingered within the bland, unfurnished four walls like a toxic cloud, he could hear whispered voices and the echoes of footsteps occasionally reverberating from the nearby hall, the admitting desk being currently abandoned.

Checking his cell, he saw it was nearing a quarter past noon and roughly a half-hour since their arrival outside the double-door glass entrance, where he'd briefly left the Camry idling while unloading the chair and exiting, nearly taking a face-first tumble onto the paved drive in the process. Wesley wheeled himself frantically inside, the staff temporarily mistaking him for the patient before he was able to retrieve Gunther from the car, the unconscious man having sat slumped over the seat with blood seeping freely from each nostril.

"Mister Grant?"

The voice startled him from his daze, the source a painfully young-looking, thin-faced man wearing an ankle-length smock and introducing himself as Doctor Markum, who immediately took a seat across from where Grant had parked his chair, a large-screen iPad placed in his lap.

"Mister Grant, I understand you brought Mister McCarron in."

"Yeah, how is he?"

"Does he have family?"

Wesley bristled, drooping eyes suddenly alert and gleaming.

"Is he gonna live?"

The young doctor held up both hands, palms-up.

"Yes, yes. What I meant is, well, relatives are normally given priority in health matters, legality-wise."

"He does have an uncle in town. Dexter McCarron."

"Does this uncle live nearby?"

"In town, yes, but hey, you can...I'm his...I'm Gun...Mister McCarron's confidant."

"Fine, fine. He's resting now. We sedated him effectively enough to ease his discomfort and have started him on an antibiotic drip. Tell me, when did his condition begin to noticeably deteriorate?"

His shoulders having collapsed upon the news, Wesley paused to sigh heavily before staring at the younger man incredulously.

"Well Doc, we are talking about a paraplegic."

"I'm well aware," the doctor replied, left brow dramatically cocked. "I mean today, this morning perhaps. Have you been with him for an extended time?"

"Since early this morning. He seemed...did seem a shade paler than usual and seemed to have a little less pep. We were...he was exposed to the elements for a half-hour, maybe more."

Doctor Markum balanced the iPad on one kneecap and begin to assault its built-in keypad.

"His blood pressure was dangerously low," he stated without looking up from the device, the tone borderline accusatory, at least to Grant's ears, which were perhaps oversensitive from building fatigue.

"His...unique health issues obviously do him no favors when it comes to what we consider proper rejuvenation and rehabilitation. Healing is a challenge from even the most minor ills, much less a near-complete collapse."

"I can relate...to the uniqueness, Doc."

"Yes, well, to put it mildly, Mister Grant, at the very least he is extremely fatigued. With his sudden loss of bladder and bowel control, he's showing symptoms of autonomic dysreflexia. Thrombosis is even a possibility. For now, he'll need intravenous fluids and extensive rest. There was blood in his urine, and although the bloodwork will take several days, I'm of the opinion he's been off at least one of his required meds while overcompensating with others."

"I don't get it. I just don't ge—" Wes ran splayed fingers through already disheveled hair. "...He showed no signs, I mean, other than looking more peaked since this morning. I was...I've been amazed at his level of energy. The last few days he's put me to shame."

The doctor handed the iPad over to Wesley, the webpage on display featuring a litany of physical issues often suffered by paraplegics.

"That's how dysreflexia works, Mister Grant. His brain wasn't receiving the warning signs due to the spinal injury."

"Yeah, I *know* the definition, Doc," he fired back with a frown, indicating his own permanently seated status with the simple downward nod of the head.

"My apologies," the young physician replied with as flatly spoken regret as was possible. "Additionally, that exoskeleton doesn't do such patients any favors. Often times it's a crutch that assists in masking potential ills. Most overuse it and this...his current state can be the result. I've never seen a model so advanced, so there's little doubt of his overdependence."

Having given the online article little more than a perfunctory glance, Wesley returned the iPad.

"Yeah, a real-life bionic man. I guess I've just grown accustomed to what it is capable of in the past few days. You tend to forget the hollow husk beneath."

"Such advanced technology is just as new to me. I've heard of them but never saw one up close. Truly sci-fi in scope and, I take it, as effective or more so."

Wes rolled his chair past the seated physician until he was able to see the hallway, where a pair of nurses, one female and one male, had repopulated the ER station just as an elderly woman and man trudged slowly through the automatically triggered double glass doors, the latter stooped over and obviously favoring his left leg.

"You'd have to see it to believe it, Doc. If I had seventy grand just sitting around the house, I'd be placing my own order on Amazon as we speak."

The young doctor arose, iPad tucked to his narrow chest.

"Well, if it does all you hint, I'm sure it's worth every red cent. Well then, back to the mines. You can see Mister McCarron if you'd like, but only for a few minutes, okay?"

"Understood." Wes nodded, backing the chair a bit more to allow ample space for the other man to pass. "Will he be moved eventually?"

"Probably later this evening or tonight. Good evening, Mister Grant."

"Thanks for everything, Doc."

Pausing to check his cell—Maggie had left a single text with the simplest of four-word messages which read "*You're in town? Jackass!*"—he giggled aloud and, forced to cover his mouth to deter a sudden, uncontrollable torrent of similar snorts or titters, repocketed the phone before wheeling himself down the corridor toward whatever room housed Gunther's withered form. Lying to his good friend and co-worker was one thing, repayable by a simple chewing out and perhaps even a brief period of cold-shoulder treatments, but continual bald-faced fibs directed at his former spouse birthed an altogether different species of potential catastrophe.

Directed to the last of a trio of emergency treatment rooms, he rolled through the opening with the low hum of the chair serving as the lone audible source within its cramped confines.

"H-howdy d-doodie, partner," blurted the room's only occupant in his familiar, baritone rasp, though noticeably weaker, frighteningly so in fact, than Wesley was accustomed to hearing.

"Doc tell ya h-how...long I have? If ya can c-confiscate a p-pen and some paper, I'll add ya to my...will."

Shaking his head in disbelief, not so much at the bedridden man's conscious, seemingly coherent state but unabashed attempt at jocularity, Wes was equally unsurprised to see the man had somehow managed to locate an episode of the seventies' cop show *Ironside* on the room's mounted plasma.

"Seriously considered just dumping you on the sidewalk and making off with that miracle walking machine."

Gunther managed a tiny grin despite the myriad of IV lines hanging from his gaunt form like clear tentacles, including the one currently spelunking his left nostril. As in some form of ritualistic tribute, his trademark beret hung from the top of one of a pair of IV stands.

"Bet you...d-did. Tell ya what, if I...k-kick off, it's y-yours, no st-strings attached. Lots of wires and st-straps but no...strings."

When Wes parked the chair to the right of the man's bed, the two were at equal heights for perhaps the first time.

"You scared me, boss. I knew you were looking kind of spent once we left the field, but no hints that taking a header into the dash was imminent."

"Guess I had been...pushin' it past my own...limitations since comin' back to town, but then...ya see, it's like I...told ya before, I couldn't risk dawdlin'."

"Gunther, there isn't an armed assassin in sight."

The impossibly thin man sneered, his left eyelid briefly sticking in a parody of a wink.

"Gi-give it till tomorrow mornin', oh ye of no faith. Sp-special Saturday mornin' edition of the *G-Gazette* m-might see 'em comin' outta th-the woodwork."

"You sound like that's the goal of all this."

Lifting a shaky right hand, Gunther was able to flash the classic thumb-to-forefinger "ok" gesture, albeit a slightly warped version.

"B-bingo."

The seated man, head tilted in obvious dismay, tossed up both hands in frustration.

"Basically a suicide mission then."

"N-no, not b-by a long d-damn shot!" the prone man exclaimed angrily, his right hand clenching into a bony fist by his equally skeletal side.

"It ain't 'bout me dyin' for some...self-servin'...cause. N-no way."

"Then *what*, Gunther?"

"*What* is n-no more passes for...t-the one or ones r-responsible. Fourteen damn y-years they've...skated scot-fr-free. W-with me wastin' away l-like some...rotted banana p-peel, who was g-gonna come after 'em? Who was left that g-gave a shit to p-push the issue? Bless my m-mom and dad, they probably fi-figured we all...*deserved* that span of s-sufferin' and purgatory in...some biblical w-way. Well, I c-call horseshit.

"It's overdue, w-way fuckin' past a reasonable sp-span that...those responsible deserve some time of...their own!"

Reaching up with a shaky hand, Wesley placed a flat, slightly sweaty palm atop the man's trembling fist.

"Sorry, man. I had no right to doubt you, no matter the agenda. No one does."

Gasping loudly as if to choke away a building sob, the bedridden man merely nodded and closed tear-filled eyes. Within minutes, with his newfound ally still gently clasping his now unclenched fist, he was fast asleep.

Friday, 1244 hours

"Thanks for coming, Mister McCarron."

"Thanks for calling."

"No problem whatsoever. You're family, after all."

Wesley had phoned Dexter McCarron—acquiring the number from a simple search—once it appeared the man's nephew would be incapacitated via chemical bombardment for several hours. The two sat at the rear of the tiny waiting room they currently shared with a young woman sitting a row away while cradling a sleeping young boy who appeared sweaty with fever.

"So the doctor said he's fatigued?"

"For starters. Thinks he's been skipping select meds."

"Select?"

"The depressants. Doesn't want to be slowed down, so he just conveniently skipped 'em. That's one rock-headed nephew you've got there, Mister McCarron."

Decked out in his characteristic all-black ensemble of jacket, cargo pants, cowboy boots and cadet khaki cap, the older man nodded agreeably.

"Call me Dex. Yeah, stubborn as a mule, just like his father. So are they looking at booking him a room in the hospital?"

"Eventually. I think they're waiting on a few tests to come back."

"He asked you to bring him here?"

Wesley laughed and instantly regretted it, though the older man's naturally stoic demeanor indicated he wasn't either shocked or offended.

"No sir, it wasn't until he took a header into the car's dash, his face paler than Casper's ghost, that I made the command decision to have him checked out."

"Yeah, that sounds about right."

"He flat refuses to slow down, Mis—Dex. I'm starting to feel guilty about willingly hauling him around and watching him deteriorate. You tell me to halt and desist and I'll do so."

"Well, this should at least delay any further goose chases for now, but truth be told, if you don't do it, he'll just find somebody that will." Dexter paused to reach up and scratch gently beneath the bill of his cap as if to carefully contemplate further dialogue. "Probably yours truly. Much as I hate to see him killing himself over his...this obsession, I am family and doubt I could refuse him, at least for very long."

"Understood. I, well, since I've only known your nephew for a few days, I felt it only right that I ask."

"You're kindred spirits," the uncle offered earnestly, staring down at his own slightly-scuffed work boots, "and I don't mean just because of the shared ills. You're very different men for sure, but there's something, a connection, that binds you. I think Gunny sensed it right from the get-go. Trust can't come easy for him, not with all the badness that's been in his world for so long, but he felt he could trust you right off."

At first unsure of how to react, Wesley's eyes darted about the room with the same spastic frenzy as his thoughts. Finally, sighing deeply and meeting the older man's intense gaze, the words flowed with surprising ease.

"Well, if that's the case, I'm flattered, though he's yet to entrust me with the whole story. I've read all the police reports, but obviously he believes there's a lot more to it than what's been typed and written in black and white."

"Indeed he does. Afraid I'm no more privy than yourself."

Hands tucked inside his jean jacket's pockets, Dexter McCarron arose painstakingly, a pained wince creasing his weathered visage.

"Maybe, just maybe, Gunny ain't so sure himself."

"Pardon?"

"Maybe I'm way off base here, but sometimes I think he's just tossing bait to see who bites."

"For the record, I think you're standing safely with both feet planted on that base."

As if to escape the nearby vicinity of the sick child, who was alternating hacking cough with wet sobs, the two men seemed to slowly and inconspicuously gravitate toward the rear of the room.

"Well, Gunny always was the stubborn, headstrong type, even as a kid," Dexter half-whispered, leaning against the back wall with booted feet crossed at the ankle and resembling an aged country crooner posing for an album cover. "Never seemed, I don't know, *contented* with whatever was going on in his life, well, 'cept for maybe when he was with *her*. Truth is, I didn't see a lot of him then, but when I did, he seemed happier than any McCarron male had the right to be."

"Must've been a very special lady, all right," Wesley replied quietly, wheeling around until he was facing the elder McCarron with his back to the rest of the waiting room.

"His eyes light up like strobes whenever he mentions her."

"She was a rare one, I hear. A real firecracker type, it was said. A real tragedy, since Wendy Hammock alone seemed to possess the power to settle that boy down."

"Sadder even, since to Gunther it's like her passing is still a freshly opened wound. I mean, in his reality only months have passed."

"That and waking up in a body devoid of all use, for the most part. No offense."

The older man visibly stiffened, reaching up to tip his cap.

"None taken. Difference is, I've had many years to grow accustomed to my limitations. He's still in his condition's infancy."

"Yep, there is that. Safe to say, this obsession of his is only gonna end one way, and sooner than later, I'm afraid. He's convinced of some great malfeasance that no one else can either sense or see."

"That he most certainly is, and no amount of amateur psychoanalysis is going to alter that perception."

The pair nodded in unison just as a female nurse of ample girth and toothy smile entered the waiting room and, following a brief, whispered conversation with the mother, took the slumping child into doughy arms and carried him from the room with the mama following closely behind.

"Listen Mister Grant, you can take off for a bit if you like. I'll take the mantle for a while."

"Call me Wes," the seated man said, sneaking a quick glance at his wristwatch. "Um, yeah, I might take a break at that. Mind if we swap cell numbers?"

Once they'd done so, Wesley wheeled toward the exit just as a heavyset black woman holding a bloody towel to her forearm bounded through as if her generous rear end were lit ablaze.

"Keep me posted on any changes," he said in parting. "If I can't answer right away, you can text."

"Will do. Take a rest," he heard Dexter say as he wheeled through the opening, careful to avoid a trail of blood spatter that led far out into the paved lot.

Friday, 2015 hours

"Um, Chief, sorry to bug you at home and all but, ugh, you got a minute to saunter on down to the station? Yes, sir. Gonna flat need some assistance here."

Donna Early's naturally mousy voice shook and rattled as if she were receiving sporadic shock treatments, a bizarre and borderline comical phenomenon that both tickled and terrified her boss in equal measure.

"Um, no sir, can't reach 'im on the radio. I called Phil in early and he's out looking for him now, but as of a few minutes ago he was still out by the Thompson Farm cutoff, which is, you know, a good ten-minute drive from home base."

A stocky, middle-aged woman in her late fifties sporting a gray buzzcut due to recent chemo treatments for breast cancer, the late shift—five PM to midnight, when the county took over duties—dispatcher's light brown eyes darted rapidly from the cluttered desktop to the window and back again as if sitting netside at a tennis match.

"Hey, Butch! You gonna bring me somebody with a badge or do I need to come in there and speed up the process?" the person behind the glass shrieked, leaning in until their moon-shaped mug practically kissed the surface. "Believe me deary, you don't want that!"

"Yes sir, as you can tell, this is kind of beyond my paygrade," Donna said through a strained grin, speaking behind a cupped hand even though she'd neglected to lower her tone to better cloak the words.

"Thanks, Chief, and please hurry."

Replacing the phone to its cradle with a shaking hand, she cleared her throat and inhaled deeply before stepping out from behind the desk and toward the glass partition, all the while secretly cursing her own carelessness in not recalling to secure the PD entrance door behind Maggie's departure almost three hours past. She'd been brewing a fresh pot of coffee at the time and it had simply slipped her mind, just one of many examples of how the recent treatments and assorted meds had shredded her short-term memory.

"Ma'am, the chief of police is on his way down, so if you'll take a seat there in the lob—"

"Wellllll then, I'll tell you what, Butchy," the person shouted from behind the glass, leaning their head away while keeping a tight grasp on the writing stand just below its lower edge, "Heap Big Chief has exactly three minutes before I commence to take this colossal waste of my time very, very personally!"

"Please ma'am, just calm down. He's close by and shouldn't take more than—"

Having raised both hands in mock surrender while maintaining a three-to-four-foot distance between herself and the front counter, the night dispatcher surprised herself by hardly flinching in the face of the vicious headbutt delivered to the center of the glass, a blow executed with sufficient force to shake a nearby pastoral-themed painting from its hooks to bounce harmlessly off the counter before rolling onto the thin carpeting.

"Clock's ticking, Butchy!" the person exclaimed with maniacal glee, a thin trail of blood trailing from their hairline and directly onto the bridge of their nose. "The head honcho best not dawdle or I guess you and I are gonna see just how much punishment that glass can take before it cries uncle!"

The knowledge that the glass barricade was the ballistic armor type and supposedly impenetrable and thus projectile resistant did little to soothe the dispatcher's nerves in terms of just how many similar physical shots of equal force it could withstand before shattering like an oversized martini glass.

"J-Just settle down, a-all right? I told y-you he'll be here in minutes, and I suggest you alter your behavior in his presence."

"Two and a half minutes and ca-ca-ca-counting!" the person screeched while backing away in a slight crouch and, pumping their heels against the lobby's hardwood flooring like an angry bull, prepping their next charge.

"Miss Jamison! Sandra!" A voice boomed from the shadows, the mere sound doing more to soothe Donna Early's brittle nerves than a handful of muscle relaxers.

Chief Crockett stood just inside the entrance, its trademark creaking upon being breached obviously having been masked by their unhinged guest's ear-splitting pronouncements.

Decked out in civvies, he stood with feet wide apart and arms raised with the palms facing out.

"What say you and I settle in over some hot coffee and a danish or two and talk this out?"

Sandy Jamison, still poised like a sumo wrestler awaiting the starting clap but with her head twisted directly at the newest arrival, cackled like a drunken teen before straightening up a degree and responding, the sneaker of her left foot squeaking loudly in protest.

"True or false, Chief of the Podunk Po-Po, do I *really* look like I need a danish?"

The chief stepped with the tentativeness of one traipsing through a live minefield while still in surrender mode with arms raised and palms out.

"Well, how about some freshly brewed java then? Donna there cooks up some of the best in the county."

Ascending to an upright standing position, her baseball cap sitting comically askew until the bill sat directly over her left ear, Sandy's unnaturally bowed gait—she appeared to lean heavily to the left, as if the pocket adorning that side of the jean jacket she modeled were loaded down with bricks—and wild, spastic gestures hinted greatly at her level of inebriation.

"All this polite diversion shit aside, Constable Crackett, all I presently desire is the location of my ex-husband."

Instinctively, the big man maintained a full arm's length distance from the visibly swaying woman, as in executing a quick mind's-eye review of her history, at least those elements Wesley had shared over the years, he wasn't about to take her potential for inflicting physical pain lightly. Sober, dog drunk or to the gills, she was apt to put up a heck of a scrap if so inclined.

"Chief Will Crockett at your service, Sandy. We...have met on numerous occasions, remember?"

"Just yanking your chain, Chief," she replied through a warped sneer. "I might currently be loaded as an entire tribe of goats, but names and faces remain as clear as crystal. Now, where's that floozie dispatcher of the Asian persuasion? This manly chick...," she paused to wag a forefinger toward the window of the records office, where Donna Early's guarded position remained unchanged, "...she's about as useful as a wickless candle."

"Well Sandra, to be fair, Donna cannot share information she doesn't have and I'm afraid Maggie has been off-duty for several hours."

"Bingo!"

"Ma'am?"

"Dollars to dog-dung he's wherever *she* is. Thick as sorghum those two. Soooo, seems all I need is the concubine's street address and I'll be right out of you people's short hairs."

Using both hands to tug at the folds of the turtleneck that appeared to be slowly constricting around her thick neck, she stumbled back a step before righting herself.

"I'm afraid your assumption is way off base, Sandra. From what I understand, Wesley is currently out of state doing some fishing."

"Well *hell*, Chief, being as I talked face-to-face with the lying sack of legless excrement just a few hours ago, whose *assumption* is more fictional?"

"Be that as it may, you know we're not allowed to release home addresses of city employees."

"She knows where he's hiding, Crockett!" she bellowed, thrusting her head forward in time with spouting the chief's family name in the same general manner that had previously jarred the glass. "Even if he isn't with her, she knows where to find him!"

"Be that as it may, Sandy, we're not able to provide Miss Childer's home address upon request. Now, what I can do is phone her and inquire if she is privy to Wesley's whereabouts. Sound good?"

"Chief, all due respect to your high crown and all, but do you really think she's gonna willingly give 'im up? I may appear dumb as a stump, but it's just a disguise."

"Sandra, may I ask why you are so adamant in tracking Wesley on such short notice?"

Stumbling forward, the husky figure was forced to briefly windmill both arms to regain her balance, forcing the chief to hop back in retreat.

"I'd been making circles around this, this...shit-stain of a town for almost two full days before I tracked him to the ball field this morning! I came down here to surprise him with an outing and he decides to pick that very day to start his first vacation in what, three years? Four? I'm pissed, Chief! Highly agitated, ticked off, perturbed. I am not leaving Crimson Falls till I corner the ungrateful a-hole and say what I need to say. He managed to slink away this morning but by god, he won't again!"

"Miss Jamison, I'm gonna need you to calm down and lower your voice," the chief said, his left hand slinking ever-so-gradually toward his lower back and beneath the lower edge of his coat, where a pair of handcuffs jingled. It was a safe bet the normally calm, cordial—if not at times obnoxious—woman's present behavior was altered in some way, either by alcohol or an unknown chemical, though at present he detected no apparent proof of the former permeating the air within the lobby.

Obviously unimpressed, their highly-irrational guest whirled back toward the glass window—displaying a surprising amount of grace considering both her size and present state—while responding in-kind.

"Awwww, why don't you go pound sand, Crockett! I'm startin' to think you're harboring his cowardly rear end right here in the building. Ye-yeah, that's it. Probably cowerin' down in your office as we speak, makin' milk duds in his drawers at the very sound of my voice!"

"Miss...Sandy, he's...Wes is not here. That I can promise," the chief reassured, the cuffs hanging loose from his left hand and tucked near his rear while still cloaked by the edge of the coat.

"Yeah, right! Chief, you could tell me water's wet at this point and I'd have to doubt the vadid...vadad...valid..ity. Regardless, somebody's gonna cough up some knowledge or I'll tear down this dump with my bare hands!"

"Sandra, I won't warn you again. Now settle down or I'm gonna have to place you into cust—"

The bullish charge, full bore and executed with nary a hint of intoxication-related clumsiness, happened so fast that the chief's feeble attempt to snag any part of her ensemble resulted in little more than a fistful of air.

Donna Early stumbled back with a shrill yelp just as the center of the window endured full impact, her left hip bouncing off the edge of the copy machine with enough force to displace it from its assigned spot and directly into the rolling file at the rear of the room.

"Damn it, woman!" Crockett exclaimed through gritted teeth, having relieved his belt of the stainless-steel restraints before posing with legs shoulder-length apart and arms spread wide.

Ricocheting from the reinforced glass like a human battering ram—her stance a slight crouch with arms tucked at her bosom and hips shimmying as from an intense electric shock—Sandra Jamison's considerable bulk seemed to seek out the big man's embrace as she all but melded into his waiting grasp.

"D-Donna, get Jerome or Ph-Phil or...some...damn...body on...the horn and...get them down...here...p-pronto!" he managed, struggling to maintain his grip on the squirming, wriggling, enraged subject, her rotund shape and loose-fitting clothes not nearly as problematic as the cock-strong physicality on display. It was while forced to use every ounce of his two-hundred sixty-five-pound frame to force her face-down on the tiled floor, that the chief recalled tidbits of ancient conversations centered around Sandra Jamison's former hobby and how it led to her first meeting Wesley.

"G-get o-off...m-me...," she spat, left cheek pinned to the checkered tile, left arm jammed into her lower back with a cuff already snapped snugly into place. "...Po-police! P-po-lice...bra-...br-bre...brutal...tality!" she continued, giggling manically at the stammering conclusion while simultaneously ceasing all struggles beneath the strategically planted knee digging at the small of her back.

"That's it, S-Sandra. Just...ease up now," the chief huffed, retrieving her suddenly limp right arm as gently as possible while lifting the planted knee just slightly. "No need for...any of this, hear? We'll need to...keep you overnight for you...for your own safety, but don't...fret. We offer all the fresh coffee you can hold and whatever...you crave as far as eats. Now...just hold still while I snap this other cuff—"

Despite dwarfing the pinned woman by nearly a foot in height and seventy pounds, Will Crockett was first jarred—his teeth ground roughly together—and then hoisted airborne onto his side from a single, vicious buck, his toboggan torn free as the right side of his head impacted—and subsequently snapped—a leg of one of a trio of high-back chairs.

Rolling clumsily in the direction of the PD entrance, lungs mostly voided of precious inventory from the initial impact with the hard tile, he was just able to crawl onto all fours and lean up when a knee driven forth like a flesh and bone wrecking ball landed with a hollow thump at his exposed breastbone, the force temporarily lifting him upward before the inevitable tumble backward and directly into the solid oak entrance door.

Crockett lay back in a spastic haze, arms splayed to either side and bald head propped against the door's lower paneling, his battered lungs begging for a refill that his gasping throat and puckering lips—like a wheezing, beached fish—were unable to syphon.

Through rapidly blinking eyes, he watched the rampaging woman scoop up the chair his noggin had so effectively crippled and, rearing it back over her left shoulder, take a short running start before chucking it toward the glass window.

The night call-taker's desperate pleas for assistance reverberated from the dispatch area, the volume of her cries rising several decibels in the aftermath of the chair's demise, its back portion split neatly from the seat and remaining legs before spilling out onto the floor of the lobby like splintered shrapnel.

Apparently giving up on successfully shattering the glass, the woman staggered over to the lone access door into which only authorized personnel were allowed to enter and, pacing a drunken path, appeared to be sizing it up. Purchased at a cost to the city of just under three grand a decade earlier, the single knob entrance—a miniature keypad for access was located halfway up the wall to its right—was a solid core, bullet resistant Armortex constructed of wood reinforced with a fiberglass composite.

The mayor at the time, Kerry Hammock by name, paranoid of possible assaults on the PD building—such an assault had

occurred in Lexington just a few months after his taking office—
insisted on the extra fortification seeing as the city's top official
had, at the time, set up shop on the building's second floor.
Nearly eight years later and with the current city head-honcho's
office located in a newly constructed city hall building located
two full blocks to the south, the tomb-like barricade and impact-
resistant glass had each seemed of late the very picture of wasted
taxpayer money. Textbook cases of extravagant overkill.

That said, at the moment Donna Early wouldn't have traded
winning Powerball lottery tickets for either.

Friday, 1654 hours

Jerome Griffey had been reaching for his ride's door handle
when he remembered the detached garage out back, a structure
nearly large enough to claim barn status.

As dusk had begun to dim the proceedings, the cold rain
mutated to a sleet/rain mix which bounded sporadically off the
bill of his cap like pea gravel. That, coupled with increasingly
gusty winds and pummeling temperatures, had encouraged a less
than thorough inspection of the Grant property, thus far limited
to the front drive, yard and porch only.

Trudging past the right side of the house, each step adding a
fresh layer of wet leaves to his already gummy boots, he'd again
considered radioing in his position but quickly declined, figuring
a quick looksee at the garage would conclude with roughly the
same time having expired.

Jerome estimated the two-door, tin-roofed structure's size at
perhaps_thirty by thirty-six with a window above the twin dock
entrances that hinted at either a garage apartment or upstairs
storage. Departing the backyard for a deeply rutted clay path
leading into the first of two garage bays, the young patrolman
paid no mind to a separate set of equally defined furrows making
a beeline into the second.

Upon finding the lone entrance secured, he stepped back with tiny pellets of frozen precip ricocheting off his cap and shoulders and weighed his options, the most sensible by far being to seek the warmth and dryness of his ride. Never mistaken for a man of reason by any that knew him, he instead sidestepped over to the first available bay door and reached for the tiny handle at its base.

"Open...sesame..." he muttered, then mildly surprised at the initial ease with which the door slid gradually upward until the occasional hitch slowed its ascension, as if the connecting cable was slightly off track. True, he possessed no official warrant for permission to search the structure, but he did have cause, which, as he commenced tugging, was no different than a routine traffic stop for a window tint violation transforming into a felony bust for illegal drugs.

That initial peek into the murky interior all but diminished the loudly creaking door's locking at the conclusion of its ascent as a nonevent, the wide-eyed patrolman literally hopping back as if suddenly aware he stood atop a trapdoor.

"Well I'll be damned," he mouthed, unaware he'd spoken aloud. "Well, hello there, charcoal colored late model Dodge Charger. People have been looking for you, pretty baby, yes they have."

Facing the hood—its high gloss dazzling despite the gloom which effectively cloaked everything past the dark-tinted windshield—he stood statue-still for several moments, hands-on-hips and mouth agape.

"Question is...," he resumed, while removing a small tactical penlight from his utility belt—one he'd purchased with his own money as a substitute for the bulky departmental light currently taking up space in the trunk of his cruiser—and sighing deeply before that initial click and narrow stream of illumination, "...exactly what *are* you doing hidden away in Wesley Grant's garage?"

That initial ray of light accompanying him with laser-beam clarity, he performed the perfunctory walk-around inspection of the vehicle, this after briefly focusing its relatively thin but intense shaft of radiance to the opposite side of the garage, where an aged, mud-coated pickup of undetermined make, model and color sat like some long-abandoned, undiscovered relic.

"Now, what was that tag number again?" he muttered, bending down near the back bumper, so badly crushed the tag beneath had been curled into and mostly engulfed within a constricted ball of fiberglass and plastic, with several chucks conspicuously absent.

"Hmm, guess it's a moot point now, right? I mean, what are the odds?" he nearly laughed aloud, still crouched as the light danced from one ruined section to the next and, retrieving the pieces of jagged shrapnel he'd appropriated near the McCarron property and half-heartedly attempting to fit them into the many voids like separate puzzle pieces. In the end, three of the half-dozen shards fit without even the slightest effort, matching seamlessly in both size and shade, the young lawman releasing a lengthy exhale.

"Well, similar to fingerprints, we only need so many matches for a hit."

Standing stiffly and blissfully unaware of the loud popping of both knees, Jerome's scalp tingled and buzzed, his cheeks ablaze and blushing with a sudden wave of euphoria, the likes of which he hadn't experienced since graduation day at the police academy.

Circling the prone vehicle like an expectant father in a hospital waiting room, his free hand tucked at the small of his back and the other swinging and swaying with the grace and fluidity of a veteran orchestra conductor with a tactical light as his baton.

"Whoa now, do not rush this," he whispered, halting while facing the driver's door, roughly every other word audible above the constant ticking and pecking of sleet bouncing off the garage's tin roof, "Cannot...*will not*...screw this up."

Digging into his jacket, he removed a pair of Eddie Bauer fleece gloves, again purchased on his own dime, and, sucking in yet another fresh lungful of chilled November air, reached tentatively for the driver's door handle.

"Nope!" he blurted, jerking the cloaked hand back as to avoid certain electric shock and sidestepping around until he fronted the passenger door. "Useable prints less likely on the driver's handle. Evidence scene protection one-oh-one, bonehead. Wanna be Officer *Dumbo* Griffey of the Podunk PD your whole miserable life?"

The fingers of his right hand lightly grasped the handle—the innermost edge as to avoid as much real estate as was possible—and tugged outward with the gentleness and care of a man cradling a palm-full of nitroglycerin, the lightest of clicking sounds hardly audible as the door pulled gradually ajar.

Even as the tinted windows had allowed zero visibility and thus offered no sneak preview as to the vehicle's interior content, he'd held little faith in uncloaking clues to its previous driver's whereabouts inside but wasn't about to call in his findings without first giving it at least a token once-over. Strangely, even while on the cusp of personal glory, the patrolman's frenzied thoughts suddenly centered around what he *didn't* have at the moment, nagging and overriding and even diminishing what should've been pure elation on what he'd uncovered through sheer determination.

In the fleeting seconds before the interior lights flashed on and the penlight slipped from his left hand to bounce uselessly off his boot, the youthful, overexuberant and uncharacteristically reckless patrolman determined he would have gladly pitched-in his own funds for department-wide shoulder-mic capability.

Sad reality was, even with what most officers nationwide considered basic 21st century equipment, all he would've had time to relay to dispatch would've been a single, shock-induced, garbled scream before the still, prone figure lying across the front seat came suddenly to life, the shiny object it brandished reflecting Jerome Brett Griffey's own wide-eyed, open-mouthed squawk just before the excruciating pain it brought forth overrode all else.

Friday, 2029 hours

Will Crockett staggered onto unsteady feet just as Sandra Jamison applied yet another front kick to the door's center, roughly the tenth such blow, delivered with a resounding grunt and yielding the same nonresult.

"—up! She's...berserk! Tryin'....in...door...—ficer down! It's...Chief....—kett!" he could make out the panicked dispatcher screaming into her mic, thus completely hidden from sight from the rampaging tank in human guise currently attempting to bludgeon her way inside.

"Just...bring 'im out to me...a-and this can...end right here and now, dammit! I don't w-wanna hurt anybody in...particular...then again...at the...moment I...ain't beyond...enjoying doing...just that!" the shrieking Panzer bellowed, clearly somewhat winded but far from having emptied all remaining shells from her inner howitzer.

The chief, still struggling mightily to refill his battered lungs, was hardly ready and barely willing—either physically or mentally—to challenge the raging warrior-woman without at least an additional few moments to recover his shell-shocked bearings. Bent over with the flats of each palm resting atop still-tremoring knees, he watched Jamison prep for yet another bull charge and realized with an inner groan he had little choice but to soldier on in the face of further destruction, not to mention the outside chance she was able to breach the door and reach Donna Early, surely as hapless a prey as the department employed.

"C-come on o-out, little pa-pa-piggy, or I'll hu-hu-huff, and I'll pa-pa-puff, and I'll blooooowwww y-your...house...down!" Sandra Jamison ranted, head whipping wildly from left to right and back again while spewing tatters of foamy spittle in either direction, her right foot drawn back and coiled, and her thick torso following suit.

Stumbling forward to within reaching distance of her cocked, slightly levitated leg, the chief reached back for his cuffs with groping fingers that found only air before recalling his earlier attempt at binding and, as if on cue, saw them swinging loosely from Jamison's left wrist.

At the first noticeable tug of the loose restraint, she turned like a feral feline, hissing through bared teeth with eyes narrowed to fine slits, this reaction nonetheless just delayed enough to allow access to her left arm as she was abruptly hauled roughly back, a loud popping at her shoulder not unlike a cork yanked from a wine bottle.

No longer the least bit concerned with the level of force used to subdue the mad beast in the guise of an otherwise placid female, Crockett jerked her toward him—the fingers of both his hands intertwined around the disconnected cuff—while simultaneously lunging forth with his bald head on point.

The crunching of the cartilage within the confines of Sandra Jamison's pug-like nose was abrupt in duration but unmistakable in origin, a veritable gusher of crimson spewing forth from both mashed nostrils in the immediate aftermath. Despite a palpable weight and overall size advantage, Crockett was pulled off balance as Jamison had, in wake of the assault, naturally lurched in the opposite direction. Releasing his hold on the cuff to prevent being slung over her failing frame and possibly taking a header into the sealed security door, he instead stumbled back in an impromptu breakdance, ending only when he was forced to plant a shoulder into the entrance door.

"G-ga-gawaaaait!" Jamison screeched, having tumbled hard onto her left side and executing a comically spastic but effective combat roll that left her semi-upright while propped on her knees and clamping both hands over the source of her self-leakage. "...Uew bra-brook by-by d-doze, yew...y-yew doi-dy m-mud-mudder f-fud-der!"

The tip of his scalp semi-numb from the blow's impact and his eyes tearing so severely he could only make out her squatting form through a wet, wavy haze, Crockett decided it best not to allow her time to recover and, in three quick strides, reached her location while striking the slightly crouched pose of a classically-trained boxer.

"Che-cheec-ken shhhh-eeeet," the squatting woman spat in a nasally whine, though less pronounced once the folded fingers of her right hand were removed from the nostrils they'd been so snugly pinching, allowing for a generous spurt of blood to sail free and spatter the boot-tip of the town's top cop.

As Jamison had used the freed appendage to instinctively cover her face from an impending blow, the chief instead went low with an old-school combination of close-quarter punches, the first landing with a muffled thump at the right side of her ribcage, its overall effectiveness limited somewhat by the thickness of her jacket and the layers of clothing beneath.

The second, a looping left hook that she was able to partially juke by ducking her head at the last split-second, what little impact there was occurring just above her right ear.

The last in the trio came in the form of a textbook right uppercut he'd intended for either of her multiple chins, a potentially game-ending jaw-cruncher that instead found nothing but a few strands of trailing, misplaced hair as Jamison flung her head back in whiplash fashion just as the wrecking ball of a fist had ascended. Amazed at the chunky, obviously altered woman's almost catlike grace and agility, the chief had no time to reload and refire—his left fist hanging limply at his side—as his own forward momentum left him leaning in and his soft, exposed underbelly vulnerable for counterattack.

As his lungs had only recently refilled from the previous hammering courtesy of a strategically placed knee, the chief employed the single second in time he was afforded for defensive purposes by dropping both arms toward his openly exposed midsection.

Instead, as if somehow anticipating this, Jamison appeared to levitate from her knees and shoot forward, head-first at an upward angle, her own imitation of a human battering ram equally effective as her opponent's own, if not more so.

With a resounding "*Ooooffffffffff*" spouted between pursed lips, Will Crockett staggered back, briefly pondering if a man's breastbone could actually be divided—split like chicken-bones by a sharp-edged cleaver—by the force of such sudden, massive trauma; this worrisome but logically irrational query was quickly dismissed by a fresher struggle: that to right his back-peddling gait just enough to avoid cracking his skull for the second time in a matter of minutes.

"How zat feeeeeeellll, Craaackit? How's yeeeww lick de-dem app-les, azzz-hool?"

At first only faintly aware of the cackling voice and the barely coherent words it spat, it was the hot, putrid breath of the source that shook the chief back to a semi-state of coherence. Lying flat on his back, left eyelid inexplicably sticking every other rapid blink, his every rasping breath was like inhaling a mouthful of razorblades, his chest cavity surely having imploded.

Sirens. Familiar, soothing. Like the faint background music overheard in elevators of yesteryear, the sounds briefly trumping the illiterate dialogue of the stinky-breathed harpy currently sitting—or perhaps standing or *dancing* a jig atop—his thoroughly pummeled torso. Faint but growing ever stronger, crisper, clearer. The cavalry, by God. Riding to his aid to remove the reeking, ranting, oversized growth currently pinning him to the tile. Never mind—at least for the moment—that he even needed rescue, or the unfathomable thrashing he'd taken to require such intervention.

His vision fading in and out between blinking jags, the twin pains at the back of his skull and upper chest, respectively, seemingly in fierce competition to see which could make him lose consciousness faster, the big man attempted to shift his shaky focus to the gradually building screech of the approaching sirens.

"Wiiillllll, can...hear me? Jus...easy...hear? Don't move...'most here," a new, vaguely familiar voice chimed in, decidedly softer and minus the severe slurring or steamy, rank breath.

"It's Phil, Chief. He's almost here, 'kay? You just lie still, 'kay?"

Will Crockett briefly came to with enough clarity of mind and a split-second's semi-clear visual—right eye only, the left still haplessly glued shut between the occasional spasm—to see Donna Early leaning over his prone form, her shaking hands resting atop his throbbing chest. Before descending yet again into a fitful state of discombobulation, the veteran peace officer noticed the jagged white bone protruding from his upper torso like a pointy flag of surrender.

From the *Crimson Falls Gazette* Sports Page
Dated Nov. 14

Fast-starting Wildcats hang on for ninth straight, 38-29 win over Cougars
(Friday Night, Adams Field)

After building a 28-6 halftime lead, the still undefeated Crimson Falls squad hung on for a nine-point win over a feisty squad from Adams (6-3), powered by a 318-yard, three-touchdown performance by quarterback Shane Mills.

Ten

Friday, 2018 hours

"So *nobody* saw him leave?"

"It appears that way, sir. Security's checking the videotape, but we figure it had to be in the last half-hour to hour. As you can probably ascertain, we are terribly short-staffed here. What I...we do know is that he wasn't transported to the main hospital. There are only four people presently on duty and, well, simply put, there just aren't enough eyes available when all four patient rooms are occupied, such as tonight."

The nurse, a skeletal-thin, gray-coifed, stoop-shouldered woman who appeared well past retirement age, regarded Wesley with a tone that was equal parts dismissive and condescending. Shielded inside the glass-encased nurses' station, she tapped away at the keys of a laptop with all the intensity and fervor of an overmedicated sloth.

"Ma'am, I can surely sympathize, but the man was a paraplegic. Even with the exo-suit, it would've taken him a half-hour just to reach the exit!"

"Sir, please keep your voice *down*. This is a hospital, after all," the lipless, scowling Angel of Mercy scolded, having already turned her attention back to the computer screen's greenish glow.

His head barely clearing the stand outside the station, his chair's polyurethane wheels shoved snugly against its well-sanitized baseboards, Wesley felt his cheeks heat with a building ire that had begun to simmer the moment he'd wheeled into Gunther's room to find it empty, the bed in disarray and a nearby dresser—earlier littered with the ill cripple's few personal items—void of any evidence the man had ever occupied the space, much less just an hour or so previous.

"Nurse...um..."

"Leckner. Denise Leckner."

"Miss Leckner. Even if he...if Gun...Mister McCarron was able to redon the suit and shamble out of the building, he had no transportation out of the area, that is, unless, well...," he paused to roll his eyes and frown as if utterly disgusted at his own stupidity. "What about his uncle? Dexter McCarron would've been here. Could he have possibly given him a lift?"

"Mister Grant, Louise and I, that is, Nurse Morrison and I, came on shift at seven PM. I have no knowledge of an...Uncle McCarron. I suppose it's possible if the man was, as you claim, a family member. The log shows no official release form signed by anyone, much less a Deron McCarron."

"Dexter."

The lipless wonder scoffed, squinting eyes unmoved from the glow of the screen while fingers tapped away at a snail's pace.

"Fine then, *Dexter*. As I stated, Gary, um, Security Officer Mills is checking video as we speak. Meanwhile, I'll give the night nurse upstairs a call to make doubly certain he wasn't transported without the last shift's knowledge. In the meantime, please be patient."

While figuratively biting his lip before saying something he would most definitely regret—though surely enjoy in the moment—Wesley backed the chair away from the station, executed an about-face and slowly rolled back into an empty waiting area, where he parked between vacant chairs and stared up at the near-muted television, which currently showcased an old black and white rerun of the classic show *The Twilight Zone*. *Weirdly apropos*, he mused, gazing at the screen through badly bloodshot eyes. The tale featured, familiar but simultaneously vague, involved a bookish man—the actor, also recognizable but whose name escaped him—who, having emerged from an underground bank vault, was wandering about an apocalyptic landscape that appeared otherwise deserted.

"Mister Grant?" A nasally voice chimed in to break his trance, accompanied by the clicking of heavy boot heels against hard tile. A chunky man sporting a mustache that literally cloaked half his face and a light blue shirt that announced him as "G. Davenport—CFH General Security" soon sidestepped around the wheelchair.

"Yes sir?" Wesley replied, the guard's limp, hangdog expression all but preordaining yet another dose of bad news.

"You inquired, um, requested video footage of the last few, ugh, several hours from the ER to the lot, um, parking lot?"

"Affirmative."

The stammering guard shuffled his booted feet from side to side like an embarrassed toddler, though in reality he appeared to be well past at least his fortieth birthday.

"Unfortunate news then, I'm afraid, on two counts. First off, Nurse Leckner did in fact verify that no transfer has taken place. Um, as for the matter of, um, a taped history, I'm afraid the results are, um, similarly negative."

The wheelchair-bound man's frown spoke volumes, though he did feel the need to expound verbally.

"Well sure, why not? Why should this be any different?"

"Sir?"

"Forget it. Proceed, please."

"Well, our...the staff's sincerest apologies, sir, but you see, um, the video system currently in use is of the old, um, videotape type, not the, well, um, not digital. It seems, um, well, that the videotape in use...malfunctioned. That is to say, um..."

Wesley stared up and over the guard's balding dome to the TV, where, ironically, a commercial for an upright walker for the elderly was being shown.

"The tape that had been inserted was comprised, um, had wound itself around the inner spools at some point in the past several days. We're just not sure of the exact timeframe."

"So, there is an outside chance the tape will reveal something?"

"Yes sir, if...when it's repaired. Not to make excuses sir, but, um, well, we've...they haven't had any type of incident in several years that would ever warrant someone checking the, um, recordings. It became, unfortunately, a bad habit not to check the tape or simply, not record at all. I was informed, however, that regular tapings had been the norm for the past several weeks, once the...my parent company performed a recent spot audit. Sad to say, using the same tape over and over does tend to cause wear. Again, the staff apologizes for the delay."

The guard, his pale complexion damp with fresh sweat and chubby hands wringing with obvious apprehension, appeared on the verge of either giving birth or suffering a total collapse.

"It's okay...all right. I get it. Small town lack of technology. Lack of manpower. Then again, it's not every day one loses a paraplegic patient, now is it?"

He heard but did not see the guard's croaking gasp, his darting eyes briefly landing back on the mounted flatscreen, where the lone survivor of an H-Bomb had just broken his glasses while standing amid an island of books that would tragically go unread.

"N-No sir, I mean, um, well, that is to say," the guard sputtered while performing an impromptu break dance that gave the impression of someone who might soon pee their pants if a bathroom weren't found. "I couldn't say if we, I mean, th-they ever mispla—"

Wesley raised his hands palms out while backing the chair a half-foot or so.

"Water under the bridge, Officer Davidson."

"Davenport, sir," the other man voiced timidly.

"My bad. Tell you what, Davenport, can I give you my cell number in case the tape is repaired and reveals anything of substance or my friend magically teleports back here sometime tonight?"

G. Davenport practically fell about himself in agreeing to said terms, even going as far as offering to retrieve Wesley's Camry, a service which the wheelchair man politely refused.

Leaving the saggy—in both deportment and uniform—security guard with a stiff nod, he then rolled from the ER at much brisker pace than normal, a cold mist wetting his face and a steady stream of condensation trailing his path as his breathing labored.

Keying the door, he immediately began to justify the man's absence and why only one means of escape made any logical sense. Peeking around a mostly empty lot while backing the chair at a precise angle to allow the driver's door's full retreat, he doubled down on that being the only reasonable answer.

Dexter McCarron *must* have transported his hard-headed nephew home at the latter's insistence, despite doctor's orders. The paraplegic had, after all, spoken of time and urgency and how his every thought and action were accelerated before the former ran out. Gunther McCarron had no patience for even the slightest delay in his maniacal itinerary. As far as the man possessing any personal health concerns, the answer was obvious. What was supposed to be several days of hospitalization, perhaps even a stint in rehab for borderline sepsis infections, he'd sidestepped, never mind the open IV wounds littering both arms.

Departing the rain-slickened parking lot with a definite destination in mind, Wesley was tempted, albeit only slightly, to drive to a location in the opposite direction, pack a few bags and get out of town like his many lies claimed he had done days ago.

In the end, nervously gnawing his lower lip and staring unblinkingly through timed wipers—a light drizzle was sporadically intensifying—all such fantasies faded almost as quickly as the temporary yellow streak briefly lining his spine.

Departing an unmarked backroad onto a narrow two-lane leading back to Main Street, he was forced to steer the Camry onto the gravel shoulder to avoid a streaking bullet of a vehicle that had seemingly teleported into his path, blue lights and sirens blaring with equal ferocity.

Still lost amid a swirl of frenzied thoughts and theories, Wesley Grant had dismissed the speeding SUV with the Crimson Falls PD emblem adorning its driver's door, blissfully ignorant that occupying its back seat was his immediate supervisor, battered and beaten by none other than his ex-wife, a fact that, if known, would've surely refueled that initial urge to flee the town at warp speed.

Friday, 2103 hours

"Where did he last ten-twenty again? Over," Phil Strickland barked into the mic, the interior windshield of his assigned Durango layered in fog from his own emissions save for a perfectly circular space his elbow had created.

Before repeating the question—he cursed his own fading memory with the same level of wrath as that associated with one Mack "The Wrench" Bain, the department's Jurassic-era hired mechanic, who obviously knew jack about fixing defective defrosters—he gave the mic transmit button the perfunctory three-clicks to indicate the need for an immediate response.

"Donna said his last transmission was around sixteen-forty-five. Took five for coffee at the Honey-Badger. Where are you now? Over."

"Just off the Hazel Path cutoff. Gonna cover the usual route before I hit the backroads. Any word from the ER? Over."

"Donna's on the line with them now. Last we heard, he was in surgery for the collarbone break. Over."

"Copy that. I'll check in periodically. Let me know when that county badge arrives. In the meantime, keep trying to run down Jake and have him take routine patrol till I find Ears. Over and out."

"Copy. Will do. Be careful, Phil. God knows we're running low on commissioned personnel as it is. Over and out."

Idling at an otherwise deserted four-way stop, the muscular patrolman reached up with the point of an elbow to wipe away a fresh build-up of film, intermediate wipers doing the same with an outer buildup of light drizzle. He felt palpable relief in that Maggie had calmed at least somewhat and that Donna Early had maintained even a semi-level head in the aftermath of Sandra Jamison's rampage. He and Maggie had been over at his place, a bowl of freshly popped corn and chilled bottles of Bud Light adorning their respective TV trays as some generic romance-is-deadly flick played away on Lifetime—he had little to nothing to say in the choice of programming these days, it seemed—when Early's screeching SOS had blared over the scanner like a braying klaxon, despite the radio's relatively low volume setting.

It had taken them just over seven minutes to arrive at the station to find the man-mountain known as Will Crockett lying flat on his back in the PD building's foyer, a jagged shard of bone sticking out from his shoulder like a prison shiv carved from whalebone.

Jamison had apparently, and wisely, amscrayed at the sound of the approaching sirens, but not before delivering a hard stomp or two to the fallen chief's scalp and collarbone, leaving the big man fading in and out of consciousness like a KO'd pugilist, drooping, bloodshot eyes that opened and closed independently, bloody drool cascading from an equally crimson-shaded set of lower teeth and a half-dollar-sized knot on the left side of his skull, just above the ear. Before hauling Will into the back seat of his Dodge and heading to the ER at full bore, Phil had instructed Maggie and Donna to lock themselves back behind the reinforced door and call the county for assistance, as in a deputy to play guard at the PD in case a return to the scene of the crime was in order.

As for that missing perpetrator, Phil couldn't recall ever actually speaking in depth to Wes Grant's ex, though he did know of her rather eccentric past hobbies, or at least what *many* might consider eccentric. Being a confessed gym-rat himself since middle teens, he had a theory that coincided with the lifestyle he and the former Sandra Grant shared. Simplicity in itself, really. Roid rage, plain and straightforward. Toss in an overabundance of booze and/or chemical substance, be it legal or illegal in nature, along with whatever beef had brought her to the station to begin with, and you had yourself a cauldron full of potential disaster that had come to full boil.

"Gonna be hell to pay, pilgrim," he grumbled in his best (or worst, depending) Duke Wayne drawl, pulling straight through the four-way on his way to the Honey-Badger convenience store while simultaneously fantasizing about getting a crack at the mad sow who had so shockingly dismantled and busted up his mentor and friend.

Meanwhile, the task at hand. *Where the hell was Jerome Griffey?*

Friday, 2046 hours

Dexter McCarron, the brim of his jet-black Stetson serving as a mini waterfall as he leaned down to address the man sitting behind the wheel of the idling Camry, sounded as haggard and worn as the man behind the wheel presently felt.

"You ride by his place? Knowing that stubborn mule, he phoned a local Uber driver directly from that hospital cot, slurred words and all."

Wesley had pulled as close to Uncle McCarron's hacienda as possible without actually nudging the porch, headlights blaring high beams in the hope of drawing out its inhabitant without being forced to exit the vehicle and wrestle with the wheelchair for at least the third time that day.

"Figured I'd check with you first. Got to admit, I'm surprised he didn't call on you first for a means of escape."

"Hardly," the standing man replied wistfully, bending down until the two were eye-to-eye. "We didn't exactly part on good terms earlier."

"Well, you know Gunther. Better than anyone."

"Sometimes I wonder if anybody truly knows 'im, or ever did." The older man lowered his head, allowing a buildup of rain to stream from the Stetson's concave crease. "Or ever will. Guess maybe Wendy Hammock did, but it must've been exclusive only to her."

To this, the man behind the wheel simply nodded—a gesture unseen as the other man's head remained bowed for an additional ten seconds or more before a gradual ascent to reveal deep-set eyes beneath a slightly sagging brim...deep-set and haunted.

"You can guess. I told 'im to drop the amateur detective bit and take better care of himself or he'd soon be toes up from the stress. In retrospect, his reaction wasn't at all surprising."

"Told you to kick rocks, did he?"

"A tad more graphic, but yeah, that's the gist. Listen, Grant...," Dexter McCarron said, pulling himself upright, "...I'd ask to come along, but if it's a calming effect you're after, my presence is liable to produce the opposite result. Still, if you don't mind giving me a ring in the aftermath, I'd be beholden."

"Not a problem. Sorry for invading your space."

Backing a step from the idling Toyota, the man in black tipped his hat.

"Appreciate you letting *me* know. That little shit may not know it, but he has at least a few good-hearted folks concerned enough to track down his pig-headed rump when the chips are down."

"Yes, sir," Wesley replied with a nod as the driver's window slowly arose with a low hum. "Rest assured I'll put in a good word for *one* such fellow. I'll be in touch."

As he backed from loose gravel back to pavement, the increasingly harried driver secretly wondered if the role he'd been awarded in the potentially tragic, way off-Broadway drama currently on display was that of court jester.

Friday, 2105 hours

"Copy. Will do. Be careful, Phil. God knows we're running dangerously low on commissioned personnel as it is. Over and out."

Attempting unsuccessfully to clear the rasp from her voice via a self-induced cough, Maggie pushed the mic roughly away.

"Maggie?" she heard Donna Early croak from the record's office, the interior lights having been purposely doused at Phil's instruction, the front entrance double bolted by the patrolman upon his departure to the ER, their ailing chief in tow.

"You hanging in there, hon?" she inquired, without yet putting forth the effort to push herself from the dispatcher's chair, a high-back leather recliner that at times was far too hibernation-inducing.

"Hon wants to call it a night," came the reply in an altogether different voice, that of Cindy Lou Harrison, a late arrival to the proceedings, having gotten there just as the department's only remaining full-time patrolman was prepping to institute a full fortress lockdown of the PD building.

"I can only imagine," Maggie sighed, rubbing the clamminess from both palms onto the thighs of her faded blue jeans, the rest of her impromptu casual-day ensemble—literally as she'd dressed down for an evening of snacking and channel surfing—including a long-sleeve green tee and a comically oversized fur-lined coat her hubby had deemed "too snug" for his own ever-expanding girth years earlier.

"As soon as that county deputy gets here, we'll have him run you home, how's that?"

Maggie took the whimpering sob that followed as reluctant acceptance.

"Can't let you walk out of here alone, Dee. You understand that, yeah?"

"Y-yes. That...woman could still b-be o-ut there...waiting."

"Exactly."

"Mag, didn't Jamison seem, well, *off* to you yesterday?" Cindy Lou inquired after a brief silence.

Sitting in almost total darkness save for the glow of the console's dual computer screens, Maggie was secretly appreciative, as her sarcastic grin might've been misconstrued if witnessed in full light.

"If your definition of 'off' includes eye-rolling, teeth-grinding psychotic tendencies, *affirmative*. Episodes like this remind me of all the textbook bipolar off-their-meds cases of the last few years, or more recently, when sucking down bath salts was all the rage."

She heard Cindy Lou gasp.

"Oh lord, *yes!* Like that Reynolds boy's suicide a few years back, right?"

"The bath salt kid? Yeah, prime example, I'd say."

"He-her eyes were weird. Like, I d-don't know. Unfocused," Donna whimpered. "Blood red and darting around like rolled marbles. And her voice was...trembly. It...s-shook. I knew, right from the get-go, that she was troubled. But I...never...never dreamed it c-could...and the poor ch-chief, he naturally underestima—"

Cindy Lou broke in just as the day dispatcher's voice cracked anew.

"Tiny's gonna be *fine*, Dee. Don't you fret about him. The big guy's taken hits before, right Mag?"

"Affirmative," the youngest of the three women replied with a cringeworthy level of enthusiasm, the instant wave of regret in doing so instantly forgotten as a series of sharp static squawks caused her to openly flinch and nearly execute a backflip from the recliner.

"CPD dispatch," a voice chimed in from the Intertalk console, the source obviously female, "Deputy Jill Ferguson. I was instructed to park at the back of the PD building and await entry through the rear entrance. Over."

Swallowing hard, Maggie retrieved the mic with quaking fingers.

"Loud and clear, Deputy Ferguson. Please proceed to the door and someone will meet you momentarily. Over and out."

Minutes later, the county deputy—short, stocky and a young woman of very few words—stood before the threesome of local CPD employees and listened patiently as Donna Early struggled to provide details of the missing perpetrator's attack while utilizing the word "terrorist" at least as many times as she paused to wipe her leaky nose with a handful of tissues.

Even as the painfully young county cop was explaining how she was not permitted to leave the premises until further notice, thus dashing the day dispatcher's immediate hopes of a protected ride home, Maggie had slunk back to the dispatcher's console.

"Unit th...Phil, the county deputy is here...on-site. Over."

For one terrible, paranoia-fueled instant, she feared continued silence from the other end, sighing with tangible relief upon that worry being eliminated via the partially broken, most mundane of responses.

"...loud and clear, headquarters. Everyone just stay put for now. Over."

"Where are...what's your twenty-three? Over," she inquired sharply, as much out of irritation at the veteran officer's bland, uninformed response as her own curiosity.

"Just departing the Honey-Badger and headed toward Main. Any word from Jake? Over."

"He's on his way. Was over in Sheffield at his daughter's place. ETA is fifteen to twenty minutes. Over."

"Okay, Mag. When he gets there, send him over to Gunther McCarron's folks' place. Over."

"Ten-four. And your destination is?"

"The Wes Grant abode. Over."

Forehead creased, Maggie paused, lips atremble, before properly forming the words bubbling forth.

"Wes...why Wesley's? Over."

"Well, what better place for that crazy bi—the suspect to be loitering? For all we know, Ol' Eliot Ness Griffey has her cornered like a feral cat over there and just needs the proper netting. Over and out."

"Keep me posted, Phil. Over and out."

Reluctantly discarding the mic with her right hand, Maggie began to simultaneously gnaw on the pinkie nail of the left, pondering the almost cataclysmic events—at least by Crimson Falls standards—of the past several hours: Not one but two missing persons, one a CFPD officer no less, a domestic terroristic attack on the PD building and its employees, the end result being a chief of police being hospitalized by the most inexplicable means possible, and with the person responsible—equally perplexing—having successfully flown the coop. It was, as Wesley was apt to say when sharing a particularly bizarre and/or entertaining slash lurid incident report, "You can't make this stuff up," or the equally apt "Real life is always stranger than fiction," each of these well-worn chestnuts usually precluded by a "You're not going to believe this one..." Toss in the fact that the individual responsible for the aforementioned terroristic siege was none other than her friend and co-worker's ex-wife and also that the friend in question was suddenly, *unfathomably* if you took into account his usual Boy Scout-honest persona, playing the role of international man of mystery, and the veteran dispatcher couldn't help but feel she'd dropped smackdab and face-first into an old episode of *The X-Files* by way of *Twin Peaks*. Blast Dan and his retro TV-watching habits, she mused silently, the whispering, barely audible voices emitted from the records office doing little to pull her from the self-imposed daze, though the familiar voice that soon blasted from the console radio did just that, nearly to the point of making her bite bone-deep into her pinkie finger.

Jake Douglas' deep drawl always sounded as if he were transmitting from within one of the many caverns in and around town.

"HQ, it's JD. Come in, over."

"Park in the back, Jake, and we'll let you in through the rear door. Over."

"Ten-four, HQ," came the static-filled retort, followed by an earache inducing serving of feedback, a reoccurring annoyance unique only to the part-time patrolman, as if he'd somehow copyrighted the sound of a snapping electric guitar string as his personal sign-off.

Despite the retired CO's droopy-dog appearance and equally listless deportment, not to mention a glaring lack of enthusiasm for the job as a whole, Maggie couldn't help but feel a measure of relief at his arrival. If nothing else, she deduced, at least he hadn't either mysteriously vanished or been bludgeoned out of commission.

Friday, 2102 hours

Wesley's eyes—burning from the gradual onset of fatigue—squinted and scanned between intermediate passes of the Camry's windshield wipers for a hint of illumination within the McCarron home's picture and bathroom windows, respectively.

He'd briefly considered trekking to the back of the house and, if similar darkness reigned through the lone kitchen window, banging on the back door entrance as a last resort. Something—a gut feeling, a premonition, basic instinct—advised against it as just more wasted time while the same mysterious, nontangible "something" was warning that there was little time to waste. The house was pitch-dark and graveyard quiet at just after nine PM, thus the odds that its sole legal occupant sulked or slept within its shadowy interior were highly unlikely, regardless of his rundown condition.

At five minutes past the hour, Wesley backed from the drive and drove not toward the city limits but instead further and further out from them, the cold, windblown rainfall alternating from light mist to intermediate sprinkle as the Camry's low beams cut through a slight but building fog.

A sixteen-minute-plus trek atop a mostly deserted two-lane state highway brought him to a destination he hadn't at all planned on traversing while parked in the driveway of the McCarron home, at least not consciously.

By the sparse count of parked vehicles in her lot—a couple of mid-size Nissan or perhaps Kia SUV's, a newer model black sedan of unknown make and an aged Ford pickup with a badly faded blue paint job—he could only assume The Prize Sow was nearing last call, but a sudden, almost painful jones for a hot cup of joe and piece of whatever pie was on special was not to be denied.

It was nearing a quarter to ten by the time he'd unloaded, unfolded and then piled onto the wheelchair, his clothes damp and his hair thoroughly flattened by the falling moisture.

Upon entering the relatively empty establishment—the place had seemed so small just a day earlier when it was packed to overflowing—he was greeted and subsequently seated by a haggard-looking, middle-aged waitress who didn't even bother to feign joy at his late arrival. As with his earlier visit to the Sow, he found sliding into the booth was made considerably easier since the seat and his chair shared nearly the same exact height.

An order for coffee and cherry pie—the lone survivor of the night's baked desserts, according to the listless server—duly placed, he sat in relative silence save for the faint sounds of a Country Western tune flowing through the overhead speakers and, while scanning the eatery's murky confines, began to mull over his options for what remained of the evening.

Turning to his left, he took little note of the older foursome conversing quietly two tables over, nor did he afford more than a passing glance to the two much younger, not at all unattractive and snappily dressed women sharing chortles and beers in equal measure at a spot nearest the entrance.

Briefly distracted by inexplicably lewd thoughts involving the latter pair, who appeared to have overshot whatever Louisville dance club they'd intended to frequent, he was forced to right his gait—the wheelchair parked snugly against the well-padded booth with its wheels locked firmly in place and thus serving as the perfect weapon of leverage—in order to properly turn his head and scan the rear of the business without falling face-first onto the hardwood floor.

Upon doing so, the dimly lit back booths initially showcased little of interest, that is until he executed a textbook double take in an attempt to verify what he'd initially deduced simply couldn't be.

A tint of light from one of the few overhead strobes still illuminated had landed upon a narrow strand of circular material of possible metallic origin. A sleek black cane adorned with assorted straps that wound around an equally slim appendage, both of which appeared more than a tad familiar upon a second, more focused and lingering look.

"Gunther," Wesley heard himself whisper, lower jaw hanging agape. "Well, I'll be damned..."

"Sir?" he heard someone inquire from what sounded like an impossibly long distance.

"Here you go, sir. Um, we do close in ten minutes," they continued to prattle before slowly blinking out like a radio station just out of range.

"Y-yeah, thanks," he heard himself mutter in response, clueless that the scowling waitress had long since dropped off his order and walked away, an order fated never to be consumed. Pushing the chair back for optimum reloading ease, searing gaze never departing the source of his fascination, Wesley wasn't at all accustomed to such flying-by-the-seat-of-his-pants behavior, though in the past several days he had grown more comfortable with it. Once situated in the chair, he initially rolled it directly toward the back booths before braking less than a dozen feet from the next to last of these and the lone occupied one. From the current angle—he'd remained as close to the passing booths as possible as to limit visibility of his approach—he could just make out the edge of the individual facing in his direction.

A black male with short, graying hair in a button-up, checkered plaid shirt and blue jeans gestured spastically over a saucer and cup to the unseen shape. The man, bespectacled and soft of voice, moved his hand from side to side and then up-and-down as he spoke, as if relaying a detailed oration of great importance. Through this hissed, inaudible dialogue, the audience of the sermon remained mute and thus Wesley was forced to roll several feet forward until he was even with the booth next to his objective in order to gain the verification desired. As he was practically brushing the booth's outer edge in order to remain unseen, Wesley gained no further visibility but was able to hear at least a spattering of the so far one-sided exchange.

"...was no usable DNA. The lab...ash...so far. As for...bribe's...nonsense. I, well, I resigned voluntarily...Hammock nothing...with it. Four and...years and...wrong profession. You can...check background if you want....the next...decades...at Dell compu—...and I'd rather...seek whatever harassment...for your...such...accusations."

The next voice to chime in—its volume cranked up a degree—was all the verification Wesley would need, though more was provided in the form of a pale hand hanging limply off the side of the table, a black strap constricting the thin wrist beneath.

"I've read the reports. Several times. I just needed to hear from you, face-to-face, that what's typed on those pages is the honest to God *gospel*. I can only take a man's word after all, and I gotta say, ya do seem sincere enough."

There came a short pause, a frightening few seconds where the chairbound sleuth could easily envision both men leaning just far enough out of the booth to uncover his amateurish attempt at subterfuge. Instead, the mysterious stranger spoke up, his words still maddeningly clipped.

"I had...motive to lie. As far as...Hammock or...'kay, I did interviews...both...as others. I detected...tell-tale signs...dishonesty."

"Noted. As long as we're bein' so upfront, I gotta admit on doin' some research of my own on your life the past decade, from leavin' the force less than six weeks after that particular case, to takin' college courses and then the gig at Dell, right in the middle of the PC boom. Nice timin' that."

"But still, you suspect...of some type...'gal and unethical...payoff?"

"Not from all that, certainly, but a Google Maps' glimpse of that mansion of yours did kinda pique the private detective gene in me. Ya gotta admit, that is one glorious spread for a computer geek."

"IT paid well enough."

"Those are million-dollar digs, pal. Maybe a quarter mil, considerin' my lack of knowledge on today's market prices."

The stranger's words, though still partially redacted, covered more ground in terms of reach as his voice box cranked the volume a decibel or two. Hearing it then, a rich bass no longer masked by the cloak of whispers, Wesley felt a brief but intense surge of *déjà vu* that evaporated almost as quickly as it had arrived.

"Well, if...that inner sleuth had done...job, he would've learned...family inheritance, a good portion...which I used to build...as the surrounding grounds. Satisfied?"

"More by the minute."

Yet another worrisome pause, this particular one motivating Wesley to back the chair almost to its original pose before bravery had trumped cowardice, the familiar voice's final clear salvo still easily comprehensible.

"Tell ya what, let's just move past that mess and, well, now that we have, I hope ya don't mind me askin' you for some sage advice, what with you easily bein' the wisest person at the table by a country mile."

As the other man had regressed to a low muttering, Wesley decided the time was right to make his exit. He had debated, though very briefly and with little enthusiasm, calmly rolling up to the pair's table to rudely interrupt, if for no other reason than to witness the looks on their respective faces, especially that of Gunther McCarron. A cooler head had effortlessly prevailed, and as he executed a graceful turn and commenced to wheel himself toward the exit—this after dropping a twenty on the table as he passed, his waitress regarding him with a pinched expression that hinted at lingering constipation—his next move had already been mentally set in stone.

Minutes later, having backed the Camry into a far corner of the lot, the front end narrowly clearing the front of twin metal dumpsters with the majority of the vehicle sufficiently hidden from the front of the business, Wesley leaned forward with elbows propped atop the down-shifted steering wheel, his scalp newly moistened from the never-ending tears of a perpetually crying sky.

It had been almost ten full minutes since he'd reentered his vehicle, folded and packed away his chair and secured the hiding spot, the last five of which he'd spent weaving and wobbling through a murky minefield of long-lost memories, before, like the blaring screech of an ambulance siren, it came to him.

Just like that, the stranger sitting opposite of Gunther was thus a stranger no longer, this sudden Eureka moment birthing less a feeling of relief than that of rock-hard knuckles to the soft underbelly.

Glancing at his wristwatch as the front entrance/exit to The Prize Sow pushed outward to evacuate the two men he'd planned on stalking from the grounds, Wesley leaned forth and stared through the thin film of precipitation coating his ride's windshield. The skeletal figure leading the way hobbled, leaned and half-stumbled his way off the planked porch, his familiar slouch intact, while shambling forth onto the combination gravel/dirt lot, as was the trademark beret.

As for whether he'd been correct in identifying Gunther's guest and most recent chauffeur, that being the tall, thinly built gentleman who followed three steps behind, the Crimson Falls

Police Department's senior records clerk could only groan aloud through a squinty, pained grimace, the type of glower so rarely generated in light of being proven absolutely accurate.

Friday, 2115 hours

Phil Strickland could not recall, at least in his formative adult years, the previous eleven of which had been spent wearing the silver and blue badge of the Crimson Falls police department, ever having experienced what others might refer to as "the willies." In fact, he had no memory of enduring a similar phenomenon, i.e., "the creeps" or any such variation since grade school, when he and a buddy had sneaked and subsequently camped out in Butler's graveyard on Halloween eve.

That night, he'd awoken from his sleeping bag well past midnight and could've sworn he'd seen the grass-covered mounds below several gravestones throb and pulsate to life, as if those long-relegated to worm-dirt status were rising up for a little witching-hour boogie. Upon discovering that his pal had long since beat feet, eleven-year-old Phil hadn't required coaxing to depart post-haste, not even bothering to gather up the sleeping bag or the cigarettes and lighter he'd snuck from his father's dresser drawer earlier in the evening.

Twenty-six years and counting since he'd sprinted barefooted and horrified from the town boneyard, Phil was reliving the moment, or at least a very similar facsimile of it.

A check of Wesley's house had yielded exactly zilch with nary a sign of life or, for that matter, light. Compounding the bizarro vibe, Jake had radioed just minutes earlier to pass on a mirror image of non-information from Gunther McCarron's place.

Nearing Main Street on the western side of town, Phil executed a U-turn at the town circle—nearly clipping the base of a homemade banner exclaiming *"GO WILDCATS! Purrrrfection is just a win away!!"* on his way to the medical center, specifically the ER unit.

Navigating a desolate Medical Boulevard at roughly twenty miles over the posted forty-miles-per-hour limit via the basketball-sized semi-clear spot his elbow had provided just moments earlier, his lips parted with a specific series of curse words in mind for a certain ace mechanic when the console cracked with static.

"Phil, what's your twenty? Over."

Thick arms bulged, gloved hands tightening their respective grips on the wheel.

"Medical Boulevard, less than a minute from the hospital. What's up? Over."

"Domestic situation at one-oh-six Dalton. Over."

Sighing, the muscular, no-neck patrolman groaned disgustedly, his left thumb levitating shakily over the transmit button. He'd foolishly assumed any call transmitted to his unit would involve a Sandra Jamison spotting.

"Send Jake. Over," he instructed hollowly while slowing to execute a U-turn at an approaching four-way.

"Jake's currently working a minor crash in the Piggly Wiggly parking lot. Over."

Maggie sounded as keyed-up as he currently felt, if that were even possible.

"Ten-four. On my way. Could you or Cindy call and check on the chief's status? Over."

"Just off the line with ER. He's out of surgery and will spend the night in recovery. Over."

"Good ol' Tiny," the veteran patrolman whispered without yet transmitting an official reply. "Never gonna hear the end of having your ass thoroughly drop-kicked by a member of the weaker sex, big guy, never mind the chick in question answering to the alias of Queen Kong."

"You get that, Phil? Over."

"Ten-four, Mag," he fired back, the grin more a toothy wince as he wheeled around a narrow, paved island and headed back the same way he'd just come. "Glad to hear it. No word on brother Jerome's whereabouts, I take it? Over."

Though he knew the answer, there it was, figuring that eventually the law of averages, i.e., Murphy's Law, dumb luck, etc., simply *had* to reverse field in their favor.

"Negative. It's like both he and Sandy Jamison fell into the same black hole as that Briggs fella. Over."

The mic parked at his lips, Phil was temporarily struck speechless by the possibilities.

"Now don't go all conspiracy theory nut on me, Mag. Did the deputy run Donna home yet? Over."

"Negative. Donna's requested to stay put for now while Deputy Ferguson has volunteered to take some local calls if we need her to do so. Over."

Ferguson? Phil nodded knowingly while stopped at the red light at Oak and Main. *Oh, yeah, short but not unattractive little ball-buster with an okay bod and wicked smile.*

"Appreciate all the help we can get, I mean, as long as you and the other gals are okay with being left alone at the station. Over."

"We...gals can manage, Officer Strickland. Besides, there's already been a couple of random calls hinting at possible vandalism-related shenanigans over at the school later tonight. Over."

"Rumor control? Over."

"Could be. Just BOLO for any unfamiliar caravans of out-of-town teens cruising our turf. Over."

"Let me guess. Juvenile delinquent types hailing from the mean streets of Dawson? Over."

"Rumor has it. Over."

"Not unexpected. Have the deputy take it if such an incident arises. I'm nearing the Harrison residence on Dalton now. Over and out."

"Careful, Phil. Karla said Rex has been guzzling Beam since noon. Pre-game celebrations and all that. Over and out."

Two clicks of the mic ensued to end the report, and as Officer Phil Strickland exited the rain-slicked Durango, the flesh of his pale cheeks instantly assaulted by gnat-sized spears of sleet, the bitter pill he crushed between tightly gnashed teeth had little to do with the impending struggle with one of Crimson Falls' best-known town drunks. The Dalton Grove trailer park was surprisingly quiet for a Friday night, save for the usual suspect(s).

"Damn *ballgame* anyway," he spat, hitching up his uniform pants and landing the palm of one hand on his taser while rearing back with a clenched fist toward badly stained, imitation cherrywood with the other.

Friday, 2153 hours

As the sleek sedan with Fayette plates backed ever-so-briefly into his line of vision—its driver bathed in partial shadow on his way to off-load a lone passenger—Wesley received the second official verification of what he'd known all along back at the Sow.

He'd watched with building ire as Gunther had struggled so mightily from the passenger's side into a cold drizzle to trek with obvious difficulty toward the side of the house, ultimately vanishing into the murk, having nearly toppled over numerous times.

In the aftermath, as the sedan executed its exit, it had taken all the restraint he possessed not to lower the driver's window, extend both hands outward and flash a double middle-finger salute to its navigator. As it was, he waited until the darkness had consumed the glow of the other vehicle's brake lights before cutting the Camry's engine and prepping for departure.

A kitchen light shone through pulled drapes as he neared the back door entrance, the door just slightly ajar.

"Come on in, partner," Gunther announced from inside just as the chair's foot-rest bumpers tapped the entrance. "I swear, between you and me, it's like watchin' a couple of dry snails creep up a greased pole."

Still decked out in full exo-gear, the host stood with his back to the door while scooping coffee from a can into a filtered brew basket, his left leg extended and noticeably crooked and limp as if he were attempting to trip some unseen assailant.

Clearing the entranceway, the guest reached back and pushed the door to a firm seal.

"You know, McCarron, for a deathly ill cripple, you are one hard man to track."

"I can be a burden," the other man replied with a soft cackle.

"You don't say? Not to sound like a mother hen, but shouldn't you still be lying flat on your back with multiple IV fluids as the meal of the day?"

"Yeah, I most probably should, but as you can see, I've clearly strayed from the itinerary."

"Clearly. Not exactly adding calendar days to the old life expectancy."

"Life expec..."

Whirling around with surprising grace, the crooked leg executing an amazing, if not accidental, textbook leg sweep, the host's pale, gaunt face was a creased mask of pained indifference.

"And what *quality* of that life am I cuttin' short exactly? Saaay, let's cover the highlights, shall we? First off, how's about the joyous stench and rash-appeal of peelin' off soiled diapers three, four times a day? Pesky, annoyin' as hell, I'd say, but nothing compared to the carnival ride that is being lit up like a fourth of July sparkler by the alternatin' of throbbin' and pulsatin' from the neck down to, without warnin' mind you, a numbness so complete you could be used as a human pincushion and wouldn't have a clue?

"I'm still debatin' what's worse, the bouts of pain so excruciatin' you wanna find the nearest gun barrel to swallow or a full-body deadness so complete you start thinkin' you've already died and your brain just hasn't got the email yet. Yeah buddy, nothin' like livin' to a ripe old age while growin' *riper* every day, am I right?"

"Gunther, I get it, okay. We've covered this ground—"

"Oh, I beg to differ!" the host railed, head tilted so severely to the left it appeared it might snap free of its freakishly narrow stalk. "Sure, the ills are similar, grant ya, but ya see, while you've been a holy roller for the past how-many years, I'm still a relative virgin to this whole walkin' veggie thing. But hey, guess I should count my blessin's, right?" he paused to gesture—the movement weirdly stiff and robotic, like a mechanical device whose battery life was running precariously low—with the flat of his right hand in a downward sweeping motion as if to indicate the whole of his frame. "I mean, what if I'd been unlucky enough to wake from a fourteen year coma at say, year six or seven? No magical bionic duds to strap on, no battery-charged limbs, no upward mobility, no movin' from point A to point B like some doped-up, barefooted rock climber scalin' a glacier wall. *Yeah well, he looks goofy as hell, but at least he ain't bein' wheeled around like a torso-shaped turnip in a wheelbarrow,* they whisper in that sickenin' tone that's supposed to be sympathetic but usually comes out soundin' at least partially disgusted at the very sight.

"So, short story made *faaar* too damn lengthy," he concluded with a slight bow of both the head and knees—a sort of motorized half-curtsy—as if awaiting a stage curtain to descend, "I've come to accept that *quality* and *life* are no longer compatible terms in this present existence. Nine short months ago, I took it all for granted, no denials. Sure you feel the same, pal, or at least to a degree.

"Anyway, that was then and this is now, right? Old me wasn't a goal-setter, obviously, and underachieved in spades.

New me, a veritable shell of his former self, is carved from a different rock altogether. Ya see, I awoke with a clear goal. It's a whopper, I'll admit, but then, I've always heard nothin' hard in this world comes easy. This goal, it's my only reason for being. It's how I tolerate the shit-show daily life has become. It's how I made it through the grueling rehab sessions. It's how I find the strength to wake up, suit up and forge on, when there's little to no motivation to do so otherwise. It's why, at least I believe, I was given another chance.

"You take cream and lots of sugar, correct?" he concluded, turning his back stiffly to the seated man, who had taken in the prolonged rant with his stubble-coated chin resting atop an upturned, clenched fist, like a wheelchair-bound version of The Thinker.

"Precisely. Pretty decent memory for a walking, talking radish," Wesley replied, resigned to having had the fire previously churning in his gut soundly doused.

The host went back about his java-brewing duties, his slightly bent back revealing the bones of his ribs and spine in such defined detail it appeared they might tear through the fabric with any additional stress.

"Nice. So what may I do you for on this fine Crimson Falls evening, Monsieur Grant?"

"Seems you hitched a ride from the ER, highly unauthorized, I might add."

"Worry-warts were dead set on a minimum two-to-three-day admission. Out of the question."

"Merciless money-grubbers."

"Bingo. Two-to-three days, my bony butt. More like a permanent booking. Anyway, what's done is done."

The seated guest hesitated over exactly where to steer the conversation, that is until his curiosity a mutated into a maddening itch he was fated never to scratch without immediate assistance.

"I caught a glimpse of your new chauffeur. Can't say I appreciate being canned without notice, boss. Personally, I thought we had a good thing going."

The host took a single step back without turning, the coffeemaker commencing to gurgle with surprising gusto.

"Don't yank my chain, Grant. You know damn well who *and* why."

"Eli Tanner, I presume."

"Eli Tanner, you presume correctly."

"I read his report. Still fresh in my mind, in fact. Saw his photo on some of the master-file crime scene pics. Other than a receding hairline, the man has aged remarkably well in the past decade-plus."

"Agreed. Probably due to his exitin' the law-and-order business while still a young man."

"So you just casually rang him up after all these years and he dropped everything to assist in your escape from medical incarceration? Seems a bit far-fetched."

Twisting his neck until the right side of his face was briefly revealed, Gunther flashed a smile beneath curled lips, showing square, peg-like teeth that nonetheless appeared strikingly predatory.

"You might *think,* but not once I explained my plight. 'Sides, he spends several months a year caretakin' his folks' old place out in Vine Hill."

"Convenient. So...," the seated guest sighed, head slightly tilted and eyes narrowed, "...as far as your investigation goes, what was the takeaway from this little chat?"

"Tanner seems an upstanding enough dude. One of the few I've run across, present company excepted a'course, with even a thread of integrity."

"Meaning?"

"Check off one former state investigator from the list as far as a knowing conspirator goes. I just needed to hear it from his own lips, face-to-face and not over the phone or texted or even emailed. The man looked me straight in the eye and answered every question without hesitation. No part felt rehearsed. I believe *he* believes every detail he's always claimed as fact."

Turning back to the suddenly noise-free java-brewer, the host took a stiff, draggy step forward and commenced lining up a pair of cups and saucers before reaching with a trembling right hand for a nearby glass container filled approximately half-way with powdered sugar.

"Seemed like a real rarity these days, kinda like an authentic bigfoot sighting, that bein' an honest man completely void of agenda. I have to assume he held the same traits fourteen years ago while totin' around a gun and badge."

"Good to hear. So who *does* remain on the aforementioned list?" Wesley heard himself say and instantly regretted having pulled the verbal trigger on that concluding series of words even as they cleared his parted lips.

"Well, I'll tell ya, partner, and I'm not real sure how to feel about it just yet, but as of this moment, it's whittled down to a nub. Lemme see now," Gunther paused, a spoon-filled left hand briefly lifted airborne as a point of emphasis, the silver utensil shaking so severely at times it seemed destined to take flight. "In order of suspicion: *Old Scratch* Hammock and his pseudo-satanic offspring...check. Coach *Big Man on Campus* McKay...check, though the ink of that particular checkmark has grown dang near transparent. The big three, essentially, well, to be fair to Farty Marty, we'll make that two and a *half*. Former State of Kentucky Police Investigator Eli Tanner did nothing to either add or subtract from that number, though he did manage to eradicate several collusion-type plots involvin' those already mentioned. So, to fairly answer your query, there remains but one name in my own personal police lineup."

"Let me guess. The first CFPD officer on scene."

The host's narrow shoulders flexed inward as the sound of a spoon clinking against porcelain could be heard.

"Awww, but you know *better*, Wesley. Officer Jeremy DeJoy crossed the river Styx 'bout halfway through the duration of my coma. One of the first police reports I purchased, courtesy of the Birmingham PD, the city from which he passed. The death investigation stated a nasty, prolonged battle with the big C, colon-type at the relatively young age of sixty, less than four years after his retirement from the Crimson Falls force and barely two since his relocation back to his home state. 'Sides, motivation wasn't just severely lacking, but nonexistent."

"Now that you mention it," Wes nodded, unable to refrain from cracking the slightest of smiles which he was able to reel in upon his host's turning to lock eyes, the latter moving toward the dining table with a cup and saucer balanced in each upturned palm and with the cautiousness of one trekking on tiptoes over a live minefield.

"Jeremy, or *old Joyless* as he was so fondly known, did pass on far too young. Think he hung up the holster about a year or so after I was hired on."

"Uh-huh. Thought so," Gunther replied smugly while managing to lay down both saucers with nary a spill. "Java is served."

Steering the chair at a right angle, Wesley parked at the table's western edge facing his host, who took a seat in one of two high-back chairs only after a dozen or more mandatory adjustments to the suit to allow manageable freedom of movement.

"So," Wes resumed, following a quick sip and subsequent grimace at the fresh brew's considerable bite, "since the late Officer DeJoy has been officially eliminated from suspicion, who exactly *does* that leave remaining in your crosshairs?"

Sipping quietly from his own raised cup, thin tendrils of smoke rising to briefly cloak the cold stare beyond—all hints of his usual mischievous spark strikingly absent—Gunther took a full thirty seconds to respond, as if contemplating a perfectly worded reply.

"Wes, you've been a godsend to my crippled old ass since day one," he said in a harsh, raspy whisper that was eons removed from the tone used just moments before. "Don't even want to think what I'd have done without ya these last few days. I couldn't have expected more from my own kin, that bein' poor ol' Uncle Dex, who isn't nearly as patient or tolerant of what he called, just today mind you, my *unbalanced* ways. So to this...," he paused to raise a shaky cup airborne and tip it his guest's way, "...I'm eternally grateful and in your debt."

"Not a problem, Gunther," Wesley nodded amiably in reply. "Glad to be of ser—"

"Let me finish, please," his host chimed in unapologetically, the steely, distant stare only intensifying. "It's high time, past time, to part ways. At this point, this *juncture*, I'm not gonna drag you any further down the cavern-sized rabbit hole I've tunneled out since comin' back to town. Wouldn't be fair. Wouldn't be *right*. Believe me, what you don't know from here on out you don't need to know. I might come off as a callous, selfish a-hole, and justifiably so, but collateral damage just ain't acceptable, especially if said damage involves one of the few people I've come to trust since crawling outta purgatory."

Pushing the saucer and cup aside, Wesley crossed his arms defiantly while attempting, in vain, to match the mega-force of the other man's stony, unyielding glare.

"What wouldn't be fair at this...*juncture* would be leaving me groping for answers. I think I deserve to be—

Backhanding his own half-full cup off the table and into a far corner, where it literally exploded into a brownish mist upon impact with the tile flooring, Gunther's tone remained surprisingly stoic and controlled in the aftermath.

"So you think my sneakin' outta that ER room like an escaped con was just some reckless, jackass whim? In my estimation, I'd already dragged you shoulder-deep into the cesspool but it took collapsin' into a quiverin' heap to realize you didn't deserve to be buried any further than ankle-high at most. You *live* in this town, man. You make a livin' in this town. You have to continue livin' here, remember?

"You'll be blackballed and shunned by some just for bein' seen with me. Don't think for a second that the word ain't already out. Small town gossip spreads faster than the clap in a cathouse, and you know it. If nothin' else, as I've only known ya for a few days, consider it payment for services rendered. You can tell 'em ya just felt sorry for a fellow gimp and that even though I was as loony as Daffy Duck on crack, you just couldn't turn down a man so obviously on his last legs."

"Last leg...? Not if you start taking care of yourself, dumb ass!" Wesley shouted, tossing both hands in the air and gesturing wildly as if swatting nonexistent flies. "You're committing suicide by idiocy, like you've no intention to survive this...this damn *witch hunt* whether it concludes to your satisfaction or not!"

The delayed reply arrived via a noticeably softer tone.

"I appreciate the passion, and more so the genuine sincerity behind it, but ya see, my...this resurrection was never about my livin' a long, rewardin' span as the town robo-cripple. I was brought back to solve a mystery and I intend on doin' so before breathin' my last. Otherwise, it's all been for nothin'."

He paused briefly to catch his breath—nostrils flaring and jaw hanging agape—but resumed just as Wes started to reply.

"Make no mistake, as egotistical and obsessive as it all seems, I at least want *you* to know that it ain't really about me at all, at least not the largest slice. Selfish horse's ass as I've been, or *was*, I can't really say I deserve to rest in peace, but Wendy Jill Hammock sure as hell *does*."

Chuckling, Gunther scanned the kitchen through haunted eyes, dark bags having formed on an otherwise ghostly-pale visage.

"Guess I'm not quite as self-centered as my pre-crip days, or I'd surely let ya go down with the ship. Now do as I say, Wesley Grant, and keep your distance. You'll be glad ya did."

His lips parting and resealing several times, the guest eventually rolled slowly toward the entrance, angled the chair to allow sufficient clearance and pulled the door ajar.

"How are you going to get around?" he asked calmly, the wheelchair halted halfway through the opening.

"I still got family here," came the reply, the source now openly straining to finish even the shortest of sentences. "'Bout time I pulled the kinfolk-guilt card on that stubborn-as-a-mule uncle of mine."

"Definitely a McCarron trait awarded at birth," the departing guest concluded, pulling the door shut behind him.

"Hey Grant!" he heard clearly enough despite the barricade between them, turning his head in the direction of the door.

"Yeah?"

"Don't forget to check those headlines in the morning!"

"Wouldn't miss it!"

"Go Wildcats!"

For once, the chaired man's smile was one-hundred-percent sincere, despite the myriad of dark thoughts coursing through his mind like a fast-spreading virus.

"Go Wildcats!"

While backing from the driveway as what appeared to be a light mix of flurries and sleet pecked the Camry's windshield, its dashboard reading 2233 hours, Wesley Grant had no choice but to allow a tidal-wave of full-body exhaustion to batter his slumped form full force.

In the overwhelmingly grim aftermath of what he'd just heard, he foresaw no probable conclusion that didn't include the word tragedy.

Even worse, this sudden flash of horrific precognition spared no one of consequence, least of all himself.

**From the *Crimson Falls Gazette* Sports Page
Dated Nov. 21**

*Wildcats 10-0 after a decisive 44-16 win over Vine Hill's Gladiators
(Friday night, Falls Field)*

Riding a 170-yard, three touchdown night by Dalton Crane and three interceptions by the secondary, Crimson Falls cruised to a four-touchdown victory over Vine Hill (4-6), who suffered their fourth straight loss. Viewed as a tune-up for next week's crucial rivalry game against Dawson High, the Red Raiders improving to 9-1 following Thursday night's 45-0 whitewashing of Carver High, the December 4th contest at Falls Field will mostly likely decide the state playoff representative.

Eleven

"Chief, you sure you're up to this?"

"Yeah, big guy. You really should be on your back pumped full of pained meds."

"They got a point, Tiny. Considering you just went under the knife less than twelve hours ago, I mean, this can't be good for the healing process."

The chief—the left side of his neck heavily bandaged, a similarly padded wrap attached to his bruised scalp, and the connecting arm in a sling—alternated weary, droopy-eyed glances at the trio standing in front of his desk from behind heavily tinted sunglasses, the latter effectively hiding the sore, swollen shiner beneath his left eye.

"Maggie, Officer Strickland, Officer Douglas, I appreciate the sincere concern, if not the amateur diagnosis. Yeah, I've felt better, but I've had worse. A plate, couple of screws and a steel rod later, and I'm good to go, or at least good enough for government work.

"And sure, normally I *would* be sacked out with Jessica or one of the kids tossing assorted opioids into my mouth at regular intervals, but you understand...," he paused, pushing himself upward with a pained grimace from the deep, comfy confines of the leather recliner he'd so effortlessly sunk into upon his arrival at the station a half-hour earlier, "...there is nothing *remotely* normal about a missing peace officer under my supervision, nor the station of which I'm in charge falling under siege and the attacker still roaming free. So, all that said, I'll happily forego any further medical advice, at least for now. What about the BOLO on Jamison?"

"County and statewide," Phil Strickland confirmed, gesturing with a single nod of his square head in the general direction of the records office. "Aggravated assault on a police officer, assault via intimidation, resisting arrest and felony vandalism. We can even add evading at this point, multiple counts. Um, boss, about the media. Rick Green and Janice Watkins are gonna have a cow once they find out we shut them out of this thing."

"Don't I know it. I...hedged about whether to involve them or not. Went back and forth on it a half-dozen times in between oxy-assisted naps, mainly because I wasn't sure we shouldn't warn the public about her still being at large. In the end, I decided to treat it as interdepartmental, at least until she's collared," Crockett replied, flashing a feeble thumbs-up with his gloved left mitt. "If and *when* she's cornered and netted, I have a sneaking suspicion we'll be adding numerous drug offenses as well. It was like, I dunno, like she'd snorted a tub full of coke and chased it with an anabolic 'roid shake. Strong as a brahma bull and bat-guano gaga. Maggie, make a note we need to get Chuck Barron and his repair crew in here no later than tomorrow AM to place a sizable bandage on the lobby. Gonna need dry wall work and some fresh paint.

"We don't want to open to the public on Monday morning with the place resembling the aftermath of a barroom brawl. Talk about raising suspicion. At the very least, we're gonna need new lobby chairs. Jake, we'll see about picking some up from city hall, at least until we can get some new ones ordered. Don't let me forget between medications."

To this, both the dispatcher and part-time patrolman simply nodded confirmation.

"As for the good folks over at the *Gazette*, they don't need a whiff of any of this, not yet anyhow. Not on the eve of the biggest night this town's seen in a decade-plus. Everybody clear?"

All nodded silently in unison.

"Good."

Walking around the right corner of the desk with a slight hunch and pronounced limp—the trio backing clumsily away to allow clearance—Will Crockett, infamous for wielding the power to maintain his composure no matter the issue or storm level, hitched his uniform belt while straightening nearly to his full height, which was at least four full inches higher than anyone else present.

"Phil, I'll be riding with you. We'll resweep Jerome's last known locations. Jake, procure the aforementioned chairs and then you get with the county boys and assist 'em as best you can on covering some of the lesser-known back roads, especially near the lake. Maggie, you and Cindy stand by for the state badges and send 'em our way once they arrive. It goes without saying that while our main priority is finding Jerome, everyone should keep an eye pulled wide open for a certain shiny, black SUV and the emotionally unstable and physically daunting suspect behind the wheel."

"Chief?" Maggie asked, hand raised timidly just as the others had moved toward the door with their shuffling leader.

"Maggie?"

"Shouldn't someone...focus on locating Wesley as well?"

The big man turned, albeit unsteadily, as the others filed out quietly past him.

"We've issued a BOLO for his Camry along with the SUV, Mag. We...*I* realize the potential dangers he's facing better than anyone. Don't forget, though, obvious disability aside, Wes was once law enforcement." The big man paused, a smile that was at least half-grimace emerging as he reached up to apply a light tap to the gold badge hanging from outside his brown suede jacket. "The way things are going, once we do sniff 'im out, I might end up swearing 'im in out of sheer necessity."

The chief's lowered head and narrowed eyes screamed potential scolding, though it never materialized, replaced instead by an exasperated sigh.

"Sorry I didn't...come clean sooner about his being back in town, or at least *allegedly* being back," Maggie said with the type of shrug a small child might exhibit in the aftermath of an accidental blunder.

"Let's just say it was that alleged part that fueled your hesitation and leave it at that," he concluded with a tip of a nonexistent Smokey the Bear cap—a narrow white bandage taped to the back of his head serving as a poor substitute.

"Thanks, Will."

"Maggie?"

"Sir?"

"I'm worried about 'im too. We'll track him...we'll track them *both* down."

"Yes, sir. I have no doubt."

The big man cocked a brow.

"Well, maybe just a little," she said tentatively, displaying the thumb and forefinger of her right hand with just a half inch or so of space between them, "and Will, it...that scares me. It scares me a lot."

"Same here, it's natural. Stay sharp."

"You too."

"Go Wildcats."

"Go Wildcats."

The chief, his voice so raspy it sounded as if he were speaking into an oscillating fan set on high, inquired one final time, his considerable shadow still visible stretching down the narrow hallway leading, eventually, to the front lobby. "That is...tonight, right?"

"Affirmative, Chief."

A resounding sigh, followed by the familiar echoing of heavy boots thumping hard tile, though noticeably less forcefully than usual.

Relieving Cindy Lou at the dispatch console a few moments later, the rest of what remained of CFPD having departed the premises, Maggie strapped on the headset and leaned back with slender arms crossed.

Never one for premonition, she'd slept fitfully if at all the previous night, as if somehow knowing for certain that Jerome Griffey *would not* be found and Sandy Jamison *would* still be on the loose come dawn's early light.

Thus, upon arriving at the station at just past five-thirty—a full hour earlier than usual and a full ninety minutes from the start of her shift, there had been little shock in the discovery that she'd been correct on both counts.

Busily gnawing a pinkie nail while sitting in the semi-dark as the clock above her station read straight-up eight AM, she was struck by a series of similar portents for the foreseeable future, the very least of which involved the high school football team's chances in that night's big rivalry game. Strange, she mused, how what had been looked upon just twenty-four hours ago as a major happening had been reduced to a less-than-trivial blip on the radar.

In a perfect world, both Jerome and Wes would be found unharmed and even amused at the level of panic they'd caused, followed by a resounding Wildcat romp over the visiting Red Raiders as dusk gave way to dawn.

As it stood, Maggie Childers would gladly settle for two out of three.

Saturday, 0805 hours

"Re-read it to me, again," the slumped man whimpered, forehead resting atop the table and bare, pale arms hanging limply on either side.

"Why bother, Gunny? It's only gonna serve to exasperate," the man sitting on the opposite end of the dining table—currently adorned by newsprint and semi-drained coffee mugs—replied morosely, his fingers staining the paper he'd haphazardly spread apart with perfectly laid prints shaped from bacon grease.

"Just need...verification that...," the other managed by talking exclusively through the right corner of his mouth, "...what I read w-wasn't just these fa-failing eyes playin' cruel...tricks."

"You sure you're comfortable? Looks painful."

"Sometimes...comfortably numb...f-feels d-dang good...after ten or...twelve straight...hours of bein' strung up...like some kinda...electronic wind-up...puppet."

Upon arrival at his uncle's pad—the elder insisting he do so upon dropping by his nephew's house at the break of dawn and bearing witness to his ultra-pale appearance, delayed reactions and slurred speech—Gunther had insisted the exo-suit be removed and his limp form be propped at the dining table, even though his uncle had at least thought to haul the only sporadically-used wheelchair along.

"Read...on, p-p-pl-please," he choked out just before a series of wet coughs ensued, wherein his limp form shook and shimmied so severely his elder was forced to lean up and prevent him from sliding sideways out of the high-back chair.

The older man did so only when convinced his audience of one could remain upright, even moving his own chair closer in case of a sudden relapse before bowing his head beneath the brim of a black Stetson and reluctantly commencing as requested.

"'Local Man's Miraculous Return and Wild Accusations Prompt more Questions than Answers' by Janice Griffin, *Falls Gazette* editor in chief."

"Ja-Janet," the slumped man blurted so weakly as to barely rate as audible despite an almost deafening silence.

"Bingo. So from there she goes on to say:

Following an almost otherworldly awakening from a fourteen-year comatose state in which he was given little chance to survive, a local man has returned to the scene of what, at least he insists, is the scene of a most heinous crime. Gunther McCarron, now aged forty-four, had only just turned thirty when near-fatally wounded at the scene of a horrific accident, as defined by both local and state author—"

"E-enough," the hunched man chimed in, twisting a disturbingly thin neck until he faced to the left, sunken eyes staring unblinkingly toward a far wall.

"Guess I...it wasn't my...imagination af-after all. De-deceived be m-my middle...name."

"You do come off sounding a might...unstable. Not exactly what she promised, I gather," the man decked out exclusively in black save for a pair of brown leather ostrich boots replied, discarding of newsprint in order to scoop up his coffee mug, the once-steaming contents now barely lukewarm.

"Story of m-my life wi-with the chicks. Well, s-save one, anyhow. Lousy backstab—she didn't drop a single...n-name 'cept mine."

The man in black responded only after a noisy sip and subsequent sigh.

"A conspiracy-to-commit-murder story that was directed at the town's beloved coach on the day of the big game? Really Gunny, you know better. As for Hammock, he'd sue that rag right out of business for slander."

"Y-yeah, well, she seemed to make it a...point to paint m-me...o-out some kind of n-nut-bag...freak of na-nature wh-whose brain didn't full...fully resuscitate."

With a final gulp of overly-cooled java, Dexter McCarron pushed the empty mug to the edge of the table and, refolding the special Saturday edition of the *Crimson Falls Gazette*—his misguided nephew's "story" found on page seven of eight, as page one and three subsequent pages had showcased a preview of that night's Wildcats-Red Raiders matchup—leaned back with arms crossed and dark brown eyes narrowed.

"So, what next? As if I *really* want to know."

"Plan B, Dex. Or is it...C or D? Hell, who cares?" the bent figure muttered, lips foaming a fine line of drool onto the table cover.

"You're fast running out of alphabet, Gunny. So plan B is?"

"Dex, I need you to set up a couple of web-net pa-pages for me."

"Web...pages?"

"Affir—yeah, webpages or webcams or whatever...they call it when ya videotape yourself...and preach a...sermon. Facebook, Tube-Youth, Tweeter."

"I think it's YouTube and Twitter you're groping for, nephew, and how very sad that you're forced to come to *me* for tech support."

The right side of his face utterly plastered to the table by his own puddled spittle, the younger McCarron executed a strained, half-grin that his uncle instantly recognized as being similar to that of an old Batman comics villain known as Two-Face.

"Desperate...times call for...s-similar measures. G-got to...spread the word somehow. G-go straight to...the people. W-what better way to...sn-snag someone's attention?"

The older McCarron groaned aloud, his normally stony visage creased with severe dismay.

"Oh, I see. Open slander in a public forum. What *could* go wrong?"

If the younger man could've casually shrugged to go along with the warped half-grin on display, he surely would've.

Saturday, 10:09 hours

Phil Strickland yawned behind a gloved hand, his haggard facial features temporarily cloaked by a rising cloud of whitish vapors. At his side stood, not quite but closer to fully erect than anyone in his current state of agony had any right to claim, Chief of Police Will Crockett, his bald, bandaged head bowed as a thick forefinger jabbed away at miniscule cell-phone keys with surprising accuracy.

The chief stepped gingerly from the modest ranch home's lifted patio into a front yard in desperate need of a shave from a buildup of winter sedges, the tiny phone stuck to his right ear effectively concealed by the oversized paw holding it in place.

"Honey, I can't be calling you back every five minutes, okay? I'm holding up fine," he said without even the slightest effort to lower the naturally thundering bass of his voice. "Now I understand the concern and I do appreciate it. You know I do. Listen, I'll give you a ring as soon as it's feasible. Yes, hon. Tell Will Junior and Samantha that the king still owns the throne. Love you too. Bye."

Sighing, he turned stiffly around to see that he and his senior patrolman were alone at the front of the house, the two state troopers that had accompanied them to the Grant property having vanished to parts unknown.

"Maybe he is holed up in some mountain cabin after all. Camrys are a dime a dozen," Phil said, meeting his boss halfway while using the flat palm of one hand to deliver an extended, vigorous rub to his own chin.

"As *could be that* or speculation-fueled *maybes* go, you think Jerome got an invite to the same cabin?" the big man replied stoically as the pair trudged toward the right side of the home over semifrozen weeds that crunched beneath their boots, eventually stepping atop aged pavement leading to the rear of the property.

"I dunno, boss. I got nothing. It's like the kid has literally vanished from the face of the earth, or at least well past the county line."

"Got to tell you, Phil," the chief replied between teeth-gnashing grimaces that coincided with every jarring step, "that Briggs kid on a milk carton is one thing. Wes is still another, but Jerome is something else altogether. The first MIA and last seen at Dexter McCarron's, the second on official sabbatical, the third several hours into a routine shift."

The heavily muscled patrolman nodded, fighting off another yawn before replying.

"That last one being nothing less than Mr. Dependability. Jerome is admittedly *Cap-pa-tan* Overzealous at times, but he's never been known to show up late or go AWOL, just stopping short of calling into dispatch whenever he had to take a dump."

Sidestepping deep tire ruts just off the pavement, their upturned edges still hardened from the previous night's hard freeze, the pair had just begun to clear the far rear corner of the house when both troopers dashed hurriedly past back toward the front.

"Sorry, Chief," the lead one, tall and lanky, offered in passing. "Got a five-car crash near the Adams exit."

"Roger that, ETA is roughly ten to twelve minutes," the other, shorter and stouter of build, was barking into his shoulder mic while sprinting past and barely avoiding tripping over the top edge of the deepest rut's curved ridge.

"Hey Chief, we'll radio in to see if HQ can provide a substitute or two, but it might not be until this afternoon's shift change," the taller trooper concluded, the roar of the gray Stingray's engine nearly drowning out the final few words of dialogue.

Watching the sleek ride vanish past a steep curve just off to the left of the property, the chief and the patrolman grunted almost in unison.

"Well, so much for that," Phil grumbled, twisting his head around to briefly eye the detached garage some twenty yards to their south.

"No matter. Another four or five hours and I'll be calling in the feds anyhow," the chief said, locking both thumbs into his utility belt and, turning stiffly, scanning the surrounding property with the same level of apathy as a grazing bovine to a passing train.

"Same route, rinse and repeat?" the stocky patrolman inquired, nodding sluggishly toward his assigned SUV, which he'd parked just past a post-mounted black mailbox reading "W.GRANT" in gold lettering.

His boss, momentarily teetering on the edge of heading in the general direction of the garage, instead joined his equally lethargic subordinate in retracing their steps to the front of the house.

"Most likely for now, but I would like to see someone, be it us or Jake and the county boys, expand the search zone to at least a dozen miles or so past the county line on all sides."

"Maybe the feds have a chopper handy. Sure would cover a hell of a lot more ground and with a much wider view."

Departing the grounds minutes later, the patrolman behind the wheel nearing thirty hours without sleep and his heavily medicated passenger, barely fourteen hours removed from surgery to repair a badly shattered collarbone, each shared a vague vibe that something vital had been overlooked, though neither had either the energy or confidence to share such a sentiment.

Saturday, 09:17 hours

"That's all there is to it? Damn. So you're tellin' me any idiot with a mic and web connection can play internet star that fast an' easy?"

"Sadly, yes. If I can figure it out, it's definitely not imbecile proof. You sure you want to broadcast this? Not too late to pull the plug."

Dexter McCarron leaned back from the office chair, a computer mouse cupped in his right hand, the PC monitor he'd faced featuring an extreme closeup of his nephew's glowering image frozen in place.

"Nice choice of words, Dex," his nephew quipped with a playful wink gone horribly awry once the lid stuck in place for a full two seconds, his voice so hoarse as to be almost unrecognizable. "And no, there's...no backin' out. It ain't like I'll...be around to be held accountable."

"You don't *know* that, Gunny," the older man shot back sharply, using his free hand to push the brim of the Stetson far enough back from his forehead so both his squinty eyes and exasperated expression were available to full view. "This is full-on self-destruction and it can stop *anytime* the user decides to blow out the fuse and simmer down. Believe it, I know of what I speak. Nothing like personal experience."

Propped on the couch—held up on either side by taped cardboard box bookends, having refused to redon the exo-suit for filming—Gunther tilted his head severely to the right, his cheeks expanding dramatically in preparation for the lengthy sigh that followed.

"Ya know, for a man...of few words...lately you've...become quite the...blabbermouth. Now, press...play, if you will. I want one...last preview before...worldwide web...publication and the inevitable power nap...that's just around the corner."

"Fine," the older man grumbled, sliding the chair back and to the left while granting his nephew's wish. "But when my living room fills with lawyers, I'm claiming full ignorance."

With that, the video footage—the younger McCarron viewed in close-up, his uncle actually leaning unseen behind the chair with a loose grip on either of his nephew's biceps to prevent him from sliding off in either direction—commenced, the audio surprisingly crisp.

"As this is my video debut, let's start with proper intros. My name is Gunther McCarron, paraplegic private eye (grins broadly) and I reside in the sleepy Kentucky town of Crimson Falls. I'm currently forty-five years of age, though I probably appear a hell of a lot older. Not exactly in the best of health, but I guess that's self-explanatory in gazin' at me, right? (laughs, coughs)

I have only recently, like in the last week, returned to the town of my birth after a fourteen-year hiatus. A rather forced hiatus at that. Gotta say, the old stompin' grounds haven't changed that dramatically, least not as much as yours truly.

Now, before I dive into the grisly details of what left me lookin' like a paler version of the Crypt Keeper, I want to give a special shoutout to a pair of Crimson Falls' finest, both of whom I hold at least partially, if not fully responsible, for why I ended up this way. Kerry Hammock, former mayor of our fine city and as corrupt and ruthless a som'bitch as I've ever run across. They should erect a statue of this soulless bastard in the town square holdin' a pile of blood-smeared cash in one hand and a severed head in the other, the former symbolizin' all the wealth he's obtained through the multitude of lives he's ruined and the latter all those he's cut down in the process.

Not to sound overly bitter, but if they assign seats in hell, you should have a monogrammed, front row recliner waitin', buddy boy.

Secondly, I can't overlook the local livin' legend that is Shannon 'Bull' McKay, gridiron great and longtime head coach of our beloved Wildcats, who just tonight are shootin' for a state playoff berth against the hated Red Raiders of Dawson High. Go Wildcats! (coughs)

Mac ol' pal, let's just say it's a good thing the majority of the population in these parts didn't know ya back in high school and those early, formative years before you backstabbed your way from lowly assistant to head honcho of the program. Ya see, those of us who witnessed the dark side of Mister Gruff-but-Loveable ain't liable to be believed amid all those who adore that won-loss record, but that don't change what we know. What we saw. What I suspect. You might wear the white hat on Friday nights, McKay, but a select few know the black one fits ya much more naturally.

But hey! Who am I but a slowly wastin' away stack of rotting bones and spoilin' meat, held together by the miracles of medicine and not much more, to speak ill of such renowned, well-respected men, right? I'm just another victim of my own self-created bad breaks, livin' the nightmare of his own makin', green with envy over the mess I've made of my own life.

To digress, I wasn't always the pale, shriveled, ghostly waste you're currently gawkin' at. I was once, not very long ago at all in my own mind, but a decade and a half in real time, a roguish, strappin' son of a gun with an appetite for mischief. Hadn't yet found my callin' but wasn't afraid to dip my toes into whatever adventuresome scenario came my way. Then one night, within the span of a scant few minutes, I was transformed into the withered carcass ya see here. Details to follow in my next installment. What few details I can honestly recall, that is. Part two will also include my personal take on former Mayor Kerry Hammock's lone offspring...the unabashedly perverted, severely twisted, bat-like entity known as Martin Hammock.

Now, I'm not gonna sit here and wallow in self-pity. Waste of time and, truth be told, it ain't like I wasn't askin' for a big ol' shiner from fickle fate, or at least testin' the fringes of what she might bring. I ain't blameless nor completely innocent.

Then again, it's damn probable somebody gave me a push down that little ol' express escalator to hell. Could be somebody wanted me out of the way bad enough to take drastic action. Fatal, final action, ya might even say. But then, that same somebody didn't expect me to about-face and start back up the escalator, now did they? I mean, what are the odds of someone lyin' prone and lifeless in their own slowly deteriorating shell for fourteen winters actually comin' to with a semblance of who they are and, much more vital, what they were brought back to do? Slim and none, yeah? Only (tilts head dramatically to the right, right eye winks) ya see, None just left the building, boys, and Slim is juuuust gettin' started in diggin' up enough dirt to cover ya both up to the neck. This is Gunther McCarron, your investigative gimp, signin' off...for now."

"So, give it to me...straight, Dex," Gunther inquired, head so severely bowed it appeared his chin rested atop his bony chest, droopy, sunken eyes upturned toward his uncle, who, upon the video's conclusion, had twisted the chair around to face his nephew.

"Just under five minutes of open baiting. You can be sure it's gonna raise some eyebrows amongst the locals, not to mention the ire of those targeted."

"My goals exactly. Now, how do...we make sure all of the above...bear witness to my little sermon?"

"Gunny, this is a mistake. I can't reiterate that strongly enough. You're bringing hell down upon yourself."

"I don't...expect to walk away...scot-free, Dex, pardon the...pun."

"So even more pain, both emotional and physical, is also the goal?"

"Collateral damage, I'm...afraid, but not without securin' the...ultimate reward in...the process."

"Gunny, you're apt not to be around long enough to reap *any* type reward."

"You may be...right. Can't say I'm all that...confident of wakin' up from the influx of...day naps these days. If and when the reaper does...snatch my hide, at least I can...kick the bucket knowin'...I tried. Just post the video, Dex. I'll...I whole-heartedly accept...the circumstances and I...promise not to...drag you into the...quicksand...once it reaches neck level."

"Last chance to listen to reason."

"Damn...the torpedoes."

"Facebook it is. No quicker way to reach the people than the *Crimson Falls Festivities* page. I would think it might hit record numbers, what with the pregame and all just hours away."

The paralyzed man practically beamed.

"Hot damn and pass the pigskin. Go...Wildcats."

Saturday, 1021 hours

Maggie leaned forward with her elbows resting atop the console, steam from her third cup of brewed caffeine from the fields of Columbia rising in billowy streams to fill her nostrils.

"Jake and the two deputies are over near the county line just past the Hammock property. So far, not much to report except for a quick detour to write up a fender-bender off the old Hawk's Bend cutoff. Over."

The chief's reply, similar to his overall tone, was ripe with fatigue. Maggie couldn't fathom how the man was sitting upright, much less in his third-plus hour of morning patrol.

"Ten-four, Mag. Keep us posted. We're headed out to the Mill Creek fork and then back into town. Everything appear copasetic within the limits this fine Saturday morning? Over."

"So far, it's church-mouse quiet. Let's pray it stays that way. Over."

"Fingers crossed. Out."

"You stay safe, Chief. You too, Strick. Out."

As she sipped cautiously from the recently micro-nuked mug, Cindy Lou wandered in from the adjacent office, dragging a high-back chair behind her before collapsing into it. The older woman's hair was a thoroughly ruffled bird's nest, her heavy-lidded eyes the envy of basset hounds everywhere. Appearing—and no doubt feeling—every day of her sixty-plus years, she regarded her young co-worker with a pained smile as weary as the drained voice that followed.

"They'll be fine, Maggie. Phil's a big, strong boy and I'd take an injured and doped-up Will Crockett over most sober men in this town in a fair scrape. Besides, we don't know for sure foul play is involved."

"You can't truly believe that Sandy Jamison's raging bull act isn't somehow tied to Jerome's disappearance?" Maggie replied, the deep frown creasing even her normally flawless features to something close to unrecognizable. "You heard what Donna said. That...screeching moose actually got the best of the chief. Tiny Crockett. I would *never* have thought that possible."

"Well, never underestimate the element of surprise or insanity-driven ferocity," the older woman nearly whispered, head bowed forward and hands lying palms up within her ample lap as if in deep meditation.

"Or the power of whatever hallucinogen that crazy bitch was tripping on."

Cindy Lou nodded agreeably, tossing in one final salvo before the dispatch phone sounded-off to disrupt the banter.

"Guess all that extra weight she put in the last few years disguised all the muscle still lurking beneath."

Before taking the call—her third since the beginning of shift, the first two about dogs running loose—Maggie's upturned brows spoke of her apparent agreement with the veteran clerk's sentiment.

"Crimson Falls police dispatch, how may I help you?" she asked flatly, her "professional" voice obviously set on a sort of robotic autopilot in wake of the multitude of distractions present.

Unlike the effect of even the stoutest cup of java, what she heard spewed from the other end of the line stretched her eyes to their maximum wideness even as she turned to her co-worker and gestured wildly toward the headset.

"Well, yes sir, if you'd like to speak to an officer about filing a re—" she began only to be cut off in mid-stammer as Cindy Lou took up a kneeling position beside her and leaned in, in a futile attempt to eavesdrop.

A full thirty seconds passed, during which time Maggie had simply leaned back with mouth agape and forehead severely creased, before a sufficient break in the other party's rant eventually allowed for an uninterrupted response.

"I'll certainly have an officer phone you as soon as one becomes available, as currently all are out and about on active patrol. Yes sir, and your cell number is?" she inquired blandly enough, though her animated expression conveyed the exact opposite as she leaned forward to type the caller's phone number into a newly opened call screen.

"Yes sir, I understand. Will do. Yes, and...go Wildcats, right...back at you. Goodbye."

"What's with the charades, Mag?" Cindy Lou inquired, still squatting as the dispatcher rolled the seat back while simultaneously removing the headset and tossing it onto the console. "I couldn't hear a blessed word!"

"Apparently, we need to check out the Facebook Falls' Festivities page for a recent video share," Mag said, standing while digging frantically into a front pants pocket for her cell.

"Facebo—who was it, Maggie? Geez, you're killing me!" the stocky senior whined, struggling to regain her feet before dashing unsteadily from the room to acquire her own communication device. Meanwhile, her younger, substantially thinner co-worker's right forefinger moved at warp speed back and forth atop the surface of her just recently purchased Apple iPhone12.

"None other than the former Mayor Mac-Big-Cheese himself, Kerry Hammock, sounding rather displeased with this recent video post. I'm talking resoundingly peeved."

"Found it!" Cindy announced with the gleeful excitement of a teenaged girl at least five decades her junior. "Come check it out on the PC monitor!"

Huffing, Maggie was hunched over the records monitor mere seconds later, as if magically teleported.

"Hey...," she muttered, barely audible, her eyes at first squinting floss-thin but gradually widening to their maximum contour as the pallid visage of the frighteningly thin host swam clearly into view. "...That's the crip—the paralyzed guy that came in earlier in the week for a background check. McCarron. Gunter or Hunter or something. You know, the comato—"

"Shhhh, listen!" Cindy Lou scolded, cranking the connected speakers to their maximum volume.

As if bearing witness to a live news broadcast of earth-shattering revelations, the two city employees stared in silent awe as the sickly man in the beret possessing an equally ill-sounding tone resumed sermonizing:

Now, before I dive into the grisly details of what left me lookin' like a paler version of the Crypt Keeper, I want to give a special shoutout to a pair of Crimson Falls' finest, both of whom I hold at least partially, if not fully, responsible, for why I ended up this way. Kerry Hammock, a former mayor of our fine city and as corrupt and ruthless a scumbag as I've ever run across.

"Uh-oh," Cindy Lou Harrison mouthed, pausing the video just long enough to regard her co-worker while donning a half-smile, half-frown hybrid that did little to quell the mischief-fueled gleam behind both her baggy eyes.

"You better *know* uh-oh," Maggie responded with an equal, if not surpassing, level of scamp-like merriment.

Less than three full minutes following McCarron's tirade, comically entitled *"Gimp's Corner: Dishin' the dirt on deserving scumbags, Part I,"* and before the ladies could properly begin to dissect or review its shocking content, the shrill ring of an incoming call intervened.

Crimson Falls Wildcats head football coach Shannon McKay, he of the gruff demeanor in the best of times, commenced to telephonically verify an even grumpier deportment in the face of what he deemed a clear case of "out-and-out slander."

Saturday, 10:37 hours

Wesley Grant lay sprawled atop the disheveled bed, his wavy hair equally unkept, the underneath of each eye sporting pronounced bags birthed from both a discernable lack of sleep and ever-increasing levels of stress.

Upon receiving the pink slip from Gunther—as unexpected as it was abrupt—he'd instinctively known to avoid the homestead and instead had driven the nearly eighteen miles northeast to the sleepy hamlet of Booneville, where he'd secured a single room at the town's lone lodge for weary travelers, the fittingly monikered Rest for the Weary motel. He'd even thought of somehow ditching the Camry for a rental before dismissing the notion as ludicrous and overly paranoid. True, Sandra was out there somewhere, sniffing him out like a bloodhound on a 'coon's trail, but thus far he'd managed to zig-zag and weave off the beaten track just enough to avoid her, well, other than that chance meeting at the ball field, where he'd managed to temporary sidestep potential disaster with the verbal tapdancing skills of the compulsive liar he was certainly was. This, he realized with no small amount of trepidation, was but a temporary respite. The whole, terrible thing was coming to a head, and soon. Sandy was in full runaway freight mode, a terrifying state he'd only witnessed one other time in their lengthy association, and one there was no reversing once effectively stoked. Casually resigned to this, he'd sought diversion for what little time remained.

Though deep REM sleep had been mostly elusive, he'd nonetheless remained bedridden for a full ten hours before venturing out for morning coffee—the room, as barebones as one could expect for twenty-nine bucks a night, did not offer either a java maker or anything resembling a continental breakfast—at a nearby café. While there, he'd been both shocked and pleasantly surprised to discover an actual newspaper dispenser in working order and a copy of the *Crimson Falls Gazette* Saturday morning Special Edition, no doubt offered this particular date not only in Booneville but county-wide for the most obvious of reasons. The headline screaming out in bold on page one said it all: *"It's Wildcats versus Red Raiders for all the state playoff marbles!"*

"So much for that promised exclusive," he whispered in a voice that sounded scraped raw with fatigue. "It appears Little Miss Scoop specializes in misleading her informants. Wise decision, actually. Nope...can't blame her one iota. Avoiding slanderous lawsuits isn't about cowardice as much as it is common sense. Let's see now...," he muttered, flipping listlessly through pages filled with more ads than actual newsprint until he'd reached the next to last page, "...oh, what's this? Shazam. Seems there *is* an article buried in there amidst all the want ads, Piggly Wiggly meat specials and Dollar General holiday doorbusters."

Upon perusing Janet Griffin's article, which clearly read more as an indictment of Gunther McCarron than of those he accused, Wesley calmly folded the dozen or so pages of the exclusive collector's edition into a neat four-sided square and laid it across a nearby nightstand.

"Well, well, what *now*, Gunther?" he lipped, barely aloud and inaudible to all but himself within the cramped four walls. "What to do when the present-day Game of the Century trumps your tragic tale of the past? Where to *go*, what to *do* when the chosen bait never quite reaches the trap."

Peering over to a far corner within his less-than-spacious digs—basically one squeaky bed with semi-clean sheets, a single wooden table lamp, slightly stained ottoman and twenty-inch plasma TV offering basic cable and little else—at his only partially folded, two-wheeled chariot, Wesley briefly tinkered with the notion of the great escape. As this particular fantasy was hardly anything new and usually involved similar plot devices: i.e., discarding all current material possessions, gassing up the ride and heading out to some tranquil, faraway paradise filled with nothing but friendly, unrecognizable faces and beginning anew with the only limitation being that of his imagination, *blah blah blah*, it was just as quickly discarded with the inclusion of a single line first extracted from the ultra-wise musings of the fictional movie character Buckaroo Banzai, "Wherever you go, there you are."

"Just a handful of hours till kickoff," he said softly with a quick glance at a nearby digital alarm clock's yellowish glow.

"Let the games officially begin."

Saturday, 10:45 hours

Chief Will Crockett leaned as far over as the recently bolted, tightly bandaged collarbone would allow, staring unblinkingly at the iPad propped atop his knees.

To his left stood Officer Phil Strickland, staring over his boss's broad right shoulder to eye the video on display through noticeably drooping eyes, the dark underneath of which appeared to have been smeared with black grease.

To his right and peering over the big man's opposite shoulder stood Kerry Hammock, arms crossed and periodically flexing jaw muscles working overtime.

Standing stiffly in the background stood the homeowner's ultra-buffed, no-neck chief of security, his own expression one of badly disguised apathy, as if on the verge of a jaw-stretching yawn.

The four men occupied the Hammock home's living room, a space that Phil Strickland had, upon initial entry, secretly deemed large enough to easily accommodate the whole of the entire police department's first floor. Sporting not one but two black leather sectional couches and a trio of similarly shaded recliners, walls adorned with assorted water, oil and pastel paintings—limited expertise aside, Strickland deduced none had been purchased at the local Walmart or Michael's—the room appeared spotless, neat and predisposed to even the most extreme checklist of OCD standards.

"I knew he couldn't leave well enough alone, but never figured on full-on slander within a matter of days," the homeowner exclaimed once the video had ended and he'd retrieved the iPad from the chief, who arose with a helping hand from his longtime subordinate.

Kerry Hammock, decked out in a river-blue shaded, slim-fit button-up plaid shirt, light brown chinos and red flip-flops, his brownish/gray hair slicked back and shining from whatever hair gel provided maximum hold, was, despite his words, perhaps the coolest, calmest example of pent-up rage the two law enforcement officers had ever seen.

"Well, truth be told, Mister Hammock, it hasn't quite qualified just yet," the chief replied once he'd steadied himself upright without his cohort providing support.

"Wait, wait, hang on...," the senior by at least a decade and a half of those present retorted with a shade more vigor than with previous annunciations, though he was still remarkably composed, considering the level of tension, "...he clearly just referred to me, for all to hear, as corrupt, evil and, most insulting of all, the offspring of a female canine. Did we all just witness the same vile dialogue?"

"Indeed we did," Phil agreed, gracefully allowing the chief to fully catch his breath. "Problem is, at least legality-wise, McCarron didn't expound any specific claims to which you might object. Now, that isn't to say we won't be having a talk with him about the possible ramifications of airing such...dirty laundry in a public forum."

"Harassment has many variants in this era of technology, Mister Hammock," the chief chimed in, already moseying for the door in a noticeably wobbly gait. "Officer Strickland and I will effectively warn Gunther McCarron against any future segments and of your displeasure and willingness to press charges if need be.

"The charge of slander is a civil, not criminal, matter. It would, of course, be your prerogative, to pursue the matter."

"I'll need to file an official report to do so, I take it," Hammock said coldly, watching the patrolman follow his superior's trail toward the front entrance.

"I would advise it, yes, if you are planning on pursuing the incident in court. Come by the PD next week and we'll fix you up," Strickland said, hitching his belt beneath the bottom edges of his jacket.

"So you'll be speaking to McCarron *today*?" Hammock's voice echoed from beyond a square foyer that separated the entranceway from the perimeter of the living room.

"We'll do our best, Kerry. We are...short staffed at the moment, but rest assured we'll find the time to visit the McCarr—'"

The voice that so rudely interrupted what was to be a parting of the parties no longer bothered with the charade of politeness or even reasonableness. It was the voice of someone used to doling out orders without the fear of refusal or rebuttal or even the slightest push back or hesitation in carrying them out. It was a bullying voice, a voice laced with an arrogance built from a lifetime of belittling without fear of retribution.

"Find the time *today*, Chief Crockett, as in within the next few hours. I'll await your call that the deed is done. You have my cell number. Don't dare think you or your...short-staffed department can sidestep or delay the issue. You were in my employment once, Will. You know I don't waste my time with casual bluffing."

Even as Will Crockett had pulled the door closed and planted a booted foot on the cold asphalt beyond, he twisted around—grimacing at a sharp stab of pain—in time to see Phil Strickland's shoulders tense, jaw constrict and eyes narrow just as the bulky patrolman executed an almost textbook about-face.

"So tell me, Mister Hammock, what is your personal take on *why* McCarron would level such hateful insults your way? I mean, what's the history between you two?"

"History, Officer?" Hammock's voice inquired after a short pause.

The two men then met roughly halfway, the uniformed officer presenting a purposely obtuse deportment as to deflect the gauntlet being tossed into the short, nylon carpeting between their respective feet; the homeowner, oppositely, revealing his obvious disdain at the question via a pained scowl that served to reveal his actual age.

"Yes sir, *history*. I mean, folks don't normally toss around words like corrupt and evil or, well, talk about another man's mama without some bad blood having arisen between 'em. Now, being that McCarron basically just crawled out of his grave after fourteen years in the coffin, I can only assume whatever did come between you happened while you occupied the mayor's office."

"Officer Strickland, was it?" Hammock queried, one arm crossed with the elbow of the other propped atop it, his cleanly shaven chin—the room reeked with Aqua Velva or probably a more expensive variant—resting on a clenched fist.

"Correct."

"You know what they say about the word 'assume'?"

"It makes an ass out of you and me, yes sir, though in this case it would be very useful for our further investigation to know what you think triggered Gunther McCarron's ire."

"Nothing I haven't already divulged, Officer. I can only chalk up these baseless attacks as part of his blaming me for my stepdaughter's death all those years ago, though clearly all logically thinking people know exactly who's responsible. Remember, those who point the finger have at least three pointing directly back at themselves."

The stocky officer nodded, peering briefly over the homeowner's shoulder to see the grounds security guard stifling yet another yawn.

"Well, I'll have to reread the incident, sir. Before my time, you understand, but I do recall there being evidence of arson, though no suspect could ever be identified."

"Correct, and as far as possible perpetrators go, I've never been mentioned as such, either by the local, state or federal law, and I won't have the lowlife scum who assisted, purposely or not, in the death of one of my own attempt to ruin *my* good name by hinting the opposite."

Emerging from a shadowy hallway in a pink jogging suit, Lisa Hammock toted a silver tray housing a trio of steaming cups. An attractive redhead in her mid-thirties—nearly three decades her husband's junior—with an hourglass figure no doubt kept shapely by consistent treks around the property and regular visits to their expansive home gym, she had assumed the role of

Mrs. Kerry Hammock number three less than three years earlier and had instantly garnered the "trophy wife" label around town. For the last two years of their marriage, she'd helped manage his Frankfort Nissan dealership, roughly an hour's drive away, though many speculated this was merely for show and that she had little to do with actually running the business, despite her once earning a degree in business management from Bowling Green University.

"Sorry it took me so long to brew this up, hon," she cooed, sporting a deep, Southern drawl that practically screamed well-schooled debutante status, no matter the utter laughability of such an outdated stereotype. "Don't tell me these boys are leavin' without a taste."

It was Will Crockett who replied in-kind, having limped to the edge of the foyer until roughly half of his massive frame was visible.

"Afraid we haven't got the time, ma'am, but thanks just the same," he said with a nod before clearing his throat noisily while eyeing his subordinate, the message conveyed crystal clear.

Tipping his CFPD ballcap her way, Strickland regarded her husband before turning on a heel and following Crockett out.

"You got our number, Mister Hammock, in case you happen to hear directly from Gunther McCarron. Allow us to get his side of the story and do not contact him directly."

The homeowner laughed aloud at the departing officer's back, a wholly humorless snicker.

"Wouldn't dream of it, Officer Strickland. Not exactly my clique, you understand."

Walking out underneath a chilly, overcast sky, Phil first assisted his slumping chief into the passenger seat of his Durango before sauntering over to the driver's side.

"Was that guy always such a snotty shit?" he inquired, backing from the paved drive.

Eyes shut, his bandaged head propped against the head rest, the feebleness of the chief's response matched his sagging demeanor to a tee.

"Actually, I think he's mellowed from his political days. I will say this," he continued weakly and with the occasional pause as his frowning subordinate steered them past a series of "NO TRESPASSING" signs that he noted had not uncoincidentally been erected since Wesley Grant had driven Gunther McCarron onto the grounds just days before—and to the edge of a newly asphalted patch of state highway leading away from Hammock property.

"Never met anyone who worked under him say they missed those days. Mayor Barker might not have been the sharpest tack in the bag, but at least he wasn't *just* about lining his pockets."

Stopping the Durango at the end of the drive, Phil shifted into park. Right would take them back to town, left further out into the county's western edge.

"So," he said, reaching up with probing fingers in an attempt to simultaneously rub the exhaustion from each eye. "Where too, Will?"

When the big man didn't instantly reply, his subordinate briefly considered he'd drifted off and felt equal twinges of both jealousy and guilt, that is until Crockett's deep rasp disproved the theory.

"Drive me to the McCarron house. If it's deserted like Jake reported Grant's place was, we'll resume the search. If Gunther McCarron *is* home, you can leave me there and get back on the road till I've taken his statement. Call Maggie and have her relay our need for either more deputies or troopers, or both if possible. We can't, *cannot*, go another full day and night without finding *someone* or *something*."

"Chief, you sure you're up to this?"

"Nope, but neither are you. Drive on, Officer."

"Yes, sir."

The patrolman made a right just as a light sprinkle of rain spattered the windshield.

"Kickoff looms in a matter of hours."

Will Crockett checked his wristwatch for confirmation.

"Yep. Might be a wet one after all."

"That's okay. The Crane kid's a mudder."

"True that. I hear tell scouts from Baton Rouge, Athens and even Tuscaloosa might be attending. Not just for Crane but Parsons and Whitman too."

"Parsons can sure enough run block, but he needs to work on the pass protection. Whitman's a monster at DT but needs to pack on some pounds."

The chief nodded agreeably, if not feebly.

"Well, rest assured whoever signs him, they'll save a seat at the table. Go Wildcats."

"Go...Wildcats," the patrolman replied wearily, pausing a few breaths before resuming the dialogue by touching on a point he knew his boss was pondering with equal curiosity but perhaps not the energy to verbally breach.

"Soooo, how long before Maggie takes a similar complaint from Shannon McKay?"

"Once he sees it, not very long. Maybe, with any luck at all, he's far too distracted with tonight's game to peruse social media."

"Maybe he is, but those teens he plays for can't go five minutes without surfing the net."

"Officer Strickland," the chief grunted, "sometimes you're too wise for your own good."

"Yes, sir. Wonder where I inherited such sage powers over the years?"

"Passing the buck to your elders," the big man snorted. "But I digress..."

The bulky patrolman groaned.

"Lord, but it's been a long few days, Will."

"Ten-four to that, Phillip. That it has. We can only pray what's to come doesn't continue the theme, or, heaven forbid, stretch it out ever further."

With that, and in the approximately eleven minutes it took them to reach the McCarron house, Will Crockett dozed, his fragmented dreams including wearing the pads, cleats and headgear of yesteryear, though instead of a familiar opponent standing opposite his trademark three-point stance, it was a bulkily-built, wild-eyed female wearing a grinning mask of madness. Charging toward him like an enraged bull while screaming mostly unintelligible drivel as thick globs of whitish drool flew from both sides of her shark-like maw, the woman sailed toward him with her head and chubby forearms leading the way.

He would awaken, mercifully, before impact and with the aid of his subordinate's gentle prodding.

"You okay, Will? Looked for a second like you were trying to duck a falling plane."

"Y-yeah, yeah. Just drifted off."

"Well, we're almost there. Hey, maybe McCarron can brew you some coffee."

"Yeah, maybe," the chief replied, the pulse in his bandaged neck pounding like a trip-hammer. Reaching down with probing fingers to his right pants pocket, he felt the prescription bottle protruding from it and sighed with palpable relief while pondering how much longer he could hold out without popping a handful.

"*Anything* to stay awake."

Saturday, 1801 hours
From 1840 AM Radio (The Falls):

"*...Unpredicted sleet and rain aside, we're just moments from kickoff here at Falls Field in what is easily the biggest* *game with the most at stake in over a decade between these two longtime rivals, the overflowing crowd present obviously undeterred by the wintery conditions.*

The captains from each squad stroll to the middle of the field for the coin toss, the home Wildcats represented by senior quarterback Shane Mills, tailback Dalton Crane and defensive end Malcom Jordan, and the visiting Red Raiders by wideout Booker Drake, linebacker Evan Tolliver and offensive tackle Randall Faraday. Head linesman Carl Williamson will execute the coin flip..."

Twelve

"He was really, really adamant that you phone him as soon as possible, Chief. Highly pissed would be an understatement, I mean, what with the kickoff in just a matter of well, hours, he mentioned some...a pregame meal in just a bit and then some type of...kind of pregame meeting with the assistant coaches and team cap—"

Breaking radio etiquette, the chief interrupted not out of frustration or anger, but to calm his friend, whose rambling, shambling dialogue was so out of character he'd recognized such an abrupt intervention was necessary.

"Maggie, rest assured I'll be ringing the coach on my cell as soon as we break radio contact. Over."

The relief in the dispatcher's tone was palpable.

"Tha-thanks, Will. Pretty sure I've been cursed and screamed at more in the last three days than in the first three decades of my life combined. Over."

"Relax, Mag. I've got this. Coach McKay will either back up a step or two in terms of aggression toward public servants, or I'm liable to allow Phil here to remind him of the correct method to deliver a pancake block. Over and out."

The radio clicked twice and fell silent.

Nearing the stop sign at Bay Drive and Main, the Durango's scowling driver completely braked before regarding his boss with a shrug of his bulky shoulders.

"Change in plans, boss?"

"Afraid so. Drop me at the fieldhouse and you go on to Gunther McCarron's."

"You sure you don't want *me* to—"

The chief raised a large, gloved paw to preclude verbal interjection.

"Give the coach a blackeye before the game of the decade? That's a definite negatory, big guy. Not to worry." He forced a grin so warped and full of spastic tics it nearly defined a stroke victim. "Mr. Big Shot gets too lippy and I'll set 'im straight right in front of his team. All busted *and* doped up in equal measure, I can still deliver a decent clothesline."

"Of that I have no doubt whatsoever," the grinning patrolman said, turning right toward the campus of Crimson Falls High School.

Saturday, 11:34 hours

Cool precipitation in the form of a half-rain, half-sleet hybrid spattered the windshield of the Camry, its interior so warm and toasty that Wesley caught himself drowsing while traversing the many backend roads circling Crimson Falls in order to reach his place of residence in the most crafty, inconspicuous way possible.

He'd eyed each and every vehicle since nearing the city limits with unnatural trepidation, half-expecting to be either sideswiped, rear-ended or T-boned by a black SUV at every turn, curve or stop sign.

His original plan upon departing Booneville was to cruise slowly by and carefully case the grounds before pulling into the driveway, this plot officially kicked to the curb upon arrival.

There was little choice but to hash out the particulars on how to proceed with the madness, as hiding out like some wanted fugitive had been nothing but an embarrassing stall.

Still, he'd sighed deeply and with profound relief upon finding the driveway deserted. Once parked, he cut the engine and scooped up his cell phone from the center console, this soothing wave of liberation providing only a brief respite from a sense of dread that was, in comparison, tsunami sized.

"Well, oh well, darling mine, where have you gone?" he whispered nervously, peering through rain-streaked glass in every direction as if expecting her to magically materialize.

It was, as he'd exited the snug warmth of the Camry for the wet chill of the elements, having already decided to first text and subsequently call her—blatant cowardice prevented reversing said order—that Wesley became aware of a low humming originating from behind the house, possibly in the area of the garage with the source most likely being that of an idling vehicle.

As specks of semi-frozen rain stung his exposed forehead and cheeks, Wesley rolled his personal wheelchair painstakingly around the side of the structure, the droning noise growing gradually as he proceeded while adding a sporadic sputter, like a wheezing engine on the verge of croaking out.

Rounding the corner—while instinctively slowing his own progression—he craned his neck so as to not to give away his presence yet, his emotions torn between hoping the as-yet-unseen and unidentified vehicle parked near his garage would be revealed as a black SUV, while also praying it wouldn't.

Squinting through an increasingly turbulent drizzle and despite a heightened state of high caution, Wesley barely had time—approximately two drumming, chest pounding beats of his heart—to identify a dark-shaded, quad-cab pickup of undetermined make or model backed nearly flush with the garage's left bay, before a sudden movement caught the peripheral of his left eye.

The bleary shadow that fell upon him held an odd, unfamiliar scent, just as the gleeful grunt of its source was both strangely alien and simultaneously recognizable.

"Hiya, buddy boy," a voice, all-too familiar, spat near his left ear, a mist of warm spittle tickling it.

"Waaay past time you and I jawed, don'cha think? Now, you can either roll that tin chariot forth voluntarily or be toted inside and leave it out here to the mercy of the elements," it concluded with a cackle that was as creepily nostalgic as it was downright nauseating. With a resounding groan, Wesley wisely resigned himself to the former and wheeled himself forward.

Saturday, 11:35 hours

Shannon McKay, decked out in a crimson and white CFHS jacket, blue jeans, black boots and a black toboggan with the word "WILDCATS" sewn across the crown in gold lettering, paced the spacious locker-room as if delivering a fiery, motivational half-time sermon to his players, though in lieu of delivering said speech at stereotypical high volume, he whispered as if to avoid full audibility from hidden microphones.

"I mean it, Chief. That adle-brained lunatic drags my name any further into that fictional swamp of lies he's cultivating, and there's gonna be more than just legal troubles. While I consider myself fairly thick-skinned and a master of self-control, what I *cannot* control is the behavior of others who will take his bullshit accusations seriously and initiate action to deter further slanderings."

Straddling one of a pair of long wooden benches between twin rows of metal lockers, Will Crockett attempted to ignore the shooting pains setting his neck, shoulder and upper arm ablaze as if literally lit afire, and instead concentrate on both the man's words and, more distractively, the familiar sights and smells of the locker room. Though it had been renovated, repainted and reorganized through the years, it was still the same general space he'd once occupied in his youth.

"You talking about your players, Coach?"

"Passionate bunch of kids, Chief, all twenty-nine of 'em. Some much more than others, and very, very protective of their mentor. Boys that age have a habit of acting out of pure instinct and are almost exclusively reactionary, as you well know."

Pacing the narrow space between benches, McKay's cheeks were beet-red and practically glowing beneath the harsh fluorescent lights, his top lip swallowed whole by the graying caterpillar of a mustache hanging beneath a bulbous nose like an overgrown shrub. "The one that brought the...that damn video post to my attention this morning did so with tears brimming at the corners of his eyes. Tears of rage. He asked me why somebody would want to spread such vileness about his coach, and on the eve of the biggest game this school's played in more than a decade. I had no answers for the kid, Chief. I still don't."

Rotating his neck gently from side to side as he replied, the chief's slumping posture, drooping lids and listless tone belied an inner fire that burned fiercely bright despite its outer shell's imminent collapse.

"And you say the two of you spoke face-to-face a few days ago?"

"Yep, over at the Sow. I'd caught wind that he'd just left Kerry Hammock's place, spouting similarly cloaked charges and threatening to 'blow the lid' off whatever fairytale that cracked egg of a brain of his had concocted."

"So, you just assumed you were next on his fictional suspect list?"

"Well, only natural to think so, right? I mean, Wendy and me *had* been engaged at the time. I just decided best to nip it in the bud before that nutjob showed up at the front door of my house or worse yet, shambled into the middle of the fifth period Algebra class I teach, resembling some kind of...mechanical zombie that just crawled outta some mad scientist's lab."

Retrieving a small notepad and Bic pen from his jacket's inner pocket, the chief propped the former on his left kneecap and commenced to scribble, secretly hoping the notes would make at least a semblance of sense upon later review, being as the inner gauge measuring his level of concentration was currently running on fumes.

"I...see. So, how did this not-quite-chance meeting go?"

"About as well as it could have, I guess. He was kinda glib about the whole thing, maybe 'cause I didn't waste any time telling, no, *promising* that I'd sue his scrawny ass if he so much as spoke my name aloud and in vain. Well, hell...," the portly man paused, rolling his eyes and tossing both hands upward in what appeared to be an overly dramatic, almost choreographed frustration, "...so much for that! Chief, if McCarron does possess the brass balls to broadcast a sequel, you might consider locking him away for his own safety, at least until the lawyers can take center stage. I know Kerry Hammock isn't one to endure similar claptrap without a fight, legal or otherwise, and we both know that son of his is unstable enough to take the law into his own hands."

"Son?"

"Martin Hammock. Lanky build, like some damn human-buzzard hybrid, stringy, scraggily hair, a tad wall-eyed. Voice like nails on a chalkboard."

The chief nodded, bandaged head lowered, while scribbling away on the notepad.

"May not look like a threat, but I've heard he cut up a couple of hardcore bikers but good a few years back down in Shreveport. McCarron is one hell of an easy target, and I highly doubt that chairbound pal of his will be of much use when the hammer does drop."

"Chairbound pal being?" Crockett inquired with a cocked brow.

"Never formally introed, though he did look weirdly familiar."

"But he was in a wheelchair?"

"Well, no, they were both sitting on opposite sides of the booth. McCarron was all strapped into that robo-gear and his pal's chair was folded up next to 'im and leaning on the edge of the booth. Kinda strange seeing a pair of well, cripples, dining at the same table. Sounds un-PC as hell I know, but it just...was."

"Describe the man."

The coach frowned.

"McCarron?"

"No, his friend."

"Caucasian, four-eyes, brown hair, severe combover, bushy brown beard with a smidge of gray. Not nearly as scrawny as Gunther, though his legs were hidden beneath the table, and I imagine they were, well, you know, kinda twiggy, depending on how long they'd been out of commission."

Even as he struggled to maintain legibility as the felt-tip sailed across the notepad's blue-lined surface, the chief's jaw visibly tightened at the ramifications of McKay's description and he felt a rush of blood exit both cheeks.

"Honestly, Chief, those two probably couldn't crack an egg between 'em and McCarron seems determined to piss off folks perfectly capable of busting skulls with equal ease as recently hatched poultry. You'd best lay out the possible consequences of such jack-wagon behavior before somebody comes along who ain't nearly as patient or understanding as yours truly."

Meeting the standing man's gaze, Crockett was somehow able to dredge up an equal level of fake sincerity in response to McKay's spouting of wholly faux concern for Gunther McCarron's welfare.

"I'll certainly take it into consideration, Coach. Now, as I advised Mister Hammock, please allow us to intercede between all parties before it can escalate. Rest assured we'll be speaking to Gunther McCarron post haste and keeping you updated."

Standing with booted feet spread, prominent gut protruding and hands propped atop matching love handles, McKay grinned beneath the massive crumb-catcher.

"I'd appreciate it, Chief. Is it okay to hold off on that update till tomorrow at midday or just after? My plate's overflowing at the moment, as you can imagine."

Masking his struggles to rise with a shaky chuckle, Will Crockett pocketing the notepad with one hand while using a nearby locker to steady himself.

"You okay there, Chief? Didn't want to pry, but what with all the bandaging..."

"Took a bad spill on a particularly slick and very solid stretch of pavement. I'll live, just won't be moving with quite as much grace for a while."

"Got'cha. That'll do it," the coach replied with a quizzical expression that all but screamed disbelief in the obviously gimpy lawman's explanation.

"The young warriors properly fired up?" Crockett asked, quickly detouring onto a safer lane of questioning. To this, the coach beamed like a typical proud papa.

"Wired for sound, Chief. You know...*knew* how it was, right?"

"Vaguely. Been many a season passed, but yeah, I did."

"We've got pregame meal in about a half hour, so I'd better shuffle on over to the lunchroom."

The chief offered his massive right mitt, which engulfed the pudgy appendage that soon accepted.

"Good luck, Coach. We'll all be rooting for 'em."

"Appreciate it. Looks like we might be dodging some of the frozen stuff after all, damn Old Man Winter's eyes."

"No problem. That Crane kid is built for the worst Old Man Winter has to offer," Crockett concluded, plagiarizing his subordinate's earlier line with nary an ounce of shame.

"And he just might need every available gear against that Dawson run line," the coach replied with a grin so wide it appeared his top lip was attempting to shed the massive cookie duster weighing it down, before the two men parted with an amiable nod.

Departing the fieldhouse's double door entrance and standing beneath what appeared to be a fairly new aluminum awning, upon which a dull rapping ensued from the descending sleet, Will Crockett paused a full minute-plus, cell phone in hand, while replaying Shannon McKay's description of the man he claimed had been breaking bread, just days previously, with Gunther McCarron. Speed-dialing the PD, he worded his immediate request even while continuing to replay both the interview as a whole and that specific nugget of knowledge in particular, knowledge concerning his vacationing and recently incommunicado records clerk, along with an earlier rumor that he'd recently been spotted nearby.

"Cindy Lou? Please have Maggie radio Phil to cruise by the fieldhouse as soon as feasible. If he's being detained, go with Jake. Yep, need a ride, post haste. It isn't getting any warmer out here. Thanks."

Pocketing the cell, the chief stared off into the far horizon, from which was visible an infinite landscape of billowy dark gray, an undulating cloak of dusk's inevitable descent, though his frenzied thoughts were equally ashen, if not more so.

At the forefront, pregnant with a creeping and palpable dread, sat the department's veteran records clerk and his long-time co-worker and friend, and the simplest of questions connecting them: *why?*

"What the *hell*, Wesley?" Will Crockett said, the hoarse whisper all but inaudible with the constant pecking overhead, a distant siren blaring in the far distance as if to respond.

Saturday, 12:19 hours

"You able to catch a few winks?"

"These days, Dex, I never know how much was actual sleep of the deep REM variety or just lyin' there unconscious in a less-permanent form of coma. How long was I undead?"

Having wheeled himself from his uncle's guest bedroom to the kitchen, Gunther appeared, at least to his last surviving elder, even thinner, paler and more frighteningly gaunt than when he'd announced the need for a mid-morning rest just over two hours earlier.

"Two, two and a half hours. Hey, just brewed up a fresh pot," Dexter announced, rising from the dining table and retrieving a clean cup from the nearby dishwasher.

"I'll give it a go, but I'm nursin' some serious heartburn since I swallowed down the daily breakfast servin' of assorted ovals. Damn, but I'm sick of rattlin' like a half-empty pill bottle."

"Here, black as the night, then," the older man said, placing the steaming cup on the table. "Best not doctor it up too much."

The seated man took a cautious sip and winced, feigning extreme disgust before revealing a sly smile.

"Mother's mi-milk."

Nephew and uncle sat in silence for a full minute, exchanging noisy slurps, the grayish hue of midday breaking through the room's lone window with its blinds fully risen.

"Hungry? Got some semi-fresh pancake mix in the cabinet," Dexter offered between sips.

The younger man, dark patches between both eyes more pronounced than ever, seemed to think it over before balking with a pathetically feeble hand gesture—more a spasm than an actual wave.

"It'll be all I can do to choke this down without spewin' it back up. Th-thanks anyhow."

An additional ninety seconds of dueling sips ensued, that is until the opening three chords of the AC/DC tune "High Voltage" echoed from the living room, the three-second ring tone repeating itself four times before Dexter pushed from the table with a strained grunt to retrieve it.

"Uh-oh, reaction to the video perhaps?" Gunther inquired, lifting the half-empty mug airborne in a shaky grip as if to pose a toast. "Racin' up the charts, I hope."

"Gunther McCarron's phone," he heard his uncle answer after approximately the fifth replay of Angus Young's opening riff. "Yeah but...you sure you don't want to talk to him...um, all right. I'll let him know."

"That was your former wheelman," he announced, reentering the kitchen and scooping his Stetson from a nearby wall peg.

McCarron replied over the top edge of the mug before engaging in a final, noisy slurp.

"Yeah? What's up with Wes?" He giggled, a wet cackle that quickly evolved into a mercifully short coughing jag. "Sounds like the title of one of those crappy reality TV shows that're all the rage."

"He wants me to drive you over to his place. Sounded out of breath and kind of, well, out of sorts, struggling to spit out the words."

"What words, Dex? What's he want?"

"He didn't say, Gunny, just that he requests your presence toot-sweet."

"Toot-sweet?" The chairbound man beamed. "Dang, how many cranium cobwebs you have to slap aside to retrieve that little nugget? That still mean as fast as possible?"

His uncle strode past without reply, rinsing his coffee cup in the sink before departing for the living room.

"Should I load up your support suit?"

"Sure, why not?" McCarron sighed wearily, rolling over to the sink area and reaching to put his own mug beside his uncle's. "There's always the outside chance the mayor will send up the crip-signal and we'll have to find a phone booth, right?"

Once his uncle didn't reply—the thumping sound of his boots growing fainter as he apparently headed down the lone hallway to the guest bedroom—the chairbound man wheeled his way to the edge of the living room.

"So Wesley didn't provide a single hint?"

The faint echo of his uncle's reply made it sound as if the older man were trapped behind thick concrete walls.

"Just said there was something you needed to see and hung up."

"Something I needed to see...hmmm, intriguin'," the younger man said, low enough to be heard thought possibly addressing only himself. "Just wish I wasn't so *beat*. Maybe the meds will kick in soon."

"Bet it's about that little vid we posted, ya think?" he inquired as his elder reentered the room with the exo-suit hanging over one shoulder, assorted black wires swinging as limply as snake carcasses.

"Wouldn't be surprised. I'll have an eye out for potential assassins on the way."

"You're a card, Dex. Fully charged?"

"You could run a marathon."

Noticing that a rare grin, however fleeting, crease his uncle's rugged visage, Gunther couldn't resist playing along.

"Never underestimate a cripple with a purpose, old man. I could finish a ten-K if properly motivated. May take me three to four weeks, but I'd shamble over that finish line with a winnin' smile, not to mention an easy-to-track slug trail."

"Ready when you are," his stoic elder fired back, all evidence of humor wiped clean.

"You're a tough crowd, Dex," the nephew said, adjusting his ever-present beret before wheeling toward the door. "Just gimme a second to go spruce up. Translation: Empty the ol' poop bag and slap on some Brut to cover the scent."

Approximately fifteen minutes later, as they pulled onto the roadway, Gunther's chair folded and placed under a tarp in the bed of his uncle's truck, the passenger noted the time displayed on his cell.

"Less than six hours before kickoff," he said flatly, adjusting the seatbelt holding him upright for at least the third time since being propped into place.

"Whole town will be there," his uncle replied, equally dully. "Practically."

"You weren't plannin' on attendin'?"

"Honestly, I couldn't care less. Waste of time. Got things to do. *Anything* but that."

"And here I thought you were a fan. You used to come see me play."

"Your folks *suggested* I show interest."

"Suggest...they bribe ya?"

The older man snorted, an act as rare a reaction, at least in his nephew's presence, as your basic bigfoot sighting.

"Not quite. Just thought you needed all the family support you could get."

"Fess up. I was a real butt boil in my time, yeah?"

"Inflamed. Both cheeks."

This time, nephew and uncle snorted in perfect unison.

Saturday, 12:53 hours

Jake Douglas and Phil Strickland stood before their superior's wide oak desk, the former sipping black coffee from a thermos cap while the latter yawned into an open palm. Slumped and sunken—at least as far as his massive frame would allow—into the recliner that was his throne five and a half days a week, not counting the occasional overtime, Will Crockett mindlessly drummed the nonwriting end of a silver pen onto the tabletop, his noticeably swollen eyes half-closed.

"You'd think just by the law of averages, right?" Jake inquired to no one in particular, resting the thermos between his thighs.

"Normally, yeah, but so far every element of this scenario has been anything but," Phil chimed in wearily, applying a gentle massage to each saggy eye, courtesy of the thumb and forefinger of his right hand.

"Scenarios," Crockett croaked, having discarded the pen.

"Will?"

"More than one situation here, as I see it, Phil. Three missing persons but nothing to show that any of them are connected in any way."

"Four."

The chief's left brow arose dramatically, though both eyes remained half-closed.

"More like two *officially* missing, one on the run and one that, as far as we know for now, is officially on vacation and incommunicado, agreed?"

"Agreed, but with all the roving eyeballs employed since this morning, how is it none of 'em have settled on either a gray Charger, black SUV blazer, white Toyota Camry or a black and white Durango with PD markings? Were they *all* suddenly supplied with cloaking devices?"

"Steady, Phil. Just a matter of time."

The veteran patrolman stiffened, his square jaw clenching and unclenching numerous times.

"It's been damn near forty-eight hours for the Briggs kid and creeping up on twenty-four for Jerome. I'm not much for speculation without tangible proof, Will, you *know* this, but my gut's telling me they *are* connected, be it via alien abduction or something similarly unnatural."

"What I also *know*, Phillip, is that much like my own, your thought process is being pulled into similarly unnatural directions from a case of severe sleep deprivation."

A short silence ensued, during which time Phil Strickland collapsed back into his chair with a reluctant nod.

"What now, Skipper?" the part-time, fill-in patrolman inquired to shatter the brief peace, this following a final, noisy slurp from his thermos cap. "You consider calling the federal boys?"

"Maggie's on the line with them now. We still have those two deputies at our disposal?"

"Headed back here after code seven."

"Where'd they go?"

"Dan's. Said they'd pick us up some turkey and cheese subs for the road. Nice kids."

The chief slid forward sufficiently to prop both elbows atop his desk, using each to push various stacks of paper in opposite directions.

"So, to summarize, no one home at Grant's..."

To this, Phil nodded feebly.

"...same at McCarron's."

The patrolman repeated the gesture, albeit even more sluggishly.

"Patrols in and around the city limits provided similar goose eggs in terms of either persons or vehicle IDs."

"Absolute zilch," Douglas said before popping a handful of mints pulled from his shirt pocket.

"You guys cover all those unnamed sidewinders around Diamond Rock Lake, Jake?"

"Affirmative, Chief. Still nada. You want us to trek over the same routes or maybe go further outside the limits? One of the deputies, the chubby one with the cheek scar, said we might want to che—"

"Those ruts...," the chief cut in, both his charges involuntarily wincing as he'd practically lunged upward in the process, inadvertently sending several sheets of paper sailing airborne.

"Will?" Phil Strickland inquired, as wide-eyed as his current state of exhaustion could muster.

"When we were over at Wesley's place, did you notice the...those tire ruts leading toward the garage?"

Even as Jake Douglas appeared comically flummoxed at the chief's sudden epiphany, the Crimson Falls PD's senior patrolman leaned forward with his square chin resting atop a clenched fist, squinting, straining and struggling to concentrate.

"We stepped right over them, Phil, never taking tangible notice of—"

"They were fresh—fairly anyhow," the patrolman finished for his boss, who nodded in response. "Steered off the path and into those saturated grounds."

Crockett nodded, lumbering out from behind his desk and almost directly into a flinching Jake Douglas.

"Something heavy enough to dig some sizeable trenches. If I recall, there was a twin-garage back there. You remember the troopers saying they checked it?"

The senior patrolman's eyes were distant with bleary recall.

"Pretty certain they received the call on that interstate crash before they ever got the chance. You thinking Wes's crazy ex might be holed up in there?"

"Could be, could be. Okay then, let's get back out there. Jake, meet up with your guys and check *both* the McCarron places."

The fill-in patrolman practically flinched.

"Both? I don't..."

"Gunther and his uncle, Dexter. The latter's located on New Union Road, just past the old chicken house. Red brick, white siding, name on the mailbox. Drives an old blue Ford or Chevy pickup."

Hopping up with uncharacteristic gusto, Jake Douglas executed an about-face and headed for the door.

"I'll go *find* those county badges," he announced in departure. "Lunch break's over."

"Keep us posted," the chief said, reaching with a probing finger toward the landline gracing his desk and punching in the extension to dispatch, where Maggie answered in a voice nearly as hoarse and unidentifiable as his own.

"Spoke to an investigator named Webster. He's checking manpower options for this afternoon and will ring us back."

"Give 'im until fourteen hundred hours to do so and then call back and ask for his superior. We're past politeness here. If they give you the old soft-shoe, let me know and I'll call 'em directly."

When there was an extended delay at the other end, Crockett decided an amendment to clarify was in order.

"I want them to provide a solid answer to when we're to expect aid."

"Oh yeah, got'cha, Will. Straight answers only."

"Exactly. Phil and I are headed back to the Grant property."

"Wesley's place? I thought y'all covered that ground already."

"We did but might've overlooked something. We'll keep you posted."

"Please do that, Chief."

Despite being battered by tidal waves of exhaustion, the two remaining law officers practically sprinted from the office shoulder-to-shoulder, met at the entrance door by a cold slap in the face courtesy of a heady mix of sleet that was, unlike just moments earlier, more ice than rain.

"Roads are gonna get slick...," the chief huffed moments later, his face a frozen grimace, while reclaiming a clear plastic prescription bottle from the Durango's glove compartment, "...so don't land us in a ditch, lead foot."

"When this is over," the patrolman said, pulling out onto a deserted Main Street with back tires spinning, "I want to borrow some of your muscle relaxers."

The chief swallowed down a pair of white pills dry, his already severely hoarse voice nearly incomprehensible in reply.

"Can't promise any leftovers. Personally, I'm planning on making a run at McCarron's coma record."

Slowing to make a sharp right onto an unmarked side road, the SUV's back tires holding up quite nicely with nary a sign of sliding, Phil Strickland gave an almost inaudible "yep, same here."

Saturday, 12:26 hours

"Put it on speaker. I need to hear both sides of the conversation."

"And just what am I supposed to say without sounding suspicious?"

"You're no dope, well...," a brief, shrieking giggle, "...not entirely. You'll think of something. Just don't tip off you're not alone."

"This is...I'm just not..."

"It's practically *done*. Even a hopeless sympathizer like yourself ought to see that we've just been prolonging the inevitable."

The shadow loomed at Wesley Grant's back, its source's warm breath tickling his neck each time it leaned in close—close enough to inhale the scent of it, the stench of old sweat and desperation and the overuse of cologne slapped on in an attempt to mask it.

"How many times do I have to tell you that the inevitable *is* gonna happen *naturally*. He was this close just a few da—"

The source grunted, its shadow leaning down as a fresh puff of putridness slapped Wesley's left cheek.

"Game's changed since then, Ace. The Briggs kid altered the plans, changed the course. Expediated the process. Besides, that walking dead look is just a disguise, as far as I'm concerned. He may have the shell of a slowly disintegrating corpse, but that heart is as mule-strong as his brain is sharp. The time is *now* and with not a moment to lose, what with the law sniffing around. We can only hope that absurd *ballgame* diverts their attention for the rest of the day. Now, make the call."

"Listen, there has to be another way."

"Negative. You don't even know the half of it, Ace, but you will. Make the call."

"He won't be alone! What did you think, he was going to hitchhike over? Roll that damn chair all the way from..."

The cell phone was snatched violently from his hand, a forefinger punching in a nine-digit number before levitating the device mere inches from his trembling lips.

"It's ringing *and* it's on speaker. Don't make me hang up and dial again."

The man peered upward and saw his own reflection from within twin mirrors of mad determination just as a sharp click followed and the line engaged in mid-ring.

"Gunther McCarron's phone."

"Yeah, Dexter, this is Wes. Wesley Grant. Could you please let your nephew know I need to see him right away at my house?"

"Yeah, but...you sure you don't want to talk to him..."

"No sir, no time to explain. Please drop him off as soon as you can, please."

"Um, all right. I'll let him know."

The hand reemerged in a blur to rip the phone away yet again and quickly disconnect the line.

"Solid job. Didn't show the slightest bit of nervousness, kind of like this whole dishonesty thing is a way of life, huh? A natural-born liar never loses their touch, no matter the time elapsed or effort given to reform. Like swimming or riding a bike, it all comes back."

"His uncle might decide to hang around, you think of that? What then?"

Instantly regretting the inquiry, Wesley realized he already knew the forthcoming answer and simply didn't want it verified.

"I'm counting on it, in fact. You have to figure by now that the elder McCarron is privy to far too much information, and besides, there is that *last living relative* thing to consider. He'll always be sniffing around for answers. Like nephew, like uncle. Gotta tie up those loose ends once the first unravels, Ace. But you see, there's a problem."

"Just one?" Wesley asked with an angry, sarcastic laugh.

"Yeah, but it's substantial."

The shadow vanished as its source repositioned until squatting before him, effectively sizing him up with a series of dramatic head tilts.

"I'm sensing reluctance, hesitation. I have a strong feeling that if you hadn't literally been forced to call via physical abduction, you'd likely have eventually tipped McCarron off."

"I've had ample opportunity before now," he replied, swallowing hard, barely able to maintain eye contact.

"True, but not since finding out the latest developments. The developments that left us no choice but to go to plan B."

"I still think plan A has a ch—"

"See? *There* it is precisely! Cold feet in the moment of truth. I worry about you, Grant. I worry about what you might do when the chips are down. What you might do to all of us."

For a fleeting moment, his anger flared to toxic heights, so much so it briefly overtook and even passed the stark fear knotting his gut.

"What I might do to—" he spat between bared, gritted teeth, a veritable pipeline of pronounced veins littering his neck and forehead. "There is no *us*, asshole! That leaky boat sailed off and sank years ago!"

The object of his ire stood with aid from his chair's armrests.

"Oh, I'm not talking loyalty, Ace. I'm talking potential incarceration in a federal prison. Sorry you misunderstood, but sadly, not surprised. After all, you never were the sharpest knife in the drawer."

"Obviously *not* to ever have gotten involved with you," he snapped back fiercely with clenched fists pounding either armrest in time with every spoken word, each blow slightly delayed for dramatic effect.

Yet again, the source of his rage refused to take the bait, instead displaying a grotesquely wide grin layered in sardonic glee.

"And yet, here we are, two peas sharing space in the same nefarious pod."

"We are *not* the same," Wesley fired back, though the flames of his rage had been doused to the point of barely smoldering, replaced by the stinging self-admission of guilt.

"Keep telling yourself that, Ace. Now, let's go over the plans for when McCarron comes a-knocking, one for if he enters solo and the other if not."

"And what if I refuse to play along?" Wesley stated as much as inquired, instantly regretting both the wording and possible implications.

The stare bore down on him with renewed intensity even as the source stepped behind his chair and whispered into his left ear, and a raw, almost primal scent of fear and desperation assaulted his senses once more.

"Oh lord, but we've chewed this same cabbage many times, Grant. It's like...you're groping for a different answer, some viable option when deep down, you know better. Fine, then, allow me to break it down one final time: Either cooperate or I'm afraid your participation will most likely be elevated to something other than mere accessory."

Forced to swallow the buildup of hot bile ascending to his throat and the back of his tongue, Wesley Grant's bleary, cataract-infested mind's-eye—having raced at breakneck speed to search out a logical, probable solution to the disaster at hand since being so roughly abducted—finally surrendered to the inevitability of the situation, snapping shut with twin padlocks fastened securely in place.

Even as the source and main catalyst of this present-day misery commenced to verbally script what would certainly be the final chapter in a modern-day Greek tragedy, Wesley's final coherent resolution before morally and mentally checking out was indeed a somber one: that he was the official co-author of the insanity-driven play on display, a play that had, finally if not mercifully, reached its closing night.

Saturday, 13:17 hours

Having slowed the Durango to a crawl, Phil Strickland squinted through straight-line sleet from the lowered driver's window.

"Couldn't hurt to check it out," he said, braking to a stop in the narrow alley and feeling the back wheels lose traction for a split-second before correcting. The vehicle in question sat slightly askew, essentially half-on, half-off the one-lane alleyway with its front bumper practically kissing the back wall of a long-deserted storefront at the southern edge of Main Street.

Will Crockett, having donned a seemingly permanent mask of discomfort, briefly contemplated.

"Black SUVs ain't exactly a dime a dozen around here, Will."

"I just...I really want to get out to Grant's without further delay. Can you tell if it's idling or occupied?"

"No smoke from the tailpipe. Tint's too dark to make out a shape."

The chief sighed while reaching up to adjust the bandage occupying a major portion of his bald cranium.

"Well, least we can do is get the plate number and run it."

"Ten-four," the patrolman replied, cautiously pulling up next to—there being little clearance on either side of the alley—and halting behind the parked sport utility vehicle with mere inches separating the Durango's fender and the SUV's back bumper, essentially blocking it in.

"Hang tight, Will. Gonna see if I can access it."

"Careful, big guy. I'll run the tag."

Hopping back into the Durango a few minutes later, the patrolman shook a sizeable buildup of icy specks from his cropped hair and shoulders.

"Locked and unoccupied, as presumed."

"It's hers," the chief confirmed. "Tag came back to a Sandra L. Jamison, 1418 Waggoner Court, Louisville. Phoned it into Maggie to have it towed to the impound till further notice."

"Logical enough, though I doubt it'll draw her out as she's obviously arranged alternate transportation. But why leave it parked not only in the city limits but less than three blessed country miles from the same PD building you just trashed?"

"Perp is not in her right mind," Crockett answered, gently tapping the left side of his skull with an extended forefinger and wincing.

Phil Strickland replied, poising bare palms directly over twin heater vents on either side of the steering wheel, "Well *duh*, boss. Pretty sure that was confirmed last night."

"In spades. Probably dumped it here without a second thought and called an Uber."

"Crazy as an outhouse rat as she appears to be, I do not doubt that. So, on to Wesley's place?"

"Let's slip-slide that way. I have a gut feeling we're about to strike paydirt."

"Lord, but I hope and pray that tingling at your midsection is right on, boss. Hey, who knows? Maybe that concussion endowed you with some kinda intestinal telepathic power. Yeah, that's probably it...ITP."

The chief eyed his subordinate with a cockeyed scowl, accented by a suitably wry smile.

"If that were the case, Phillip, all the missing would be present and accounted for, and you and I would be at our respective domiciles performing a synchronized version of dueling snores."

"Ah yes," his baggy-eyed subordinate crooned horribly off-key. "Paradise by the lamp-table light."

In silent reply, the chief, not at all mystified by the late '70s classic rock reference, flashed a lazy thumbs-up that just as quickly wilted.

"Four and a half hours till kickoff, Chief."

"Strange," the big man responded soberly. "Keeps slipping my mind."

"Worse, I only thought of it because of your solo interview with McKay."

"Priorities, Phillip, priorities."

The digital clock reflecting 13:27 hours, the veteran patrolman steered the bulky SUV away from its smaller, compact-by-comparison kin, tires crunching along the alleyway's pavement as hailstones began to accumulate substantially despite a temperature hovering several degrees over the freezing mark.

Saturday, 1822 hours
From 1840 AM Radio (The Falls):

"...So with just over eight minutes remaining in the opening quarter, Dawson prepares to kick to the home Wildcats, who will go on offense for the first time following the visiting team's successful opening drive; a twelve-play, eighty-four yard march to paydirt that took nearly seven minutes off the game clock. The icy rain has subsided to a light mist, the damp grass field is slowly transforming into a muddy quagmire that will make establishing an effective passing game most difficult as the night progresses and temperatures remain just above the freezing mark. Dawson's strategy of keeping it on the ground definitely worked to the Red Raiders' advantage in that methodical opening drive, as they attempted nary a single forward pass. The squads are lined up for the kick, Dawson's Craig Graham sprinting toward the teed-up pigskin and sending it end-over-end toward the Wildcats' waiting return man, Slade Travers ..."

Thirteen

Saturday, 12:48 hours

Slightly hunched and squinting, the figure stood at the living room window, peeking through narrowly spaced blinds.

"Headlights. Too distant to recognize the source. What does the uncle drive again?"

Having parked his wheelchair half-in, half-out of the living room/kitchen entrance, Wesley Grant's expression conveyed quiet desperation.

"Faded blue pickup, Ford, I think. A beater," he whispered, the clarity of which improved the instant his raw, sandpaper-over-chalkboard tone amped up the volume several degrees. "Why the continued charade? He's oblivious, damn it. If not, I would've surely picked up a sign over the last few days."

"Man was in a coma for fourteen years, Grant. Who knows what supernatural skills he inherited in whatever Netherworld he inhabited during that span. No way it was all just blackness. Or maybe, having been the convicted liar he was in that younger, heathier incarnation, he's honed said skill to a razor's edge. Either way, you're surely no judge."

"He...doesn't...know..."

The figure allowed the blinds to seal while backing a step.

"You're asking the impossible, Ace. You're asking that I trust the instincts of one so hopelessly gullible he practically dove into this shit-show with his eyes wide open. So spare me your opinion and just sit there looking clueless, as usual."

With an assumed drop-of-the-mic, the figure openly smirked while moving back to the window.

"Yeah, so how about you?" Wesley shot back fiercely, his cheeks glowing beet-red. "You planning on hiding in the hall closet and only attacking when the unsuspecting paraplegic has his back turned? I've heard such fearlessness is your specialty."

"Still contemplating my entrance, thanks. Wish this dump had a chandelier I could swing in on."

"You promised a civilized meeting. You said we could end this without unnecessary viole—"

"Pickup slowing, slowing," the figure interrupted, narrowing the opening in the blinds until only the thinnest of openings remained. "And...turning in. Okay then, you said he always enters through the kitchen door..."

"Well, yeah, but it's not like this is a common thing..."

"We'll just wait to see where the knock originates."

"Front door has a bell."

"Whatever. Regardless, I'll duck into the opposite room and let you play greeter, then pick just the right time to hop inside for formal intros. Now let's see if we'll be entertaining just one McCarron or the entire remaining bloodline."

"Let's just assume Dexter does decide to join the party."

"It appears no amendments to the original script will be necessary," the subject said flatly, removing his fingers from the blinds and turning on a heel. "The pickup in question just backed out of the drive. Worry-wart."

"Listen, can't we just act like civilized hu—" Wesley began only to be cut off yet again as the figure squatted directly in his path, a hand placed lightly atop each of his knees.

"Because he isn't now and never *has* been civilized, Ace, and for your own sake, do *not* give away the surprise. Do we understand each other?"

"Surprise...what is this, some TikTok gag? You planning on going live on Facebook? What the hell is wrong with you..."

The slap, sudden and forceful, arrived in a streaky blur, the impact to Wesley's left cheek jerking his head hard to the opposite side, the flesh of his skin instantly reddening with a burning sting. Grant's trembling hands, both tucked snugly beneath the blanket, remained cloaked despite the abrupt trauma to their host's central control center.

"Get your jollies slapping around cripples?" he spat, teeth clenched so tightly he thought he might shatter a molar. "Seems to be a pattern."

The figure backed away a step and sighed, though apparently more from disgust than regret.

"Remember your place, Ace. Remember why we're here and just put on the same act you've apparently nailed down to a fine art these last several days."

"Yeah, sure, right," Wesley mumbled beneath his breath, having wheeled his way into the kitchen at the sound of a light knock at the back door, with the same enthusiasm one might display if heading to their own execution.

Moments later, the door swung inward with aid from a blustery wind, the host's noticeably puffy cheeks slapped by a frigid mix of misty rain and near-microscopic ice pellets.

"Greetings and salutations, Wesley," the visitor bellowed cheerily, though the underlying tone sounded as haggard and weary as that of the homeowner's. "So what's the hubbub?"

Backing the wheelchair to the inner edge of the living room entrance—as if unconsciously backing himself into a corner—Wesley discovered that feigning even the slightest of smiles was a physical impossibility.

"Come on in out of the blizzard, Gunther...," he managed with the weariest of nods. "...We need to chat."

With that, his guest ambled inside and struck an uneasy pose at the dining table, each gloved hand filled with tubular black canes that he utilized whenever moving forward, and instantly reminding Wesley of a blind man surveying the path ahead.

"Sounds intriguing," Gunther replied with an inquisitive tilt of the head, while obviously straining to remain upright despite the fully charged exo-suit's ever-sturdy existence. "By all means, let's jaw."

Saturday, 1854 hours
From 1840 AM Radio (The Falls):

"...Mills avoids the rush and flips it to Crane at the Red Raiders forty-three with a convoy of blockers leading the way...Crane shakes a tackle...two tackles...he's at the thirty-five, the thirty, streaking down the sideline...he's at the twenty...the ten...TOUCHDOWN, Wildcats!"

Saturday, 13:36 hours

"I know what you're going to say."

"Do you, now?"

"Fairly certain, yeah."

"You mean, something along the lines of: *Even though it might save us a minute or two, you really ought to avoid Donner Pass and stick with the main roads.* Sound about right?"

Phil Strickland gunned the engine in futility, matching winces with his superior in synchronized perfection, the younger cursing under his breath as the rear of the Durango spun around an additional foot or so, the tires digging an increasingly deeper groove into the mushy shoulder while creeping precariously closer to a nearby ditch that measured at least five feet in depth. The unmarked one-lane dirt path, nicknamed for the tragedy-filled trail of Western history lore due to its narrow, overly curvy, crevice-infested track—especially dicey when oversaturated or in this case, muddy and semi-frozen—had long been mythicized as a time-saving shortcut between Main Street and a half-dozen, mostly non-connecting backroads.

"Spare me, boss. I've cleared this particular hill dozens of times in similar conditions," Phil huffed, shifting from four-wheel drive back to park with an overly exaggerated, comically exasperated slapping motion.

"Dozens? Well then, the hill was clearly *due*," Will Crockett exclaimed calmly, peering over into the backseat. "Didn't happen to pack a dogsled team?"

"Droll. No canines, but I do have a couple of flattened cardboard boxes packed away from the Thanksgiving meals-on-wheels deliveries. If you're so inclined, Chief Crockett, would you mind taking control of the bridge while I position those items beneath the tires for additional traction?"

"That I can do, though I'm fairly certain I fully quality for DUI status upon taking the wheel."

"I swear to not uphold the law," the bulky patrolman said, raising a gloved right hand airborne as if to take an oath.

"Go to it then, Phil. Time is slipping away. I'll radio into Maggie and have her give Mac Frame's garage a ring in case we need a tow."

Hopping from the driver's seat directly into ankle-deep slush, Phil Strickland again cursed the fates, if not his own stupidity.

Saturday, 1912 hours
From 1840 AM Radio (The Falls):

"...Le'Floyd Reynolds leaps over the mass of humanity piled at the Wildcat goal-line and rolls off the pile...(pauses) and...has a Dawson Red Raider touchdown. (Pauses) This completes a ten-play, seventy-nine-yard drive, and with just over two minutes until the half, Dawson takes a 13-7 lead with the extra-point try upcoming..."

Saturday, 12:57 hours

"You sure you don't want to sit? You're looking kind of, well..."

"Rickety? Wobbly, Wabbly, Tottery?"

"I'd have gone with unsteady, but well, yeah, any and all of the above would work."

"Just a disguise, Wes, I assure ya. Underneath this façade of paralysis, I'm a man of pure granite, though lately I have found regular use of these damn walking sticks sadly mandatory,"—he paused to showcase each cane by briefly lifting them airborne—"Long as they hold out, I'm steady as an oak. Well, a slightly rotted oak anyhow."

"Well, you're the doctor. Feel free to snag a chair if you change your mind."

The two men locked eyes only briefly, the awkward vibe present a first since their earlier introduction days, before settling into their perspective poses: Wesley Grant remaining parked half-in, half-out of the kitchen slash living room, Gunther McCarron with painfully thin thighs propped against the dining table with his back to the entrance/exit way.

"So what's up, Doc? Dex said ya sounded kinda edgy, which I personally hadn't witnessed in our travels together," the latter said, reaching up to straighten his trademark beret, which the gusty winds had so rudely repositioned. As haggard and weary as he appeared, there was a definite gleam in his eyes that belied the sickly physical appearance.

"Spill, bud, before I do, and I mean that literally."

To this, Wesley gestured toward the table serving as his guest's impromptu third crutch.

"It's, well, complicated and likely to be a tad longwinded. Sure you don't want to give the bionic a rest?"

McCarron waved him off with obvious impatience.

"I'm good, damn it. You're actin' kinda weird, if ya don't mind my sayin'."

"No offense taken nor do I resent the remark. Coffee?"

"Had my fill, just ask my adult diaper. Now quit stallin' and spit it out already. Ya know time is at a premium for *some* of us."

Wesley nervously stroked his beard—uncharacteristically disheveled—before executing a series of spastic neck stretches as if prepping for a strenuous physical workout, the bizarreness of the movements not going unnoticed by his frowning, perplexed guest.

"What's it gonna be, two out of three falls?"

"Sorry. To the point then. I guess it is better that way."

"Dude," his guest responded with a cocked brow, "you're startin' to scare me...sincerely."

"It gets scarier, I'm afraid," the host replied, clearing his throat before resuming. "I need to ask you something right up front."

"Shoot."

"How much of that night do you remember?"

"*That* night referring to?"

"Don't be obtuse, Gunther. You're the one fighting the clock."

"Just wanna be clear. You speak of the night I transformed into the modern-day Rip Van Winkle?"

Wes nodded peevishly.

"Everything is sparkling crystal to a point, then bits and pieces at the conclusion. Mostly bits."

"Check. Let's cover, then, what you *do* recall."

"Wait, so I'm doin' the talkin' then?" Gunther spat, his expression a pale, rumpled mask of annoyance. In reply, his host held up both hands, palms-out.

"There's a method to my madness, I promise."

Gunther's deeply sunken eyes briefly peered downward, a faint whistle escaping pursed lips.

"Gonna hold you to that, Grant, 'cause the truth of the matter is I don't at all enjoy voluntarily revisitin' the details you seek."

"Understood." The seated of the two nodded. "But to properly paint a picture requires those initial strokes to the canvas."

"Dude, you are officially freakin' me out," the upright of the two offered in response before inhaling as deeply as his limited lung capacity would allow.

Unseen by both, a figure cloaked in shadow leaned with its back against the living room wall and eavesdropped onto the conversation happening less than six feet away.

Saturday, 1924 hours
From 1840 AM Radio (The Falls):

"...and as the final seconds tick away and both teams head to their respective locker rooms, I can only surmise the Wildcats' coach Shannon McKay is less than thrilled with his team's turnover issues in the first half, having lost two fumbles and an interception, the bright side obviously being that the home team trails only fourteen to seven despite those potentially fatal miscues..."

Saturday, 1317 hours

"...fade to black. That was all she wrote. The rest is a great big black haze of nothingness. If I'm gonna be completely honest, since wakin' from that record-breakin', super-extended nap, even some of what I was sure *did* happen before is in question. That's just between us cripples. Don't go around quotin' me on it. What pisses me off the most is that every day I wake to *less* clarity. Afraid I grow denser every minute of the day."

With that, the nearly ten-minute narrative complete, McCarron gingerly backstepped until he leaned against the back kitchen wall, spindly arms folded—the black canes crossed like dueling swords—and head bowed as if on the verge of sinking to the floor in a crumbled heap.

"I can't imagine, Gunny," his seated host chimed in only after his guest's head had rearisen and the two locked eyes. "Considering what you've gone through, it's amazing you retain memories at all."

"Yeah well, the hospital staff echoed similar opinions during rehab, I guess blown away that I didn't come to with all the intelligence of a plate of collard greens."

"I've got to ask," Grant stated following another lengthy pause, "not that you're obligated to answer..."

His complexion so pale it practically glowed, McCarron's response was a faint whisper, whatever vim and vigor he'd possessed upon arriving at the rural homestead having gradually ebbed. "Fire...away."

"With what you have recalled, why not pass this updated information to the feds or, at the very least, the local cops?"

McCarron first winced before managing a pained smile rife with sardonic glee.

"To what purpose, Wes? The original narrative might change, sure, but only from a brain-addled gimp left for dead, who's still possibly a suspect in his girlfriend's death. No matter how logically or passionately stated, to those adorned with badges it still comes down to the accusations of a delusional, crazy-ass gimp out for revenge against old enemies.

"Sure, I'm nobody's genius, but I'm not rock-stupid either. No proof, no evidence equals same...old...dead...end, no matter what new info I bring to the table, and to be honest, I'd probably brush me off, too."

"Then why put yourself through this? Can't you see it...it's..."

"Killin' me? Sure as shootin' do, but ya see, I've always known this magical trek back into the land of the livin' wasn't of the extended type. Like I've told ya before, I *truly* believe it was the man upstairs allowin' me just enough time to uncover the culprits. Maybe I misread the message, but damned if I'm gonna stop diggin' just cause the inner pilot light is growin' dimmer by the day. Hell, by the *minute*."

"By digging I assume this includes going on Facebook to publicly trash the culprits you suspect?"

"See that, did ya?" McCarron inquired, eyes suddenly gleaming with mischief, a warped smile breaking through an atypically grim visage.

"Oh yeah, I saw and heard," Grant answered with a gentle shake of the head. "Speaking of which, any word from their respective attorneys?"

"Nah. Didn't really expect anything so dramatic, though I'm bettin' both of 'em had a sudden case of instantaneous *anal-pucker-itis*."

"You ever hear the expression 'poking the bear,' Gunther?"

"Sure, 'cept in McKay's case, it was more like 'pokin' the kitten.' Fat bastard is all manly poses and hot air. As for Hammock, it was more like tossin' pebbles at a feedin' vulture. Pissin' in the coach's Wheaties was just a lark; I don't so much suspect 'im as just don't like 'im. Oh, I'm sure he was capable of imaginin' such nefariousness back in the day, but in the end just didn't possess the testicular fortitude necessary to actually carry it out. Nothin' but an overfed, overrated chicken-shit used car salesman that I would love to see humiliated on the biggest stage possible. Maybe tonight," he winked. "Go Red Raiders.

"As for the former mayor, I don't just *think* that sociopathic conman was behind it...," he paused, visibly straining to raise a hand airborne and extending a forefinger to emphasize the point, "...I'm damn *certain* he was. I remember enough of what Wendy told me about 'im. I also remember talkin' to other folks durin' his mayoral regime who behind closed doors found him less than commendable. The general consensus was that he was one person in public, all agreeable and amiable, and nothin' short of a mustache-twirling, fork-tongued devil in private. He was more than capable of either bein' directly responsible for that night or hirin' someone else to see it through. When I say someone, that ratty perv offspring of his probably woulda done it for free."

Rolling forward just enough to clear the space between living room and kitchen, Wesley stared first at his immobile boots for several seconds before returning his gaze to his guest, who had pushed from the wall following this latest soliloqy, the former struggling for words as his lips squirmed nearly as actively as the gloved hands wriggling spastically at his blanketed lap.

"So that's it?" he finally managed, suddenly unable to match his guest's stare.

"In a nutshell. Why, sound too farfetched for ya? I mean, experienced police records clerk and former Johnny Lawman that ya are, I'm sure you've heard sim—"

The sudden interruption, executed as a hissing whisper between pursed lips, served to instantly melt the mocking grin from McCarron's face.

"Gunther, did you *read* the police reports?"

"The poli—"

"The reports I dropped at your place the morning after you arrived back in town."

McCarron snarled and stumbled forward a step, his momentum halted only by the table's edge.

"Did I—of course I read the damn reports! What'd you think I did, line my adult diaper with 'em? Though honestly that might've been a better use."

"Selective reading perhaps?" his host inquired, his right brow cocked inquisitively.

"Okay, enough already. Just...enough. What exactly are you diggin' at, Grant?"

The voice that boomed from the living room had dramatically different effects on the two already conversing, the seated of the two flinching so severely it appeared he might swan dive from the wheelchair, while the one standing remained wholly unchanged in both deportment and expression.

"Allow me to fill in the blanks!" the mystery source had shrieked before practically sprinting into the room and sliding across the tiled floor in stocking feet and taking up position directly between the two other men.

Remarkably, it was Wesley Grant who appeared the most shaken at the newest arrival's blatantly stagy entrance, his guest's shockingly casual reaction a single blink of the eyes and the forming of a smile as wide as all the great outdoors.

"I'll *be*," Gunther McCarron practically beamed, reversing the single step he'd progressed moments earlier. "Well, ain't this a kick in the gonads?"

The new arrival, all swinging arms and overly animated gestures, was scarecrow thin but simultaneously weirdly graceful and agile, alternating wild, spastic glances between both men.

"Well, hello there, Mac. Surprised?"

"Not at all, when I properly dwell on it," Gunther answered giddily, resembling a downhill skier with each arm stretched wide to either side and the slick black canes effectively propping him.

"So glad ya could join us, Martin."

To this, Martin Hammock executed a slight bow, rising to display a black-handled handgun curled into his right palm.

"Oh, believe me, the pleasure's gonna be *all* mine, Gunny."

Saturday, 1947 hours
From 1840 AM Radio (The Falls):

"...*So with the game clock reading just over seven minutes left in the third stanza, the Wildcats have evened it up at fourteen, courtesy of a Shane Mills to Jeremy Dixon twenty-six yard TD pass, Dixon leaping over solid coverage to haul in Mills' toss and somehow managing to get the tip of a cleat down in the far-left corner of the end zone. That aerial hookup, the fourteenth of the season between the all-county pair, capped a ten-play, eighty-one-yard drive that ate up nearly eight minutes off the clock. Dawson will now receive the ball for the first time in the second half, and just as a light drizzle of sleet and rain resumes for the first time...*"

Saturday, 13:28 hours

"C'mon now, is the hardware really necessary between such trusted old friends?"

"Mandatory."

"I look dangerous to you?"

"Always."

Marty Hammock held the handle of the firearm tucked tightly against his own ribcage with the sights trained directly at McCarron's narrow midsection, his aim as unwavering as his tone, his bony frame holding up an ankle-length black duster that appeared to be at least three sizes too large.

"Cuts me deep, dude. Extremely hurtful," the intended target quipped, briefly peering over Hammock's shoulder to his seated host, whose crinkled face expressed either sadness or disgust, or perhaps a hybrid of each. "We used to be so tight."

"You know better, smartass," Hammock fired back through a thin-lipped grin of pure malevolence.

"Do I now? So amid such a long checklist of skills, you now claim mind reader as well? Marty, you are one talented degenerate."

Using his free hand to wipe away lengthy, overlapping strands of stringy, light brown hair from his path of vision, the new arrival performed a slight curtsy though careful to remain perfectly on-target with the other.

"Oh, my apologies, your highness. Let's just say I considered our relationship more of the client-customer type."

"Never said we swapped spit, Weasel."

The armed man's right eye twitched, his gun hand flinching ever so briefly, as if from a mild electric shock.

"Some things a man never forgets," McCarron continued, winking playfully. "Especially a nickname so damn fitting the source material."

Taking a single step back until he all but hip-checked Grant's wheelchair—the seated man's complexion having transformed to a sickly green in a matter of minutes—Hammock raised what appeared to be a nine-millimeter of unknown brand until the front sight sat directly across from the standing man's nose.

"That so, is it? School-yard insults at this stage in the game? Well then, as long as we've rolled shoulder first onto memory lane, might as well stop wasting time with the small chatter and, as someone we in the general area used to refer to as Captain Crank might've said, tear open that box of Scooby Snax. I'm talking rip that *lid* right off and *dunk* that prime *rocket fuel* right in the *trash*, what say, Mac?"

Even as McCarron's smile had for the most part, save for a few slight tics, remained glued in place for the duration of his captive's nonsensical rant, Wesley Grant had lowered his head into both hands as if either deep in prayer or overwhelmed by a sudden wave of repulsion.

"Hooo-kay. Still sprinklin' paint chips into our mornin' cereal, are we?"

The armed man's rounded shoulders instantly sunk, as did his stubble-coated chin.

"Sure, Mac, sure. I get it," he eventually replied, eyes rolling. "Maybe you figure I'm wearing a wire or have some random mic tucked away in my undershorts or even had a camera surgically inserted into my left nostril."

"Not...really, dude," the captive said, briefly raising each cane knee-level as if to mimic exposing bare palms in confusion. "Just don't have the remotest clue of what you speak. Or for that matter, why the hell you were hidin' away in this man's livin' room only to attempt some cheap jump scare for whatever reason, and most of all...," he paused only long enough to again gaze past his captor toward the homeowner, whose hangdog expression had yet to alter, "...what's the purpose of holdin' a couple of cripples at gunpoint? I can only think of one reason. Well, maybe *two,* if you're here as dear ol' dad's stand-in. Hey, you're holdin' that piece, Marty, so we're goin' nowhere, at least nowhere *fast.* Can't speak for Grant, seems your sudden entrance struck him mute, but me—I'd give a month's worth of pain meds for a few answers. Actually, make that a week's worth, since stockin' up past that seems downright foolish at this point."

Tucking the handgun at his side while simultaneously lowering its trajectory back to his captive's upper chest and midsection, Hammock sighed heavily before offering up a surprisingly taciturn reply.

"Y'know, all my life I've heard the term 'selective memory' and always deemed it outright horseshit, a convenient excuse for lying assholes who made a habit out of misremembering whenever it best suited."

Head tilted, eyes squinting and mouth partially agape, McCarron slid a step forward—with no small assistance from the twin canes—to presumably make up the back-stride his captor had executed earlier.

"Correct me if I'm wrong, Marty, but are you callin' me a liar?"

The gangly, weirdly disproportionate man smiled broadly, revealing gold-plated incisors.

"Without a doubt."

"Again, I'm both disappointed and dismayed."

"I rest my case."

McCarron shrugged shoulders so rounded they resembled ball-bearings balanced atop broom handles.

"Whoa now, I'm gonna need a prime example on just how you reached this diagnosis."

Completely turning his back on their seated host, Hammock hopped away until the pair stood and sat, respectively, thigh to shoulder.

"Oh, I can do a hell of a lot better than that, Mac. I can go deep into the count. Ring a few of those rusty bells in that foggy noggin of yours, you might say."

"Jesus, Marty...," Wesley Grant mumbled from the armed man's right, still unable and/or unwilling to lock eyes with his fellow paraplegic's intense stare.

"Hush, Wesley. Hey, you wore a badge once upon a time. Weren't you trained to read the body language of suspects, you know, to know if they're lying and all that?"

"Just leave me out of th—"

"Get to it already, Weasel," McCarron interceded sharply, the left cane raised and pointed accusingly at his armed captor. "Got no time for all-night tap dances with the likes of you, unless of course the final waltz includes a complete confession."

Hammock snorted, gesturing with his free hand for his detainee to lower the cane, to which McCarron replied as his long-standing grin was quickly replaced with a half-snarl, half-grin hybrid.

"Not likely, Mac, at least not the admission you're hoping for."

Lunging forth a step—narrow chest bowed and canes smacking the hard tile with shocking force—McCarron's forward momentum nearly tipped him directly into the gun's front sight.

"Then th-the *HELL* with you, Hammock!" he screeched, frothy spittle sailing airborne following each emphasized word. "If you're here...to cover dear old dad's ass...you can go ahead and use that...peashooter, but spare me the...*BULLSHIT!*"

Calmly, the armed man—who, shockingly, hadn't visibly budged in the face of his captive's enraged, overt aggression—addressed this with uncharacteristic poise, and his aim had yet to waver.

"I'm not here to cover up anyone's sins, Mac, least of all yours or mine. I'm just here to address 'em as I saw 'em. Now, I don't know if you're lying through those peg-corn teeth or if surviving fourteen years as a cabbage did manage to flush away the bloody shrapnel from your own past actions. You claim you've come back to Crimson Falls on a mission, some unfinished retribution the gods have seen fit to grant you. See if you feel the same way in the face of the cold, hard truth of the matter..."

Saturday, 1947 hours
From 1840 AM Radio (The Falls):

"*...Dawson's Miles Randolph takes the screen pass from Booker Jeffries and rambles untouched to paydirt, and, with just over two minutes left in the third quarter, Gary Tiffin's extra point gives the Red Raiders a twenty-one to fourteen edge. Now as Tiffin prepares to kick off to the Wildcats, Vern Williamson and Shantel Clarke waiting near the goal line, a*

light snowfall has replaced the earlier band of sleet, slowly adding an ivory glaze to an already messy, muddy field.
"

Saturday, 13:41 hours

"That double-wide trailer that used to fill space right off the highway a mile or two down Jensen Acres, called it 'Bootlegger Alley' until about a decade back," Hammock began, pausing with an index finger raised.

"I'm familiar with it," McCarron replied calmly. "Fact is, I took Wes there on a little magical mystery tour a few days ago. Not much left but a dead patch where the ol' homestead once sat."

Leaning against one of the high-back dining chairs with a cane firmly planted on either side, Gunther McCarron had managed to assume a half-sitting, half-standing pose without removing the X-suit, his captor kneeling next to Wesley Grant's wheelchair with his gun hand balanced atop the right armrest.

"Sweet. Now then, hop in that creaky old time-machine with me to late summer in the year two-thousand seven."

"Remember it like it was yesterday," McCarron nodded stiffly. "Well, more like nine months ago...literally."

The slim narrator, the baggy duster cloaking his slight frame like the flaps of a circus tent, snapped the fingers of his free hand before using the same appendage to again clear a few stray locks of scraggily hair from his line of sight.

"Never thought of it that way, but yeah, I guess you did lose the majority of fourteen years to one hell of a power nap. So why the fuzzy brainpan? I'd think your memories would be all the fresher."

McCarron's forehead severely creased, his right brow arched over a squinted eye.

"You would *think*, but it seems that long a mental sabbatical has a tendency to wipe clean a large portion of the slate, flashback-wise."

"Yeah, whatever. Medical science was never my specialty."

"Understandable, considerin' your talent for charmin' underaged girls, sellin' skunky weed to their little brothers and trollin' the elementary playgrounds for up-and-comers."

"Oh, so I'm the lowlife? That's how you remember it?" Hammock smirked, briefly glancing over to Wes Grant, whose slumped shoulders and blank stare into the carpet at his feet had remained unchanged since the impromptu interview's opening barbs.

"So sorry to have offended, but it does prompt the question: what profession did such a clean-cut, upstanding citizen such as yourself claim at that time?"

"As I recall, kinda hazy ya understand, at least about any Crimson Falls-related paychecks, but I do know in Nashville I worked both full- and part-time gigs as a handyman for hire, mostly for nearby apartment complexes."

"Handyman...," the kneeled man giggled behind the palm of his free hand. "...Oh shit, this is priceless. Seriously though, I guess one could define your way of making ends meet within the community as a handyman of sorts. Permission to refresh the foggy recesses?"

Suddenly stone-faced and gnawing into his pale lower lip, McCarron merely nodded his approval.

"Great. Personally, if I were tasked with writing the job description of one Gunther McCarron a full decade after his many gridiron heroics had been all but forgotten, I'd have to begin with the natural skills he'd shown in the field of homegrown, homecooked goods, followed closely by a penchant for salesmanship."

In lieu of a verbal response, McCarron ceased the incessant lip-chewing and arched both brows.

The narrator's reply was direct but blandly delivered, as if with the understanding that what he was about to divulge was already a well-known fact despite whatever fervid denials might surface.

313

"You were a chef of sorts. A chef who specialized in providing his dishes through personal delivery, or for a fortunate few, a drive-thru service. Ring a bell?"

"Cut to it, weasel," the clearly irked captive snarled in reply. "Or spare me the continuation of this little mental tap dance and shoot me already."

Shrugging, Hammock addressed the seated man without breaking eye contact with the standing one.

"I'll take that as a definite 'no' then, what say you, Wesley?"

"Leave me out of this," Grant spat, jaw muscles clenching and unclenching at regular three-to-five-second intervals.

"Oh sure, no problem. My bad. Forgot you haven't yet been called to officially testify. Fine then, straight to the chase."

The man holding the firearm stood with aid from the wheelchair's armrest, bony knees crackling from the effort.

"Bluntly put, you cooked meth and sold it."

Following a brief pause, in which Gunther McCarron's left eye twitched spastically, he first turned before tilting his head to the left, lifting a spindly arm—having left the cane propped against an equally thin thigh—to his ear and extending the generous flap outward.

"Come...again?"

Hammock sidestepped gingerly until he stood directly behind the wheelchair and its solemn, pouting passenger.

"Clear and concise, Mac; you were, admittedly, a low-level dealer but with big aspirations, that is until my stepsister stepped in to gum up the works."

"Horseshit, weasel," McCarron said, the spastic tic having traveled to the opposite eye, the lid briefly sticking every few blinks. "Try again."

"Oh, your words say no but those beady little eyes speak otherwise. C'mon now, Mac, concentrate. Coma-induced pudding-brain aside, I can see you fighting what you know is the truth. Drop the mitts and jut the chin, brother, the jig is definitely...up."

McCarron appeared to ignore the request, turning his gaze to the wheelchair's Golem-like inhabitant.

"So Wes, please tell me you were sabotaged at gunpoint and *not* a willing participant in this garbage."

Through haunted, dead eyes, the seated man peered slowly upward.

"It's true, Gunther. All that and so...much more. Heaven help us all, so damn much more."

The back door exploded inward just as McCarron's quivering lips were prepping a reply, however moot, the bulky figure responsible strolling calmly inside wearing a smug, frozen smirk and an object slung over a shoulder that was of vague familiarity to the startled captive.

"Well, 'bout time you joined the party." Marty Hammock grinned while delivering a gleeful smack to Wesley Grant's left shoulder, the recipient openly shuddering, wide-eyed and mouth agape, as if death himself had just entered the fray.

Saturday, 2006 hours
From 1840 AM Radio (The Falls):

"...Dalton Crane takes the pitch from Mills at the Wildcats' forty-four. He's streaking down the sidelines with one man to beat! He's at the Red Raider forty...the thirty-five...thirty...the twenty-five...breaks a tackle at the ten...five...paaaay-dirt, Wildcats! With just over eleven minutes left, this contest is an extra point try away from our third deadlock!"

Fourteen

"Well, well, ain't this special now?" the newest arrival brayed in a comically nasal whine both alien and vaguely familiar, kicking the back door shut with a blind back kick delivered with a mud-packed work boot before turning swiftly to address a wide-eyed, slack-jawed Gunther McCarron. "Howdy, sunshine! Long time, no see. Don't you resemble hammered shit!"

Stumbling several shuffling steps to the right until his hip bumped the edge of the kitchen sink, McCarron's lips squirmed as if he were unable to articulate a coherent counter punch, his eyes spastically darting as he deliberated the identity of this newest and easily most intimidating of entities.

"Well, don't just stand there gawking like some backwoods inbred, Mac, say hey to an old friend," he heard Hammock quip while vaguely aware of a low moaning sound originating from the general vicinity of Wesley Grant.

"I don't...know...do we...know each other?" McCarron babbled, clueless to the fact that he'd raised the cane, gripped in a badly shaking right hand, positioning it like a fencing sword aimed directly at the new arrival's midsection.

"Oh, come off it already, handyman. All those lost years aside, it should seem like just yesterday when I was greasing your palm with cash on a bi-weekly basis."

"Greased...p-palms? I just...but...no, there's nothing...," Gunther stammered, the cane slowly descending.

"Get a load of those plate-sized peepers," the heavyset stranger resumed in sarcastic awe, alternating glances between McCarron and Hammock. "The lower jaw all unhinged, the spazzy twitching of those stringy limbs. All the stereotypical signs of utter confusion. Amazin'. High as a kite and still able to pull off a pretty damn convincing act, though for what purpose is a mystery beyond this girl's solving."

"He is the *limit,* isn't he?" Hammock chimed in while applying another light tap to Grant's shoulder, the latter openly flinching though able to maintain a steely focus on the most recent intruder to his longtime residence. "But I gotta tell you, at this juncture I'm not so sure it is an act."

"He knows, Martin. He's always known. Fooling my soft-hearted, soft-headed ex over there is certainly no Herculean feat."

To this, McCarron's gaze departed the large and definitely in-charge form of Sandy Jamison—sleek, black baseball bat slung over one shoulder, a black and silver *Vegas Raiders* windbreaker and baggy jeans doing little to conceal her imposing girth, and what appeared to be wads of rolled up tissue paper protruding from each reddened nostril—for that of his former escort, whose own predatory-like glower remained frozen on that selfsame individual.

"He is...*was* clueless," Grant whispered, in reality his voice barely audible but its overall effect that of a bellowing screech through a bullhorn. "If you'd just...waited...held off, none of...*this* would be necessary."

"Nope. Negatory." Sandy shook her head, raising a meaty hand palms-out toward her onetime life partner, stepping directly into the kitchen's bright LED spotlight to reveal a myriad of physical wounds, including a severely swollen nose complete with the tissue-packed nostrils, a blue-shaded shiner beneath her left eye and a quarter-sized bruise at the center of an otherwise pale forehead. "Honestly, sweetums, but you're a weak-minded fool. All he had to do was limp along by your side, crap his pants a few times, require an ER visit or two or just wax nostalgic, and he had you hook, line, and sinker. You were unable to separate your shared hardships, baby. Be that as it is, you don't get a vote here. I knew when you started running from me, avoiding me, hiding from what you knew was gonna *have* to come to pass, well...," she shrugged massive shoulders, "...that's when your precious Plan A got shoved through the shredder."

"Jesus, Sandy, you get the plate number of the truck?" Hammock inquired, leaning forward with eyes squinted to better take in the myriad of wounds.

"You should see the *other* guy," came the nasally reply, delivered through a tight, sadistic smile.

"St-steroids," a voice suddenly echoed within the relatively cramped, surely overpopulated walls—deep, hoarse, raw—and if nothing else, shockingly revealing in its blatant frankness. Not at all the choreographed utterings of a veteran thespian, but a genuine, heartfelt revelation spewed forth in a moment of spontaneous epiphany.

"I sold...ya De-Deca-Durabolin injections a-and or...Anavar tabs, s-sometimes...," McCarron continued, eyes gleaming and turned upward, mouth agape between stammers. "...Dianabol. You...were competin' for...for the Olympics or...or...somethin' similar."

"Miss Olympia, genius, IFBB sponsored," Jamison snarled, twirling the ball bat until it rested on the opposite shoulder while regarding McCarron with a deep scowl that spoke of her disdain and disbelief in his abrupt remembrance.

"You...had opened a gym in Carver Hills, *no,* Benton," he concluded, glazed, rapidly blinking eyes finally locking on her own.

Jamison swapped glances with both her ex-spouse and Marty Hammock before turning back to the subject of their collective dressing-down, the ball bat now balanced between ample thighs.

"If it is an act, boy, I must say you deserve one of those gold statues."

"Nope. Not falling for it," Hammock exclaimed with a vehement nod, stepping out from behind a shell-shocked Wesley Grant to stand shoulder-to-shoulder with his female cohort, who appeared to outweigh him roughly by half. "Little too miraculous, isn't it? Why the sudden recall?"

"You're truly...*truly* an imbecile, Hammock. An honest-to-god...mental...midget."

Twisting around to face the source—his gun hand and accompanying aim remarkably unchanged—Hammock's nonverbal reply consisted solely of a comically exaggerated frown. In response, Wesley Grant simply resumed in the same flat, emotionless tone he'd utilized since McCarron's arrival.

"Think about it, Einstein: If his so-called act was all about masking his knowledge of your involvement, why would he change that and instantly incriminate himself?"

"Ask him, smartass. I'm no psychic."

"Doesn't matter," Jamison chimed in, sweating profusely while pacing a small circle and staring down her ex even as Hammock refocused on their shared adversary, who appeared to be gradually sinking to the tiled floor in a slow-motion squat. "End result's gonna be the same regardless."

"Stirring amphetamines into your steroid soup again, dear?" Grant inquired, regarding his ex-spouse with sincere disgust and, if his follow-up snarl were to be believed, as pure a loathing as he normally saved for himself. "You look about one hit away from a massive coronary."

With that, Jamison halted her incessant stride and stood at mock attention, tossing the bat roughly from palm to palm, overly dilated eyes drilling into his own.

"Keep it up, shit stain, and I'll surely reserve that one last swipe for you."

Hammock merely nodded as if not to take such threats lightly while watching with dismay as Gunther McCarron slunk slowly downward, only the bulky suit strapped to his frame preventing a more accelerated descent.

"You..." the slithering cripple whispered, knobby knees half-bent and stringy arms and hands hanging limply at his sides, "...you were...all there. That night...a-all of you. E-even...," he paused, sunken eyes rolling counterclockwise like marbles in a slot machine until landing firmly on the seated paraplegic parked barely a reach away, "...even you. That was...you were the...law."

"Uh-oh, it appears you've officially been i-den-tee-fied, Deputy Grant. Guess a scraggly beard, balding scalp and an extra layer or two of padding can only be so effective as far as disguises go," Marty Hammock exclaimed grimly, reaching out with a socked foot to apply a light kick to the chair's right footrest.

"And you!" their accuser resumed, a bony forefinger pointed directly at his armed captive. "You...sick fr-freak. It was...you."

"Uh-huh, here we go. Appears he's going for both best act-tor and best support—"

Hammock never finished whatever quip he'd so cleverly ad-libbed, instead freezing with mouth agape and thin lips atremble as the target of the group's collective ire resumed speaking in a voice drastically altered from the one that had initiated the allegation.

320

"You murdered Wendy. It was...*you*."

For the first time since Sandy Jamison's raucous home invasion, a ten-plus second silence ensued, during which the only audible sound was the suddenly harsh breathing of the accused.

Surprisingly, the initial verbal response belonged not to Marty Hammock but the paralyzed man sitting immediately to his left.

"Well, well, it does appear a rewrite of that moldy fourteen-year-old script is in order."

Saturday, 2019 hours
From 1840 AM Radio (The Falls):

"...*Booker Jeffries outruns the pursuit and dives for the pylon...that's six points for the Red Raiders.*

(long pause amid a spattering of hoots and applause)

The visitors from Dawson are an extra point away from taking a seven-point lead with just under five minutes remaining in the contest. This as the ever-present cold rain and sleet seem to be picking up in intensity..."

From the time his ex—her only vaguely familiar traits from when they were a couple—that honey-dripping Southern twang, so sickly sweet it sounded manufactured on some Hollywood soundstage, and of course, the refrigerator-with-a-head physique—had bludgeoned her way into the room with her usual lack of finesse, Wesley had fallen into a self-imposed haze. As such, though while still acutely aware of the assorted movements and sounds around him, an inner projector had been switched on that allowed for a private screening within his mind's eye: a program showcased, strangely, in black and white images more akin to a silent picture of old. Fitting in some ways, considering the memories flooding forth to break through a dam forged of denial and cowardice seemed comfortably at home in such an archaic setting when in reality, the story it displayed was but fourteen winters old.

He'd tracked Sandy to the trailer, feeling a twinge of guilt that was easily dismissed by thoughts of the potential big bust at hand. It went without saying that his fiery spouse was liable to be less than thrilled that he was out to bust her dealer and was essentially using her to do so. He had even debated—albeit ever so briefly—about not going through with it before deciding that, cliché as it sounded, it was a matter of sworn duty to bring the dealer to justice, and it wasn't as if all other leads had been exhausted by both him and the department. It also wasn't as if he wouldn't take his lumps, even if the bust was the complete success he'd hoped.

Both he and Sandy had partaken of the illegal substance in various forms (everything from Deca-Durabolin to Equipoise to Winstrol) for most of the past year, though his had been more of the semimonthly cycling of mostly the pill variety just to bulk up, she'd also been injecting regularly for a forthcoming IBB competition in Louisville. He'd never pushed her on where she'd obtained the scripted drugs, though she had mentioned in passing that her trainer had "loaned her" the goods on the few occasions the subject had been breached.

In the aftermath of whatever glory and accolades the arrest and subsequent seizures would bring, he knew a detailed grilling would be in order from his superiors once he fessed up on just how he'd managed to track down both dealer and stash. Making matters worse would be that it was obvious, what with his own bulked-up appearance—the other deputies had nicknamed him "Stay-Puft"—that there'd be no denying his own illegal usage over the past year or so.

Sandy had opened up the gym roughly six months earlier and struggled to make a profit past rent and maintenance fees while also failing miserably to strike any fear in the lone competition in Crimson Falls, a long-established sweat-and-strain joint run by a former all-state wrestler called the "Pump, Press and Flex."

With an investment of just over sixty-grand in free weights, benches, racks and assorted universal machines on the verge of going permanently into the red, she'd gotten desperate enough to branch out into illegal steroid and human growth hormone sales, buying in bulk from her dealer and selling individually to a growing list of customers, some of whom weren't even clients at her gym but at the aforementioned competitor's.

While they'd used together—she'd convinced him that as a "power couple" they must first impress prospective clients with their own buffed physiques—he'd begun to suspect rampant illegal activity, the final indictment being that she'd begun to spend more freely and seemed far less stressed out as months progressed, despite the gym turning a modest profit at best. It had taken some detecting, but he'd eventually discovered a hidden cache consisting of rolls of unreported cash and the ledgers she'd used to calculate debits versus credits.

That night, as he'd trailed her while off duty—he'd told her he was working an extra shift to assist the Benton PD with a possible meth bust on the eastern edge of the county—and having borrowed an aged Pontiac Grand Am from the county's drug-seizure impound lot, he'd understood he was more than likely sacrificing his marriage for nothing more than a clap on the back and possible future promotion considerations. Saddest of all, he'd resigned said trade-off as perfectly acceptable. He and Sandy had been drifting apart for years, spending less and less time with each other, and were strangely detached and disconnected even when together.

The sand hourglass had drained dangerously low by that point, though there were still times he wondered if he'd made the right decision to put that final nail into the coffin. It was only when logic intervened that his actions had, at least temporarily, cut off a major meth supplier from the locals, that Wes accepted that the right call had been made.

It had been approaching eleven PM when Sandy had exited their bed and snuck out to make the buy, as he had confirmed with a quick peek at the clock-alarm on his side of the headboard. Wide awake but feigning exhaustion, he'd long since suspected such an action was imminent via her restless, ill-at-ease behavior that evening.

As he'd run two to three minutes behind her, he'd been forced to guess a direction—east or west—leaving town and guessed right, spotting the brake lights of their gray Chevy Impala along state highway six, headed out of the city limits and directly toward Booneville.

Approximately twelve minutes later, after traversing a perpetually curvy two-lane—briefly a four-lane to allow for the passing of slower traffic, mostly rumbling semis and farm tractors—he'd followed her down an unmarked, semi-paved stretch that was as sporadically hilly as it was curvy, switching off his headlights once she'd braked onto a dirt path cloaked in overgrown evergreens and azaleas, grateful for a brighter moon that was hardly typical of a late fall night in eastern Kentucky.

The trailer—a massive double-wide with light brown paneled walls, its foundation effectively shrouded in a faux brick paneling—sat roughly fifty yards from the dirt road, and, considering its seemingly strategic, tucked-away in a dark corner locale and the fact that it was weirdly void a visible mailbox, appeared as the comically stereotypical structure used for the manufacture and sale of illegal substances.

Wesley sat idling inside the irregularly sputtering Grand Am on the dirt path which showed no signs of a nearby dead end while curving further into the forested landscape, and was just able to make out his wife's substantial shadow departing the Impala, which she'd parked in a wide clearing fronting the *trailer. Barely visible past the front end of the Impala was the front end of a dark-shaded pickup, parked underneath a tight grouping of oaks and maples, their mostly bare limbs having shed the majority of their summer cargo.*

In eventually cutting the engine of the noisy Pontiac—he'd feared an impending backfire—he became instantly aware of a spattering of bellowed profanities and screams, both male and female in origin, echoing from the trailer's general direction.

Never one to hesitate in the face of mortal danger—in his two-plus years as a commissioned deputy for the county, he'd often been referred to as not only overzealous but downright reckless—he'd hit the ground running with his departmental thirty-eight already freed from its holster.

The voices grew louder, shriller, angrier and more desperate as he leaped the four wooden steps leading inside, toward the front entrance that was pulled ajar.

Wesley would like to think, at least in that moment and time, that this latest example of youthful recklessness was due to marital concern, but in truth, and especially as the years had gradually worn away the façade of that particular mistruth, the mad rush into that mystery structure had been all about showcasing the guts to obtain the glory.

Regardless, what he'd dashed headfirst into at the rear of that trailer—looking twice as spacious inside as observed from out—had surpassed times ten all probable options his frenzied imagination had manufactured beforehand.

Amid the makeshift laboratory: tables overturned, glass shattered, the overwhelming aroma of chemicals freed from their constraints, a trio of bodies standing upright and shifting rapidly and one down and unmoving.

To his right stood his estranged spouse, armed with, of all things, a baseball bat—she would later testify to not knowing exactly where she'd acquired said blunt object but could only guess at the trailer's living room or hallway—her breathing labored and strained, mouth hanging agape as if she'd just completed a strenuous set of squats.

To his left, a lanky, longhaired male brandishing a large, serrated hunting knife, whose thin face and pointy goatee he'd found faintly familiar as if perhaps he'd once viewed it in a mugshot lineup.

To his right-center and backed nearly to a far wall stood the man later identified—first by Sandy and then in local newsprint all over the state—as Gunther James McCarron, shirtless and barefoot, a pair of blood-spattered blue-jean shorts his lone form of clothing. As far as weaponry went, McCarron was waving around a small handgun of some sort in his right hand, the flash of its silver handle obvious beneath a trio of fluorescents burning brightly from above.

As for the still form, it was definitely a female and, unlike the skinny longhair flashing the cutlery, much more to Wes than just weirdly familiar; her severely bludgeoned face had been pulped nearly into nonexistence—an obvious case of psychotic overkill—a single bloodshot brown, glazed-over eye stuck ajar and staring accusingly upward. Decked out in a once-pink blouse—recently altered drastically via thick streaks of dark crimson, blue jeans (ditto) and white sneakers, one of which had vacated the host to sit upside down near the bare foot it had departed—it was apparent that the corpse had endured quite the beating even after its living host's pulse had ceased. At the sight, mercifully brief, of her overly pale features and one-eyed death stare, Wes openly gagged, his tongue splashed with a misting of hot bile that threatened to erupt volcanically if his look lingered.

The four had screamed, shrieked and screeched over each other for a full minute, perhaps more, the main gist of the non-conversation consisting of accusations of betrayal—Sandy toward Wes, Wes in-kind back to Sandy and the as-of-yet unidentified male soon to be introduced as Martin Hammock toward both Sandy and Gunther McCarron. As easily the most hysterical amid stiff competition, McCarron's overly dilated eyes bounced like loose marbles while exchanging spastic glances from the trio of invaders to his turf to the cooling corpse taking up floorspace to his right.

Of the few words of comprehensible dialogue Wes could clearly recall from their obviously enraged and possibly psychotic host, the majority had been the multi-use of the word "NARC," "traitor," and, most notably "set up," all spat in the direction of the dead body with great emotion, its originator's gaunt cheeks lined with fresh tears while both nostrils spewed forth thick torrents of clear mucus.

Whatever had occurred before his arrival, whatever had led to the death of the fresh-faced waif lying in the corner, Wesley Grant understood in that moment that the man most likely responsible had suffered, at least in his own chemically-altered mind, the ultimate in betrayals.

He also understood, reluctantly and not without a period of stubborn denial, that a certain county deputy with more ambition than brains was equally responsible.

In light of McCarron's googly-eyed stuttering accusation, Marty Hammock executed a textbook face-palm, perhaps unaware that he'd dropped the firearm to his side in the process.

"You were alone with her when we...*all* of us arrived, genius. There's only been one feasible suspect since day one. Find a mirror and you've found 'im."

Gangly legs splayed out in front of him, the twin canes folded across a nonexistent lap, McCarron stared up toward the ceiling as he spoke, as if envisioning projected images he alone was privy to.

"That night I...she was...told me that she was...a...narc, an informant. DEA or county or...some such agency lookin' to stamp out the meth trade in the area. She...said that our...that meetin' me at the game that first night was hardly by...by chance.

"The night she...it all happened, she had called and...wanted to meet at the Old Spaghetti Inn over in Adams. It was...one of the special places, ya might say. One of our first official, well, dates. Funny, she was supposed to be back on campus.

"After a bite we...left her car there and drove over to the trailer for a...fix. Said she knew what I did, even though I'd never...told her outright. Smart chickie, I used to call her. It was...on the way that she...started to talk. Told me every...damn...thing. Strange"—he paused, gaze dropping and then shifting toward his fellow paraplegic—"I've forgotten more than I can remember 'bout that night, but one thing that's still clear as crystal is, while she was spillin' her guts as we sat together on the livin' room couch, there was a wave of dizziness that almost knocked me to my knees. Natural paralysis, ya might say. Never felt such...so betrayed by anyone, much less the one and only person I'd grown to fully trust.

"I finally just had to get up. Had to move. Had to get the hell outta dodge. I recall her callin' my name, not screamin', mind you, just calmly repeatin' it over and over like she did sometimes whenever we kidded around. As she had a bad habit of leavin' her keys in the ignition, I jumped in her ride and just drove. Left her there alone without even thinkin' about it. About what she might see if she walked to the rear of that trailer. By the time I did, I found I really didn't give a damn."

"Convenient. Just needed to blow off some steam, right?" Hammock intervened, having reclaimed a slightly wavering aim near or around the speaker's skull.

McCarron resumed as if either oblivious to the statement or utterly uncaring, his focus now at his own splayed boots.

"I couldn't have been gone more than twenty minutes, tops. Just to the Hazel Path four-way and back, all the while tryin' to figure out what I was gonna say or *do* once we were back face-to-face. The trailer door was hanging wide open when I pulled up and quiet as a church as I strolled back in. Might've taken me a minute, two tops, to case the other rooms before makin' it back to the lab. Now, that room was double padlocked as a rule, but there was that steel-plated, two-inch thick door standin' as wide as the front had been and I faintly recalled leavin' it unsecured the night before as a higher up in the organization had called earlier about a surprise inspection or some such shit. A rare occurrence but far from a virgin experience.

"I took...two, maybe three steps inside, not even surveyin' the damage, and it was extensive, before findin' her exactly the way you three did upon that...group trespass."

While Hammock openly scoffed and Jamison released a sarcastic giggle while twirling the bat like a baton, Wesley Grant alone remained both verbally and nonverbally uncommitted.

"Funny thing, though," McCarron resumed, infinitely aware and donning a warped sneer aimed directly at Grant, who managed to maintain eye contact despite wearing an expression that was guilt defined, "...those CFPD police reports didn't even hint at what Wendy knew or why. I can only *guess* why. Riddle me that, Mister *former* stalwart law dog and so well-respected po-leece records clerk."

As he replied, Grant alternated glances to all present, the deadness behind his eyes accompanied by a similar tonc: bone-weary and leaden in the act of confessing to the one person not already privy to the story.

"She was a great kid. Determined and so damn serious about everything. Sure, I used her. Used her youthful exuberance, her willingness to help. She was fresh off getting a degree in criminal justice. Wanted to be an agent: FBI, CIA, DEA, ATF. Wherever she could do the most good, she said, to make a real contribution.

"It was off the books at the department. No one knew. It would've cost me my job, putting a civilian in such potential danger. Might've meant doing some time. At that age, I thought it worth the risk.

"She was mentioned as a person of interest by the state, but nothing ever came of it, just another dead meth-head, despite her...such a privileged upbringing. Poor little rich kid done in by the evils of drug addiction. Wrong place, wrong time, tragic accident. End of story as far as most were concerned. Kerry Hammock hired an assortment of private eyes from Lexington, Louisville. Even flew one in from Denver. That explosion and fire covered our tracks damn well."

"Well, considerin' you ignited a thermal charge on site, it's a damn wonder there was still a tree standin' fifty feet away."

"Not guilty. Nope, not that," Grant fired back, removing his left hand from underneath the ever-present blanket covering his lap and waving a forefinger back and forth.

"Hate to agree with my spineless former *less*-half, but I concur," Jamison chimed in, utilizing the ball bat as a cane with the fat end propped crookedly onto the hard tile.

"Make it three. We didn't blow up shit," Hammock concurred, actually holding up his left hand and flashing the famous "three-finger salute" of Boy Scout fame. "It lit up damn well on its own once those chemicals caught. Between the battery acid, the acetone and the red phosphorus, it went up like dried kindling from the first spark."

McCarron's laugh was more a raspy, hacking cough, his unblinking, unwavering gaze never departing Grant.

"Yeah, well, since Deputy Devious over there saw fit to tase me into oblivion, who exactly sparked the kindlin'?"

"Can't speak for Marty, but the two of us left together," Jamison retorted with a snarl while nodding toward her ex as dime-sized droplets of perspiration formed on her cheeks and forehead.

Grant swallowed hard and laughed bitterly before chiming in for what was obviously a reluctant concurrence.

"San...she's right. Only the back of the trailer was burning as we...as we..."

"Shagged ass...," his ex-spouse concluded with an exaggerated roll of the eyes, "...but not until Mister Hero with a badge there decided to pull your worthless carcass out and haul you twenty or thirty feet up the driveway."

"Murder just rubs me the wrong way, sweet cheeks," Grant retorted sarcastically. "Guess I was in the minority."

With what appeared a Herculean effort, McCarron raised himself upright—with no small aid from the twin canes, which he'd dug into the tile as if burying railroads spikes on either side—and, his breath coming in short raspy bursts, struck a decidedly bowed pose, leaning hard to the right.

"I thank you from the bottom of my paralyzed rear end, Deputy, but somethin' still preys on my mind and has since comin' to all those months back.

"Leavin' Wendy's body behind was no mystery. Somebody wanted nothin' left but ashes, I get that. The dedicated lawman over there had zapped me into submission and then, so y'all say, dragged me outta that burnin' lab." He paused, shooting lazy glances at the trio who'd formed a makeshift semicircle in the relatively small kitchen before coming in for a visual landing, yet again, on Wesley Grant. "So how exactly did I end up with a shattered spine? Wes here *drag* me under somebody's wheels 'fore they just happened to drive off? Sooo, somebody clue me in. Was I wearin' car tread tattoos on both cheeks or *what*?"

Gradually, both Wesley Grant's downtrodden and Sandy Jamison's spastic gazes, respectively, turned to Marty Hammock.

"You gonna tell 'im?" Jamison inquired, wiping her sweat-drenched visage with a thick forearm as the ball bat leaned precariously against an equally copious thigh. "Truth be told, I wouldn't mind claiming it, though at present at least two here would know I'm fibbing."

Firearm newly raised and aimed directly between McCarron's eyes, Hammock took an additional half-step forward.

"Let's just say, seeing my half-sister's fast-chilling corpse curled up in the corner didn't exactly motivate calm, cool behavior on my part. Simply put, I wanted you dead, asshole. I didn't want you walking away only to see some DA or liberal judge show mercy with a handful of misdemeanor drug charges and maybe a pled-down reckless endangerment."

Hammock grinned, shuffling forth another half-step and stretching out his gun hand until the barrel tip levitated mere inches from its proposed target's forehead.

"All that said, once Grant saw fit to uphold his precious moral oath, I disagreed with the call...vehemently. I waited till he'd laid you down in the grass at what he figured was a safe distance from the blaze and, well, commenced to dance a bootheel jig on your murdering ass. By the time he ran back to shove me away..."

"I had to cuff you and it took both of us to haul you away," Grant chided in with all the emotion of a houseplant, having returned a blank stare onto the blanket cloaking his lap.

Jamison nodded in apparent agreement, although no one bothered to notice.

"...that he did, and they did. But I'd definitely heard some bones snap in the time I'd been allowed to work out some very justifiable anger issues. Ribs, spine, who knew? I'm no doctor."

Leaning to the left just enough to clear the path of a would-be bullet, McCarron winked playfully enough, though his tight-jawed expression spoke otherwise.

"No great shakes at murder either, but I guess ya get points for tryin', right? You're a sick pup, Hammock. Like father, like son."

"My father didn't have a clue his stepdaughter had signed up as a drug informant, much less that she was courting a local dealer. He's always laid her death squarely at your door, Mac, as have I. Tap dance all you want with what little time you have left, but we all know the only viable suspect that night was you.

"As for my less-than-auspicious debut as your would-be eradicator, I can just about guarantee better results this time around."

"You ain't got the gonads, freak," McCarron spat, thrusting his head forward until the barrel dug into the pasty flesh. "Your dear ol' dad didn't give a shit about her, bro, once she'd threatened to turn 'im in for payin' her those occasional nocturnal visits durin' her middle school years."

Hammock's eyes widened, his nearly nonexistent chin descending, his oversized nostrils flaring wildly.

"Bullsh—"

"Wonder what that new young wife would think 'bout ol' Kerry's penchant for trollin' middle school playgrounds in faraway counties. It does appear the deviant fruit don't fall far from the parent tree, now does it?"

The handgun's shiny blue barrel began to shimmy, stabilized only by the barrel tip's firm hold on McCarron's utterly motionless dome.

"You're a lying piece of sh—"

"At least she didn't have to worry 'bout bein' groped by the grubby little stepbrother. Seems the Weasel here got his sick kicks with those young'uns possessin' similar equipment, if ya catch my drift."

The gun hand had graduated from slight tremor to full-blown rummy-with-a-cheap-wine jones, the tip rubbing a faint red welt into an otherwise ultra-pale surface.

Standing a mere two feet away from the sparring pair to the left, a series of wet, bawdy giggles escaped the pursed lips of Sandy Jamison, to which Hammock shot a brief glance of shocked indignance.

"He's making all this...what th...wha...she s-said th..."

"Hey, whatever blows yer skirt, junior...," McCarron resumed with a weak shrug, "...'cept a little bird told me that your mom wasn't all that thrilled the day she came across that stack of nudie mags stuck between the mattresses. Mags with titles like, I dunno, maybe *Long, Hard and Hunky* or *Butts of Iron*."

With that, the handgun's barrel full retreated several inches, wavering an inch or more either side with each subsequent huff from its comically flummoxed handler.

"Wise ass son of a bi—"

"Why so uptight, Weasel?" McCarron concluded with a final jab accompanied yet again by a deliberately drawn-out wink that, this time, was anything but jokey, the words themselves spewed out in an almost reptilian hiss. "I mean, after all, we're well into the twentieth century and I hear Pride month is right around the corner. Pray tell, do peds have their own celebratory month yet—"

A sudden shift of movement, hardly anything more than a frenzied blur to the naked eye, was followed by the echoing retort of a discharged firearm so resounding it all but completely masked the enraged growl that accompanied it.

Saturday, 2033 hours
From 1840 AM Radio (The Falls):

"...Shane Mills takes the snap and surveys the end zone...pressure from the corners! Mills tucks it and dashes up the middle...he bounces off Julio Waddle at the ten...dodges Luke Jackson at the five and dives forward...TOUCHDOWN!

(long pause, wild applause)

Folks, the hometown Wildcats are but a kick away from tying this game at twenty-eight apiece with just over a minute left on the game clock!

(long pause, continuing applause)

What's this? Unbelievable! Oh gracious! Folks, it appears Coach Shannon McKay has elected to go for two and the win as Shane Mills, Dalton Crane and company are huddling up to run a play to perhaps decide once and for all who will represent this county in the state playoffs! There's a Dawson timeout on the field so we'll take a final commercial break (long sigh), during which time your friendly Falls radio crew are gonna whisper a group prayer while perhaps simultaneously seeking out medical assistance for the aftermath to come in what has to be, simply has to be, the biggest single play in Crimson Falls High School football in several decades! Stay tuned, folks, and whatever you do...don't touch that dial!"

Saturday, 1358 hours

"Ten-four, Maggie. We're less than five from the Grant place, barring another unforeseen catastrophe. I'll keep you posted. Over."

Chief Will Crockett's naturally deep, raspy voice had acquired a shrill rawness that defied description other than to say it mimicked a lifelong smoker of the aged, female variety...a hollow croak with just a tint of screechiness that his subordinate and longtime friend would've normally taken great joy in ridiculing but instead barely noticed as the two shared similar, potentially dangerous levels of fatigue.

Dangerous, as Officer Phil Strickland's severely dulled reflexes behind the wheel had already managed to land them in one muddy swamp of a ravine, costing the search nearly forty-five minutes as they'd had to wait on a tow.

Dangerous, as both men shared similarly foreboding vibes about how the situation was going to play out before dusk fell and the stadium lights at Falls Field burned a wide chasm into the growing murk.

Doubly dangerous in the face of their collective bone-weariness being akin to a pair of gridiron gladiators facing a third or fourth overtime period and having thoroughly spent their respective inner-fuel reserves a quarter or two earlier with no magical "second wind" in sight.

Additionally, Will Crockett had secretly been in dire need of a pain pill for what seemed like days—or a handful of them—having ingested his last such serving over six hours earlier, sharp pains like wasp stings sporadically assaulting his neck, scalp and shoulder before trailing the length of his arm and all the way to the fingertips. The temptation to numb his pain to at least an equal level with his current fatigue-ridden mind was building steam with every second of continued consciousness, though it was not nearly overpowering enough to trump a relentless sense of determination and dedication to task. It was one thing for a stranger to come up missing in his jurisdiction; it was altogether something else when the list of mysteriously vanished included one of his own.

Thus, no chemical alteration other than a trio of two-hundred milligram ibuprofen—swallowed dry just as they were awaiting rescue from that mud-and-ice layered ditch—would be allowed to pass his badly chapped lips until Jerome Griffey's whereabouts had been resolved. As for those similarly hiding out, either purposely or by unknown circumstance, Wesley Grant and his clearly psychopathic ex, the chief had fallen securely in line with the belief that all the above were somehow linked. If so, he would need all the mental coherence he could muster when strolling voluntarily into the mist of such a potentially precarious mystery.

"McCarron might just not be answering the door, you know. Strange bird, that one. Trust his gimpy rear end about as far as I can toss it, boss," Phil grumbled, reaching up with a free hand and carefully probing fingers to massage increasingly droopy orbs.

"She said Jake all but kicked in his door, but you're right on both counts," the chief replied, staring out into a field of flattened sea grass with all the vitality of an animatronic in dire need of a recharge. "Not sure how serious to take those reports of him and Wes palling around though. You know, nothing but bad happenings since Gunther McCarron rolled back into town, no pun intended. It's like, well, like he'd lassoed a few select black clouds full of past spites and ancient grudges and dragged 'em directly over the town limits."

Agreed and may I say, quite poetic verbiage considering your state of semiconsciousness," the driver said while very gradually picking up speed as they traversed a steep hill growing increasingly slick from a noticeable lack of accompanying traffic. As was generally the case in similar tiny Southern hamlets, whenever frozen precipitation descended in any form, the wiser or those blissfully virgin to driving in such alien elements stayed home to prevent ending up grille-first in the nearest ravine.

"It's all coming to a head, Phil," Crockett said without a tint of the attempted levity of his subordinate. "I can feel it in these aching bones."

The veteran patrolman sighed, slowing for a series of extreme curves and wisely refraining from braking even as the rear tires slid a bit more dramatically with each adjustment of the wheel.

"Yep, very well could be. Wish I felt better prepared for whatever shenanigans lay ahead. My kingdom for a powernap of, say, eleven or twelve hours."

His superior's stoic, straight-faced response was delivered in a croaky half-whisper, as if not meant to be heard by anyone but the speaker, though the low hum of the vehicle's heater did little to sufficiently drown it out.

"Buck up, soldier. There's no napping in fox holes."

Phil Strickland's dark-shaded, sagging eyes instantly widened while turning to his passenger with a look of utter befuddlement.

"You really think we're going to war, Will?"

The big man's lone response was a click of the tongue, neither affirming nor denying, though his own searing gaze spoke volumes.

Saturday, 14:01 hours

"So I'm guessin' from this jackass behavior that merely leavin' me paralyzed all those years back didn't quite do it for ya, Weasel?"

Resuming his previous pose—a hard, slightly askew lean against the bare, eastern-side kitchen wall with the matching ebony canes crossed in an *X* in front of splayed legs almost equally thin—while cupping a bloodied hand over his left ear, McCarron had unconsciously bellowed the inquiry, the shot serving not only to rip the lobe from the cradled appendage but its booming retort partially deafening all those present.

"*YOU'RE A LYING SACK OF SHIT, MCCARRON! A COMPLUSIVE BULLSHIT ARTIST, CONMAN AND MURDERER!*" Hammock screamed in reply, the barrel of the firearm hanging limply by his side emitting a thin tendril of smoke. "*I KNOW IT...THEY KNOW IT...AND DEEP DOWN SO...DO...YOU!*"

Two distinct acts had prevented the bullet bound for the center of the intended target's forehead to veer a scant few inches down and to the left, the first and most critical being the intended target's surprisingly swift reaction and subsequent head-juke to the right, the second the grazing collusion of wheelchair to the left calf and shin of the shooter, the shock of impact just enough to cause a subtle flinch and yank of the trigger.

"All I know for sure is that you are one lousy target shooter! I mean, *hell's bell's,* Weasel, if ya can't nail a cripple from barely two inches away, ya need to seriously consider tradin' in that meat-smoker for a bazooka."

McCarron's grin, a toothy grimace seemingly pasted into place, wavered only slightly as he briefly pulled the hand from the leaking wound just long enough to wipe the sticky wetness onto the thigh of his cargo pants. The light brown wall behind him had gained a dime-sized cavity at approximately the exact height of his previously upright head.

With the aforementioned wheelchair parked strategically between the two men, Wesley Grant alternated uneasy glances from one to the other, apparently either unaware or uncaring that his hulking ex hovered wild-eyed and drenched in flop-sweat within easy reaching distance of his seated form, both her beefy fists clenching and unclenching with spastic regularity.

"I said back away, Marty!" he shouted between teeth so tightly gnashed the clarity of the demand seemed an impossibility save for the intervention of a nearby ventriloquist.

"OR WHAT?" Hammock shrieked, bending down until the tip of his pointy snout sat directly across from Grant's own with barely an inch of space between them. "*WHAT YOU GONNA DO, FRACTURE MY TOES? SHATTER MY SHINS? HONESTLY, GRANT, I OUGHTA SLAP YOU OUTTA THAT DAMN COASTER AND RUN OVER YOUR GIMPY ASS WITH IT! YOU FINALLY SPROUT SOME BALLS AND USE THIS SUDDEN BRAVERY AGAINST ME? JUST WHAT THE HELL DO YOU THINK YOU WERE DOING PLAYING HERO FOR THIS MURDERING SON OF A BI—*"

His spittle spewing, saucer-eyed rant cut off in mid curse, Hammock froze, mouth agape with a droplet of fresh drool hanging precariously from his lower lip, thighs trembling from a mixture of rage and being forced to hold the same hunched pose for longer than intended.

The tiny firearm, instantly recognizable to all present save for perhaps Sandy Jamison with its stubby, distinctively shaped gold barrel and curled black marble handle, as a Deringer of perhaps Colt manufacturing, protruded from beneath the edge of the lap blanket, the pale hand guiding it as steadily as its intended target was antsy.

"I didn't agree to a group lynching, Hammock, nor did I sign off on your being the self-proclaimed judge, jury and executioner of anything similar," Grant stated coolly and at near-normal volume as the effects of the earlier blast had begun to wane, the round, gold barrel levitating less than six inches from the base of Marty Hammock's neck, from which a vein visibly pulsed.

The son of one of the county's richest men snarled but otherwise froze in place, his thighs trembling beneath the lengthy duster that lay about him like a magician's cape.

"What *did* you think, Grant? We were all gonna sit around and wax poetic about all the great times we shared the night my sister was murdered and left to sizzle and pop into a black pile of ash?"

"Jesus, Wesley, what the hell?" Jamison blurted in a Southern drawl that seemed to grow thicker as tensions did the same, her ample arms spread wide—the horsehide punisher gripped at the thick end and swinging freely at her side—and staring down at her ex as if his balding noggin had just sprouted antennae while strangely hesitant to step closer into the inner circle of the current Mexican standoff. "Figured it went without sayin' our presence here is two-fold: to correct an ancient wrong while maintaining our current reputations."

Beret-covered head falling back against the wall with a light thud, McCarron's half-guffaw, half-growl garnered looks from all but Wesley Grant, who had yet to blink since unveiling what he had to figure was his lone trump card.

"Current rep...and what status do each of you currently *claim* that warrants cold-blooded, premeditated murder?"

"Oh, shove a cork in it already, McCa—" Jamison began dismissively but openly flinching at the crippled man's sudden burst of rage, the rawness and furor of this latest oration reducing all that had come before to casual small-talk status.

"First in line then, a pill-poppin' 'roid-rager whose only concern is the financial bottom line and the potential ruination of her precious business ventures if the truth ever got out."

Eyes sliding with predatory, shark-like coldness to the hunched man currently staring down the barrel of a pointed firearm, McCarron offered a cynical wink.

"How 'bout a lifelong moocher, known pervert and small-time gambler whose many crimes against society have either been bribed or lawyered into nonexistence practically since the day the jackal gave 'im life?"

Dropping the blood-drenched mitt from a saturated ear, his final salvo—completed while yet again propping himself upright into a decidedly distorted stance with the canes providing invaluable assistance—was aimed directly at the back of his fellow cripple's head.

"Saddest of all is a former peace officer of great potential reduced to a muted, spineless shell by regret. Regret that eats 'im alive for fourteen winters to the extent of not even havin' the balls to pack up and leave behind his greatest failure, instead hangin' around like some legless phantom payin' an infinite pittance for simply not standin' up and doin' the right thing all those years ago."

Lumbering forward a single, awkward step, McCarron recklessly lifted the right cane and, his fragile frame looking as if it might collapse onto itself like an upturned accordion, lightly tapped the back of the wheelchair.

"For the record, that *right* thing bein' holdin' somebody accountable for the murder of that young, eager, bright-eyed, and sadly naïve young girl who he himself doomed with his own blind ambitions. Honestly, Wes, you're the sincerest disappointment here. The behavior of these two...," he paused briefly to sway the cane toward both before returning it to prop status, "...is par for the course from what I dug up about 'em. Well, me *and* a private dick I employed a few weeks after wakin' up in that veggie ward. Common white trash of the stereotypical lowest order, though only one of 'em can honestly claim murder as the ultimate resume topper."

Following a moment's pause, during which time all focused on their crippled accuser, Sandy Jamison twirled the bat like a majorette with an oversized baton while obviously addressing her "stereotypical" cohort.

"Enough pointless chit-chat already. Let's do what that damn coma should'a."

Marty Hammock sneered, rising gradually upright while simultaneously lifting the gun to shoulder height and leveling the front sight at the center of the propped man's narrow chest cavity.

"Agreed. We're just going around in circles and ending up at the same dead end. Daddy told me long ago you can't argue with either stupid or crazy, and this dried-up husk here is a lethal mix of both."

"Yep, and besides, *this* ain't murder," she concluded, shouldering the bat with the thick end pointing upward, "...it's justice for the girl he *claimed* he loved."

Mimicking ski poles, McCarron tucked the cane grips beneath each arm pit and pushed back until he was flush against the wall, thus allowing perhaps a three-to-four-foot distance between himself and his would-be assailants.

"Well, if you're both bound and determined, please allow for a final request...." He shrugged with inhuman calmness considering the scenario, immediately resuming as if to avoid rejection, "...I just gotta know. So the plan is to shoot the paralyzed man at close range and *then* bludgeon 'im with that Louisville lumber?" Yet another short pause proceeded a final quip, uttered in conjunction with a dramatic facial transformation from whimsical jester to sinister, Kubrick-like psychopath, complete with lowered chin, squinty gaze and lipless snarl. "Damn, I'm either one supernaturally powerful cripple or you two are the undisputed king and queen of *Pussy-World*."

"God...just...d-damn it, STOP!" Wesley in a barking huff so weak and hoarse it escaped as more of a croaking plea from a man trapped behind a thick wall or the bottom of a deep cavern, the petite handgun swaying wildly at a seventy-degree angle between each before finally resettling in the general vicinity of Marty Hammock's upper chest, neck and chin.

—small black plugs popped free from the bottom edges—beforUnfazed and possibly even amused, Hammock refused to visibly acknowledge the appeal, instead offering only a sarcastic snort that spoke volumes on how seriously he took the potential threat.

"This is for my sister, you sick, twisted, delusional motherfu—"

Two distinct actions proceeded as if executed in a surrealistic realm where all movement was reduced to either half-speed or deliberate slow motion.

A descending thumb lowered a silver-plated hammer just as a forefinger began to press inward.

Thick arms reared back, guiding hard, wood-stained hickory of precisely thirty-six ounces of weight forward in a looping arc, accompanied by a banshee-like shriek that sounded as weirdly muted as it appeared badly out of sequence from the source's lips, like a poorly dubbed movie.

Oppositely, a third action—in reality a twosome of cloned movements in the guise of one—played out in an equally unnatural speed, only this time so swift and seamless as to be all but invisible to the human eye.

Like a veteran gunslinger, Gunther McCarron flipped the twin canes forward and, in the split-second allowed, thumbed a tiny trigger mechanism just beneath the handle of eache executing an inward, crisscross sweeping motion that saw each flay out as blackish blurs.

Sitting a mere reach away, one of the cane's plugs actually ricocheting off his left shoulder, Wesley Grant's beginning pose altered very little in the aftermath save for the gradual relocation of the Derringer's aim from an awkwardly ascending angle to one more of shoulder range while trailing his initial target's stumbling breakdance: first to the edge of the living room, then a brief lunge forward and finally a complete, arms-windmilling collapse that resulted in all but a pair of mud-caked boots taking up residence outside the kitchen's limited parameters.

Marty Hammock's wet gurgles, as if he were choking on a mouthful of marbles, went unseen and were mercifully brief.

Meanwhile, either by instinct or divine intervention, Grant rolled his chair back just in time to avoid being battered full force by his lurching ex's flailing bulk, who sailed by in reverse with both hands wrapped tightly around her own throat.

Eyes bulging, lips quivering, cheeks puffing and deflating like a beached fish, Sandy Jamison backed into the kitchen's western wall, shattering the outer glass and several stacked dishes within a free-standing China cabinet, before bouncing forward face-first onto the tile.

"Gaaaaaa....daaaa...whaaattttheee...," Grant stammered, dropping the tiny handgun onto his lap while gagging between each nonsensical emission, this visceral reaction due to the wheelchair's skidding action as he'd first backed into a thick spatting of crimson leakage and then, having instinctively rolled forward, slid straight into yet another fresh stream.

"Wha...what did y-you...how d-did?" he inquired, nostrils flaring from a sudden, overwhelming stench of copper, a purely nauseating assault on the senses he hadn't encountered since a certain night fourteen years ago.

Seemingly unshaken, Gunther McCarron stood directly between the still squirming body of Sandy Jamison and the upturned boots of Marty Hammock, the canes balanced atop narrow berms like shouldered rifles. His expression held no joy, no satisfaction; nor was it a blank slate devoid of human emotion. If forced to properly define, most would have probably described it as melancholy or even downright glum, the most obvious visible clues being the haunted eyes and downturned mouth.

"Ya know somethin', Wesley? There ain't no pleasure in takin' the life of an innocent, even if that person had done ya dirty. Killers...murderers, they deserve the same kinda death they doled out. Do ya...think this makes me no better than them? I mean, one of these..." he paused to gesture with separate nods toward the prone bodies on either side, his left shoulder and upper chest being sporadically dotted by pea-sized, crimson droplets from a pair of four-inch straight-razors protruding from the corresponding cane's sharp-tipped edge,"...just didn't warrant the same punishment. They...but they forced my hand, ya see? You did see that, didn't ya?"

Grant turned his head from the carnage, instead focusing on the clear, shattered glass littering the tile floor, along with broken pieces of ceramic from the dishes that had toppled from a nearby cabinet.

"Th-they were...well, w-were clearly going t-to...," he began to respond only to feel his tongue lock at a sudden surge of motion in the peripheral of his left eye.

Sandy Jamison's lunging assault was as shockingly catlike and graceful—a controlled, tumbling combat roll that saw her spring upright at the last second—as it was miraculous, considering the blood loss on display.

Her chin, neck and hands appeared to have been dipped in red paint, the majority of the silver and black windbreaker similarly re-shaded and oversaturated.

Bounding upright in a slightly hunched pose, she clamped groping fingers onto the thin shoulders of a wide-eyed McCarron—who'd actually appeared to smile and giggle from either the sad resignation of his own impending demise or the sheer preposterousness of her resurrection—and tossed him effortlessly airborne, the bloodied canes sailing from his grip as his upper back impacted the dining table.

Grant raised himself as far as his straining arms would allow from chair-height but was unable to visualize any part of his downed fellow cripple, though he could only surmise the odds of surviving such ragdoll treatment were slim at best. A muffled, hacking cough originating from behind the misplaced furniture almost instantly proved him wrong, its significance not lost on his former better half, who replied with a series of angry, wet squeals.

"San...Sandy, s-stop! *Enough* DAMN IT!" he cried out, finding his voice as splayed fingers probed blindly for the Derringer hiding within the deep folds of the blanket atop his lap.

His ex-spouse stared at him, head tilted as if dumbfounded at the audacity of the request, her shredded vocal cords unable to dredge up anything past a wet groan as a fresh stream of leakage erupted from between pursed lips to spatter kitchen tile already claiming enough random smears and pools to qualify as abstract art.

Stumbling past, her bloated cheeks a surreal mix of ghost pale and devil red, she applied a forceful slap to her ex's left cheek, the surprisingly well-aimed blow causing his chair to roll back into a makeshift barricade supplied by Marty Hammock's upturned boots.

"Fuuuuukkkk yuuuuuuu," she hissed, the sound like a shrieking security alarm filtered from beneath rushing ocean waves, before shambling toward the overturned table, currently sitting on its side and thus providing a temporary blockade for McCarron's unseen but surely crumpled form.

Having reclaimed the Derringer, Grant rolled his chair in a tight semicircle until he sat directly behind his ex-wife's hulking form, the wheels having left a twin trail of spilt rosiness in their wake. Lifting the tiny pistol with a hand shaking so fiercely it took the opposite hand's hooking beneath it for a semblance of stabilization, he clicked back the tiny hammer and spouted a final plea that sounded pathetic and weak even to himself: the definition of defeatism in the face of desperation.

"Sandy, stop...just *stop*. Da-damn it, y-you need...help. You're...there's too much blood."

His one-time love, business partner and fellow juicer of illegal HGI products ignored the hollow gesture, pausing only to kick away one of two overturned dining table chairs in order to scoop up the baseball bat hidden beneath.

At her back, her ex rolled the chair until the wheels struck the cabinet doors in order to extend the aim of the Derringer, which shook and shimmied in a grip that appeared ravaged with late-stage Parkinson's.

"Sandy, don't...don't make me...*force* me t—"

Grant halted in mid imploration upon Sandy's sudden, full-body spasm, her head flinching back as if struck, her thick body convulsing as if the edge of the dining table she'd reached to grab held the power of electrocution.

It wasn't until she stumbled back a step—and another half as her heel slid in her own spilled life-source—and turned partially around that Grant eyed the cane protruding from her upper abdomen at an ascending angle, her blood-drenched right hand finally yanking it free to reveal the same three-to-four inch, sharp-tipped razor that had previously opened the tender flesh of her neck. Not surprisingly, such an abrupt removal resulted in a fresh torrent best described by the township's given name, this one initially resembling an arterial spray before settling into a frighteningly steady stream.

"S-S-San...oooh gaaa...," Grant heard himself stutter, unable yet again to maintain a proper aim as his arm fell limply to the chair's side.

Wearing a bloody mask of comical perplexity, Jamison turned toward him with a look of sad desperation; wide, gleaming eyes conveyed a "what now" message her quivering lips were unable to verbalize.

In turn, Grant executed the hapless shrug she was unable or unwilling to accept as anything more than a final gesture of goodbye and thus whipped her head back around—her damaged and dying form following suit but with obvious delay—toward the dining room table and the person directly responsible for her impending death.

To their immediate left, the kitchen door swinging gradually ajar went unseen, as did the increasingly substantial gusts and swarm of sleet this ever-widening cavity allowed.

"Muuuuthurrrrrrrr foooouuuuukkkkkk...," she stuttered madly, slinging the bat up and back in her right hand while lurching forward and, using her left to send the tabletop spinning into a far corner to ricochet off the wall and directly into Grant's path, stomped forth with far more vim and vigor than anyone not hopped up on illegal muscle meds had any right to.

The blast echoed like an internal thunderclap just as Grant raised the Derringer and applied pressure to its miniscule trigger, for a split-second contemplating whether the deafening roar might have actually originated from the tiny two-shooter, the Glock's earlier discharge like a child's popgun in comparison.

Tossing up both arms in an impromptu "touchdown" gesture, Sandy Jamison was blown sideways as if swatted by a giant flyswatter, landing on her right side directly atop the shins of Marty Hammock, a large portion of lower intestine unceremoniously dumped between his splayed legs from a freshly excavated crater found just below her left rib cage.

Grant, scrunched expression still frozen in mid-wince, eyes half closed, initially stared at the diminutive handgun curled into his palm and pondered just how it not only had managed such a canon-sized shot but also curved a hard left before boomeranging back to strike the target.

Having dispelled such an impossibility on both counts, he was snapped back into a semblance of reality via a whispering inquiry from somewhere behind the upturned dining table, the voice as familiar in accent and delivery as it was alien with such timidity.

"Wha-...what the hell...hap...is...who's th-there? Who the...is a-anybody...still th-there?"

"I'm here, Gun...," Grant started to reply, rolling forward through a cloud of fading smoke and the smell of spent gunpowder, all the while keeping an eye peeled on the kitchen's back door as he'd only a moment earlier realized it sat ajar. Halting his forward momentum, his tongue locked in neutral upon seeing the long shadow posing motionless just outside its perimeter.

"Who's...Wes? Did ya...n-nail her?" He heard Gunther's raw, gasping question but remained involuntarily mute as the shadow took shape with a single step forward.

"I guess timing *is* everything," the figure announced grimly, cradling a Winchester twelve-gauge with a still-smoking barrel laid lazily across a heavily cloaked forearm.

Backing the chair hard left, Grant found his voice just as the figure seemed to levitate into full view.

"Mister Grant," Dexter McCarron nodded solemnly before retraining a tight squint into a far corner and reaching up with a free hand to reset his ever-present black Stetson.

"Gunther, you're looking well," he quipped, stone-faced. "Really, no shit, I mean, compared to how I figured to find you."

From the same corner emerged a sarcastic laugh and assorted dragging noises.

With the scent of recent death hanging in the air like a toxic black cloud, Wesley Grant had the sinking feeling there was more to come.

Saturday, 2036 hours
From 1840 AM Radio (The Falls):

"Okay then, here we go, folks. This is, pardon the vulgarity, one straight-up ballsy call by Coach Shannon McKay. The whole ball of wax, as far as a state playoff berth goes, all comes down to this. (Pauses)

Mills takes the snap from the shotgun and pumps once...twice...a third time! Pressure coming from Banks and Holder from up the gut! He's backed up to the fifteen...the twenty...he's going to have to throw it away...Holder's got him by the ankles...he pumps a final time and tosses it short to the left...Dalton Crane makes a one-handed grab just inside the fifteen! Crane jukes hard to the left and shakes Justin McCray at the ten...he's headed to the far corner pylon with Deshawn Holder in pursuit...he's at the five with Holder riding piggyback! Crane dives for the pylon...

Fifteen

"Dex, you are...one serious sight for...sore eyes," Gunther said, panting heavily as his uncle gripped him beneath one stick-thin elbow and pulled him gradually upward.

"Wish I could say the same, Gunny. Can't take you anywhere, can I?" the elder replied with a huff, his grim visage seemingly carved from stone.

Righting one of the kitchen chairs, Dexter plopped his feather-light nephew onto it and hesitated before backing away to ensure a semblance of stability had been obtained and resuming what, to a man known for few words, qualified as a full-blown grilling.

"You knew this was a trap, right? *Hoping* it was?"

Dropping to one knee and shooting Wes Grant a cautionary glance, the older man scooped up one of the razor-equipped canes and eyed it without any readable emotion before tossing it aside.

His nephew, still catching his collective breath as his narrow chest heaved and swelled to its maximum girth, raised a shaky forefinger airborne as if to indicate a reply was impending. His grayish/brown mustache was tinted on either side by reddish smears and his left cheek, raw and bleeding, looked to have been dragged over cement. Portions of the X-suit appeared to hang loosely from both his left leg and right arm, the battery pack limp and swinging like a pendulum. Almost supernaturally, his trademark beret appeared unfazed and perfectly fitted.

"The odds kinda favored it, yeah. Ya toss out...enough bait...a nibble or two is...pretty much...guaranteed."

Rising with resounding pops from both knees, the elder strolled wearily over to the pair of chilling corpses forming a human barricade from the kitchen to living room.

"I told you. Didn't I tell you from day one not to make waves? To quietly, completely *without* fanfare, put the house on the market and get as far away from the Falls as the profit would take you? As a stopgap, I would've gladly loaned you the necessary fun—"

The younger man interrupted his elder with a raised, trembling fist. Red-faced with a veritable roadmap of veins visible on both his pale forehead and the narrow stem holding it erect, it was apparent a second wind had been procured via an abrupt burst of rage.

"You never did get it, Dexter, and apparently...you're just not...capable. One of those...*them*...," he paused to point the clenched bleeding paw toward the recently deceased, "...killed...murdered the only...the *ONLY* person I've ever loved enough to avenge. You...*can't* understand, I get it. Failed marriages one...after the other. Nothin' personal, Dex, but...how could you?"

"I loved them *all*, Gunny. Things...change. People change. That's neither here nor there."

Head lowered, the beret seemingly superglued into place and unmoved, Gunther's tone decreased in both fury and volume.

"Good to...know. Sad thing is, I never...Wendy and...we never got the...chance to see it fail *or* properly succeed, thanks to...one or both of those shit-stacks."

Even as Dexter McCarron's lips parted for the inevitable reply, it was Wesley Grant who intervened, rolling forward until he sat directly between the two with little to no room to spare on either side.

"Gunther, she...Wendy was on *assignment*. Face it. Whatever your feelings for her, just know her own might've...were more than likely compromised by not only that, but the fact that she'd broken the golden rule as far as informants go. She *used* the product and, as was too damn common with that specific poison, acquired a taste."

"Says the lowlife scum who led her down the road to addiction," McCarron responded with a tiny smile and slight tilt of the head while focusing over Grant's head at his uncle, as if unwilling to meet the sitting man's gaze. "You didn't *know* her, and sure as hell didn't *know* me. How then could you possibly know how we were together? We were gonna run away that night, ya know? Together. She'd given me her word. I believed...*knew* she meant it. Saw it in her eyes, ya see, heard it in her voice. She wasn't blowin' smoke, fellas.

"The plan was to leave all the dopin', drama and smalltown back talkin' behind us."

Lowering his gaze to the man sitting within reaching distance, McCarron leaned back into a slump so severe it appeared he might tumble from the chair with the slightest jolt, and tucked both hands into the pockets of his jean jacket while simultaneously crossing bony ankles mere inches from the wheelchair's footrest.

"Honestly though, Grant, I can't altogether hate ya as much as I'd like, 'least wise not enough to add ya to that pile of soiled garbage over there, since well, you *did* bring me and Wendy together. Maybe not with the best of intentions." He paused to sneeze, a light maroon mist shooting from both nostrils, resuming after wiping across both with a skinny forearm before re-stashing the hand to hidden status. "But hey, it was what it was. Fate is fate, no matter the bogus circumstances surroundin' the chess pieces, right? 'Sides, grew kinda fond of ya this past week, whatever our individual agendas."

Grant executed a brief glance over his left shoulder to see McCarron's uncle standing stoically with the shotgun slung behind his neck and laying across both shoulders before turning back to the slouching guest of honor, whose almost smug demeanor was grating on his last nerve.

"But, wha, why that?" he moaned in desperation, a buildup of hot tears smearing his vision as he nodded without actually looking at the bodies. "Is this bringing her back, man? Sandy...was a very troubled woman but...hardly capable of killing someone over the possibility of her steroid use going public."

The slouching man scoffed, the scrape on his jaw practically glowing as the flesh around it visibly reddened.

"Dude, tear away the rose-colored specs. The two of ya were legally spliced at one time. You never saw her on a true rage, did ya? Well, I sure as hell did and she was *damn* capable, especially in the heat of a moment. You saw her luggin' that bat like it was a third arm, right? Remember Wendy's face, man? Like raw hamburger through a woodchipper, right? Two plus two.

"I mean, were your eyes sewn shut the last few minutes? Premeditated all the way, baby. As for all those years ago, well, crime of passion, I think you law dogs call it.

"As for that panty-sniffin' perv layin' under her, even if he was innocent as far as Wendy goes, well, let's just say justice is still served for *all* those he victimized in a lifetime of rapin', robbin' and runnin' over. I'd even go as far as to say society owes me a big ol' thank y—"

The voice that broke in and the message it conveyed easily matched the outer elements in terms of sheer iciness.

"Neither death was justified, Gunny, least as far as young Miss Hammock was concerned."

"All due respect, Dexter...," the younger McCarron berated, the usually unbudgeable beret visibly shifting from the swiftness and viciousness of the head turn he executed toward the other man, "...but you probably know less about this than anyone in the ro—"

"They didn't end her life." The older man intruded yet again, staring straight ahead and into the relative darkness of the living room.

Incredibly, his nephew's already creased facial expression grew even rubberier, a comical wince *slash* frown usually associated with either severe stomach cramps or the insertion of a syringe in the most tender of spots.

"Really? Well then, elder of mine, don't tell me *you* belong in that fast-dwindlin' camp thinkin' I'm the culprit? If so I gotta tell ya, Dex, it's a slap to the face with a cast-iron—"

"It was me, Gunther."

Following a moment's pause, during which the paraplegics present exchanged a shockingly tranquil glance, though accompanied by arched brows (Grant) and rapid blinking (McCarron), the younger of the McCarron clan chuckled, coughed, snickered and sneezed, in that specific order, before regarding his lone remaining elder as if his Stetson had sprouted antennae from its felt bill.

"Good lord, man, why would you feel the need to cover for such bottom-barrel trash? Please expound, uncle of mine. I'm...," he surveyed his own comically saggy pose, his narrow rear hanging on to the chair's edge for dear life, "...bound to hear this. I can only guess former Deputy Sheriff Grant feels the same itch."

Grant remained mute but highly attentive, head tilted upward toward the shotgun-cradling McCarron, his own undersized firearm resting on his lap with both hands overlapping.

"The deed to that trailer held my John Henry, so to speak. Sure, the lot it sat on was registered to and owned under a false name that was later traced back to my boss in Lexington."

"The...boss?" His nephew sneered, struggling to stay upright with only his spindly arms gripping the chair seat to prevent him from sliding to the tile. "We talking Kentucky fried mafia then?"

His uncle resumed in the same flat monotone that was as much his trademark as the polished Stetson and all-black ensemble.

"As such, he was able to distance himself from the incident with what I presumed was a sizeable bribe or two and subsequently gave up a name to represent a local scapegoat. This took nearly three full years from the date of the incident, but the smoke trail eventually ended with me. From what I was told by my own counsel, I missed out on death row by an eyelash. As it was, I served just over four years at Green River, was paroled and wisely refused to narc out anyone up or down the chain of command. In the seven years since, I've kept my nose clean. Relatively anyhow. If you weren't bombarded with accusatory questions upon waking from that coma, and I take it you weren't, it's because I reiterated to at least a dozen state and federal agents that your presence at the trailer that night was purely accidental and they couldn't prove otherwise." He paused, peering up just beneath the Stetson's lower edge at his fidgeting nephew, whose own gaze darted spastically about the room as both hands similarly drummed to some unheard beat.

"Believe me, Gunny, the whole lot of 'em wanted to lay her death at your feet. Hammock senior was similarly obsessed. In the end, there just was no proving it. Wasn't no means of nabbing the true culprit, not after I doused enough of that volcano juice around to scorch half the county."

As Gunther had donned a seemingly eternal mask of denial, complete with sporadically rolling eyes, lipless grin and the occasional, barely audible snort, Wesley Grant's natural curiosity and former law enforcement instincts kicked in, shifting his mobile transport until he faced the shotgun toting storyteller face-to-face and wheelchair to cowboy boots.

"The state reports listed a mix of gasoline, turpentine, paint thinner and a few other ultra-flammable chemicals," he injected with a hint of awe and inadvertent fervor that he quickly dialed down. "Can't remember anything specific, but a few sounded pretty far-fetched, stuff you'd find in most people's food pantries."

"Quite the mulligan stew, all right," Dexter nodded solemnly. "Linseed oil, nail polish remover, even some baking flour and Florida oranges. The higher-ups supposedly employed a military-trained chemist with a pyromania addiction and employed 'im to brew up what they called Satan's lighter fluid. I'd been told to keep a five gallon can handy just in case the need arose. That night, it definitely did the trick. Took about forty minutes to turn those grounds to scorched earth and the trailer to a mound of ash."

Remaining conspicuously mute, the narrator's nephew struggled and strained to push himself upright in the chair, broom-handle thin legs splayed out on either side of the chair like warped boat oars.

Dexter, meanwhile, stared down at his own mud-spattered boots and resumed with the same lack of emotion or sincerity one might emote if speaking directly into a brick wall.

"Unfortunately, modern DNA was able to ID some of the ash as human and the teeth as belonging to Kerry Hammock's stepdaughter. That night, I heard her car's engine rumbling in the distance and...left before I finished what I'd started. If I hadn't, well, let's just say nothing resembling teeth would've been left on the scene."

Grant chimed in, right eyebrow cocked quizzically.

"I don't recall seeing another vehicle nearby that night when we...the three of us left the scene. Where was your ride?"

The older man's response was without hesitation nor a hint of regret.

"There was a one-lane dirt road about a half-mile north of the trailer. Only those with a need to know were privy."

The room fell awkwardly silent just long enough for Wes to alternate squinty glances from uncle to nephew and back again.

"So, you added rocket fuel to the...that fire and just left your nephew there, still alive but most likely on the *verge* of dying?"

"I took the time to check Gunny's condition. Felt a pulse. Pretty stout one, if I recall. Dragged him a dozen feet or further from the blaze but knew he was in no condition to be hauled around the countryside. I hadn't even reached my truck when I heard the sirens. Took EMS and the fire department less than ten minutes to reach the pl—"

The eruption, abrupt and akin to a screeching Klaxon blared through a bullhorn, caused the wheelchair-bound man to flinch as if physically struck. Oppositely, Dexter McCarron budged nary an inch nor did his carved-in-marble expression alter even a twitch.

"*HEY! ASSHOLES! CAN'T YOU SEE I'M...SITTIN'...RIGHT...FUCKIN'...HERE!*" Gunther bellowed between cupped hands, instantly dropping the clenched mitts and lowering the volume to half the pervious glass-shattering level once properly recognized. "And just for the record, I couldn't have given a shit less about my own means of survival that night. How 'bout we shift focus back to the one who wasn't so fortunate? You know, the one identified via some egghead peekin' into a microscope after the fact?"

"Gunny," the elder McCarron stated calmly, turning to regard his nephew with the tone and demeanor of an adult correcting an ill-informed child, "Wendy Hammock was warned of the potential dangers of being a police informant. She played it reckless and paid the price."

Gunther wrung his hands as if chilled while studying the felled bodies through a floss-thin squint.

"Fine. *Whatever*, Dex. Flap those gums all ya want, and I will probably *never* understand who you're coverin' up for or why, but as far as I'm concerned, that long-overdue bill's been paid in full, what with that pair of matchin' scum lyin' over there stiffenin' up."

"The trailer had been *made*, Gunny," the older man insisted, hands held out and palms up. "Feds were sniffing around. I went there that night to torch it, per orders from higher up. The call you took about a site inspection was bunk.

"Sad, bottom line is that I found the front door open and her inside. Hate the timing for her, but it was what it was. I took no joy in doing what I deemed necessary. I considered...briefly I have to confess, just knocking her silly and dumping her into a nearby thicket, far enough from the blaze for safety. But then, she'd seen my face and, Lord forgive me, I wasn't about to go back to stir."

"Horseshit. Enough already."

With that, the younger McCarron seemed to have dismissed all further discussion save for an impending parting of the ways.

"Wesley, do you mind retrievin' my canes? Afraid the ol' bionic suit is runnin' on fumes and I'd like to avoid taking a face-plantin' onto those soggy tiles."

Grant, searching out the requested items while expertly maneuvering the chair to avoid as much of the existent spatter as possible, addressed the elder in a tone befitting a man once trained to interrogate.

"Why the sudden urge to confess, Dexter? I mean, as far as anyone in this room is concerned, it might be that her killer *is* one or both of those two with neither in any shape to deny it."

The elder McCarron, having propped the shotgun barrel up against his right side, used his left hand to briefly remove the Stetson and the right to run splayed fingers through thick, tar-black hair infested with sporadic streaks of gray.

"Maybe I...maybe it's a quest. Something I've searched out, desired, at least subconsciously, for decades."

Wesley, having successfully completed his own expedition—and handing the items in question to Gunther—paused in the aftermath, inquiring only when it seemed an answer was not forthcoming.

"That quest being?"

The elder McCarron replaced the cowboy hat, wandering eyes finding his nephew.

"A clear conscience. Haven't slept more than a solid hour a night since...Gunny revived and showed back up here. Sometimes, even bad men can't rest easy from their deeds."

"Enough already, I said," the younger McCarron interceded with a raised finger pointing out the back door. "You two need to think about shaggin' ass."

Grant shook his head and managed a smile.

"Gunther, this is *my* house."

"Oh yeah. Slipped my mind. We'll...work on it. Dex, you'd better make tracks. If I'm plannin' on takin' the fall and makin' anybody believe I managed...," he paused to nod toward the bodies, "...that on my lonesome, we're gonna need less loose ends gummin' up the tale."

"Gunny, I'm not go—" his uncle began, only to be talked over as Grant again rolled between the two to face the younger McCarron with arms outstretched and gesturing wildly, as animated a response as he'd displayed since the two had shared company.

"Premeditated murder isn't *waived* due to disability, Gunther, unless you plan on convincing state and possibly federal investigators that those razor canes are a regular part of your daily ensemble."

"I'm not leaving, Gunny," Dexter added, shouldering the shotgun and taking a step toward his nephew. "You are."

"Like hell I am," his nephew growled, raising the canes and crossing them in an X-shape as if to ward off a vampire. "I ain't sayin' it again. If there's a rap to take, I'm takin' it. It's up to Wesley if he wants to follow my lead to wash away some of his own guilt or try 'n' play innocent victim of the whole shitshow, but you ain't got no reason..."

The elder McCarron turned on a bootheel like a solider practicing a drill, the shotgun remaining firmly in place.

"Grant *is* innocent, other than placing that girl in harm's way all those years ago," he exclaimed in obvious desperation, staring out the semi-ajar back entrance, a few wet, ice-coated stray leaves having made their way in to warm on the edge of the tile, "but there ain't no way he'll explain away all this carnage, not to mention what's in his garage."

Gunther and Grant silently regarded the armed man as if he'd just announced an alien spacecraft as their means of escape.

"What did you...do, Dex?" his nephew inquired, frowning deeply, dropping the canes to waist level.

"I've...been...I even brewed up some of the old volcano juice just in case, well, the whole thing went tits up like it obviously has. Gonna have to burn it all down again, the house, the garage, the bodies, the whole shebang," the elder stated blandly, as if announcing the leaves outside required raking, his back still turned and using his right boot to pry the entrance door further ajar. An icy gust instantly dropped the temperature inside the room by double digits.

As Gunther had fallen conspicuously mute, head bowed as if in silent meditation, Grant was the first to break yet another brief but stilted silence, this while rolling his chair back until it struck the fleshy barricade of Marty Hammock's bootheels.

"What's in the garage, Dexter?" he inquired as calmly as he could manage despite his every functional nerve ending tingling as if he were receiving a full-body electrical shock.

"Some snarky, eager-beaver reporter out to make a name at our expense. From what I gathered, digging well deep into both my past and Gunny's and was leaning toward making up his own facts to whatever end. Said he knew Gunther's secret and was gonna make it known. Cocky little shit told me that right to my face on my own front porch before the chief and his boys ran 'im off. Said the McCarron clan, or what was left of it, was, in his words, 'lying on borrowed time.'"

Having instinctively reclaimed a double grip on the tiny Derringer—the right serving as the official gun hand and the left cupped underneath the former for support—Grant gradually stretched out both arms until the line of fire was roughly between the standing man's shoulder blades.

"You said bodies, as in plural," he managed to say with nary a shaky note, remarkable considering the wobbly status of his aim, "You talking about in here or out there?"

The elder McCarron's shoulders visibly slumped as he took a half step forward and nearly to the back door's outer edge. Still another strong draft saw a swarm of icy specks blow over and past him to invade the space beyond.

"Local badge. Stout kid. If I hadn't caught that one totally by surprise, we probably wouldn't be conversing."

If possible, Grant's grip on the suddenly weighty firearm grew even ricketier, actually wobbling off target for a split-second before righting.

"Jerome Grif-...you killed a uniformed police officer?"

"Noisy law dog was sniffing around like one of the Scooby gang and found the reporter's car. Lucky I was in the act of moving the latter's body and was able to get the drop on 'im."

Like an immense weight being hoisted by crane, Gunther McCarron's head gradually arose, his expression no longer displaying either bewilderment nor anger, but the blankness of utter disconnection. His arms hung limp, his legs splayed in a wide V and equally lifeless, rapidly blinking eyes drifting from Grant's outstretched arms and wobbly aim to his uncle, who stood with legs spread shoulder wide like an Old West gunfighter posed dead center on a dusty street awaiting first draw.

"De-Dexter, ya...got a...sss-second? Ne-need some h-help h-here," he stammered, audibly wheezing, a single cane resting across his thighs, his eyes sporadically rolling back into his head.

As the elder McCarron turned to his ailing nephew, Grant instantly dropped the firearm to his side, tucking it next to and just underneath his chair's blood-smeared spokes.

"You just hang on, nephew...." He heard the elder McCarron whisper to his younger kin, the man falling to one knee with the shotgun's barrel resting against his left shoulder, pointing toward the ceiling.

"I'll drive you over to my place and we'll toss a few essentials in the ol' beast and head south, what say? Maybe torch this place nice and proper before heading onto the interstate. 'Course, there is one more loose end to tie up 'fore that can happen."

Just as a Stetson shrouded head turned and a purely predatory gaze fell upon Wesley Grant—who'd slickly maneuvered the wheelchair so it faced the McCarrons and effectively cloaked the Derringer—the target of the brazenly unveiled threat raised the pistol with surprising quickness and grace, magically recalling younger days on the target range.

His aim focused directly between the elder McCarron's wide-set eyes, Grant's trigger finger gradually eased while he used his free hand to back the chair as far as barricades, both human and nonhuman, allowed.

A wet, hissing sound, like steamed air escaping a ruptured hose accompanied Dexter McCarron's backward stumble, the shattered end of the walking cane protruding from his neck whipping back and forth like a windshield wiper set on an intermediate setting.

Miraculously, the elder managed to stand erect, the shotgun slung beneath his left arm with the barrel out while his right clenched the razor-end of the cane, clutching, slashed fingers trailing increasingly copious streams of dark red leakage.

"Gnnnn...neeee...," he gasped, eyes round and accusatory and boring into his suddenly very aware nephew, whose playing-'possum strategy had apparently worked a second time in ten minutes.

Leaning forward, knobby knees bent in and back hunched, the picture of the younger McCarron's face read far less indignation than mourning.

"You tra-traitorous...murderin' b-bastard. My own...flesh and...blood. Took...a-away my...my life...my...my everything."

Astonishingly, Dexter McCarron stood statuesque, having apparently discarded all thoughts of removing the spear jammed into his jugular notch like some freakish, elongated tumor, and swinging the shotgun drunkenly around toward his betraying kin.

The Derringer tore a dime-sized hole in his left shoulder just as he'd managed to at least somewhat steady his aim, the shotgun blast tearing away a chunk of plaster and wood a foot above Gunther's head.

Teeth bared in silent rage, the wounded elder staggered a step forward while whirling the shotgun around to his latest attacker, the two-shot pistol's sharp retort like a Black Cat firecracker in comparison to the latter's.

Despite the extreme close range, Grant's succeeding attempt at halting his potential assassin had little more effect than the first, digging a deep trench into the shambling man's left cheek before cleanly shearing away an earlobe on its way out the open back door and into parts unknown.

The elder McCarron stumbled back the step he'd previously gained, but somehow remained upright, the cane protruding from his neck appearing to act as a rudder of sorts as he locked eyes with the shooter and, bloody teeth bared, reset his earlier aim with the smoking barrel a reach away from the intended target.

Naturally panicked in the face of imminent death, Wesley Grant raised the spent Derringer only to have it batted from his grip via the twelve-gauge's descending barrel, his gun hand shoved into his own lap and his thumb instantly and severely crushed via the scorching metal hammer.

Dexter McCarron, bloodied lips pursed and wild gaze squarely focused, slid forward yet another half-step, planting the shotgun's red-hot muzzle flush against Grant's heaving chest, the latter still groaning in anguish in the aftermath of the battering of his wounded hand.

Shrieking, Grant was in the process of reaching with his good hand in a panicked, last-ditch effort to shove the barrel aside when a lurching blur caught the periphery of his left eye.

Struck in the side of the face by the passing figure, his black-framed glasses knocked askew and quickly corrected by groping fingers, the former deputy executed a series of rapid blinks at the surreal scene playing out a mere three feet away.

The two figures growled, grappled and groaned in a grisly dance of imminent death, one a head taller and, at least in appearance, twice as thick as the other, though the struggle itself appeared an equal draw.

"Gu-Gunny?" Grant muttered weakly, the image of Gunther McCarron *standing* upright—when not being briefly hoisted airborne like a straw husk—seemed some insane, stress-related hallucination.

Nephew and uncle wrestled near the open back door, either a particular stout gust of wind or equally vicious jerk of the head dislodging the latter's trademark Stetson, the former having assumed a veritable death grip on the shotgun's barrel with one hand and the cane spear with the other.

For a frozen moment in time, their faces posed mere inches part, four bloodshot eyes locked: one in apparent disbelief and the other with unfathomable rage.

"Guunnnnn...dooooooonnnnn...," the elder McCarron hummed through tightly pursed lips that spewed forth a fountain of blackish crimson, eyes widening with a sudden, terrible realization...that his brother's only child meant to end his life and, most horrifying of all, possessed more than the capability necessary to do so.

Understandably, all were oblivious to the incessant hammering at the front door or the raspy screams—the ringing of their respective ears effectively eliminating any chance of further audible input save for perhaps one of the nuclear variety.

The shotgun's second and final shot freed a sizeable chunk of plaster from the ceiling above their heads, this as the smaller of the two men by roughly half was able to first shove the thick wooden shiv deeper into his uncle's ravaged throat before yanking it out with equal ferocity.

Releasing the spent firearm without resistance, Dexter McCarron stumbled back into the breach of the open door, both hands clutching and fingers searching with futility to somehow cork the collapsed dam at the base of his throat.

Knees buckling, he dropped on all fours into a pool of his own spillage, head bowed briefly before arising to regard the two men responsible for his demise. Blood-spattered lips parted as if to convey a final message even as a rapidly flaccid, haunted gaze fell solely upon his nephew, a message never fated to be verbalized as badly shaking arms folded inward and a disheveled gray crop of wavy hair smacked the sticky wet tile with a resounding thud.

The front door of Wesley Grant's modest but neatly kept home—only recently transformed into a nightmarish slaughterhouse—splintered inward with a sharp crunch just as the thumping sound of approaching footsteps echoed through the back entrance.

With a resounding sigh, the lone remaining member of the Crimson Falls' McCarron clan shuffled awkwardly toward his fallen elder and, rounded shoulders slumping, gradually turned to face the seated man also presently claiming survivor status.

Grant's tilted head and scrunched, disbelieving expression required no words to convey the burning question at hand.

"I...was savin' it to use for strategic purposes," Gunther answered the unasked question, waving his spindly right arm high to low as if to indicate his bony frame as a whole, the left shouldering the shotgun that, from Grant's perspective, appeared thicker and far too hefty for the arm holding it upright.

"You know, catch 'em by surprise," he resumed, his ghostly-pale—save for bloodied nostrils, several noticeable scratches and the bleeding rash atop one swollen cheek—visage having donned a mask of doomed sorrow at the tragic finale its author had never foreseen. "Wait till just the right time and...hop up like one of those Hollywood horror flick jump scares. Re-Revel in their shock, ya know? I mean it ain't like this mighty physique don't look the part, right? Shame it...didn't quite...sure as *hell* didn't turn out...the way...I'd hoped." He shrugged weakly and fell mute, backing up a step while allowing the shotgun's barrel to descend outward and tucking the stock against a bony shoulder.

"McCarron! Drop the shotgun...*NOW!*" a deep, raspy voice boomed from just beyond the open entrance.

"Wesley, are you all right?" still another inquired, not quite as deep but equally hoarse, this one originating from the living room.

Neither the command nor the inquiry was adhered to or answered, respectively, as if the target of each was either purposely or inadvertently oblivious. Instead, the one ignoring the command to drop his weapon faced the one garnering the concern and, head slightly stooped and eyes upturned, gradually lowered the shotgun's barrel.

"Ya know, Wes, when all is...said and done, I can't *quite* forgive ya...," he paused, possibly for effect while gradually lowering the shotgun's barrel toward the tile as yet another command—similar in dialogue but louder in delivery—rang out from behind him, "...yet I find I can't quite kill ya either."

The seated man took in the whole of the sickly pale, scrawny specimen standing before him with assorted wires and latches from the battered X-suit hanging free like rogue seaweed and, warm tears blearing his vision and hands trembling, coughed his words more than spoke them.

"G-Gunther, I-I'm...truly, truly so—"

The standing man shushed him, forefinger of his free hand tucked horizontally against lips spotted and smeared with semidried blood.

"You've paid a pricey enough penance, brother. Ya see, I heard all about your...the accident that put you in that chair. I can only figure that carryin' around such guilt is just another form of gut cancer, slow and painful. And hey, unlike the others," he concluded with a playful wink, narrow neck, bony thighs and round shoulders visibly tensing, "at least you had a conscience."

"D-don't!" Grant was able to screech just as the thin man swung around on a heel with the shotgun directly on point, the feeble attempt drowned out by a chorus of similarly themed cries ringing out from opposite sides of the room.

Two shots—and a single, hollow click—rang out almost simultaneously, the first live round penetrating the X-suit's back plate directly between the wearer's prominent shoulder-blades and, ironically, snapping his thoracic spine; the second blowing a quarter-sized crater into his left check and exiting through the base of his skull in a bone-fragmented arterial spray.

Even as the first had pushed his frail frame forward, the second served to shove him back upright to his original stance, the shotgun acting as a counterweight to the remains of the suit tumbling from limp fingers.

Gunther McCarron's collapse, like a structure felled by explosives buried at its base, appeared to occur in sections from top to bottom: bony ankles folding inward and finally buckling, followed by the knees, coming together with a solid smack before splaying apart as if pulled in opposite directions.

Like a puppet with severed strings, his frail upper body soon followed suit, trademark beret dislodging to land on the upper back of his prone elder, the nephew's final resting spot just a reach away, his skeletal arms forming an impromptu "touchdown" gesture.

In the scant thirty seconds it had taken Will Crockett and Phil Strickland to step over the separate pairs of lifeless forms blocking their respective paths of entry—living room to kitchen and back door entrance, respectively—Wesley Grant had commenced to openly sob.

Saturday, 2037 hours
From 1840 AM Radio (The Falls):

"...they're saying Holder stripped the ball from Cane before it crossed the goal line! Coach Shannon McKay is livid! He is literally being physically detained from getting at the referee and folks, I can't I blame him! That...call just cost his team a trip to the state!

(Long pause amid a mixed chorus of boos, hisses, whistles and cheers)

Sad to say (sighs) that unlike college or pro ball, there is no instant replay to possibly reverse the decision. As such, the scoreboard's current display of zero time remaining and a score of twenty-eight for the visitors and twenty-seven for the home team will go into the history books just that way.

As the Red Raiders' team and coaches celebrate at midfield and beyond, I see scattered Wildcats' players and fans huddling together in consolation, a few of which openly weep..."

Epilogue

Eight and a half months later
The Glutton's Dream
2255 hours

Hands cupping a mug of freshly poured coffee, the man quietly cleared his throat, silently contemplating the trio of revelers still present at the table talking over one another about various topics to which he was blissfully ignorant in the moment.

As the gathering had begun at just past seventeen-hundred hours, his tongue was tired and his ears on the verge of similar exhaustion, though he had to admit it felt good to be among those he considered his only close friends.

The previous months had involved many acquaintances but nothing more. As such, within mere minutes of sharing space with all the good folks who'd sacrificed their Wednesday night for his return, there had been a familiar, warm feeling of belonging, one that not long ago, he'd thought lost forever.

Sipping noisily and secretly marveling that, unlike the feebly brewed java he'd grown accustomed to upstate, the present concoction held nary a hint of bitterness, he watched Maggie motion toward Dan for another round of drinks. The lanky proprietor, he of the perpetual frown, waved his acknowledgement and soon disappeared behind the bar to load up a tray with draft beers for Will and Phil and another gin and tonic for his soon-to-be-staggering wife, who would sporadically reach over and playfully pinch or punch the guest of honor.

"So how you doing, Wesley?" he heard Will ask in that impossibly deep baritone, the chief leaning forward with elbows atop the table and wearing that toothsome grin that was a true rarity to behold. Decked out in a black and gold tee, blue jeans and UK baseball cap, the Chief was in rare, full casual mode.

"Good, Will. Top notch."

"Hope this wasn't too awkward, but Maggie figured, well, truth be told we *all* figured you needed a night out with the old crew."

"Well, can't say I wasn't reluctant, but she was right as usual."

"Darn tootin' I was, Wheels," the party planner, or at least *dinner and drinks with friends* planner announced, with a raised glass void of all but a few small chunks of ice. With a lingering grin birthed from a previously ingested four-spot of libations, she slid a slender arm across the table and delivered yet another slap to their guest's exposed hand.

"Well, it's like I've always said...," Wesley beamed, leaning forward to return the favor, "...you're more than just a great pair of legs."

"I second that motion!" Phil Strickland chimed in with a roguish wink while raising a mostly drained beer mug.

The present foursome, at the request of the chief, had earlier been joined at the Glutton by Cindy Lou Harrison, Jake Douglas, Charles "C.J" Jacobs and the latest addition to the department, a fresh-from-the-academy, twenty-one-year-old guy named Derek Banes—Jerome Griffey's replacement within their ranks and in terms of by-the-book eagerness, at least the murdered officer's equal. Dan Childers even closed for regular customers, a first as far as Maggie could recall. Burgers, baby back ribs and barbecue chicken with all the fixings had effectively cloaked a pair of pushed-together tables, as well as drinks aplenty, all willingly donated by a man famously known for his penchant for frugalness.

"That new kid working out okay, Will?" Wes inquired with a cocked brow directed at both the chief and his most experienced officer.

"He's a go-getter. Green as fresh-cut spinach when he got here, but as fast a learner as I've come across since, well," Will paused to reach over and deliver a gentle slap to the broad shoulder of the veteran officer to his left, "since this one here. Might as well have been holding a sign that said 'learn me' written in the brightest bold."

Phil Strickland sneered playfully at his boss before addressing their guest of honor.

"We'll never keep 'im longer than a year or two. Stepping-stone officer for sure, and we're just that first rock to hurdle off of."

The chief nodded as if to reluctantly agree. "Maybe. We'll see. The city did authorize funds for an extra badge, though. Got a female recruit from Lexington incoming next month."

"Cool beans. About time y'all got some help."

"Cool be—ah, the return of Mister Hip," Maggie blurted drunkenly, smiling like a Cheshire cat with a mouthful of canary. "No stretch in the pokey is gonna dumb down that flower child vocabulary."

Though a smiling Wes flashed her a double-fisted thumbs-up gesture, there were cleared throats and an unmistakably stilted silence in the aftermath of the buzzed dispatcher's breaching of a subject that had, up until that point, been conspicuously avoided.

The sentence—pled down to a stretch of just over six months—had originally been five to seven years for conspiracy to commit murder for the most recent deaths and, from fourteen years earlier, criminal conspiracy charges in the burning death of Wendy Hammock and the near-fatal injuries and abandonment of the now-deceased Gunther McCarron. The trial had, predictably, been a media circus and easily the most discussed in decades within the state, not to mention within the city limits of Crimson Falls, which had been besieged by a steady stream of news vultures and sightseeing tourists, the latter of which had yet to completely dissipate.

Thus far, Wesley's release had been kept as low key as possible, though he doubted that particular dam would hold up to the flood waters to come once the media did catch a whiff of his presence amongst the locals.

It was, predictably, Maggie who continued down the same taboo path of questioning, unable to curb her naturally curious nature.

"So, how was it, Wes? I mean, were you treated...any differently?"

"Well, Blackburn was no picnic, but I heard from several of the guards that worked both units that it's a regular Holiday Inn Express compared to Green River, especially for those less...physically capable. Had a private cell and a desk job, so I'm not gonna complain after the fact."

When the group fell silent once again and appeared to share a knowing glance among their ranks, Wesley grinned and resumed with a shrug of the shoulders.

"And no, I was no one's bitch. Cripples weren't exactly a desired commodity."

At the conclusion of the "no one's bitch" segment, Maggie executed a textbook spit take, a mouthful of gin and tonic spewing forth from between pursed lips and spattering both the tabletop and a nearby napkin holder.

Once a semblance of seminormalcy had been established—the chief being forced to apply several firm slaps to his veteran officer's V-shaped back to prevent the latter from choking on a mozzarella cheese stick—and a fresh round of drinks delivered, a more somber tone settled in.

"So you gonna sue the pants off that Grimes jackass or what?" Phil Strickland fired first between noisy sips. The perpetually buffed—and currently buzzed—officer's reference held no need for clarification among those present. Randy Grimes, former *Dayton-Post Dispatch* ace reporter and current best-selling author had pumped out the true-crime novel *Crimson Falls: Deceit, mayhem and murder in the heart of small-town America,* a mere four months after that tragic winter night, the less-than-positive reviews doing little to detour its meteoric rise up the nonfiction charts. As if to pile misery upon misery—a common theme in true crime novels—he'd even added a chapter, and the occasional blurb, covering the Crimson Falls' Wildcats controversial, last-second loss to their most bitter rival on the night of the murders. Grimes had conveniently left out that Dawson's Red Raiders had been routed in the first round of the 2AA playoffs, as if doing so would've provided a soothing salve to an otherwise devastated fanbase.

"No grounds, I'm afraid. Interview was on the up-and-up and pretty much word-for-word."

"No lie? You...oh wow. I just, I mean, we just assumed he...that you'd never..."

Wesley quickly interrupted Phil's stammering defense *slash* apology with a mild shrug and the wave of a hand.

"He'd hounded me for weeks for a meeting at the unit and I finally caved, figuring if I didn't put the truth as I knew it out there, either he or his publishers would surely take liberties."

"Man, if all you said was true, that second conspiracy charge was as bogus as hell. If anything, you were trying to protect McCarron."

Wes stared down at his own upturned palms, sighed deeply and paused as if to thoroughly articulate his thoughts.

"Can't really say, Phil, not if I'm being completely honest. I just know at the end, I didn't want to see *anyone* hurt, particularly him. In just a week's time, I saw that man's passion in his every act, every word and every gesture. I just...didn't know...I couldn't find a way to divert him off the whole 'revenge for Wendy theme.' Same with Marty and Sandy's belief that Gunther was gonna be their downfall, never mind that none of the above was a killer.

"Strange. I'd taken turns over the years suspecting any and all of them, but at the end I was positive none were responsible. Just wasn't able to derail the madness. Arming myself was questionable in retrospect, though I guess living on the state dime does beat dying."

The chief nodded as if to wholeheartedly agree, even as Maggie whispered an emphatic "amen."

"Grimes did some impressive digging in such a short time," the former said, to which the veteran officer by his side openly scoffed.

"Still a smarmy jackass."

The chief, Wes agreed, had been spot on, Phil's reluctance to give credit aside.

"I noticed he gave posthumous credit to that Briggs kid at *Tail Wags Dog* for the inside scoop on Gunther's condition."

"Truly mind-blowing," Phil said with a slight shake of the head before a long swallow and barely audible belch. "Never was truly paralyzed, but faked it for fighting advantage."

Wes nodded sheepishly.

"Ended up saving my bacon instead of his own."

Wearing a sad smile, Maggie reached over and squeezed her former co-worker's hand.

"Then it wasn't all for naught, was it?"

"The good Lord does work in mysterious ways," Will added, pushing his own half-full mug to one side as if to cut himself off from possible inebriation. "The Briggs kid had bribed that orderly for the goods about the fakery but then made the mistake of trying to blackmail Dexter with some deep, dark secret about his nephew."

While Wesley and Maggie nodded in silent agreement, Phil swallowed down the remainder of his brew before chiming in.

"Bribed the wrong dude."

Leaning back with meticulously manicured nails tapping to a seventies-era southern rock tune being blasted in from overhead speakers, Maggie added to the continuing narrative with only a slight slur present.

"That Dexter McCarron was dead serious about not serving anymore time."

Wesley sat his own mug aside and, staring down into its mostly empty interior, replied, donning a pained wince, as if the recall itself were enough to trigger physical discomfort.

"Weird though, and damned sad this was, but that man lived his last acting as Gunny's protector. I'll never forget that look on his face when probably the only person on the planet he still trusted betrayed him. I mean, that had to be excruciating. In the end, it wasn't *solely* about saving his own hide, but the McCarron bloodline."

With that, Wesley excused himself to the men's room, rolling his chair through a single door entrance pre-propped open for his convenience.

Parked atop the porcelain throne within a less-than-spacious handicapped stall, Wesley allowed himself a brief rest as nature's typical delay in taking its course ensued.

While serving his sentence in relative peace, he had rarely allowed his thoughts to be consumed with the events of that faithful week in early winter of the previous calendar year, instead focusing on what future he might build for himself once liberated.

Now nearing dawn on his third full day of renewed physical freedom, he allowed himself what was to be, at least he hoped, the beginnings of self-healing via flashbacks and subsequent evaluation of them.

The thought then, of his ex-spouse, whose court-ordered autopsy revealed a bloodstream rich with not only three separate HGH variants but enough crack cocaine to fell a Clydesdale. It seemed the decade and a half of guilt-ridden stress had found her weakened mindset ripe for addictions beyond those merely associated with bodybuilding. This, of course, helped explain her erratic, borderline psychotic behavior, the latter on full display not only the night of her own death but in the near-fatal attack on a six-foot-five, former gridiron great turned police chief within the walls of his own police station.

Try as he might, any tears he shed in the aftermath of Sandy's demise were more closely tied to his own sense of failure to aid in helping her to identify and treat what had become an obvious drug addiction than her inevitable passing. Sadly, the screeching, wild-eyed, baseball-bat wielding version of Sandra Dee Jamison he'd watched perish that night wasn't remotely the same individual he'd once promised to love and cherish till death chose to separate them. Still, if he dug deep enough, there existed a faint tug of sentimentality but mostly and ultimately, regret.

Just the fact that she'd left him her SUV in a newly written-up and certified will was sufficient to tug at vulnerable heartstrings, at least as long as a pair of the darkest-tinted rose-colored glasses imaginable remained set firmly in place. As for her late arrival on the night of the murders, it was discovered that she'd parked a rented Honda Civic less than half a mile away from his home.

He thought then of Martin Hammock and his arguably jinxed lineage. Given the man's track—not to mention criminal—record before, during and after the Gunther McCarron saga, Marty was the lone fatality that even Wes would be hesitant to define as being completely tragic. Fact was, Wesley had long suspected Martin of being his stepsister's killer, especially after witnessing the man's merciless ways up close and personal that night at the trailer, said hunch disproven only in the moment that he'd heard Dexter's shocking confession. Kerry Hammock's only son had earned his rep of mean-spirted ruthlessness through decades of dirty dealings, double crossings and (long-rumored) pedophilic tendencies.

He thought then of Dexter McCarron, the soft-spoken—and of few words at that—man in black, the surviving family patriarch by day, former hardcore convict and veteran dope dealer by night, a rarely seen man-about-town, who, despite his undeniably shady past, had always seemed harmless enough. The archaic idiom that spoke of it being unwise to judge a book by its cover had never been more fitting.

As for the senior McCarron's victims, Wesley thought of the eager young deputy who would never see the potential he'd driven himself so relentlessly to reach, all due to what had probably been no more than a split second of recklessness. Jerome Griffey's natural curiosity, teamed with uncharacteristic carelessness, had been his undoing.

As for Kevin Briggs, e-zine rag reporter of all things tabloid sleaze, it was determined his death was truly of the "wrong place, wrong time" variety; that and hinting openly to Dexter that Gunther was harboring a secret so dark and dirty that it would surely bring the Crimson Falls community to its collective knees. In saying this, the mouthy young Mister Briggs had unintentionally painted a bullseye across his own acne-scarred forehead. State police reports speculated that the senior McCarron had first used his tow truck to ram the kid's Dodge, asphyxiate its driver—with such force as to crush his trachea—and then tow the damaged vehicle back to the one place he'd decided would serve as the perfect temporary hiding place, that being the spacious two-car garage deeded out to one Wesley Grant.

Of course, he thought mostly of Gunther James McCarron, a troubled, multi-faceted individual whose countless complexities were belied by an outward persona of good-natured goofiness and exaggerated machismo. A literal time-traveler miraculously revived with but a single, simple mission: to extract revenge on the individual or individuals deemed responsible for stealing away the single good thing he'd had from a past otherwise littered with self-doubt, crushing disappointment and ultimate failure. No matter Wendy Hammock's deathbed—perhaps *trailer* was the correct term—confession that fateful night and his own acknowledgement of it, the man's feelings before and after the fact had met the truest definition of unconditional love, her admitted betrayal barely registering a blip on his heart's radar.

Wesley then considered how he and Gunther had bonded over shared disabilities—or so he'd thought—in the matter of just a few days. To this moment, he could manage a wry smile when considering the colossal fraud that had come to light and the deep-seated guilt this had birthed from the one truly *without* the power to stand and walk.

As far as his passenger's Houdini-like sleight-of-hand—or *legs*—he smiled yet again when considering the videotaped footage from the Crimson Falls' ER, obtained mere days following that final, fatal fall night. Blurry in spots and showcasing no better than mid-eighties era video quality, there was no mistaking the broom-handle thin form of Gunther McCarron strutting down the hallway with rounded shoulders pulled back and knees rising to comically goosestepping heights, the bionic suit tossed over the former and dangling down his emaciated form like flapping tentacles. Wesley often pondered if this blatant display hadn't been somehow purposeful? Surely Gunther had realized that cameras were commonplace in a medical setting. Was this somehow a sly, sardonic, conclusive shot? A final thumbing of the nose to law enforcement, or better yet, Kerry Hammock and all those still firmly planted in the enemy camp? A safe bet, Wesley had ultimately deduced, as Gunther had surely wagered it would be viewed posthumously.

Mostly, he thought of how, at the conclusion of that frigid night of horrors, when all had gone tragically awry, a battered, wobbly, barely one-hundred-pound man previously hellbent on a single-minded mission of cold-blooded retribution had literally leaped into the line of fire to essentially save the life of a man he had labeled an enemy only days before.

He then thought, actually *obsessed* over on a daily—and nightly—basis, how the same man had, in the last act of a mostly tragic existence, so casually expanded his own single-minded agenda from that of final vengeance to a sacrificial, almost messiah-like mercy. As such, a frozen image of Gunther McCarron's resigned smile, equal parts sad and sardonic, stretched over a pale, gaunt death mask, would forever remain filed away in whatever nightmare gallery of photos the darkest section of Wesley's mind might permanently hoard.

Concluding this surreal rewind, fourteen-plus years in the making, Wesley thought of how fate had chosen him out of a lineup of five potential candidates to claim lone survivor status. If he had somehow been deemed the most deserving, why exactly? His sins were certainly comparable with all but Dexter's, and at least equal to those of his former spouse and Marty Hammock. Perhaps the decision was based not on the degree of guilt, but of its overall level. If so, a veritable landslide had surely been in order, all catastrophes considered. In the end, he decided his was not to question, but simply to appreciate a second chance to make things right in his own terminally culpable mind.

Sandy's chemical addictions aside, he knew little to nothing of Marty or Dexter's own culpability issues in that almost decade-and-a-half span, but it was safe to say none had gone from level-headed, strict teetotaler to mean-spirited boozehound in the months following the trailer incident, nor had they crashed through a metal guard rail at eighty-plus miles per hour while claiming an alcohol level of 0.280 (considered *well* past blood-poisoning level), following which, Wesley's lower back resembled a corkscrewed pretzel. In a matter of just under eight months, he'd lost his career, his mobility, and essentially, his marriage. He had, in time and with unimaginable difficulty, corked the devil inside the bottle—the almost two full years of rehab having been a roller coaster of nightmare proportions—though there had been a trying span where alcohol had handed the mantel of addiction to Percocet and hydrocodone. The eventual hiring at the CFPD had helped him turn the corner toward an existence where positivity finally overtook negativity as the daily norm. Friendships had been made, responsibilities accepted, and the nightly dreamscape was no longer quite as inundated with the horrors of the past.

Still, the eternal question lingered: Was it merely luck that had decided how individual events transpired, or was he chosen to survive for some tangible reason only the outcome of future endeavors could dictate?

Options had been weighed and reweighed, *ad nauseam*, and hard decisions had been made.

Only time would tell the wisdom of said decisions, but the first and perhaps most difficult step would be to thoroughly test that well-worn cliché to its max.

Before departing the strangely soothing quiet of the otherwise deserted men's room—Dan had obviously added some extra-stout deodorizer to the nearby urinals and the scent of recently burnt incense permeated to dominate the normally heady smell of stale piss and spilled suds—Wesley had inhaled deeply and sighed, determined to maintain a semblance of dignity. Not exactly a strongpoint of late.

Upon wheeling back into the main room, he first noticed that the trio had turned their chairs away from the table in order to face him, both Will Crockett and Phil Strickland sitting with the high-back portion tucked against their respective chests— each man having donned tight-lipped smiles as if privy to some as-of-yet unexecuted prank. As for Maggie Childers, she stood cross-armed and droopy-eyed next to her own chair, a booted foot propped on the seat. Spilled tears had carved jagged lines through her makeup and down both cheeks, and it was obvious she was fighting off additional waterworks. Braking as he neared this human barricade, he then took note of a large cardboard box centering their table and wrapped in what appeared to be holiday-themed paper.

"Well, don't you three look pleased?" he inquired through a wide, cheesy grin.

It was Will Crockett who naturally took point, the unquestioned leader of not only local law enforcement but pretty much any company he kept.

"Just thankful you took so long in the john," he said with a wink before nodding toward the mysterious package. "Two minutes shorter and you'd likely have spotted drunky Phil here pawing it out of his trunk and lugging it inside with all the speed and dexterity of a sea tortoise on Ambien."

Phil merely grinned sheepishly in reply, his dark blue UK tee sitting comically askew on his buffed frame. As the chief resumed, it was a perpetually sniffing Maggie that turned to retrieve the box.

"Wes, we know you've got a long haul in the morning, and since it's well past midnight and these two are oiled-up way past legal limits and tomorrow is a school day, we're gonna need to shut this little bash down. That said, we didn't want to forget our little going away present."

With assistance from her visibly wobbly boyfriend, Maggie positioned the wide box between herself and Wes, who then rolled his chair until it sat directly on his right side.

Two days earlier, while visiting the PD building for what would be the final time, he had parked his chair in front of the chief's desk and announced his plans to both the man in charge and Maggie, both of whom took the news with obvious disappointment, especially the veteran dispatcher, but without any expression of shock or real surprise. Wes had previously turned down Will's kind offer to resume as the PD's records clerk, complete with a dollar an hour raise, this coming mere days after his release on parole. Though admittedly there had been a twinge of temptation to step right back into a situation and job so familiar and comforting, two distinct factors weighed as heavy cons versus a long checklist of pros. The first was Kerry Hammock, a wealthy and still very influential power broker within the county who had made it known to all—via multiple newspaper and TV interviews—that he placed the blame for both his son's and stepdaughter's deaths on the former county deputy and veteran police records clerk. Wes understood that the senior Hammock wasn't apt to take kindly to the recent parolee's return to Crimson Falls, much less to his reinstatement as a city employee, and that the former mayor would likely make life miserable for those responsible for his rehiring, with Will Crockett sitting high on the hit list.

The second factor, strange as it might sound to anyone else, was that Wes himself at least partially *agreed* with such thinking, and he had to figure a sizeable headcount of Crimson Falls' citizens did as well. The thought of all the backbiting and bad-mouthing he'd endure, especially if so suddenly and shamelessly reinstated to his previous position, was reason enough to seek out new climes and challenges.

He'd reached out to an old friend from his police academy days whom he'd recontacted via Facebook while in stir, and the man had offered him both a position and living space, and though central Montana sounded a world away from eastern Kentucky, a part of him openly invited such a drastic change of scenery. Being as he'd never traveled further west than Little Rock in his life, he figured to be long overdue for such a radical road trip.

"Hmmm, now what have you jokers gone and done?" he inquired, looking over the square mystery box as if sizing up some as of yet unrevealed, unidentified alien artifact.

"Hey, don't look at me, pal," Phil said with a glance over his shoulder toward the kitchen area, where Dan's shadow bounced around like a windblown cape. "I cast my vote for one of those lifelike blowup dolls," he concluded, reaching over to apply a playful pinch to Maggie's left thigh, to which she balled up a fist and socked his bulky right shoulder.

"Shall I?" Wes grinned, his right hand resting on a yellow ribbon tied across the top of the mystery carton. "I mean, she might be having a hard time breathing in there, right Phillip?"

"*Bingo* Wesley." Phil winked, flashing the classic thumb-tip to forefinger-tip gesture.

Maggie rolled her eyes while matching the pair's imbecilic smirks.

"Just open it, knucklehead," she said, giggling like a girl half her age.

Moments later, ribbon removed and wrapping paper peeled away, Wes read and re-read the words revealed atop the slick black boxing.

"Guys, I'm...how did you..." he babbled, exchanging brief glances with each of the trio, "...how were you able to swing *this*? I mean, I priced these things while...once Gunther showcased his last year. Not exactly chump change, especially this particular brand."

The words Phoenix SuitX were featured prominently beneath his open palm, while just below and in smaller lettering read "Medical Exoskeleton," with a 3D image of the product itself.

"Hey, what's one less new Explorer for the fleet?" Will Crockett shrugged. "Baines will just have to rough it in a used model till next year's budget. Call it a rookie paying his dues."

Slapping the top of the box, the giftee's voice noticeably cracked upon response.

"I...seriously don't know what to say but, hey, thanks. I've often wondered, especially after Gunther's daily demos, just how well such a thing even worked. The cost was, obviously, always a roadblock."

Sauntering over to stand on the chairbound man's opposite side, the chief laid a hand atop his left shoulder.

"You may need to seek out technical assistance to maximize those new bionic powers, though I did notice an instructional video is included."

Wesley merely nodded, fearful that a verbal response might trigger a full-blown sob.

A half-hour later—Dan had locked the door behind them with a brief but meaningful nod Wesley's way—the box tucked snugly inside the Camry's trunk, the remaining trio stood facing the driver's door in varying poses of awkwardness.

"You sure those hand gears aren't gonna wear out on such a lengthy trek?" Phil Strickland inquired, indicating the Camry's brake and accelerator handles, located on opposite sides of the steering wheel.

"They build 'em for the long haul," Wes replied from the driver's seat, crisp, cool air escaping the cab as the A/C fan blew at its maximum setting. "I'm planning on three nine-hour shifts with a hotel stop in between. Should arrive in Big Sky country around noon of day four."

"You make sure to call me along the way," Maggie said, leaning in to apply a light kiss to his stubble-infested left cheek, "or at least shoot me a daily text."

"Will do, Maggie. Chief, you gonna make sure these two public intoxicants arrive home safely?" he said, leaning out the window as the three slowly backed away from the running vehicle, a sheen of sweat coating his forehead despite the A/C's best efforts.

"Most assuredly. Keep in touch, Wesley, and if you find those wide-open spaces aren't all they were cut out to be, well, you're always welcome back here, my man."

"Definitely," Phil Strickland echoed with a thumbs-up, wrapping his free arm around Maggie's shoulder before removing it just as quickly and shooting a worried glance toward the Glutton.

"See you around, Wheels," Maggie yelled as he pulled from the mostly empty lot with his right hand executing a continual wave out the window.

"Not if I see you first, Legs!" he bellowed, pulling out onto the highway with a short blast of the horn, a gnawing feeling at his chest cavity that was the textbook definition of bittersweet.

~ * ~

He exited the Crimson Falls' city limits at just past seven AM the next morning and approached the western edge of the county a half-hour later.

At precisely seven-thirty-three, he pulled the Camry onto a dirt and gravel shoulder just ahead of a narrow two-lane bridge, a faded road sign proclaiming the shallow water flowing beneath as a portion of Winder's Creek, named after the eighteenth-century explorer said to have discovered her.

Just over fifteen years earlier, he'd steered a Pontiac Grand Prix into and through the rails of the same forty-foot stretch of overpass at just over eighty miles per hour, roughly thirty-five over the legal limit—this after ingesting a full fifth of Southern

Comfort on a mostly empty stomach just an hour earlier. There were specific details of that crash and its aftermath he was unable to clarify.

The first was whether or not he'd simply lost control or had purposely meant to test the bridge's aged W-beams.

The second, being that he'd never again driven or even ridden over the same stretch of roadway since, was the possibility that he'd developed a phobia or, equally unlikely, simply sought to avoid a place of such painful recollection.

Regardless of his continued inability to truthfully answer the first of these enigmas, the cure to the second was easily enough tested and remedied in one fell swoop.

The Camry passed smoothly over the slightly cracked asphalt without incident at just under thirty-five miles per hour, its grim-faced driver not even hesitating to test the fates any further with a lingering gaze through the rearview mirror.

His eyes moving back to the path ahead, he casually reached to power up the XM radio dial just in time to take in the final chorus of The Rolling Stones' "Hang Fire," to which he could've sworn he felt both feet tap rhythmically in time.

For the first time in recent memory, he daydreamed of running on healthy legs, chest burning and lungs afire with a wholly satisfying discomfort while sprinting toward something worthy of his pursuit.

Two and a half minutes later, Wesley Grant passed over the county line of his birth for the final time.

In his mind, at that very moment, heels temporarily unaffected by full paralysis clicked joyfully together.

Meet Terry Lloyd Vinson

Born and raised in northern Alabama, Terry Lloyd Vinson is an Air Force veteran and former corrections officer who has authored over a dozen published novels. Having previously resided in five states and overseas, he currently homesteads in Hendersonville, Tennessee with his wife Liza and a killer Maltipoo named Dexter.

Other Works from the Pen of

Terry Lloyd Vinson

Sea of Bones – When wading the most treacherous of waters, the lesser of two evils can oft times prove to be the deadliest.

The Purgatory Inn - Not to be found on any existing map. To truly tempt fate is to take the 'VACANCIES' sign literally.

Letter to Our Readers

Enjoy this book?

You can make a difference.

As an independent publisher, Wings ePress, Inc. does not have the financial clout of the large New York publishers. We can't afford large magazine spreads or subway posters to tell people about our quality books.

But we do have something much more effective and powerful than ads. We have a large base of loyal readers.

Honest reviews help bring the attention of new readers to our books.

If you enjoyed this book, we would appreciate it if you would spend a few minutes posting a review on the site where you purchased this book or on the Wings ePress, Inc. webpages at: https://wingsepress.com/

Thank You

Visit Our Website

For The Full Inventory
Of Quality Books:

Wings ePress, Inc

Quality trade paperbacks and downloads
in multiple formats,
in genres ranging from light romantic comedy to general
fiction and horror.
Wings has something for every reader's taste.
Visit the website, then bookmark it.
We add new titles each month!

Wings ePress, Inc.
3000 N. Rock Road
Newton, KS 67114